THE FRANCIS CONNECTION

THE FRANCIS CONNECTION

Frank James Unger

ISBN: Softcover   978-1-4931-7347-1
             eBook   978-1-4931-7346-4

This book was printed in the United States of America.

Rev. date: 03/20/2014

To order additional copies of this book, contact:
Xlibris LLC
1-888-795-4274
www.Xlibris.com
Orders@Xlibris.com
541082

Contents

"All the darkness in the world cannot extinguish the light of a single candle."

Saint Francis of Assisi

Prologue

Making a permanent life-choice isn't easy. Fortunately, such weighty events don't happen often. *Un*fortunately, when they do, it's at a time of formation when confusion reigns, somewhere between childhood and adulthood. At that tenuous point, the decision of what to do with one's life is overwhelming because the rule allows for only *one* choice. A person can't very well be a clown in a circus while at the same time be practicing medicine.

So, making a wise *first* choice is practical and prudent. Seldom does one get a chance to choose path number *two* if path number *one* doesn't work out. Many people, facing that reality, grudgingly acquiesce, accepting their first choice and plodding through life in misery, boredom and unhappiness.

It was different for Frank Chase, DDS. During his seventy-seventh year, he was handed an amazing document that gifted him a second life, one that ran concurrent with his first. Under the mantle of a single persona, Frank thus traveled two simultaneous journeys.

The extraordinary nucleus in Frank's case was an elusive and perplexing prayer written and concealed by Saint Francis of Assisi centuries earlier. The prayer was remarkably beautiful but strangely divisive and discriminatory.

Frank's saga actually began in 1997 when a major earthquake devastated the Franciscan Basilica in Assisi. The quake revealed a document that had remained there from the thirteenth century. The writing gave birth to an inexplicable and unfathomable mystery: the creation of Frank's second self, a unique human person who shared the same soul as the man who called him to life. Amazingly, that second person lived according to *his* vocation and *his* vision, inspired by virtue and driven by a passionate commitment to his religious vows as a Roman Catholic priest.

Make no mistake, *The Francis Connection* is a fictional story. But it is rooted in the historic legacy of Francis of Assisi and consistent with the saint's life and actions in Assisi. The reader is forewarned that some of the unexpected twists and turns, while contrary to conventional wisdom are, nevertheless, rational and sustainable.

It is clear that the two men within Frank Chase manifest the same strengths and weaknesses while they share life in the same city of Chicago. Each man is a quiet leader with the gift of letters and each brandishes a charm that attracts lifelong friends. In *most* cases, those are commendable qualities. In others, they are traits that generate a plethora of complexities.

In its essence, *The Francis Connection* is a story of love, an account of the strenuous personal issues indigenous to any path on life's journey, especially the struggle to honor lifetime commitments. Those prove no more or less arduous in the 21st century than they were 800 years ago in the life of Saint Francis of Assisi.

For Frank Chase and for *Father* Francis Chase, the challenges of leading *two* lives toward a heavenly reward are fewer than imagined, because he treasures both. Moreover, he is inspired by a rich and true conscience. Having laid that predicate, it is a wonder to imagine a different life for any of us had we chosen that *second* path instead of the first, and lived to witness its conjunction and coexistence with the first.

This story is not of sadness, death and dying. It is of joy, life and living, a tale of faith, hope and love among family and friends. It describes the plentiful enjoyments and adversities of a fine and noble man, one who lives twice after experiencing *The Francis Connection*.

Introduction

I sat at a booth near the bar, savoring one of my favorite sports, people-watching. As a further adjunct to sipping my beer, I scanned the shoes on the customers sitting on a long line of barstools. The shoes were all attached to legs attached to men, mostly *large* men.

There was a surprising diversity in the selection of footwear: soiled tennis shoes, shiny penny-loafers, canvas sneakers, flip-flops of all materials, sandals, slip-ons, and moccasins of all colors.

Breaking my concentration were loud voices. *Carl's Sports Bar* serves $.75 drafts from 2:00 p.m. until 6:00. It was nearing 5:30 and the natives were restless and noisy. Add 60's rock music to the mix, blast it from dozens of speakers, and you have a major ingredient for audio pollution, exactly what the customers want at *Carl's*.

Legitimizing its claim as a "Sports Bar," 42 flat-screen TV's hang eight inches apart and surround the perimeter of all four walls. Fortunately, they need no sound because the action speaks for itself: a soccer game between Chile and Brazil, a tennis match from Abu Dhabi, a hockey game from Calgary, an extreme sports show from Reno, golf from San Diego, an ESPN report on every sport in the world, and the rest of the 42 sets dedicated to the pastime of the season. On this particular day and month, it's baseball.

Ah, yes, things were great in Venice, my place of retirement for the past ten years. For most of that time, *Carl's* has been my favorite watering hole, just around the corner from my home. By the way, that's Venice, *Florida*, on the Southwest coast of the State.

I've grown to love just about *everything* here. It's where I live with my wife, Annie, without much conflict at all, only peaceful skies, lovely clouds and a blue and friendly sea. But that's about to change. I'm going home to Chicago, to end all this . . . by dying!

But before I do that, I'm heading for another exciting destination, without a map or compass, across the uncharted waters of another lifetime. And in spite of overcast skies, I'll enjoy the rays of a most remarkable sun, one that dramatically brightens the last year of my life. Like the footwear on those men at the bar, surprising diversity will mark my days.

The Illness

The setting was grimly familiar: several pieces of colorless furniture encircled a bed, three innocuous pictures hung crookedly on the walls, and a stench of stale air wafted through the room. Even though he had visited here many times before, this was different. It was Frank's turn to be the dying patient in the hospital bed, *his* time to face the most catastrophic death of all . . . his own.

Though the *setting* didn't arouse any particular sensations within him, facing his own death did. Frank didn't expect this right now. In fact, like most humans, he didn't expect it at *any* time. But he had read the warning in scripture and personally witnessed its traumatic effect enough times to believe it: "The day of the Lord will come like a thief in the night."

And so the thief was coming. He was knocking at the door and there was no way to stop him. Frank was never a huge fan of endings and he wasn't exactly happy to face his own. It did bring him joy, however, when he recently and abruptly ended his chemo sessions because the side effects were grim and the treatments had no chance of saving his life. Other than that single exception, Frank's personal endings weren't happy.

Now, in spite of an impending dismal conclusion to his life, Frank would experience a most remarkable event that would make him happy . . . and dramatically change the final months of his life. Indeed, Frank Chase was handed an opportunity to create a cathartic scenario that would end his life with great satisfaction and

1

unexpected flair. His wife, Annie, his four children, and his most informed friends had no idea what was climactically approaching. Nor did he.

From his bed at St. John's Medical Center, just yesterday, Frank had issued a mandate to his family: "Stay away from here for one day," he dictated, figuring they'd had enough of his depressing room and its cranky inhabitant; and besides, this could go on for several more weeks or even months, and visitations were becoming an aggravation more than a comfort. His diagnosis was adencarcinoma, inoperable glandular cancer of the pancreas. It had already spread to his liver and lymph nodes. Now, after six months of treatments, his discomfort was worse and the prognosis remained the same: the illness was terminal and the most optimistic guess for his lifetime was another six months.

For a while now, either because of the therapy or simply because of the *aging process*, Frank had been wandering off on tangential mental flights and having a difficult time concentrating and conversing. It was not an uncommon pattern when a myriad of mind-altering drugs collided with the mental handicaps of a 77-year-old man. Normally, Frank was a peaceful, likeable, spiritual guy who loved just about everything and everybody. But these past months had brought out the worst in him. He was bitterly impatient.

His psychological malady was, arguably, causing as much discomfort as his cancer. He called it the "why me syndrome," a belligerent refusal to accept the fact that such a fierce illness would dare to befall *him*. Up until his initial diagnosis, he believed he was impregnable and immune to diseases with fatal conclusions. He had also become extremely cynical of the hospital experience. "Repair shops," he would call them, "places where people denied the inevitability of death and struggled in futility to extend life, if only for a day or a week."

In his practice of dentistry, Frank had occasionally contributed to diagnosing cancer in his patients. But to hear the word applied to *him* was unthinkable. He had studied the disease during his undergraduate work at The University Notre Dame and later during his graduate studies at The Ohio State University. So he was familiar with the frustration in providing treatment for a cancer as deadly as the one that attacked him.

In spite of his "new normal" attitude of antipathy, Frank was now looking forward to a break in his hopelessness. On issuing his mandate for the day, Frank excluded one person, his close friend, Father Tony Tonelli, pastor of Frank's parish in Chicago. The two had remained friends since Father's ordination some thirty years earlier and they remained close during Frank and Annie's ten-year temporary relocation to Venice, Florida. With the priest's Italian lineage, it was most appropriate that he be assigned as pastor of Saint Francis of Assisi Catholic Church in suburban Chicago.

Frank's illness struck him after he and Annie lived in Florida for nearly ten years of retirement. Now, after that relatively short time in what Frank called a "paradisiacal environment," they were forced to return to their roots to be closer to a more diverse selection of high-level medical professionals. It was also timely and sensible to be located nearer to their children and grandchildren. Frank's internal gyro told him it was the right move though he resented the fact that they were *forced* to return. He loved Florida and detested harsh winters. He had done enough snow-shoveling.

Frank and Annie were born in Chicago and made it their home for most of their married life. Frank's practice of dentistry was, by all standards, extremely successful. It helped that Frank was both pleasantly gregarious and professionally superior.

Further, Frank was well-respected among his fellow members of the American Dental Association. Because of his prowess as a writer and public speaker, he had been called on frequently to be a guest at the Annual Convention of ADA. He had fostered a gift for writing and speaking in front of large audiences as far back as his days as a student of dentistry during his undergraduate and graduate programs.

Most of Frank's peers were envious, not hostile or resentful, just *envious* of his articulate and erudite skills. They thought it surprising and even somewhat inappropriate for a man involved in a heavily scientific career to be so gifted in speech and writing. He did, nevertheless, continue to apply those talents well.

He also had frequent speaking engagements as a Past Grand Knight of the Knights of Columbus, a Roman Catholic fraternal organization. His membership provided him with an excellent forum in a uniquely friendly speaking environment. Recently, however, he had to limit his engagements because of his illness.

Replacing that enjoyment, one of the rewards in returning to Chicago was being near family and also being closer to Father Tonelli. The current gyrations in geography notwithstanding, Frank balanced the benefits and liabilities of the move back and accepted its shortcomings. He and Annie were amazingly adaptable to change.

For the moment, Frank was upbeat. He was most anxious to visit with his priestly friend who had just returned from a trip to Rome, not his first to The Eternal City; but Frank hadn't seen him since he came back over two weeks ago and he was looking forward to the stories about Father's audience with the Pope and about other visits along his Italian itinerary.

In his role as a priest and friend, Father Tonelli had been a reliable source of strength for Frank and Annie and the entire Chase family, especially as they faced the latest challenge of a terminal illness. Frank was reluctant to ask Father for more help because he had certainly paid his dues as a mentor and counselor for many years, willingly appearing to share a sad tear or a moment of joy during the family's stereotypical soap-opera plots and subplots.

Thinking of Father and many other friends past and present as he lay alone in bed, Frank reflected on the very *concept* of friendship. It was not unusual for him to ponder such common facets of life and then tediously dissect them and record them in writing. Now, he noted those reflections, rambling sometimes, but expressing rich profundities.

He began by stating his belief that "The friendship you seek is less important than the friendship you bring," and "A kind mouth multiplies friends." It was on that foundation of selflessness that he constructed his personal friendships.

For whatever it was worth, this was the first opportunity in his life that Frank actually had time to dwell heavily on his ideas about *friendship*. Playfully, he divided his friends into three categories.

"First," he wrote, "there are friends we all make because we have so much in common with the person. It's probable that our personalities and interests brought us together. Or maybe it was a common demographic, or our education or religion. Things like that.

"In a more restrictive delineation, there's a second category that's quite a bit different. It includes the friendships people hold onto for many years, primarily because they shared so much time with another person. Even though they may never have had much in common, they remained close simply because they knew each other for so long. Those friendships," Frank would argue, "are held together primarily by the glue of longevity. That's not to say the friendships are any less meaningful than those in the first group. Perhaps they're even stronger because they're endowed with the qualities of endurance and perseverance, remaining undaunted in spite of geographic obstacles and the shortcomings of aging.

"Then," Frank reasoned, "the strongest of all friendships is a combination of groups one and two, a merging of the shared denominators of commonality and longevity." In Frank's analysis, "This is the ultimate friendship, the kind that a person experiences once in a lifetime. It is usually rooted in the special quality of love."

Harboring that conclusion, Frank thought that such a friendship ". . . should be treasured as conscientiously as a valuable gem," (acknowledging his trite metaphor.) He placed his exceptional relationship with Father into that lofty category, bonded by trust and mutual respect. And Frank wasn't at all reticent to say that he *loved* his friend, to the nth degree. In fact, he would stake his life on Father Tonelli's fidelity to his vows of celibacy, chastity and obedience. He was sure the man would die a priest and a virgin.

In his current state, Frank's recollections also transferred him back to his ten-year home in Venice, Florida. It was a psychic as well as a physical "place" where he recalled a small circle of retired gentlemen who became close friends. Since his first session with the "Coffee Boys" he had experienced quite a ride, mostly observing, occasionally contributing, and always enjoying conversations that were anything but mundane. All of this over morning cups of coffee.

Using his bountiful amount of spare time in the hospital, Frank tediously recorded remembrances of the group as a legacy to their friendship. During the exercise, he dictated through a voice-recognition system on his computer. Until recently, he regarded *DragonNaturallySpeaking* as another "gimmicky piece of software." But now, at the urging of his oldest son, Frank acknowledged that it proved a handy tool that afforded him a more efficient means to an end.

Since he actually had no lap as he lay in bed, typing on his *laptop* was ergonomically impossible. He had thus, reluctantly, become proficient in the use of "Dragon" and boasted of his newfound skill to anyone who'd listen. His recorded experiences were written so explicitly that they became an excellent personal source of literary pride as well as whimsical reflection. Annie especially commended him on his writing as he vividly described "The Coffee Boys."

"Imagine your father or grandfather drinking daily, morning coffee and sharing stories with best friends. Not a terribly unique situation, but it takes on a new dimension when you're part of the dynamic. Sitting between such men, I feasted on the verbal meal, absorbing massive amounts of wisdom and energy slowly. The listening was easy. And because the conversation was so healthful, digestion was assured.

"There were adventurous tales of the past, profound appraisals of the present, and bold prognostications of the future, all enriched by a tasty seasoning of humor. In every case, the stories were as savory as the black blends of coffees that were consumed. (Additions like cream or sugar were disdainfully called 'the tutti-fruiti stuff.')

"With these guys, there was more harmony than discord, more conciliation than argument . . . no boasting, no showing off, no competition. In a culture of victimhood, these men were secure

enough to blame no one or any thing for unfortunate events in their lives. They were optimistic, always.

"Rarely did physical concerns commit these guys to a Physician's care. My current illness is an exception and I'm forgiven for it. We still remain in touch through frequent emails and they readily assure me of their prayers.

"There is also a prevailing manifestation of selflessness among these men, a quality that impresses more than most others. Though each of the seven members is capable of repeating a favorite story many times, the listener listens, again and again, with equal attention to each repetition. 'We've heard that one before,' has never been uttered. The men are too tolerant and kind to voice such a crude reality.

"Unarguably, the essential fuel that keeps these men running is compassion; a close second is love for one another; and third is the desire for peace in the world. Surely, in this microcosm of a small community, sturdy minds and hearts of dear friends are cemented in loyalty and understanding.

"Since we moved away, I deeply miss the daily gatherings (Sundays excused) and the unique individuals that forever remain my friends. I'm frequently reminded that they miss my company, too. That warms my heart as a compliment and a gift I'll carry to my final destination."

Annie had printed the writing of those two pages from Frank's computer. As he read them repeatedly, the papers became mutilated from overuse. He'd neatly fold them and store them inside a small book that Annie had given him for the recording of personal thoughts. The book inhabited a safe place in the drawer of his bedstand, resting alongside a tattered book of prayers, a rosary, and a small statue of Saint Francis of Assisi, all given to him by his mother before her passing some two decades ago.

After his energetic foray into writing about his Florida buddies, Frank was weakening. He paused and committed to saving his strength for Father's upcoming visit. In the meantime, he buzzed the nurse and asked for something to drink. His wish for a cold Heineken for himself and a Guinness for Father was not granted, however. The two men had enjoyed those libations to a background of an inconceivable variety of sports telecasts. Such events were excuses for them to get together at Frank's house. Annie encouraged the gatherings even though the odor of their cigars lingered in the house for days.

Frank was wincing a bit as the pain-killer was wearing off. When the nurse arrived for her periodic visit, he planned to ask her to refresh some of his meds. Then, he changed his mind, wanting instead to be at his sharpest during Father's visit, at least moderately alert and conversational. If he dozed into incoherency, well, Father had learned from experience how to accept and accommodate that reoccurring condition.

Frank waited eagerly to see his black-clothed friend enter his room. Over their many years as friends, Frank had assessed Father as a good man, full of practical wisdom more likely found in a much older person. His sense-of-humor and the gift of self deprecation were also admirable.

Frank also appreciated Father's ability to talk straight, explain himself clearly, and display a knack for simplifying complex issues, especially when related to matters of his church. Permeating all of that, he remained commendably jovial and humble.

As Frank readied for Father's appearance, a nurse he had never seen before entered his room. He hoped she wouldn't expect to pass the time of day and cover *her* history as well as his. It was uncommon for him to bully nurses, but this time, he was prepared. At that moment, he saw Father right behind her. He quickly asked the white-clothed woman to help him move from his bed to the adjacent recliner. But first, she'd have to help him get across the room and into the "john."

"Mr. Frank?" she asked loudly as she approached his bed.

His answer was quieter and quicker than her question.

"I'm not *Mr.* Frank," he said. "Frank's my *first* name. *Chase* is my second name. And if you must know, it's *Doctor* Frank Chase." The terse comment demonstrated Frank's unacceptable impatience. He apologized for that display of exasperation.

Frank thought the nurse, however, should be embarrassed by her ignorance. He was disappointed that she showed no remorse, but instead, grumbled about his request to be helped across the room. She obliged, but not without a growl and a struggle to move his lifelines around the bed, into the bathroom and back to the recliner while still attached to his body. Frank didn't like the lines that hung from tall metal poles and dripped fluids like slowly thawing ice. The apparatus rolled around on little wheels that squeaked as they moved. To avoid the annoying noise, Frank simply avoided the bathroom until such moves were absolutely necessary.

To break the spell of the awkward moment, Frank turned to face the doorway where Father entered. The priest had seen the rambunctious maneuvers, controlled a chuckle and threw a wink and a wave of his hand to let Frank know he had arrived. Frank motioned for him to come in as the nurse left.

Father whispered, "Reminds me of Nurse Ratched in 'One Flew over the Cuckoo's Nest.'" Frank laughed and nodded in agreement, adding only, "She's not going to drive *me* nuts like she did Jack Nicholson." Frank greatly appreciated Father's incredible gift of recall, especially when it came to movies. From that time on, at least behind her back, Frank would refer to the new nurse as "Nurse Ratched."

"Looks like you're still hanging in there," the priest said politely as the two men shook hands, smiled broadly, and feigned a hug. (Neither was a man-hugging-man type, unless it was a close relative . . . maybe.)

"Honestly," Father said, "you actually do look a little better than when I saw you a few weeks ago."

Frank silently mouthed the words, "Thank you."

There was a pause before Frank burst into conversation. "Damn, Father, it's good to see you. Sit down here. Maybe you can bring me some good luck and help me get this over with. Got any prayers to help an old man die?"

Father frowned and laughed as he got comfortable in the chair. It was October and already chilly in Chicago. The grandkids had decorated Frank's room with all kinds of Halloween stuff: finger paintings of pumpkins, cutouts of black cats, and black and orange streamers around the perimeter of the ceiling. Father scanned each one and smiled.

"I like your taste in art, Frank . . . very high-class."

"Yeah, more like *art* class. I thought you'd appreciate it."

"Tell me, seriously. How are things going?" Father asked. "Are you in pain? How's the family holding up?"

It would take awhile to respond to each question so Frank addressed them one at a time. "Family's fine," he said, "all six Grandkids involved in Halloween as you can see. Nothing big happening." He paused, hearing his own words as he purposefully dodged the issue at hand, then finished his sentence, ". . . except me sitting here dying. The worst part is not knowing exactly how long I have and how the final hours are going to play out. I don't have to tell you, Father, that in spite of my faith, I'm scared."

Father shook his head compassionately and said, 'Remember, my friend, adversity is the parent of virtue.'"

"Never heard that. Very profound. Who said that?"

"To be honest, I read it in a fortune cookie!"

Frank laughed at Father's successful attempt to break the somber mood. He followed it with the comment, "So then, I guess I can count on becoming extremely virtuous, right?"

Father slid his chair closer, removed his jacket and hung it over the back of the chair. "I know it's trite to say this, Frank, but it's true . . . you have to trust in the Lord. He's got it all worked out and He'll take care of you as He always has. You've led a good life and should have no fears."

Frank pretended not to hear what Father said as he laid his head back and maneuvered a small pillow under it. A deep sigh was his only reply to Father's comment. The two men sat in silence as they gathered their thoughts, for longer than they had ever endured silence before. But neither had ever carried so much on his conversational agenda.

Frank turned to look into the priest's eyes to say, "So, you had a good time in Rome. Tell me about it, Father. It's my favorite city in the entire world. I always told Annie that if I was dying and had only one city to visit in my final days, it would be Rome. A bit ironic as I think about it now." Frank frowned and closed his eyes for a second or two.

"Love that city," he continued, "for a lot more reasons than its being the headquarters of the Church. The food, the people, the antiquity, the zest of the Italians . . . the *energy* is unreal, unmatched by any culture in the world. We attended a convention there once and I never forgot the experience. Greatest city in the world!"

"I agree," Father said. "You'd be a good one for their Chamber of Commerce. I learn more about the place every time I visit. It's been four times now that I've been privileged to go over there and I always learn something new."

"What was it this time?" Frank asked with childlike enthusiasm.

"Well, it was the first time I got to visit Assisi, the birthplace of your namesake and my parish."

"Ah, Saint Francis and Assisi. Gosh, I always wanted to go there and never had the chance. How was it?"

"Not disappointing, that's for sure . . . awesome, *inspiring* is a better word. It touched me personally and I wasn't prepared for that kind of deep emotion."

"How long were you there?" Frank asked.

"At first, only a few hours. We took a tour bus from Rome. The whole day was incredible." Father abruptly changed the subject with the order, "Frank, I'm here to talk about *you,* not my trip. Tell me how you're handling this . . . up here." He pointed to his temple.

"You mean mentally?"

"Well, more *spiritually* than mentally. But if you give me one answer, it'll cover both."

Frank had to think quietly for a couple of minutes. Father appreciated that and shifted in his chair as he turned his head away from Frank. Frank hadn't talked to Annie or anybody else, deeply, about what he was really thinking or feeling about the time ahead. So this was the first time he was pressed to verbalize his inevitable death and the unknowns ahead of him.

As he gathered fragmented thoughts and looked at his friend, he felt someone had placed an anvil on his chest. Tears welled in his eyes. It was sudden, like nothing he had yet experienced, hard to explain . . . a *spiritual* sort of outburst, perhaps inspired by the presence of "a man of God." It was the fact that he believed he would *meet* God face-to-face, like, maybe tomorrow, or the next day or the next week . . . that soon. It was the realization that he'd be leaving his beloved family, all of them . . . and Father Tonelli.

He was uncharacteristically overwhelmed by self-pity. That's what it was, self-pity. He could feel his cheeks, all of his face, begin to shudder with the expulsion of the tears.

Uncommonly, he felt the gravity of it all. This wasn't some character he was watching in a movie. This was him, Frank Chase, now facing death. And there was nothing anybody could do to stop the vicious onslaught.

He broke loose and cried, not loudly, but in *contained* sobbing that only Father could see and hear. And they were real tears. He wasn't good enough at acting to "fake it."

Then, as quickly as it came, the indulgence left. And he said to Father who had observed quietly, "Sorry about that. I hit some downtime there. No way to explain it. Sorry to interrupt your story. I'm embarrassed. Let's get back to Assisi. Tell me all about it. And don't spare any detail."

Frank laid his head back again, wiped the tears with a single tissue, then, with another one, blew his nose, loudly enough to get a smile from his visitor. Father settled back and appeared to be comfortable and ready to resume his narrative.

"Okay," he said, "so the bus ride to Assisi was absolutely wonderful. We passed these lush vineyards that rolled with the hills and valleys. Just gorgeous. All around us on every horizon, we were surrounded by green mountains and these tiny villages that just hung from the mountainsides. The only drawback was the fact that it rained on the entire trip. The windows on the bus got wet enough to distort the scenery, but the effect was still breathtaking.

"I sat next to an elderly woman who was happy to remain focused out the window . . . and silent. That pleased me. I wasn't dressed in my 'blacks' so neither she nor anyone else knew I was a priest. I like traveling like that sometimes."

Frank smiled and responded, "I'm sure it's nice to be inconspicuous once in awhile after all the attention you get around here. I mean, everywhere you go in the neighborhood, people know you're a priest."

"Doesn't really bother me. Kind of keeps me in line as I monitor my every move: how I drive, how I respond to strangers, my personal remarks to reckless drivers." Father laughed as he made a gesture to indicate zipping his lips.

"Ever since I was a little kid," the priest continued, "my mom taught me to be inconspicuous. She said that people blame the *worst* things on those who are *seen* the most. So I grew up not liking the spotlight for fear it would get me into trouble. Then what do I do? I become a priest. I commit to one of the most conspicuous careers in the entire world. I wear black so that people will notice me in public, broadcasting to the world by the very clothes I wear what I do for a living. And that can easily be mistaken as a sign of thinking I'm better than everyone else.

"You know I'm a pretty quiet person. It takes me a long time to get to know people," Father continued. "Remember when I first met you and Annie? It took several years before I felt comfortable with you and the kids."

"That's true, Father," Frank said as he shifted to the other cheek on his sore bottom. "So what does all that have to do with Assisi?"

Father apologized for his diversion. "Sorry," he said, as Frank returned to his role as listener.

"So I'm sitting on the bus and remaining *inconspicuous*.

He accented the word, frowned and continued. "But when we arrived at our stop in front of the Papal Basilica of Saint Francis, this literally *monumental* structure, everyone made a mad dash for the two exit doors on the bus. It was a minor stampede and quite irreverent. And here's me, a Catholic priest, being knocked and bumped and shoved around.

"But I asked for it by being 'out of uniform.' And because of that, I was the last one off the bus, the last in line to follow the tour inside. So I got what I deserved. And because of *that*, I had to wait for a second group to form from another bus. It was kind of a mess. But it was a lesson in patience as well as in humility. I can always use more of both.

"At that point, I decided to wander the Basilica by myself. I followed a printed brochure that explained all the details of the site. The way it turned out, it would have been less to my advantage to wear my 'blacks' even though I might have gotten some privilege for the status-effect."

"I thought you didn't like formal tours anyway, Father. I remember many a time when you opted to walk a historic setting on your own rather than follow a guide."

"Yeah, that's true, Frank, but in this case . . . well, anyway, here I am wandering the magnificent Basilica of Saint Francis all by myself, loving every minute of it. I truly believe that I learn more that way than with a guide or with one of those recorded headphone gizmos."

"So, bottom line?" Frank interrupted.

"Bottom line is . . . it was better that no one knew I was a priest because I wouldn't have had the privacy. And it gave me a great opportunity to meet a truly remarkable person at the *Sacro Convento*. That's *The Friary*, a part of this huge expanse that was originally, and still is, the home of the Franciscan Friars."

Frank followed his friend's narrative closely. He had seldom heard the priest demonstrate such enthusiasm about anything as serious and revered as the birthplace of Saint Francis. Maybe a fourth quarter come-from-behind victory for the Bears, but nothing this heavy ever brought such energy and so many words from Father Tony Tonelli. It was a pleasure for Frank to watch him and to share in his exuberance. It also piqued his interest in what Father was preparing to say. Frank was completely distracted from his illness and felt no pain.

Assisi

"Are you comfortable? Is there anything I can get for you?" Father's compassion was showing. "I feel kind of bad bending your ear like this but I've been so excited to tell you this story, primarily because you and I have such a deep devotion to Saint Francis . . . and, of course, you *are* named after him."

"And so is your Parish. I don't think I have to remind you of that connection. You've got an equally close relationship with him. And by the way, you're not exactly 'bending my ear.' Your words are like *music* to me, and the suspense you're building is a great distraction from my misery in this bed. I'm anxious to hear where your story goes. And do I have anything better to do?" Father smiled and ignored the rhetorical question from his friend.

"Speaking of my bed," Frank said quickly. "Maybe you could help me get back in there. This chair is killing me . . . there I go again with a classic unintentional pun."

Father performed as he was asked and helped Frank climb and crawl his way back into bed. Frank grumbled under his breath, "Look at this damn thing, Father. Just look at it. This bed has been made for 'little people' and I'm over six-feet long, er, tall. How am I supposed to be comfortable in here? It's discrimination, clearly discriminatory. How can somebody my size be expected to stretch out in this? My feet stick out at the bottom of the sheet, my head is . . ." The cranky patient caught himself and apologized to his friend. "No excuse," he said. "The outburst was uncalled for. Sorry."

"Don't worry about it," Father said as he returned to his storytelling. The interruption didn't bother him. He simply again ignored what Frank had said, thereby demonstrating his love and understanding by remaining silent.

"I think I was about to tell you about the Basilica," Father said. "I brought back a video that I'll show you when you get out of here. So I'm not going to give you all the historical stats right now. What I do want to tell you about is an extraordinary experience I had while roaming the church alone. You'll be interested because eventually, it's going to affect you."

Frank replied quickly, "I'm all ears!"

"Well," Father said, "I ended up following this tour group and its guide around the church and near to the entrance of the crypt. The crypt is below the Upper and Lower Basilica where the tomb of Saint Francis is located. I tagged along at the end of the line, pretending to be part of the group so I wouldn't be 'conspicuous.' As they moved on, at one point, I drifted back and was studying some of the awesome frescoes as we left the main Basilica. They're all done by late medieval painters and are just stunning in detail and color."

Frank shook his head in wonder, vicariously walking every step on Father's journey. He didn't want to appear envious of Father's opportunity to visit the historic site, but in a small way, he was.

"So we went down into the crypt," Father said, "and I froze in front of the remains of the great Saint, not simply because of the aura emitted by the tomb, but because I noticed someone kneeling in the shadows off to the right. I can still picture exactly what the image was like . . . a small person on a kneeler off to one side. It was a beautiful sight right out of a fresco from upstairs. I swear I saw the glow of a halo around the person's head.

"So . . . you've got to picture the tomb of Saint Francis, my friend. You remember, his body is uncorrupted after 800 years. His burial place was discovered in 1818 . . . okay, so there's this ancient stone coffin with iron ties bound around it." Father demonstrated by stretching his arms open and wide. He used his hands abundantly and graciously to supplement his descriptions. It's a long-standing quality that Frank attributed to the Italian blood running through the priest's veins. He'd tease Father and laugh loudly when he did that to excess.

Father was not distracted, speaking so fast that Frank had trouble following him. "Then the coffin is enshrined in a space above the altar," he said. "In 1934, Francis' most faithful brothers were entombed near him in the corners of the wall around the altar.

"So anyway, here I am, kneeling on cold hard stone in this historic and silent space, praying to myself (actually for *you*, Frank). That's when I realized I wasn't alone, when I saw that figure off to the right moving slightly. The person was half-invisible and sharing the dimly-lit area but I could see that he was dressed in the clothing of a Franciscan Brother.

"Well, you know me, Frank. I can't let this opportunity pass without seizing the moment and filling it with conversation. I just *had* to speak to this person whom God had placed beside me in this most obscure place on planet earth. We were meant to be here together, I firmly believed, to meet here at the same time in such a remote location. It was undeniable destiny, for both the Brother and me.

"I finished my prayer and watched as the man rose with me. We stood almost face-to-face as we both moved awkwardly in the same direction, toward a narrow archway that exits the area of the tomb. We exchanged smiles and I offered him the right-of-way, stepping to one side. He smiled and motioned for *me* to go first. We stood together, locked in place. Neither one of us wanted to take the initiative to move forward. Then, the Brother slid through just in front of me.

"I didn't know if he understood English so I did my best to manage a greeting in my awkward Italian. He smiled at my attempt and responded in excellent English, though influenced heavily by an Italian accent.

"Have you lost your group?" he asked.

"I told him I chose to remain here alone for awhile. 'It's so different,' I said, 'so unique, to be here alone—or *almost* alone—with this great Saint.'" He shook his head in approval.

"I am sorry I stole your aloneness."

"Not at all. It's good to meet you,' I told him. 'It's a privilege. My name is Tony Tonelli. I'm a Catholic priest visiting here from the United States.' He introduced himself as Brother Pietro, a resident of the Friary of Saint Francis. He said he'd lived there for over 60 years. I figured him to be in his early-eighties.

"We talked for only a few minutes in the cramped quarters. Then he invited me to follow him to the courtyard of the friary. It stands next to the Basilica. It was my introduction to the *Sacro Convento*. Again, you have to picture all this, Frank."

"I'm doing quite well, Father. Keep the pictures coming."

"Well, as we walked, Brother explained that the high walls have a total of 53 Romanesque arches with these huge buttresses that support the complex. It towers over the valley below, giving the impression of a fortress. It was built with pink and white stone from Mount Subasio and was already inhabited by the friars in 1230. But construction took a long time with a result that there's an intermingling of different architectural styles, mainly Romanesque and Gothic. You'd really love it there, Frank. You'd appreciate all the fine art and sculptures.

"There I go. I promised not to give you all the details but to save them for the video. I got carried away. Sorry."

"Father, don't apologize. Do I look bored? I'm enjoying every minute and every word of your 'details.' Go on."

Frank shifted his rear quarters again and moved the pillow under his head to the side so that he could have a better view of Father. At his subtle urging (though he didn't need it), Father resumed his narrative.

"I'll just tell you one more thing about the Friary," he said. "It now houses a huge library with all kinds of medieval writings, a museum with works of art donated by pilgrims over the centuries and more than, I believe the Brother said, more than 50 works of absolutely *priceless* art. The tall, imposing belfry was finished in 1239.

"I mean, Frank, this is an old place, a *really* old place. Imagine that this was built over 200 years *before* Columbus came to America. I'm telling you all of this so you can envision it as I go along here. You'll see how important that becomes later on."

Frank said to Father, "I was going to say that I'm *dying* to hear how this ends, but thought twice about my choice of words. So I'll just say that I'm getting more and more curious the deeper you go. Before you do, though, would you please pour me some fresh water? I'd appreciate that very much."

The good priest obliged and helped Frank take a sip. His throat was as dry as if *he* had been doing all the talking. It was a side-effect of his medications. So he drank eagerly from the straw that stood sternly above the edge of the cup. He needed a *new* straw, too. Again, Father obliged. Frank was embarrassed to ask his priestly friend to wait on him like that. But because of their friendship, it was more *humbling* for Frank than it was humiliating. The saving grace was that he knew Father excused his frequent requests.

As soon as he again gave Father the floor, the soft-spoken priest continued. Frank was fascinated, though he knew that he'd remember only a small percentage of what Father was saying. It seemed that both men knew Frank would do better retaining the *visual* aspects of what was being described.

"Sorry for the interruption, Father," Frank said. "Just throw me an extra pillow from over on the chair, please, and you can start whenever you want." His needs were again quickly accommodated and Frank resumed his position, settling back as comfortably as possible.

"Where was I?" Father asked with his hand on his chin.

"You and the Brother were talking in the courtyard."

"Yeah, okay. So he's giving me this great history lesson on the Basilica and the Friary and I'm enjoying every minute of it when I see him glance down at his wristwatch. I instinctively did the same. We both realized it was approaching four o'clock in the afternoon, nearing the time when all the buses had to leave to return to Rome. I guess because we were having such a good time together and we seemed to hit it off so well . . . because of that, he made a suggestion: 'I must drive into Rome tomorrow morning for a meeting I have scheduled at the Vatican,' he said. 'Why don't you stay here tonight and you can drive back with me then?'"

"It sounded like a great idea. When I told Brother that I didn't want to impose on him, he explained that it was no imposition and that he'd enjoy continuing our conversation over dinner. I was delighted to have the opportunity to spend more time in that sacred place as well as with Brother Pietro. I looked upon it as a rare gift, a sort-of 'thank you' for being the pastor of a church bearing the name of Saint Francis."

"Boy, I'll say it was a privilege," Frank replied. "So then, you stayed there, in the living quarters with the Brothers? By the way, before you go on, straighten me out on something. Do they refer to themselves as Brothers or Friars?"

"Good question, Frank. Actually the two terms are interchangeable because *Brothers* are informally called *Friars*. So it really doesn't matter which you use."

"Okay, sorry for the interruption. Go on. I had just asked if you stayed in the living quarters with the . . . uh, *Brothers*."

"It was *near* their quarters," Father answered. "They gave me a modest little room set aside for guests of the Friary, people who were members of the Order or members of the Brother's families. The only window overlooked the courtyard.

"Brother Pietro set me up in the room with fresh linens, and then told me that dinner would be served in about an hour. He gave me directions on how to find the dining hall. He was extremely accommodating. I apologized for not bringing an extra set of clothing, but he said jokingly that he'd be sure to keep his distance the next day."

It was time for Frank to shift around in his bed again and Father provided the assist, adjusting the pillow behind his head and giving him fresh water. They were familiar with the drill. Frank expressed his gratitude.

Reluctantly but necessarily, reality set in as both men were forced to abruptly shift from the peaceful room at the *Sacro Convento* back to the very dismal hospital surroundings. Frank explained that they'd soon be bringing his dinner. It was approaching five o'clock. As much as they hesitated to interrupt the flow, duty prevailed. Father explained that he was obligated by multiple needs at the rectory and said he'd be back in the evening to complete his story.

Frank certainly did not underestimate the priest's zeal. He returned promptly at seven o'clock and Frank was off again on his delightful visit to Assisi. It came as no surprise that Father knew exactly where to pick up his narrative.

But Frank had a question before they got started. He said he'd like to know what Brother Pietro *looked* like. Father had given his approximate age but Frank was curious about his physical appearance. Father obliged.

"Frank, rather than *describe* Brother, I anticipated your curiosity and brought you a few pictures I took while at the Friary. They were a little nervous about picture-taking inside the building, but Brother stepped outside where I snapped these."

Father stood at Frank's bedside and leaned over to help his friend better view the printed pictures. Frank wasn't surprised at Brother's appearance. He was short (Father said about 5'6"), very thin, not much hair on top, and he sported a robust white beard that began at each temple and ended several inches below his chin. The beard reminded Frank of facial hair he once grew when he was in his twenties, an attempt to, at least *visually*, join the "hippie" generation of his time.

Brother smiled broadly in each picture as he posed before a blooming bush of red roses behind him. He appeared as a stereotypical Italian Brother of the Order of Saint Francis. Frank was pleased that he could now visualize him exactly as he was. Father said he gave his age as 92 though Father's initial guess put him at "more like 82." He had smooth skin and very few wrinkles.

After that brief break in his story, Father moved back to his chair beside Frank's bed and resumed the conversation.

"After a delicious dinner . . ."

"What did they serve?" Frank interrupted.

"Well, there was excellent wine made from the vineyards of the property and fresh-baked bread the likes of which I've never tasted in my life. It had an aroma of garlic and wheat that was almost as delicious as the flavor.

"And then there was some pasta with a buttery sauce and mushrooms. I'm telling you, Frank, the taste was completely unique, especially when I compared it to the Italian foods they serve in the United States and even throughout the places I've been in Italy, for that matter. I complimented Brother on the excellence of the raw materials, unique herbs and spices, and the cooking talents of the chefs at the Friary."

Father's description made Frank's mouth water as he felt the pangs of the hospital's institutional food. Fortunately, he was fed only a bland tuna salad sandwich for supper so the stomach distress was minimal. Father once again eagerly returned to his story.

"When we finished dinner," he said, "Brother Pietro invited me to sit with him in the garden. We sat on adjacent straw chairs. The night was brisk but the rain from the daytime had stopped and the air smelled fresh from rain-soaked soil.

"Just before we walked into the garden, Brother handed me a small glass of Italian brandy. He toasted with the words, 'To your health, my friend. And may the blessing of Francis be with you.' We sipped from the glasses. I could feel the warmth of the smooth drink touch me inside and out. I had already developed an unusual, a *spiritual* closeness to this good Brother who sat beside me. I felt I could trust him and that the prayers I requested for *you*, Frank, would be in good hands. Little did I know that my request would culminate on a grand scale.

"Right up front, I took it upon myself to explain about your illness, about how courageously you were facing the fact that it was terminal. To my surprise, that simple and common request for prayers triggered an uncommon response. Brother smiled, sipped from his drink and shook his head up and down, indicating that he would, indeed, remember you in his prayers.

"But what was most unusual was the illumination in his face as it glowed with enthusiasm. He immediately began to tell me a most intriguing tale. It wasn't that long ago and, thankfully, I can recall his words pretty accurately."

'I am going to tell you something that not even most who live here have heard,' Brother began. 'It is something that has been kept very quiet for over fifteen years, something we have held from most visitors and from the secular world. You will understand when I tell you why we are obligated to keep it concealed and private.'"

Father said he was honored that Brother would confide in him after knowing him for such a short time. He was as proud as he was curious to hear the *private* story. He told Frank that he could actually feel butterflies in his stomach from the anticipation. Frank acknowledged that he now felt the same.

"Brother spoke with a thick Italian accent like I said before. But it was fortunate that he spoke very slowly and deliberately. I thus had no problem understanding everything he said. It was as if each syllable and each word knew exactly where it was going and where it belonged in a sentence. He was truly an amazing man. These are the details of his story."

'You probably remember the earthquake,' the Brother said, 'the earthquake that shook this very ground on the morning of September 26, 1997. There were actually two earthquakes that hit in succession. They registered 5.5 and 6.1 . . . which is bad.'"

Father said that he told Brother he had been saddened to read about the quakes and the fact that they caused severe damage to the magnificent Basilica. Brother continued.

'There was devastation all around this part of Italy. Our Basilica was not spared. Later, and very tragically, while a group of repair specialists and friars were inspecting the damage, an aftershock shook the buildings.'

"While he was explaining about the earthquake," Father said, "Brother Pietro paused and pointed toward the Basilica that was affected. Brother and I both waited in silence as if to expect the ground to shake one last time."

Brother Pietro continued. 'The quake caused the collapse of the vault in the Upper Basilica and two of our Franciscan Friars who were among the group and two of the specialists were killed during their inspection. We still grieve for them. Less critical but also of grave importance, many of the most beautiful frescoes of the life of St. Francis were destroyed in the collapse. That made it necessary to close the Church for two years of restoration.'"

Frank was compelled to interrupt Father to ask questions: were the frescoes ever restored to their original beauty, and where was Brother Pietro when the quake hit? Father's answers were thorough.

"The restoration is *a work in progress* and it may actually take decades to complete. Brother Pietro was helping to prepare breakfast in the kitchen when the quake struck and he and others in the room quickly protected themselves beneath tables. It was the best place to hide from falling debris." Frank encouraged Father to go on with the story.

"So, Brother Pietro and I are sitting there sipping our brandy in the garden. I heard the bells strike midnight and we were still vitally involved in our conversation. Of course, Brother was diligent in refilling our glasses from time to time. It was a teacher/student relationship that had developed between us and I listened to his every word. At that point, things *really* got interesting."

Frank was mesmerized by the suspense in Father's story as the priest offered more details. Surely, everyone involved had mastered the art of fine story-telling, complete with anxiety, embellishments and expectation. The Brother told an excellent tale and Father was now up to the task of relaying it to an enthusiastic listener. It seemed appropriate, an inconsequential item for sure, but one that Saint Francis himself would have found delightful. He was said to be a poised conversationalist and never at a loss for words.

'One of the restoration artists,' "Brother went on," 'while he was removing the damaged plaster from the surface of one of the frescoes on the wall, he felt a large bubble of air just beneath the surface. He dug carefully with a tool, a small, sharp spade, and the bubble burst, in spite of the fact that he had been so cautious. At that moment, a short scroll tied and wrapped in burlap appeared from the cavity inside the wall. It tumbled gracefully from the wall onto the dusty floor. It *fell from the heavens,* brother said as he smiled and pointed his hands toward the sky. Then, he continued.

'The scroll had obviously been tucked into a crack of concrete and then painted over by the creator of the fresco. Even though it was visibly wrinkled, its contents were protected by the outer shell of burlap, plaster and paint.

'And now I tell you the most astounding element of the discovery,' Brother said, 'the most amazing of all. In his *Legend of Saint Francis* painted on the north wall of the nave, just to the right of the entrance, the artist, Giotto di Bondone, created a pictorial narrative of the Saint's life. In one of the frescoes, the one designated # 5, *Renunciation of Worldly Goods,* Saint Francis is shown reaching his hand up to heaven. As if breaking through the sky, a hand is reaching down, a realistic human hand reaches down toward the standing Saint. It is clearly a representation of the hand of God.

'You may find this hard to believe, Father,' "the Brother told me," 'but it was directly *from* that hand painted on the wall that the document dropped. And that is the truth!

'Of importance also . . . art experts admire the paintings of Giotto as being so vivid that it appears as if he had been a *witness* to the life of Saint Francis.'"

Frank was spellbound, his attention riveted on the eyes of Father Tonelli. But he was excusably compelled to interrupt him for a desperate visit to the bathroom. All the water he had been drinking was taking its toll on his bladder and it was important to relieve himself. Father helped him negotiate with his *appendage on wheels* so that he could get into and out of the bed and bathroom safely and quickly. Frank apologized and asked Father to remember where he left off in his story. There was little doubt that he could and would.

The Prayer

When Frank was comfortably back in bed, Father resumed his story. His patience was being tested by the interruptions, but he was happy to pay such a small price for the opportunity to entertain his good friend.

"Well," he continued, "Brother Pietro expanded his story and explained more about the restoration artist's discovery. He told me that, in his words, 'The artist was so alarmed and shaken at seeing the scroll fall onto the floor below him that he immediately climbed down from his scaffold and, with no pause and little discretion, opened it.'

"So, Brother goes on to tell me that the artist expected to find notes left behind by Giotto, the original artist, probably written in Latin or Italian. But instead, he held in his hands a delicate, well-preserved document written in Italian but in a dialect the artist didn't recognize. He told me the restoration artist was so frightened by the astonishingly excellent condition of the document that, with great care, he carried it to Brother Giacomo, the head of the Friary at that time.

"Giacomo examined the delicate manuscript closely but he couldn't translate many of the words from a dialect he found unfamiliar. He then deferred to the man who held the reputation as a linguistic scholar and the primary historian of the Friary, Brother Pietro. The shocked Brother was as excited as he was perplexed by the clear handwriting with the distinctive signature at the bottom appearing to be that of Saint Francis himself.

"Pietro then told me that when he received it, he opened the thin parchment and measured it to be exactly twelve inches wide and fifteen inches from top to bottom. The words were written in the same language that Francis used to record his well-known *Canticle of the Sun*, the Umbrian dialect of Italian, an extinct Italic language. The *Canticle* is believed to be among the first works of literature, if not *the* first, written in the Italian language.

"The scroll was dated with the first three digits 122. The fourth digit appeared to be a 4 or 6 but the ink had been smeared after the numbers were written. So it could have been the year that Francis is said to have first revealed the *Canticle*, in 1224, or the year that he died after a long illness, in 1226."

Frank immediately asked how a parchment scroll inside the wall could still contain discernable words after so many years, so many *centuries* of aging. Father admitted that at the time he heard it from Pietro, he also was in disbelief.

Father continued without answering Frank's question because he knew it would be addressed later. "Well, Brother told me that the preservation and condition of the scroll was a significant part of the extraordinary mystery, almost as inexplicable as the uncorrupted body of Francis.

"At that point in the discovery, the humble Pietro didn't want the personal responsibility of verifying the authenticity of the author's signature and the handwriting on the scroll itself. But he was certain enough that he could judge the relative age of the parchment to determine that it was near the same age of the painting that concealed it for almost 800 years. The Church was begun in 1228 and was completed around 1240. So the manuscript must have been placed inside the concrete some time between those years. The best estimate was the year 1235.

"Brother Pietro told me," Father said, "that he knew immediately that the scroll must be submitted to Rome where it would be subjected to close scrutiny by scholars and linguistic experts for confirmation of its source. But not yet!

"The ambitious Brother Pietro was determined to do his own research with the help of his fellow Franciscans who shared life with him in the Friary. They would attempt to solve the mystery of the scroll which contained, in his words, *proprietary information.*

'The manuscript belongs to our founder,' Brother attested, 'and we shall be the first to translate it. *Then,* and *only* after our initial examination, shall we pass it on to Rome.'

"So ownership was one issue and pride was the other. Both were motivating forces that inspired the Brothers to attempt to translate the document themselves 'without the help of the theologians and documentarians of the Church of Rome.' "By the way, did I mention that Pietro was enjoying himself immensely as he told me all this? It was obvious that he was having a grand time and directly reinforcing his reputation as a propitious story-teller."

Frank became increasingly interested in the discovery of something new from the mind of Saint Francis, something found in the 21st century but fresh from a man who had been dead for over 800 years. Frank had a generational bond with the great Saint of Assisi . . . he received the name "Francis" from *his* father who took it from *his* father who took it from *his* father. It went back as far as the family-tree could be traced. So it was no mystery that Frank *connected* to the Saint.

Now, "Frank IV" greatly valued his "inside track" on something so personal and something so vital in the life of his family and his Church. The story Frank was hearing was, indeed, as fascinating as it was relevant to the history of a fond and most beloved friend, Father Tony Tonelli. Having confided so much in him thus far, the priest approached a critical phase of sharing his Assisi experience.

"So Brother and I are still sitting in the garden talking and sipping our brandy," he said, "conscious enough to assure our sobriety throughout the important conversation. And Brother continued to verbally connect the scroll to the famous *Canticle of the Sun,* the religious song of Saint Francis that was said to be composed while Francis was recovering from a serious illness. According to tradition, the first time it was sung in its entirety was while Francis lay on his deathbed and enlisted the accompaniment of two of his original companions, Brothers Angelo and Leo. That was confirmed to be in 1226.

"As the bright and well-educated Brother Pietro started putting all the pieces of the puzzle together, he determined that the writing on the newly-discovered scroll was penned at about the same time as the *Canticle* and in the same Umbrian dialect of Italian. This, for sure, complicated the translation process of the new piece because of the extinct nature of the dialect.

Brother Pietro was an excellent translator of Italian, Latin, and English, but being accurate with the Umbrian dialect was a challenge he wasn't prepared for at the age of 92. Pietro reasoned, however, that his cohorts at the Friary could collaborate to provide the expertise he himself lacked."

This time, it was Father who needed a breather in the conversation. He politely excused himself, stood, stretched, and explained to Frank that he had to take a short walk to the hospital cafeteria. It closed in ten minutes and he needed a "coffee fix" as he put it, something to energize him for the remainder of the story. Father returned within five minutes to complete his narrative. He needed every bit of the energy just gained from the caffeine. Frank turned down an offer for coffee because even decaf wasn't allowed in his diet.

Frank understood his friend's need for the break, although he was nervous and fidgety the entire time he waited. He took advantage of the opportunity, however, to stand and stretch, to straighten his disheveled bed sheets, and to return to the bed just in time for Father's reappearance.

Father carried his filled cup of coffee and sat down again in the chair beside the bed. Frank had no reason to doubt the accuracy of what Father was saying because he had been baffled by the priest's extraordinary memory over the many years of their friendship. The extreme tests of his qualities of recall were demonstrated through his knowledge of dates, places and people as they related to history, film and sports. In Frank's words, "The man could win a fortune on *Jeopardy!*"

Father began again with the following statement: "Hang in there, my good friend," he said, "because at the end of my story, you'll learn that there's something in this for you. I wouldn't be consuming your precious hours if I didn't think it was important enough to tell you." Frank trusted Father and waited in an advanced stage of curiosity. If the story was nothing else for Frank, it was an intense distraction.

"So I'm going to pick-up with the thoughts of Brother Pietro again," Father said. "He told me that he worked tediously with his cohorts at the Friary, laboring over dozens of lengthy translation sessions. It was important to be accurate. After all, there was strong evidence to support gut feelings that the words on the parchment were those of Saint Francis.

"Sometimes, the team of seven—an uneven number chosen to prevent a tie if the men disagreed—spent entire nights without sleep as they perused the document. Pietro admitted that the holy and learned men had heated disputes over the Umbrian dialect used to record the words. Especially difficult were articles, adjectives and adverbs. Nouns and verbs were easier and caused fewer linguistic debates.

"Brother explained that, 'after more than five years of dissecting the words and sentences on the mysterious parchment, in early 2002, the Brothers still remained at odds over key phrases. Our translation of every word had to be *absolutely perfect*,' he said."

"Brother went on to explain more. 'The problem becomes complex when you translate into Latin or Italian from the *Umbrian* dialect of Central Italy. This dialect has its roots in Classical Latin and is sometimes preferred as the International Language of study. But it was less familiar to all of *us*.

'We were fairly certain that the precious Umbrian writing did conclude with the unique signature of Francis. From the very beginning, that was the easiest part of our undertaking. St. Francis himself had chosen a large and mysterious *tau* or letter *T* which he was wont to use as his signature. It was the 19th letter of the Greek alphabet and its use by Francis was asserted by St. Bonaventure. So our greatest doubt wasn't who *signed* the manuscript, but who penned the words in its body. Brother said that his team made suppositions that were based on reason and logic.

'The heart of the document,' "Pietro told me," 'was probably recorded by one of the two men present at Francis' death, either Brother Angelo or Brother Leo. It was of little consequence to know which one, but if they were both present at his death, as the history of the *Canticle* tells us, and this was possibly composed at that time, around 1226, one of them must have recorded the words on paper. We could assume, then, that Francis *spoke* the words as another man wrote them down. That process of dictation led us to expect and to accept minor grammatical errors.'"

"Brother then told me that in spite of such discrepancies, each of his seven translators concluded that the structure of the words and sentences and paragraphs supported the idea that this newly-discovered written piece was . . . a prayer.

"If that prayer was composed and dictated by Francis on his deathbed, the translation of the heading at the top of the document was reasonable. It was accurate to assume then that the new document was what it claimed to be . . . *A Prayer for the Dying*.

"It was known that Francis suffered terribly during his last days and weeks of life, especially while he endured the agony of the *stigmata*. He would have reasonably expressed compassion, then, for the plight of any and all people who were in the process of dying. A prayer would be generously appropriate.

"Most dramatically, The Prayer appeared to be an amalgam of many of Francis' most popular works, especially the *Canticle of the Sun*. In fact, *The Canticle of the Sun* refers directly to Francis' interest in and focus on dying.'"

Father then told Frank that Brother Pietro had memorized those portions of the *Canticle* and recited them to Father: 'Be praised, my Lord . . . through those who endure sickness and trial. Be praised, my Lord, through our Sister Bodily Death, from whose embrace no living person can escape.'

"Those were, indeed, undeniable facts that confirmed the Saint's near-obsession with death. Since the new prayer could be related to the last breath of Francis himself, it was most logical to assume that its relevance could affect others who were about to face their meeting with God.

"But this is where the Brothers ran into a baffling conundrum, one that nearly propelled the new prayer into oblivion. As Brother Pietro told me, 'Just as we were about to celebrate our accomplishment in translating the difficult Umbrian piece of literature, a contentious argument erupted among the members of the translation team, namely, the interpretation of a request by the great Francis. It seemed that he had instructed his friends, Angelo and Leo, to *restrict* the public distribution of this, his final prayer.

'The conflict arose in the *introduction* that preceded The Prayer but, nonetheless, was a vital part of the document. It gave directions on the application of The Prayer, on how it should be used. So here we were, seven "experts," and we were unsure of how to interpret the Italian and Latin meaning for several key words in the Umbrian manuscript.

'As we translated from Umbrian to pure Italian, we largely agreed; but when we went from Italian to Classic Latin (which was customary for such translations) the dispute became more acute. Unfortunately, each step was necessary to develop a translation that was flawlessly acceptable to the Vatican.

'The words at issue were *numquam,* the Latin word for "never," the Latin *haud* meaning "not at all," and the Latin word *aliqua* meaning "some." Transitioning from Umbrian into Italian and then into Latin, the equivalent of those three words was used by Francis several times. And that is where the conflict arose.

'Three of the Brothers on the team insisted that by using the words that translated into *numquam* and *haud,* Francis meant that The Prayer's public exposure should be "never" or "not at all," thus reserving it exclusively for the Brothers. Three other Brothers insisted that Francis, more than once, used an Umbrian word that translated into the Latin *aliqua,* thus, not necessarily *forbidding* but merely *restricting* his prayer to discretionary use by people outside the monastery. In that context, Francis wanted The Prayer to be used "sometimes."

'It was in this state of limbo that the document floundered for nearly three years . . . until the team decided to place the resolution of the problem entirely in my hands. It was a logical decision since I was the eldest in the group and I had the most experience in Italian and Classic Latin translations.'

"At that point, I interrupted Brother Pietro and asked if all the Brothers didn't concur that the most important part of their job in translating The Prayer was to capture its spirit and meaning rather than its *application*.

"He said that was, indeed, the primary concern. 'But if we could not recommend its proper *use*, then our hard work was in vain.' "He went on to explain his conclusion."

'I favored the meaning for the word, *aliqua,*' he said. 'I believed deeply that the Saint who was the model for our lives would not have wanted his prayer reserved for the Brothers' eyes only. It was more logical and more consistent with the personal theology of Francis to concur that he desired his prayer to be used by everyone, at the very least, "sometimes."

'This deduction, the one we eventually agreed upon, allowed the use of The Prayer by faithful followers of Francis. It would be released to our fellow Brothers first, then to the closest friends of the monastery, and, of course, eventually submitted to theologians and scholars at the Vatican.

'Within our family of friars, the judgment of who would receive The Prayer was left to the discretion of the seven of us who executed the translation. In due time, the responsibility would be passed on to others within the Order who assumed *our* responsibilities through attrition. All of these conclusions were submitted to Brother Giacomo who remained the head of our Order. He concurred with our judgment and presented The Prayer, along with our findings, to Rome, in 2007. By that time, we had also translated the document into English which was the easiest of the translation obligations.

'So today,' "Brother said to me," 'today, even though we wait for the authority of Rome to release our precious prayer in *all* languages, we feel justified in offering it to our personal friends.

And we dispense it selectively. Consistent with my own strict rule, because of my faith and trust in you, Father, I will privilege you with a copy of this blessed document, *A Prayer for the Dying*, most likely written by our own Saint Francis.'"

"I told Brother that I was humbled by his trust. But I was, at the same time, troubled by one serious issue. I said to him, very directly and with no insult intended: You used the words 'most likely written by . . .' do you accept the possibility that the document was *not* written by Saint Francis? I know you said you were *fairly certain* that it was his signature, but do you have some doubt about that? And will final attribution be confirmed and announced by the Vatican?"

'Yes,' "he answered" . . . 'yes, to both questions. A small doubt does remain about the origin of the signature. And yes, that will ultimately be confirmed by the Vatican. There are forensic examiners who are now studying the very unusual symbols Francis chose to use as his signature.

'But as we view it today, the translators agree that The Prayer itself, the sensitivity and delicate choice of the words, even if they were *not* the words of Francis, they are uniquely inspirational. It is that which we honor and appreciate most. And it is *that* which we believe will attract the attention of Almighty God, regardless of who authored those words.'

"My final comment to Brother was that, given the time, I would enjoy debating his rationale on the importance, or lack of same, in determining The Prayer's author. His last words on the subject of authorship were barely intelligible, 'I remain as certain as I am about anything,' he mumbled, 'that our founder, Saint Francis of Assisi wrote *A Prayer for the Dying*. I would defend that premise with my life!' "I left it at that!"

"Brother then said a few more things about his gift to me. 'Tomorrow, I will give you a numbered copy of The Prayer before you leave. I expect you to use it sparingly. Release it only to dearest friends and members of your family. Apply it only when death is imminent and incontrovertible.'

"Then, in a near whisper, as if he was afraid someone might hear his words, he said, 'I would be most pleased if you offered it to your friend who is dying.'"

"He added more. He gave me what I'd call a 'qualifier.' He told me that reports from beneficiaries of The Prayer claimed that no dying person had ever been spared from his or her impending death. It was an exception that the Brothers noted clearly, an *exclusion* they accepted. He said that many other results, answers to The Prayer, are on record.

"There was once a dying man who used The Prayer repeatedly, and before his death, was reunited with a son he hadn't spoken to for many years; there was a young girl whose dying mother used The Prayer faithfully for over ten days and her missing daughter was found after being lost in the wilderness; a family dispute was settled with forgiveness just minutes before a woman passed to God; and a mentally-disturbed man found peace before he died. These cases are all documented and verified by witnesses, not declared *miracles*, you understand, but answers to intentions attributed to respectful use of the newly-discovered prayer.

'These and many other requests,' "Brother told me," 'have been granted, but not in a single case has a prayer been answered to save one's own life. Be certain to pass this on to your friend.'"

"As he had promised, early the next morning, Brother Pietro handed me an English-language copy of the document. I didn't know exactly how to treat it, where to put it. I knew it was merely a copy, but it had such tremendous significance and was such a treasured gift that so few people had seen. It was actually unnerving to think of carrying it back home, especially while assuming it was still a very private document created in the holy mind of the great Saint Francis of Assisi.

"From the time Brother gave it to me until I returned to the rectory, it never left my person. I tucked it into a waterproof pouch along with my passport and I carried that pouch in the safest place I could find, on a strap around my waist. It did make it back safely and in good condition. No doubt, a few prayers of my own helped protect it."

Father Tonelli, as Frank stared at his movements, reached into his jacket pocket and withdrew a wrinkled piece of copy paper that had been folded twice. When fully opened, it measured 8½" x 11" with typed words bleeding through one side. Frank felt that looking at the paper was intimidating enough but seeing it in such an unpretentious form bordered on sacrilege. It resembled nothing more than a mundane note, like a grocery list or an appointment reminder.

Together, the two friends stared at the paper. As Father handed it to Frank, he said, "It's my honor to give this to you, my friend. It's the most exceptional gift I've ever given."

It was, indeed, titled *A Prayer for the Dying*. Frank held it tightly as he also held back tears. He was speechless and in disbelief. He stared at Father and the paper simultaneously. Father smiled, overcome with joy. It was one of those rare, *silent* moments between two friends when neither needs to speak to tell the other what is in his heart. Father recalled the final comments of Brother Pietro and shared them with Frank.

"As we Brothers witnessed the power of The Prayer to grant special intentions over recent years, as it has affected our friends and family through unusual manifestations, we became even more certain that it was the work of our beloved founder. We also learned to appreciate just why Francis limited its use. He most assuredly received the inspiration of the Holy Spirit and he felt, in the goodness of his heart, that the power of God should be manifest in restricted situations only through the humble judgments of his family of Brothers."

Frank interrupted Father Tonelli at this point. He posed a heavy and legitimate question. "I want to go back to something you said earlier, about the signature. Why did you doubt the words of Pietro, the words of such an obviously holy man? What is it that troubled you about his belief that the signature was genuine?"

"It was simply my human nature, Frank. As I listened to Brother, I was puzzled by his hesitation from time to time. I was reminded of his age of 92 years and I thought, perhaps, that his entire story could be attributed to a fertile, aging, but extremely dedicated and enthusiastic mind.

"Let me make it clear . . . I never doubted his intentions or his genuine passion for wanting to believe the document was the work of his beloved founder. It was really hard for me to doubt him, but that thought did linger. I, too, preferred to believe that it was the loving work of the wonderful Saint Francis. But I guess we'll have to wait for the people in Rome to pass their final judgment before we can be certain that Brother Pietro was correct and that his story contained no fabrications, no fiction. I asked him again about just why, in his personal opinion, Francis placed restrictions on the use of his prayer."

'It was said that he harbored a personal fear that the granting of intentions through The Prayer might be perceived as "magic," that The Prayer might be expected to grant wishes in the same way as "a genie in a bottle!" He prevented this by limiting its use and trusting the discretion of his loyal Brothers. So we care for The Prayer,' Pietro explained, 'as we care for our own lives, for our faith, and for the affirmation of Francis' holiness and his devotion to the teachings of Jesus Christ.

'Today, significant elements of the mystery remain unsolved, especially details about the placement of the document behind and inside the precious fresco. Questions are abundant: in the 13th century, how did this prayer of Saint Francis pass from the hands of Brother's Angelo and Leo into the hands of the artist who placed the document inside the wall?

'And why would the Florentine painter, Giotto Di Bondone, have been an accomplice in such a clandestine act while working on an assignment as important as the walls of the Basilica with scenes from "The Life of Saint Francis of Assisi?" And why would the closest companions of Francis entrust Giotto with such an invaluable document? He was, after all, a very young artist seeking to establish a reputation. The only *clear* part of the mystery is its *lack* of clarity.'"

Father Tonelli explained his difficult farewell to the saintly Brother. "I was sad to see our visit come to an end," he told Frank.

"But I promised him that he would forever be in my prayers. I told him that I so envied him for living his life in the habitat of the great Saint Francis. And do you know what he said to me? He said, 'The spirit of Francis does not live in *this* habitat alone. It lives in *you*, Father. It lives in the hearts of all those who voice his name, in the souls of those who pray to him, in those who believe in the power of his intercession.

'So, one might say that the habitat isn't nearly as important as the inhabitant. Saint Francis is in your heart as purely and as completely as he is within the walls of these buildings, the material structures that sheltered his body. Remember that, my friend. Francis lives within you, *and*, I might add, within your parishioners who praise him every time they utter the name of your parish.'"

Father Tonelli and Frank were both exhausted by the hard work of telling and listening to the intense story. Frank carefully fingered the folded piece of paper and fumbled to find appropriate words to thank his friend for the overwhelming gift. He held the paper tightly but did not open it fully. Frank reasoned that since it was the culmination of Father's mission to deliver The Prayer, then its reading should be saved for a privately spiritual time.

And so, the words and the power of the gentle prayer were passed from Saint Francis of Assisi to Brother Pietro, then to Father Tony Tonelli, and eventually, into the hands of Frank W. Chase in Chicago, Illinois. The dying man would now apply The Prayer with caution and care, conceiving a final wish before he passed his life to God. Though the task was daunting, Frank's eager acceptance was endowed with hope and trust.

The two friends spent another five minutes together after the transfer of The Prayer into Frank's hands. Frank remained motionless for some time as Father arose, returned his chair to its place against the wall, retrieved his jacket, blessing his friend before leaving.

Frank fought immediate frustration, blurting out, "So you're leaving me alone with this responsibility, this *burden?* Am I supposed to come up with an intention all by myself? Can we talk about it a little while before you walk out of here? Geez, Father . . .

I mean, what am I supposed to do? Where do I go from here?" His words sounded indignant and ungrateful, especially after just receiving an exceptional gift carried half-way around the world. Father stared silently at his friend.

It didn't take more than a minute of reflection for Frank to come to his senses. His conscience was troubled because he knew he had offended Father.

"Man," he said as he awkwardly paced beside his bed, rolling his lifelines beside him. "This is just awful, Father. Damn! I don't know what I'm saying. There's no excuse for jumping all over you like that." He sat down on the edge of his bed, ruffled his hair, and bowed his head. He was excused the instant he displayed the need for forgiveness.

Father promised that they'd soon have more time to talk about what was on Frank's mind; but for right now, the priest must get back to the rectory. It was after eleven o'clock and both of the men needed sleep.

In leaving, Father said to Frank, "Sleep on this, buddy. Give it serious thought before you come up with an intention. Pray over it tonight and I'll be by tomorrow some time. I'd like to hear what you come up with. The only advice I can give you now is to weigh your decision carefully. Remember that it's *God* who'll answer your prayer, not Saint Francis. The Saint is merely an emissary to carry your wish to our Lord. In the end, be prepared to accept God's will regardless of whether his answer is 'yes' or 'no.'

"My gosh," Father said, "I forgot to tell you something. You can use this idea to pass your time. I know you've got your computer here in the room and they've got wifi in the hospital." Father walked closer to Frank, glanced around the room, and whispered as if disclosing a secret.

"There's a 'live webcam' at the tomb of Saint Francis in Assisi," he said. "I urge you to do this, Frank. Just *Google* 'The Basilica of Saint Francis' and navigate your way to an external link that'll guide you right to the webcam, actually 'live' at the crypt. It's stunning, incredible! It'll warm your heart.

"And while you're at that 'Basilica' website, go to the 'Legend of Saint Francis' by Giotto. Study the painting that Brother described, the one with God's hand reaching down from heaven, the place from where the scroll fell. Remember, panel #5 called *Renunciation of Worldly Goods*.' I'm telling you, to see it after our talk will blow your mind. Good night, Frank. See you soon. Sleep well."

As Father left the room, Frank mumbled to himself, "Yeah right. He expects me to sleep well after all this. Maybe I'll try Annie's technique for sleeping in spite of stress. She's always telling me ". . . try to think of *nothing*." And I come back with, "When I think of *nothing*, I'm thinking of *something* as part of that very act. Yours is a good trick if you can manage it," he'd say, "but for me, it's like a dog chasing it's tail. I can never reach the point of catching it. It creates an even greater challenge than the one that's keeping me awake."

Exceptional Intention

Predictably, neither Frank nor Father Tonelli rested well that night. After telling Pietro's story for the first time, Father rehashed the details throughout the night, double-checking his facts and doubting slightly that he recalled everything exactly as it occurred.

At the same time, Frank struggled with the complexities of choosing a worthy intention for The Prayer. Dictated by his faith, he believed there was a high probability that his request would be granted. He thus cautioned himself to make a decision based on sound wisdom rather than instant emotion. The intention required tedious deliberation. His safety net was to have his choice reviewed and approved by Father Tonelli.

Father, on the other hand, had minimal ruminations during the night. His concern was that Frank not be intimidated by The Prayer, that it won't frighten him so much that he avoids its use. Between the two friends, they would examine and dispel their doubts.

Father called Frank around noon the next day. He said he'd come by the hospital around three in the afternoon. Frank explained that the time would work perfectly since Annie and two of the kids had spent the entire morning with him. He then promised Father a surprise. It was *his* turn to play with unexpectedness.

When Father arrived, the visual jolt was greater than he had imagined. Frank sat in his chair, cleanly shaven and hair combed neatly, fully dressed in street clothes and tennis shoes.

41

"What in the world?" Father asked.

"Told you I had a surprise."

"Yeah, but this?"

"Worked it all out. I talked to the doctor when he came by this morning. Told him I had to get out of here, if just for an hour, to get some fresh air, to take a walk in the outdoors, and to visit with you in an environment other than this medicinally-scented hospital."

"And he said it was okay?"

"Absolutely . . . with the condition that I take it slow and not abuse the privilege. I'm still pretty weak from my weight loss, from eating that hospital diet-stuff, and from lack of exercise."

"Then let's get out of here! Where'd you like to go?"

"I'd like to walk somewhere nearby. I'd like to sit down in a quiet place where we can talk . . . over a cold beer. I've got tons of stuff to ask you and I really need your counsel right now."

"There's a place only a block away, Father said. "It's a sports bar and at this hour, I don't think it'd be crowded. Follow me. You're sure you can have alcohol, buddy? I mean, with all the meds you're taking?"

"That was approved by my primary-care Physician, as long as I skipped two of my meds. And I've already done that."

Father led Frank to the elevator, down to the lobby, out the door and up the street into Geno's Place. Along that path, they walked very slowly and deliberately with Father holding Frank under his right arm each time they approached a step or an unexpected obstacle in the pavement.

Frank was, indeed, weak and unsteady . . . physically, that is, not mentally. He had lost 70 pounds, dropping his weight from 240 down to 170. It was a much healthier weight for his 6'2" frame, but he found it ironic that since he was dying and in a "healthier" weight zone, it really didn't matter. But "he was determined to die healthy," as he would say to friends.

Annie had a dear aunt who developed the theory that God gives us excess weight during our healthy years so that when we lose dramatic amounts due to an illness, there's still enough left for us to subsist on for the maintenance of good health. "It all balances out, she'd say." Frank never did agree with the theory but he admired the attempt at excusing excessive eating.

Geno's Place suited the two friends perfectly. Sports memorabilia covered the walls, large-screen TV's poked between autographed pictures, and not more than a half-dozen customers were spread-out over a small and intimate environment. The two men chose a comfortable booth near the rear and ordered their favorite drinks, a Guinness Draft for Father and a Heineken for Frank. The discussion promised to be of monumental proportions.

"Father, I was taught to be really careful about what you ask of the Lord," Frank said. "Because He just might grant your request and you'll be stuck with the outcome for the rest of your life. 'Every time you pray, be sure you're willing to accept what God gives you.' That's my belief. You agree with that?"

"Totally! If you pray for a special intention, be prepared for your wish to be granted. That's what faith is all about, believing that your prayer will be answered, maybe not always in the way you expect, but it *will* be answered."

"Okay, then . . . this isn't just *any* prayer. This is a prayer written by a man whom the Church judged great enough to declare a Saint. So don't you think I oughta weigh this thing even *more* carefully? I mean, this could be the most meaningful favor I ever ask of God."

"True. That's very true, my friend. And yes, I'd weigh it *very* carefully. Why, did you come up with something already? You know, you don't have to tell me if you're not comfortable with that. You've always been an excellent decision-maker. You've been judicious in making excellent choices. You can do this thing on your own, you know. Have you talked to Annie about it?"

"That's a lot of questions, Father, and I haven't even started answering the first one yet."

"Sorry, go ahead."

"Well . . ." Frank hesitated. "Of course I feel comfortable talking to you about it. As a matter of fact, I didn't mention *anything* about the Brother's story or The Prayer to Annie and the kids. I think it's a little heavy for them right now. Maybe later on.

I've got to think about it and get your feelings on that, too. But for right now, I want to run my reasoning by you. I hope you're ready for this. You've heard a lot of crazy things from me over the years, but this is something completely off-the-wall."

"Fire away!"

The men sipped from their beers. Food wasn't an option since Frank's doctor advised him to eat no solid food but his diet from the hospital (maybe a few pretzels, he allowed.) For liquids, the only exception was the freedom to enjoy that beverage of choice. Conversation and *that beverage* would do for now. Both stimulants were in equal and adequate supply.

"To bounce my idea off of you, Father, I've got to go way back into my past. I've told you a lot of this before, so you'll have to excuse the redundancy; but now that these things are important in a different way, I've got to look at my ideas under a stronger microscope."

"I can understand that."

"Okay. So you know that the sixty-plus years that Annie and I have been together are, unquestionably, the happiest years of my life. For each of us, we know we made the right choice in committing to one another forever. We agree on that totally. Never had any doubts about Annie being the right one. She's the greatest wife and mother who ever lived and I'm honored that she married a guy as imperfect as me. I love her more than I ever thought I could love anything or anybody. No regrets. Now . . . store that away as I explain the rest.

"Oh, another thing," Frank added. "The kids and grandkids . . . they're all just incredible *perks* to the marriage, blessings I don't deserve. So my choice to enter marriage as a vocation was the right one.

"But there was a time when I stood at an intersection, a kind of "Y" junction, with two roads going off in different directions. One was the road leading to the vocation of marriage. The other was a road leading to *another* vocation, the vocation of priesthood. Two separate directions but only one choice. Man, I can tell you that at the time, it was tough as hell. I was between thirteen and fourteen when I faced that lifetime decision!" Father Tonelli, having been in that place himself, identified with the difficulties by nodding his head in understanding.

"Now here's my problem," Frank said, "and you're going to think I'm crazy for even thinking this . . . but I've wondered what it would have been like, what *I* would have been like as a priest. No regrets, I've got to say that again, no regrets that I didn't choose priesthood over marriage. But there *have* been thoughts over the years, wondering what it would have been like to be a priest. You understand that?"

"Of course," Father said quickly. "But I think I can answer one of your questions already. First of all, chances are that you would've been the exact same person you are as a husband and father and grandfather, the very same person acting as a *priest*. The career-path doesn't matter. You would've had the same struggles and successes, the same failures. Oh, the people and the experiences would've been different, for sure, but you would've been the same person that you are now, at least *inside* . . . the same morals, conscience, integrity, and weaknesses."

"I knew you'd say that," Frank responded. "But I think your answer is an over-simplification. It's too easy a way to look at it. It's too logical and it's devoid of emotion. It doesn't address my most serious questions."

"And what are those, Frank?"

"Well, for openers, I've studied priests we've known over the years and I've wondered . . . would I have been like 'Father So-and-so?' Would I have been a good homilist, a decent administrator, a good leader of a parish? Would I have had a sharp sense-of-humor or been more or less judgmental than I am now? Would I have been tempted by women? What about those things? They're far less tangible than the things you've been talking about.

"Importantly, too, would I have enjoyed the work, found it interesting and satisfying? Or would I have been bored to death but still remain faithful to my vocation?

"There's another thing I'd like you to tell me, Father. Do you personally believe that I'd have a greater chance of getting to heaven as a priest or as a husband and father and dentist? C'mon now, be honest. Which path do you think gives a guy better odds of getting through the pearly gates?"

Father laughed out loud, shook his head in disbelief, and muttered something about Frank's questions being unique. His only answer was, "I think you know the answer to that one, my friend. When you're judging the 'odds' of getting into heaven, it's not the career or the walk-of-life that matters as much as the person and his or her obedience to the rules of God."

Frank interrupted and laughed as he acknowledged that he knew the question was absurd and didn't really expect a serious answer from Father. He simply wanted to get a "rise" out of him, to see if he was paying attention to the lengthy monologue.

"Keep talking, Frank. I know you're going somewhere with this, a little farther than what you've said so far. I'm still listening."

"Okay! I know you attended a seminary out-of-state for the Oblate Fathers. But you probably remember that I went to the High School Seminary here in Chicago, 'Quigley Prep' as it was called. I was in my final year, my fifth. From there, it was on to Saint Mary's College in Mundelein. And then, I ran into serious doubts. I just liked women, *girls*, too much. When I told my confessor at Quigley, he said it was a clear sign from God. For some reason, God just didn't want me as a priest. He had other things in store for me.

"I remember feeling terribly guilty at that point, apologizing to the priest and telling him I was ashamed of myself for taking the easy way out. He looked me straight in the eye and said, 'You're not taking the easy way out at all, Frank. The path you're choosing is going to be much more arduous than priesthood.'

"And do you know, over the years, Father, I've thought about that a lot, every time Annie and I ran into problems in raising the kids, or a financial impasse, or the common challenges in keeping a marriage fresh and healthy. With every thought like that I figured the priest was right. Marriage *is* tougher in many ways, not *all* ways, but in *some* ways, *different* ways.

"The biggest difference I've seen is . . . at least in marriage, a guy's got somebody who really cares, a wife who's eager to share burdens, a *partner* who cares about him, unconditionally. But that makes me wonder all the more about what kind of priest I might have been. Could I have handled the problems unique to priesthood, like the loneliness? What if I had become a priest and failed, dropped out, left the priesthood, run off with some woman? Would I have been happy? Do those issues, those questions make any sense to you? Did you entertain thoughts like that before you were ordained?"

"Of course," Father responded. "You're not alone, my friend. You can't imagine the high percentage of men, like you, who've had the same questions after leaving the seminary, or especially just prior to ordination. It's part of the human condition when facing a huge decision like that. We just don't know for certain that the choices we make are the right ones. The only measure you can use is to tally your score as a husband and father.

"Judge yourself, Frank. If you've been happy and have done a fair job in your different roles, then you've certainly made the right choice in selecting the married way-of-life over priesthood. But it doesn't mean that you would've made a bad priest, either."

"Do you see, that's not really the issue here, Father. I know all that. It's just that I wish I had the opportunity to have done both, been a married man . . . and then, been a priest. How am I ever going to know how the *real* me would have behaved as a priest?"

"Did it ever occur to you that any *woman* can wonder about the same sorts of things, Frank? Don't you think she, too, stood at an intersection at some point in her life, with a choice of which way to turn? Annie chose to be a married woman and might have wondered all her life how she would have handled being single and pursuing a career in nursing or teaching or music."

"Yeah, of course. I think about that, too. Women are human beings like men, and as such, they also face those difficult choices. Or maybe that's not saying it right. We all face a decision to make one choice. And we want to make sure we make the one that's right for us. That's a no-brainer."

"Don't forget, Frank, you've got to include me in that equation. Don't you think I've wondered over the years about the same kind of things?"

"Sure. But we started out talking about a very serious decision I'm facing right now. I have a choice to make, a chance to have a prayer answered if it's God's will, a chance to leave this planet a little better, maybe, than it was before I walked on it. So what I'm getting at here is the idea that, I think, with your approval, what I'd like to ask for through that prayer of Saint Francis. And I'll share something else with you . . . I haven't even read The Prayer yet."

"So what's your intention, Frank? You're making me very nervous with this build-up. Tell me exactly what you're going to ask for. Get it out and maybe you'll feel better about it."

"Okay. I'm going to ask God, through The Prayer created by one of His favored creatures . . . I'm going to ask Him if I could lead a life as a priest, like right now! I'm not asking to go back in time, to reject my decision to be married to Annie. But somehow, in some creative plan that only He could come up with, give me a chance to live my life all over again, as a priest. Now, what do you think about that, my priest-friend? That's it. Am I crazy or what?"

Father shook his head, frowned, exhaled deeply and said, "Well, it's certainly a unique petition, something I never heard of as a special request. I guess it beats asking for the Cubs to win the pennant, or for world peace, or for your kids to win the Lottery. I don't mean to make light of it, Frank, but that's an intention that's new to me, something *really* different. It's most probably already brought a smile to the face of God. And quite honestly, I don't think you have a prayer in getting it answered."

"Was that an *intentional* pun, Father?"

"Accidental at first, but intentional as the words slipped out. *Spontaneous* fits better. Gives more honor to my genius!" Frank sneered in friendly fashion.

"So you don't think I have a prayer," he said. "I don't quite understand that. Why are you pessimistic about this intention of mine? If God can move mountains, why can't he do this? Just because you never heard of somebody asking to live two lives doesn't mean God couldn't grant that as an answer to a prayer. The way I see it, I think I *do* have a prayer . . . and it's a mighty good one, a prayer from Saint Francis of Assisi."

"Hey, it's *your* intention, Frank. I didn't think you'd be so sensitive about it. Go for it! Who am I to stop you?"

"Well, let me tell you something, Father. As I lost sleep over this last night, I felt terribly selfish. I mean, here I am, this old geezer who's got only a short time to live, here I am asking for something for *myself*. All I'm thinking about is myself. If my wish is going to be granted through this prayer, shouldn't I be asking for something positive for somebody else, like something for Annie or someone else in my family, like improved health for Annie or one of the kids, like . . ."

Father interrupted. "You're forgetting something important about that prayer, Frank. Some eight centuries ago, Saint Francis wrote it as *A Prayer for the Dying*. And you're the only one who's dying that I'm aware of. So if you're going to apply the influence of The Prayer in any way, it's not selfish to apply its benefits to you and to your own life.

"Regardless of how you look at it, Frank, it's your call, your decision. Through my serendipitous meeting with Brother Pietro, or perhaps it was Divine Providence that brought us together, maybe that meeting was destined by God to allow me to gift that prayer to your bedside here in Chicago. Don't you think that's a strong possibility? You've got to look at the big picture here, Frank."

That thought really got Frank's attention. He had never reflected seriously on the plausibility of God intending the blessings of The Prayer be given to him personally as a special gift. Perhaps something good he had done in his life got the Deity's attention and that lead Him to reward Frank in this most exceptional way. Father helped that thought sink deeper into Frank's psyche. And Frank did feel less selfish, though he was humbled at receiving The Prayer. Father had something to add.

"I know that you've always been extremely scrupulous about not being selfish, Frank, ever since I've known you. It's a haunting and daunting thought that you've always been plagued by.

Addressing that, let me digress for a minute. You might appreciate what I'm going to say.

"While I was in Rome, I attended a Mass at a beautiful little Church that sits right beside the Fountain of Trevi. It's dedicated to Saint Rita of Cascia, a Benedictine nun. While at this Mass, as a part of the congregation, I heard a wonderful homily by a visiting priest from Boston.

"This priest talked about something he called, "The Forgetfulness of Self." He explained some of the philosophy of Saint Augustine. And he said that in order to love God completely, in the way God intended, we must temper our love of self, sort of *forget* about our selves and make *God* number one . . . *The Forgetfulness of Self*. And he explained that the thought could be applied to love in general. 'Forget about our *selves* and give our love totally to someone else. Turn our love *outward* rather than *into* our selves.'

"And I'll tell you something, Frank. As I knelt in that gorgeous, historic Church at Trevi, I thought about *you*. I really did! I remembered how you beat yourself up so often in your attempts to do nothing selfish, to always think of the other person first before you ever consider yourself. So in this instance in which you're asking Saint Francis to intercede for you to God, to grant an answer to a special request, I cannot see anything wrong in that at all. My advice is, with humility and sincerity, ask God to grant the answer to your prayer. And be prepared for something you'd never expect."

Frank was so taken back by the words of his friend that his initial response was, "Wow' . . . followed by "I never expected my simple statement about being selfish to trigger something so profound. I always learn so much from you, Father."

Father was ready to go on with the subject at hand. "You know something, Frank," he said, "About asking for a shot at another type of career and life right now . . . maybe it's not quite as wacky and absurd as it sounds at first blush.

"Not long ago," Father continued, "I read a story in the sports pages about an NFL player by the name of Benjamin Utecht. He's 6-6 and 245 pounds and he played for the Indianapolis Colts. But he suffered five known concussions and decided to leave the game. He landed on his feet by becoming a classical singer, a vocalist for touring musicals. He said that he had twin dreams growing up: to play football and to sing.

"He admitted that he got plenty of teasing in school for trying to combine those two. But when it came time and it really meant something special, he made a whole new career for himself. And right now, he's an extremely happy man as a professional singer."

"I know what you're saying, Father, and I appreciate that. But *my* request is different. I'm not asking for a 'new career.' I'm asking to go back into my life and come out as a different person with a different focus . . . simultaneously, the *same* person but a *different* person. It's so damn hard to explain. But I know God's going to understand when I present this to Him, through the hands and the prayer of Saint Francis, of course."

The two friends continued sipping from their glasses of beer, enjoying every minute of their stimulating discussion. Father caught himself, from time to time, pondering the loss of this good friend. He already experienced the vacancy in his life. It made him focus on a greater appreciation of times like this. Occasionally, that appreciation forced a lump in his throat and a tear from his eye. Only once when Frank was speaking did an errant tear follow a path downward from his eye, down his cheek and directly across his upper lip. He wiped it without notice and coughed once or twice to conceal it.

"You know, I had another thought, Father," Frank said. "Last night as I laid there trying to sleep, I thought about Saint Francis himself and the fact that he once changed his life dramatically. As I've read, he was a very worldly guy before he became a religious. He lived the high life, became a soldier, and probably did a lot of things that even you and I wouldn't dare do. So then, he abandons all that and spends the rest of his days forming an order of religious, dedicating himself to the poor and a lot of other saintly missions. I'm sure he had early friends who thought he had gone mad.

"So even a man as great and unselfish as Francis of Assisi, even he had second thoughts. Well, maybe not *really* second thoughts. But kind of like I've tried to explain. He wondered about another kind of life and lifestyle. In his case, of course, he abandoned one life and discovered something totally new.

"On the other hand, what I'm asking for is to have *two* lives, one that I've already lived, and another that I can only imagine. I still have doubts about that being a legitimate intention for *A Prayer for the Dying*, primarily because I'm motivated more by curiosity than by anything else. But if I could live a second life, perhaps there are some people out there that I could help as a priest, some parishioners I'd get to know who needed me as much as my family needs me, maybe just somebody who needed my love."

"I overheard two people on the airplane on my way back from Rome," Father said. "They were talking about the nature of love. The one believed that loving someone dearly was like seeing the face of God. Right now, I can't find anything wrong with you wanting to 'see the face of God' through more and different people with Saint Francis as the conduit. It's a tall order for *any* Saint to make that happen. Just give Him time."

"Yeah, but that's one thing I don't have right now, time."

Both men smiled as Father patted Frank on the shoulder and they prepared to leave Geno's Place and head back to the hospital. It had been a wonderful visit that they both would treasure for as long as they had left together, and beyond. Along their walk back, Frank had another thought.

"Last night, during one of the few times that I slept, I had this crazy dream, Father. It was like a scene from the movie, *Avatar*. I was jumping off this really steep cliff, down into a deep, green valley, without a parachute of any kind. And as I jumped, I feared dying when I hit the ground. But instead, I'm falling downward and I sprout these wings. And they take me down to a soft landing. And I'm okay.

"I thought to myself in the dream, 'You know, Frank, you still believe in fairy tales.' And that's been a problem all my life. I'm more of a dreamer than a realist. And there have been times that my line of reasoning has gotten me into big trouble. You've already heard of my follies when I dabbled in real estate. By the way, are you laughing *with* me or *at* me?

"Maybe now, though," Frank continued, "my dreaming is going to lead me to something that's good for me, something that'll help me find another kind of peace in another place, somewhere where I can do some more good. I don't know if that'll be *after* I die . . . or while I'm still alive. I just don't know how God can possibly position anything this complex and unwieldy . . . actually, *contradictory* in the purest sense.

"It's a challenge to the Almighty, that's for sure, Frank."

"Plus, I've still got a lot of work to do on my own. I have to read The Prayer as many times as I can and hurry to get my message to Francis, first to him and then to my God. You know of any shortcuts, Father? Like you said, my request is 'a tall order' for the best of Saints, maybe even for Almighty God. I'm not at all sure how to *word* my request so that it's clear and without question."

"I wouldn't worry about that, Frank," Father added. "You underestimate the Deity. Remember, He has a count of every hair on the head of every human. I doubt He'll have a problem understanding your request. How He chooses to answer it, however, is a different story. Remember, 'no' is an answer."

Frank had a reply, something he had pondered many times while in the hospital. He humbly offered it to Father.

"I've been thinking a lot lately about God answering my prayers. It's easy to love a God who says 'yes' but it's so much harder to love Him when He says 'no.'"

"That's an obvious reaction, Frank. It's that way in all relationships. I'm sure when Annie says 'yes' to you, it's a lot easier to love her and stay close to her; but when she disputes something you say or she gives you the 'thumbs down' on a request, it's tougher to love her, isn't it."

"Yeah, but it's different with God. I mean, He's the source of everything. And He has it within His power to say 'yes' to everything we ask for. I'm ashamed to admit it, but sometimes I get a little upset with Him when He doesn't grant my wishes, like immediately. My love for Him becomes more of an obligatory thing rather than a heartfelt passion."

"Don't lose sleep over it, my friend. It's the kind of conundrum that's part of a human nature that's full of imperfections. God understands that. After all, He chose to create us that way."

"Can you believe," Father said, "that we're actually sitting here imposing conditions on our love of God? Shouldn't we love Him *unconditionally* regardless of how He answers our prayers, whether the answer is 'yes' or 'no'?

Father and Frank each bowed their heads, ashamed of their spin on this topic of discussion. Frank decided that he'd accept God's answer, whatever it might be.

The Best Marriage

It was no secret that after 57 years of marriage, Frank and Annie's relationship was showing signs of wear and tear. And well it should after raising four children, running a stressful business, and handling the care and loss of both sets of parents. In the final analysis, when all was said and done, they had held together better than most under the same set of circumstances. And they still loved each other more deeply than ever.

Frank recalled a conversation between the two of them, just before he received his tragic health news. He and Annie had a mild dispute about . . . well, neither one could remember what it was about after the first five minutes. But it contained a muddled conflict over empathy and understanding. Annie hadn't been feeling well and Frank was frustrated because she refused to see a physician for a diagnosis.

"You know," he said, "It's really driving me nuts seeing you in discomfort like this."

"So, as usual, it's all about *you*, right?"

"It's not about *me*. It's about my worries about *you*, my frustration at trying to convince you to see a doctor."

"That still means it's about *you*."

"Don't you understand? I'm trying to help you. I'm trying in vain to get you to take better care of yourself and to see a doctor to find out what's going on in your stomach."

"After 60 years of marriage . . ."

"Fifty-*seven*."

"What?"

"I'm correcting you. We've been married fifty-*seven* years."

"All right, after these fifty-*seven* years, you still don't know much about women, do you?"

"How can you say that?

"Because what I'd like to hear from you right now is . . ."

"I know exactly what you're going to say." Frank shrugged his shoulders and rose from his chair at the kitchen table.

"What am I going to say?" Annie asked.

"You're going to say that what you want to hear is . . . 'I'm sorry that you're feeling sick. I'm sorry you're in pain. And if there's anything I can do for you, let me know . . . right?'"

"Yes, something like that."

"I try to say that all the time."

"I haven't heard it in a long time. Instead of saying that, you complain about your own frustration and your own discomfort in witnessing *my* discomfort. It's all about *you*."

Frank stopped his pacing and exited the room. Within sixty seconds, he returned, approached Annie from the back while she stood at the kitchen sink and wrapped his arms around her waist. He gently turned her head to face him and they kissed, like young lovers.

They both said they were sorry for the harsh words. And that was the end of it. Annie promised to make an appointment with her doctor and Frank promised to work harder at being more sensitive to what Annie really needed. It was a typical confrontation . . . brief, forgiving, loving . . . with no hard feelings.

Annie concluded with, "I love you."

Frank replied, "I came not to *be* loved, but to love." His wife slapped him gently on the arm and smiled, acknowledging his distortion of a familiar remark by Jesus Christ.

There were more such encounters as they entered the ranks of *senior citizens*. They had agreed that their patience wasn't nearly as strong as when their marriage was 30, 40 or even 50 years old. Nor was their health as good as it was in the past. But they coped as best they could with the pains of arthritis, bursitis, sciatica, RSD, IBS, and a wide variety of other ailments not uncommon to the elderly. Though they didn't feel or act like they belonged in that category, they were honest and reasonable enough to grudgingly admit it.

One of their favorite pastimes was to enjoy lunch together at a dozen or more favorite restaurants. It was a habit of Franks to stare into Annie's deep brown eyes from across the table and remind her of how much he loved her and how beautiful she remained at the age of 76. She was, indeed, an attractive woman, unusually svelte for her age and gifted with perfectly symmetrical facial features. Combined with her pleasant personality, she was easy to love.

"I am so lucky," he'd say, "because I get to look at someone so beautiful. And all you have to look at is *this*."

Annie was quick to respond as she'd reach across the table and hold Frank's hands in hers. "First of all," she'd say, "I enjoy looking at you every chance I get. And secondly, you're the man I chose to marry, the most handsome man on earth. It's an equal pleasure for me to look at you." Such mutual admiration at this stage of life was extraordinary.

There was another running disparity between the couple, no more serious than the others. Ironically, it involved death and dying. Annie's approach was to be realistic about the inevitability of death yet optimistic about every hour and every minute she had left in her life. She thus studiously appreciated everything from a sunrise to a drop of rain. She clung to every daily experience. And she treasured conversations with her Frank, her children and her grandchildren, whether in person or by phone, email, or text.

Frank, on the other hand, focused more on death than on life since he learned of his prognosis six months earlier. That focus wasn't his choice but something he dared to say was, "beyond his control." Initially, he had extreme difficulty grappling with the thought of death "coming too soon."

"Why don't you breath every breath like it was your last," Annie would say. "Appreciate every second of life." She used that approach only once, however, because it became hurtful and indiscreet. Besides, within a month's time, Frank had taken control of himself, learning to accept the bad news and surrendering totally to God's will. That involved not a small amount of love and compassion from Father Tonelli and the entire family. Annie soon felt ashamed for the times she had scolded him for having little faith.

Actually, Annie turned her husband around so completely that he wanted no more literature on "Death and Dying." Instead, he preferred "More worthwhile subjects about life and living." He was grateful to Annie for her courage and encouragement and he quickly became an exemplary patient.

The only other difficulties between the two elderly lovers were the stereotypical products of aging; e.g., depreciating quality time in the bedroom, mutual accusations of hearing loss, equal accusations for not speaking loudly enough, tardiness for appointments, and persistent forgetfulness. Though each of those human failings was unwillingly accepted, they were heroically tolerated.

The most serious affliction of any marriage, infidelity, was never an issue with either Annie or Frank, at any time in their lives. For her, because of her dedication to her husband and her moral and virtuous consistency, her marital vows would remain intact, "until death do us part." She had no interest in other men, save for the enjoyment of an occasional compliment or an innocent flirtatious comment from one of Frank's friends.

For Frank, it was slightly different but with the same result. He, too, would remain faithful forever. But he would face several female encounters throughout his marriage. He never perceived those as "temptations," he'd say, but rather, "opportunities." He made the differentiation clear. He would never allow himself to be *tempted* because there was no desire to be with any other woman.

The humanness of Frank's nature, however, did recognize infrequent *opportunities,* each related to his business of dentistry: two were offered by married secretaries and the third by a promiscuous hygienist. All were dismissed. Such fidelity in the hearts and minds of both Annie and Frank was attributed to their love and faith in God and in each other.

The final judgment, then, in scoring the marriage of Annie and Frank Chase was that it was as close to a perfect "10" as any could be. It was a partnership "made in heaven" and recognized with gratitude to God. The secret to their marital longevity? An abundance of the three c's: compliments, compromises and contrition (manifest through more than a dash of apologies.)

Throughout their long life as partners, of course, they knew that *forever* wasn't exactly *forever*. It was a very long time on earth but in the next life it was *eternal*. The time for beginning that eternity was now approaching, at least for one of them. And it was approaching as boisterously as a dangerous thunderstorm rolling from over a hill into view.

Frank felt that he had lived long enough. He had traveled the world with Annie, witnessed the growth and happy marriages of a son and two daughters, and the very happy life of a daughter who remained single by choice. They had all enjoyed a full life with minimal worries and no regrets. It was not a bad time for Frank to leave. Besides, he was increasingly curious to see what lay beyond human life. He was always that way, from childhood to now, abundantly curious . . . to a fault.

In a very real sense, Frank was heroic at the prospect of meeting his God. He was actually *eager* to discover the surprises of the afterlife, certain that they would exceed his expectations. He was also prepared to accept a just punishment for his wrongdoings. Any anxiety was overcome by that faith. There was minor concern, of course, but he felt it was needless. If God was as good as he knew Him to be, his trust in Him would be manifest through complete and eternal joy.

As Frank saw it, the ultimate reward in dying was personally meeting almighty God. Then, after an introduction, God would place before his loyal servant the resolution of all the mysteries of the universe, the mysteries of science and medicine and people and other-worldly places and things . . . all the answers to all questions would unfold before him. "Isn't that something to await with excitement," he would ask?

So Frank had rationalized his death with a controlled level of *enthusiasm*. Not that he was happy to leave his loved ones, but his approach was effectively cushioning his last days. If it was God's will that he die now, he was obligated to show acceptance and trust.

Frank's only sorrow wasn't in leaving but in leaving *alone*. He had selfishly prayed for many years that he and Annie would go together, like in an auto accident. Fortunately or unfortunately, that wasn't her wish. Contrary to Frank, she had a desperate fear of dying in an automobile crash. And this being one of only a few occasions, she prayed for an intention opposing her husband's. It wasn't that she wanted to stay alive while Frank passed on, it was that she wanted to die in some less bloody manner than an auto accident, and more importantly, she wanted to spend additional time watching the maturation and development of her grandchildren and, perhaps, even great-grandchildren. Of course, none of that really mattered since, like most conventional people, neither Frank nor Annie had much to say about the sequence or the timing of their deaths, Doctor Kevorkian's methods excluded.

Frank's death right now would also be a severe test of *Annie's* faith and love. Both she and Frank had counseled and consoled many older friends and neighbors during their ten years in Florida. But this was dramatically different. This would create a personal void in Annie's heart and soul, the emptiness of which would be difficult to fill and more challenging to face than any other experience in her life.

On the material side, Frank had taken care of her monetary needs. The house was free of debt, plenty of investments had paid off, and her future was secure for longer than she could live. In addition, there was a trust for each of the children and grandchildren. She would compliment Frank on being "a good provider." But she would also emphasize that it was the *intangible* more than the tangible that would leave her poor. It was "her Frank's presence" that she would find irreplaceable. Though she was surrounded by a loyal and diligent support group of family and friends, Annie would, nevertheless, endure incomparable pain and loneliness.

And so, during the past eight months, she had already adjusted to the absence of her husband around the house. But she and the children were faithful visitors to the hospital. They saw to it that each day, one member stopped by for a chat, sometimes long, other times short. Regardless of the length of the visit, those times were touching, always accompanied by uplifting, conversational *songs of joy* in an otherwise somber environment.

Privately and at regular intervals, Frank said *A Prayer for the Dying* at least three times daily since Father Tonelli gave it to him two weeks ago. He'd recite it after waking in the morning, repeat it at noon, and say it once again just before falling asleep. In the meantime, his physical strength was ebbing at the same rate that his faith was swelling. Though his speech was becoming slurred, he would recite The Prayer out loud each of the three times, provided no one was around. When that occurred, he'd wait until he was alone again.

There was one slip, however, at a time when "Nurse Ratched" was leaving his room. She heard him speaking out loud and thought he was calling her. As she turned, she saw Frank reciting words with his eyes closed. With unabashed indiscretion, she asked what he was saying and why his eyes were closed. Frank opened them, stared at her and answered, "It's because I'm praying."

Nurse Ratched wouldn't let that pass without a personal comment, a distasteful one. "Who you prayin' to?" she asked.

"I'm praying to Saint Francis of Assisi, if you must know."

"Hell, why don't you get yourself a 'medium' and be done with it? Get your hands on that book by Shirley MacLaine. She'll teach you how to talk to dead people."

The nurse was disarmingly ignorant and offensive. Frank replied quietly, "I don't need stuff like that. I talk to my friend without any intervention. He's always there for me. He listens to every word I say. And I don't need a *medium*." With that, Frank closed his eyes and the nurse left, never again to trouble him with spoken questions about his praying.

After that encounter, Frank worked hard to memorize The Prayer. Although he struggled valiantly against the opposing defect of forgetfulness, each time he recited it the thoughts seemed fresh and original. Brother Pietro had not exaggerated when he praised the beauty and sincerity, the elegance and imagery of each word and phrase. Frank appreciated those qualities with each reading and was quick to forgive himself for flaws, figuring that neither the Lord nor Saint Francis would hold him accountable for such shortcomings.

He marveled at the structure of The Prayer, its simplicity and symmetry: 25 lines, 300 words, 3 lines per verse. Did Saint Francis plan such perfection, or was it by chance? How did the author assemble such a page that was so inspirationally creative and organizationally perfect . . . as he lay dying? The Prayer itself was a miracle, a gift of the Holy Spirit, an amalgam of many of the other writings of the prolific Saint.

Throughout his long days, Frank kept closely in touch with Father Tonelli who, just a week ago, had anointed him with the Sacrament of the Sick. They discussed The Prayer briefly during personal visits but avoided talking about the *intention*, even though Frank still felt a conscious spiritual connection to Father. Regardless of that, he winced at the thought of placing so much attention on himself, in spite of the priest's urgings to convince him otherwise. It still made him uncomfortable to talk excessively about himself. And this was no time for unnecessary discomfort.

Frank also remained committed to his original decision to avoid speaking about The Prayer or its intention to anyone in his family, for the same reason. Plus, he feared he could no longer remember enough of the details to adequately explain The Prayer's amazing appearance. His special intention was reserved for the ears of God and repeated every time he uttered The Prayer. "Please God, may I live as a priest, as a man of God in Your Church." He believed deeply that God, through the intercession of His Saint Francis, would somehow answer that prayer.

If there is a difference between *falling* or *slipping* into a coma, Frank *fell* into this one. It was immediate and without warning. One minute he was chatting with his nurse, and the next, his mouth, mind, eyes and ears were inactive.

Nurses, physicians, a cardiologist and an oncologist responded quickly, but no one could break Frank's comatose condition. He was completely out-of-touch with his world!

Another Life

I was eleven years old in 1946 when I first thought about becoming a priest. And I was serious about it.

I was an "only child" growing up in a small apartment on Chicago's north side with my mom and dad and grandma. She was my mother's mom. All of us shared a wonderful life centered on our Roman Catholic faith. It was natural for me to think about priesthood. Without forcing the issue, my family nurtured my vocation.

Besides that heavy influence at home, I was also affected by a large and thriving parish-family called *Our Lady of Lourdes*. It was staffed by a saintly Monsignor and three full-time associate pastors. The parish was also blessed by occasional visits from two absentee associates who were serving as Military Chaplains in the U.S. Navy. They appeared while on furloughs from their duties; then, after retirement from the service, they were re-assigned to our parish.

Every one of our priests at *Lourdes* was an exceptional role model for a young boy like me who was contemplating priesthood. I was impressionable and wanted to be like each one of them, without exception.

During those early years, I prayed a lot, attended daily Mass and served as an "altar boy" at most of those Masses. We lived only a city block from the church so walking to those morning services was no problem, even during winter snowfalls when my passage was severely slowed. But I was dedicated and committed to never missing an assignment or being tardy.

By the time I reached my twelfth birthday, I was receiving training to prepare me for serving High Masses and events like Holy Thursday, Good Friday, special weddings and funerals, and to serve as Master of Ceremonies at many of those events. It was a great honor that my family and I were proud to share.

Along with other servers my age, we were instructed by seminarians who attended Quigley Preparatory Seminary in downtown Chicago. The minor seminary offered a five-year high school program that was a required starting-point for studies to the priesthood.

The seminarians who trained me were also a powerful influence on my life and on my priestly vocation. They were solid, down-to-earth young men whom I admired for their holiness, their moral character and their exemplary Christian behavior. They were all competent students, excellent athletes, and superior role models. They established high standards for the kind of priest I wanted to become.

When I was 14 years old, I graduated from grade school and entered Quigley. There was only one small glitch during my priestly high school studies. Her name was Nancy! She was a neighbor whom I knew since kindergarten and couldn't avoid seeing because she lived only two houses up the street. We were both 15 years old when we got interested in one another.

Nancy wasn't exactly beautiful, by any measure, but she was a very nice person who just happened to have pretty legs and a great smile. We got along amazingly well, took long walks down to the shores of Lake Michigan while holding hands, and slowly became each other's best friend.

If you can believe it, my relationship with Nancy never seriously interfered with my dream to become a priest. It just complicated the matter and dictated the question, "Which do I want most, Nancy (or someone like her) or priesthood." In direct contradiction to my dream, Nancy and I frequently discussed marriage, children, and the possibility of one day becoming man and wife. It was youthful, flirtatious chatter and wasn't anything even close to an engagement to be married. Neither of us knew anything about that more serious stuff.

But Nancy and I *did* kiss. I can vividly recall the first time. I was scared to death and, making it worse, the fear wasn't mutual. We stood in the garden at the back of her house at the twilight hours of a summer night, a romantic setting that was no accident. It had been carefully set up, by me. I worked hard to pick the right time and the perfect location.

Somehow from somewhere, I mustered the courage to make the first move, to lean toward her face . . . and to kiss her on the mouth. It was the kind of kiss that was dry and short, the very first of very few in my life. It meant something to both of us. One *could* say, "Our friendship was sealed . . . with a kiss."

During that friendship, like I said, Nancy and I didn't kiss much . . . a goodnight peck was about all, and no "necking" or that sort of thing. Actually, I was most impressed with her morality and purity since she had no spiritual motivations to be good, at least none that she ever talked about. She was an uncommitted Protestant.

If Nancy was to be my one-and-only girlfriend in a lifetime of bachelorhood, she was a perfect choice. She left me with good memories and no regrets for doing anything sinful.

I continued to find girls in general very attractive and a permanent obsession. I worried about that and, from time to time, deeply questioned the roots of my vocation to the priesthood. Several different confessors and counselors advised me to "remain on mission," to pray hard for the strength to overcome my problem, and to be watchful in protecting my eventual vows of poverty, chastity and obedience. I took all of that very seriously but had not yet experienced exposure to opportunities. It didn't affect me that my favorite aunts insisted I was good-looking, so good-looking that I "shouldn't waste it on the priesthood," as one admiring family-member would offer. But that didn't bother me. I was too busy to be aware of my appearance.

As I progressed through the five-year program at Quigley, Nancy and I saw less of each other. I had been counseled to lead in that and to focus on the ideals of priesthood instead. As it happened, by the time I reached the age of 18, Nancy had found another guy at her school and I was far less distracted. I was happy that I never met her new "boyfriend" and I did feel some sadness at the end of our happy times together.

For the next seven years, I attended the College program at St. Mary of the Lake Seminary in Mundelein, Illinois. The years went by quickly and I grew closer to my seminary family of friends and teachers . . . and to my God. I was ordained on Monday, May 1st, in 1961, at the age of 26.

My 33 fellow seminarians and I were ordained by His Eminence Albert Cardinal Meyer in the chapel of the Immaculate Conception on the seminary grounds. We had a great class and I stayed in touch with my closest friends for many years. I had instantly become *Father* Francis Chase.

I celebrated my first Solemn Mass on May 7th at 12:15 p.m. in my home parish of Our Lady of Lourdes. I was most gratified to see my mom, dad and grandma sitting proudly in the first pew. Neither they nor I could refrain from tears of joy throughout the Mass, especially when I walked down to my mother and gave her my first personal blessing, a tradition for new priests. It was the thrill of my life and one I had dreamt of through all the 12 years of my studies. It was well worth the wait. And so was the consecration of bread and water, changing it into the body and blood of Jesus Christ. The honor and privilege were overwhelming.

After Mass, there was a small reception for family and close friends in the school cafeteria just across the street. It too, provided unforgettable memories.

My first assignment was to serve as an associate pastor at St. William Church, an older parish founded in 1916 and located on the west side of Chicago. I got along well with the soon-to-retire pastor, Monsignor Cletus Devereaux, and I worked closely with the nuns who taught at the parish school as part of an eight-year elementary education program.

Early in my assignment at St. William, my love *for* and ability *at* writing and public speaking proved invaluable. I was asked to preach at Parish Retreats, a variety of Holy Day services, and special Masses for our schoolchildren. Every such assignment was a pure, personal joy. Generous compliments from parishioners reinforced my confidence and gave me an extra appreciation for my undeserved gift.

When I joined the Parish, there were fifteen teaching nuns assigned to our school, all of them well-qualified and eager to work in collaboration with the priests. We joined forces in teaching religion classes for the preparation of sacraments. The Sisters were members of a religious order called BVM's, *Sisters of Charity of the Blessed Virgin Mary.*

The nuns wore a modest black "habit" that hung from their shoulders down to the ground. Their head was covered with stiff, black and white fabric that revealed only their face. The habits marked them distinguishably as Roman Catholic nuns.

One of the Sisters, Sister Mary Rose, taught the fourth grade. She was a very mature 21 years old when I first met her. She explained that she had recently received her B.A. Degree in Education from Loyola University of Chicago and had joined the convent just prior to her graduation. The young Sister was as beautiful as she was energetic, as gentle as she was vivacious. She would be a force to reckon with!

In the secular world, this nun could have become a model and never wanted for income. She had a bright smile and a thin frame classically stretched over a height of no more than five feet. The shape of her face was perfectly symmetrical, an elusive ideal sought but rarely found by classic artists. In short, Sister Mary Rose was a vision of loveliness . . . in black and white.

I wondered many times about her hair. Since it was hidden under her habit, it remained a mystery: was it blond, brown, black? Was it naturally curly or straight? All I knew for certain was that it was short. My curiosity was prompted by human nature as well as by personal interest.

Early on in our friendship, I tried to explain to Sister that she reminded me of a nun in a 1957 movie called, "Heaven Knows, Mr. Allison." The nun was portrayed by the actress Deborah Kerr. Sister didn't see the film, wasn't familiar with the actress, and couldn't figure out if my comparison was a compliment or an insult. It was, of course, an intentional compliment.

The primary physical difference between the actress and Sister Rose was Sister's slightly darker complexion, acquired genetically from her parents who were native to Lima, Peru. Sister was proud to be named after the wonderful Saint Rose of Lima.

As the young nun and I became closer friends, we worked well together in classes that prepared students for their first reception of Holy Communion, Confession and Confirmation. She was popular with parents, children, and all the priests of the parish. The parishioners adopted a shortened version of her formal name and simply called her "Sister Rose," mainly because a Sister *Mary* was already serving there.

I should have heeded the inherent warning signs, but I was naïve enough to deny the dangers that surrounded my friendship with Sister. That was either naïveté or denial, but not both. I wasn't sure. What's more, Sister Rose was completely unaware of my unhealthy admiration for her, both physically and emotionally.

I concluded that Sister was too young and too holy to recognize what was going on. I was smitten by her innocence, beauty and personality. She was the most delightful little woman I had ever met. Throughout my life, I had behaved awkwardly with most females. To say I was *shy* is an understatement. But here and now, around Sister Rose, I was extremely at ease, confident and comfortable.

As an indicator of my previous distress around females, I recalled that as an eighth-grader, I was invited to a round of graduation parties by a classmate named Barbara. I was to be her escort. But I had a near nervous breakdown just *contemplating* the events. So I created a credible excuse: "Quigley Seminary frowned on attendance of seminarians at activities mixing girls with boys." My classmates bought the excuse and my lack of social skills with girls remained a guarded secret. I had saved face and was admired for my noble sacrifice.

Sister Rose required no such devious measures. I had already worked closely with her for six months before I recognized the augury that faced me. This was my first encounter with a woman since my ordination and it was a trial and test of the solidarity of my vocation.

The problem was easily explained: I enjoyed Sister's company and we had a lot of fun together. It was the kind of relationship *not* recommended for either a nun or a priest. In the seminary, we learned the obvious no-no's of this sort of thing but this was the *real* thing. I was encountering a real woman whom I found very likable in daily, face-to-face situations. I had to admit that being around her had become a dangerous habit (pun intended) resulting in madly frustrating enjoyment. And it was no laughing matter.

As a student of temptation in a theological sense, I had privately divided temptation into three stages: the first was *potential*; the second, *opportunity*; and the third, the actual *temptation*. If it progressed to an end, I called the final stage, *the fall*. Those were not exactly the words of Jesus Christ, but they were parts of a rationale that I applied to myself. I also viewed every category, if handled properly and rejected, as a step to sainthood. No step was easy to climb, but aspiring to be holy and saintly was enough motivation to keep me on the ladder.

As I analyzed my current situation, however, I had experienced the *potential* to be tempted into wrongdoing and I was rapidly entering the *opportunity* stage; but with confidence, I was certain I'd never come close to an actual *temptation* much less a *fall*. I would never allow Sister (or myself) to be tempted into breaking our vows. But whatever words I used, I knew they were a smoke-screen that messed with a final litmus test of honesty with myself. I admitted that my growing affection for Sister Rose could, indeed, jeopardize my fidelity to priesthood.

There was not a single day that passed without my praying deeply and intensely for this ominous problem. "How can I be doing this?" I'd ask myself. "How can I be feeling this way about a dear and devoted nun? This is *me*, Father Francis Chase." Each time I said that, I shook my head in disbelief. And the situation worsened the longer and closer we worked together over a period of almost two years

Potential

I was not proud of my behavior and/or my private thoughts about Sister Rose, though they never wandered anywhere near indecent. They were thoughts only about my friend and how much I enjoyed being in her company. There was one instance in particular that shrieked of *potential* and moved dangerously close to *opportunity*.

One evening, mid-way in our friendship, four of the Sisters and I (Sister Rose included) were working on assembling printed materials for a class that was preparing seventh graders for the reception of the sacrament of Confirmation. No kids were present as the four of us sat at a long table and folded papers, passing them down a sort-of production line. I was seated at one end and Sister Rose at the opposite. In-between us were the three other Sisters. It was a comfortable and practical configuration.

When it reached nine o'clock, three of the Sisters, the three seated in the center, announced that they were retiring for the night. That left Sister Rose and me alone, with three empty chairs in-between us. It was awkward and inefficient. We were still folding papers and couldn't reach to pass them to one another. I got up from my chair and moved to sit beside Sister. It was logical. She didn't stop her work but smiled as I sat down beside her. Our conversation was playful.

"Do you have any paper burns?" Sister asked me.

"Dozens," I replied. Do you?"

"Millions," she said. We both laughed.

"Millions? Do you actually have *millions*?"

"Absolutely! Look here. Look at this finger."

Sister boldly held her right thumb high so I could see the thin lines of cuts made from the edges of paper. Since it would have taken a microscope to discern the depth of the injuries, I held Sister's finger in the palm of my hand for a closer look. Her hand was soft, without a single blemish, save only for the tiny ridges of *burns*. I enjoyed the moment immensely. She smiled, looking into my eyes from a distance of no more than 12 inches. I noticed, silently and surreptitiously, that she was even more beautiful from up close.

"See, I told you," she said.

"What a sissy! Can't you stand a little pain?" I replied.

"Not that kind. It hurts . . . and paper burns last a long time. They never heal."

"Of course, they do. By tomorrow, those skinny little lines will have disappeared and you won't ever feel them again."

Without thinking, with no premeditation and still holding her finger, I took it to my lips and kissed it.

"There," I said, "now it's healed and will never hurt again."

Sister blushed and retracted her hand, claiming I was unsympathetic. She gently slapped my fingers as we returned to folding papers. I recognized that we were behaving like two small children. It was embarrassing.

There was more conversation, some of it about her family and her growing up as an "only child." It was one of many things we had in common. We continued to flirt like those little kids in the classroom.

"Did it ever bother you to be the only one?" she asked.

"Never. I never even thought about it. And you?"

"Sometimes. I wanted a playtime partner," she said. "A sister would've been nice. But it never happened. I think my mom was lucky to have *me*. She had some health issues that couldn't be fixed. I overheard her and my dad talking about it once but

I never pursued it. I thought it was their business and nothing I should be hearing in the first place."

When Sister talked, I listened to every word, watching and admiring the movement of her lips . . . and the rapid blinking of her dark eyes. She seemed to blink more than anyone I'd ever consciously noticed blinking, especially when she spoke. It was a unique and entertaining characteristic. I called it to her attention.

"Did you ever watch yourself blinking, I mean in the mirror, when you're talking?"

"You are so silly," she said. "Why in the world would I do such a thing?"

"Because I suggested it. Go do it some time," I said. "Look in the mirror and talk to yourself. You'll see that you blink very unusually, really much more than you have to. Doesn't it impinge on your vision? There must be thousands of blinks every time you say a word. Don't you feel it? And by the way, you can call me *Francis* instead of *Father*."

Sister giggled like the young girl inside her. It was wonderfully innocent. I had tried hard to deliberately make her self-conscious of her blinking. And it worked. She became acutely aware of the habit and that awareness inhibited her speech. The result was hilarious. She'd close her eyes for long intervals, and then open them for the same length of time. And she tried to speak normally while she did all that. She was noticeably blushing as I smiled but didn't say a word. Hilarious!

The eyes and mouth of the self-conscious little nun could put on quite a show. I focused on every move, though my conscience kept nagging at me to refrain from getting so personal. At that point, however, I believed I was in total control and there was nothing inappropriate in my actions.

Both Sister and I engaged in laughter, *hard* laughter that caused us to shed tears. Sister pulled a folded tissue from under her habit and wiped the moisture from my eyes and cheeks. That stopped our laughter. We both froze, recognizing how close we were to each other's face. Our mutual stares were so comforting that they forced the playfulness to end. We were both aware of what we were doing.

"Look at what we've done," Sister said as she assembled some of the papers. "None of these are in the right order. Everything's discombobulated."

"What was that word?"

"What word?" Sister asked as she spun around defensively to look me straight in the eye.

"I don't know, that's why I'm asking, something about discom . . ."

"You mean 'discombobulated?'"

"That's it! What in the world does that mean?"

"You've never heard that word before? I'm surprised at you, Francis. It means *disturbed*, like messed up, like the shape these papers are in after all our hard work." I never forgot the word, though I never had occasion to use it.

As we continued to fold papers and stuff them into folders for distribution to the kids, we continued to "mess up" as Sister called it. Near the end of our workload, Sister stopped suddenly, smiled, and stared at my hands working clumsily.

"Whoever said, 'Many hands make light the work' never watched Father Francis Chase stuff Confirmation folders." With that, Sister grabbed one of the papers from my hand and re-folded it, this time, properly.

We both laughed again as we moved away from each other and completed our work, more conscientiously than before. Both of us were embarrassed by our childish behavior. We were like two Pre-K toddlers enjoying the game of teasing but not making much sense of it. It was a pattern we could not have executed in public.

That acknowledgment alone illuminated a subconscious sign that read, "Entering the Danger Zone." At that point, we were both wise enough to recognize a *potential* and an *opportunity* occurring at the same time. We knew it could lead to a much more serious event. But, oh, we had such a good time. Could something feeling so good really be so bad?

As we split for the night, I confronted myself with that question and our evening of felicity. I was deeply guilted and certainly not conscienceless. But, at the same time, when I examined my inner voice, I concluded that I was simply a human male who greatly admired a human female who just happened to be charming and beautiful. It was a most innocent, natural reaction as old as time itself. As long I took no sinful action or harbored any sinful thoughts, my innocence was in tact. At least that was my excuse for going where I didn't belong.

Sister Rose soon became the best friend I ever had, even closer than my friends at the seminary. We shared stories of our past, challenges of the present, and hopes for our future as members of the *religious* within our Church and our community. From my early youth on, I had valued the security of a lasting friendship. It was a gift from God that allowed mankind to share burdens as well as joys. And it was never meant to obstruct saintliness, purity or virtue. It was, on the other hand, created by Almighty God as an adjunct to selflessness.

In and of itself, of course, there was nothing wrong with my "friendship rationale" regarding Sister Rose, with the exceptions of *priesthood* and *sisterhood*. With those factors added to the equation, the reasoning weakened. Even though there were no sexual intentions or devious motives that troubled either Sister or me, there was something inherently wrong with our friendship. Facing that conundrum repeatedly brought me back to two elements that made it incorrect: our commitments to God and a promise to ourselves. It didn't take a Doctorate to come to that conclusion.

There was another incident that magnified the nature of what we were facing. It happened on a weekday morning as I was preparing to celebrate Mass. I was in the sacristy (the private area that priests use to vest themselves for Mass) and I was due to step into the sanctuary where Mass itself is celebrated. Two young servers dressed in their own room adjacent to mine.

On this occasion, when I placed my vestment, the chasuble, over my head and shoulders and attempted to close a short zipper under my chin, the zipper got caught in a small piece of fabric. My efforts to close it were unsuccessful. To say the least, I looked quite unkempt and was not presentable to a congregation. It was 7:57 a.m. and the Mass was scheduled to begin in three minutes.

My first thought was to solicit the aid of the servers. But they were in the fourth grade and too short to reach the zipper under my neck. I was 6'2" and they were about 4'2". Then I remembered that Sister was helping the boys vest for Mass and she was in the room right beside mine. I hurried over there and said a quick "Good morning," then quickly explained my predicament. I asked her for help. But as she came close to examine the zipper, I encountered the most trying test of my priesthood to date.

If I describe this as a delicate situation, I'm making a gross understatement. Sister was inches from my face, standing on her toes to reach the zipper under my chin. She was no more than six inches from my chin as she struggled to release the zipper. I smelled the fragrance of flowery soap on her face. I studied the unusual blinking of her eyes. And I watched the movement of her generous lips. I actually began to perspire.

"Boy, Francis," she said, "you really did a number on this."

My reply formed slowly but I managed a nod of my head and a meaningless sentence: "Please, if you can help me and save the comments 'till later, I'd appreciate it. I've got about two minutes to get out there for Mass."

"You should come to church earlier, Francis."

"I've been here since 7:30."

"I'm doing my best and I cannot get the zipper to move."

I shifted from one foot to the other, several times.

"Would you stand still? You're rocking like a pendulum," Sister said with authority.

"I'm doing the best I can under the circumstances."

"Now what does that mean?"

Throughout her struggles with the zipper, Sister was typically expressive, distorting her mouth and over-using her tongue in a vain effort. It was as if she were attempting to thread a needle in a darkened room. None of her contortions helped at all but were, nevertheless, as amusing as they were unintentional. My laughter was uncontrolled.

"If you could see yourself in a mirror," I said. "I can't keep from laughing."

"What do you mean, 'see myself in a mirror?'"

"I mean . . . you're making some of the most hilarious faces I've ever seen in my life. You belong in a circus. You could be a wonderful clown." I laughed harder. And so did Sister.

"I don't want to undermine your efforts," I said, "but I'm down to about 60 seconds 'till launch."

The zipper closed. But that closure included a small chunk of skin from my neck. It was actually bleeding, but only a bit.

"Ouch!" I cried out instinctively.

"Sorry," she said, fumbling with her fingers and gently moving the zipper to release my skin. She also dabbed a small bubble of blood from my injury.

She smiled and held her hand to her mouth. "I'm so sorry," she whispered as she again dabbed the wound. "I think the bleeding has stopped now. You'd better get out on the altar."

"Thanks, Sister," I said quietly. "Your help is appreciated."

"I come not to be served, but to serve," she said with a smile as she walked away. The encounter was fun and typical of the many we faced together. It began with the incident of the zipper and ended with a quote from Jesus Christ. I noted the irony.

That night, I had serious trouble falling asleep. It was becoming a bedtime habit: struggling with insomnia while reliving the happy time I spent with Sister. On this occasion, I smiled every time I pictured the faces she made as she tried to repair my vestment. That imagery eventually put me to sleep. But I fought a conscience that told me I shouldn't be doing what I was doing.

Throughout my seminary years, at both the minor and major seminaries, I had made many close friends. The closest were Bill Crosby and Kenny Zalinsky. Even after going our separate ways after ordination, we had remained in touch. We met frequently for local sporting events and/or at local restaurants to talk and to share stories. Neither of these friends knew anything about my personal problem with Sister. But they were about to hear it in great detail. Sister and I had already worked together for nearly two of the best years of my life and it was time that my two buddies heard about my personal predicament. If they were my close friends, they'd be willing to hear about my struggles as well as my joys, and hopefully, offer some thoughtful advice.

Counseling

The three of us met at Maggio's, one of our favorite Italian restaurants that was equidistant from our parishes. The food was good, the atmosphere quiet, and the beer cold. It was ideal for what I had to say. Both friends knew immediately that something was amiss. I was atypically serious and they were typically jocular. Bill was the first to address the fact that I was behaving "strangely."

"Okay, buddy," he said as he chomped on his BBQ wings. "What's up? Something's going on here."

I smiled at his perceptiveness and told him he could read me like my own father.

"Well," he said thoughtfully, "you haven't been this quiet since the night before ordination."

"I've got a lot on my mind now, just like I did then."

"So tell us about it. I'm sure that's why you called this meeting, right?" I smiled at him, took a sip of my beer, and leaned back in my chair.

"Okay, you guys. I need your help. I've gotten into a real mess and I don't know how to extricate myself."

"What's the category?" Kenny said as he leaned toward me.

"The category is one you won't believe."

"Like what? You in trouble with the Pastor, say something dumb to some parent, smash your car?"

"I wish it was that simple. I'd take any of those in place of what I've done."

Both friends now gave me their undivided attention which is what I wanted in the first place. I prepared to explain and had rehearsed my opening to make it easier on myself.

"You won't believe this," I said again, "but I've gotten involved with a woman."

Bill almost choked on a wing. Kenny knocked a salt shaker onto the floor. And I stared at both priests.

"You've got to be kidding," Kenny said.

"A woman? Involved with a *woman?*" Bill added.

"Yeah . . . you haven't heard the worst of it yet."

"What could be worse?"

"The woman is . . . a *nun!*"

"That *is* worse! My God, a nun?"

Both men threw their heads back and immediately ordered another beer and more wings from our server. Needless to say, the guys had been rendered speechless. They never expected that I'd have a problem of that nature so early in my priesthood . . . or *ever,* for that matter. We all sat in silence with our heads bowed for at least a minute before Bill said, "I can't believe this. Fill in some of the blanks and help us comprehend this thing."

I had to make a long story short because both Bill and Kenny had short attention spans. They also appeared to be terribly nervous and uncomfortable with my news.

"Well, it's like this," I said. "Nothing extremely bad has happened and the Sister hasn't a clue as to what's going on, I mean what's going on inside *me.* I can't help myself. I'm crazy about her."

Bill started the questioning. "Maybe it's not that important to ask, but what's she like. I can't believe I'm actually saying this but . . . what attracted you to her?"

"She's young and beautiful. She's got an incredible sense-of-humor and we have a great time together."

It was Kenny's turn to quiz. "What do you mean by *beautiful?"* he asked.

"Man, don't make this any harder than it already is."

"Just give me some details. I've got to know what you're up against if you expect me to give you advice. Tell me what she looks like."

"She's short, has a pretty face, long eyelashes, and she's got ways that she blinks her eyes and moves her mouth that I've never seen before. She drives me nuts, in a pleasurable sense. Every little thing about her gets to me, frustrates me, because I don't know what to do about it. The best description I can give you is to ask you to picture . . . well, did either of you see, 'Heaven Knows, Mr. Allison?'"

Two heads nodded in the affirmative. "Then you've seen Sister Mary Rose. She looks *exactly* like the nun in the film, Deborah Kerr. And I mean no less beautiful and even more charming." Incoherent mumbling followed.

"Okay, so there's some physical attraction there?"

"You bet there is!"

"You ever touched her?"

"Only by accident or to be mischievous. Just touched her hand once or twice by accident. It was so soft and I got the smell of her soap on my fingers. Drove me wild!"

Bill couldn't control himself any longer. "I can't believe I'm hearing this from you, Francis. You, of all people. I never thought you had much interest in the opposite sex. Actually, you always led us to believe that you were scared to death of women. Have you been deceiving us all these years?"

"Never had a problem like this before," I said. "I never paid any attention to women. It was more like I had a *fear* of them. But I never had an opportunity to get close to one. This Sister is something I never dreamed of. She's got something, *everything* that I find so attractive: the way she talks and walks, the way she looks at me, the way she says my name. It all comes together. It wells up inside of me. She makes me feel safe and comfortable, inside and out. And I can't tell her or . . ."

Kenny interrupted. "Why can't you tell her?" he demanded in a firm voice.

"Are you crazy?" I said. "I should talk like this to a nun? She'd think I was crazy, or immoral, or some kind of letch."

"Well, aren't you? You do understand what's at stake here, don't you?"

"I'm innocent, I tell you, totally innocent."

"Yeah right! You're so innocent that you called us together to talk about a woman, specifically a *nun* who 'drives you nuts.'"

"Look," I said calmly but with authority. "I got you two together to counsel me, to empathize with me. So just listen and try to digest what I'm saying."

"Okay, so finish your confession."

"The bottom line is that I really don't know what to do. Do I tell my pastor what's going on? Do I try to explain it to Sister like you said? Or do I just let it go and enjoy my time with her, knowing that it's bound to end some day? One of us *will* be transferred sooner or later."

"I can tell you one thing," Bill said. "You cannot just 'let it go.' You've got to create a strategy that ends it, like *today*."

"I agree with Bill," said Kenny. "It's too volatile a situation to let go much longer. It's dynamite. And it's going to explode soon. But I don't think you should explain it to Sister. From what you say, she's unaware. She's too young to understand what men are all about, what *priests* are all about. You could possibly ruin the rest of her life. You've got to come up with something other than approaching her with the problem."

Bill added, "And I wouldn't go to the Pastor. He's over 70 years old and wouldn't understand what you're talking about. I mean, Francis, you *are* a priest, a man of God committed to celibacy. And with a *nun* involved? You've got to handle this *without* the Pastor . . . with a level of discretion you haven't practiced so far."

I appreciated the comments from my closest friends. I excused them for their shock at what was going on in my life, because it *was*, after all, deeply disturbing and inconsistent with my prior behavior. I remained puzzled as I offered a speculative solution.

"Okay," I said. "I admit that I'm behaving like a little boy ruminating about his girlfriend. I know how silly it all sounds, especially coming from *me*, not exactly what I'd call a 'flirt.' I mean, I'm mature and intelligent and I do love my God above all else."

Kenny interrupted. "You just used the word *love*. Was that a Freudian slip or do you . . ."

"No, I don't believe I *love* her, not in the sense of man and woman and *romantic* love. I love her like I love all human beings . . . well, maybe a *little* differently."

"You're talking about serious stuff here, Francis. And from what you've told us so far, I think you're in love with this woman."

"Now I lost my place. You said you'd let me finish."

I paused to gather my thoughts. "Okay," I said. "I was saying how I love my God above all else. And I do. This Sister is just something, *someone* that God placed in my path as kind of an *opportunity*, a challenge, something that can help me grow."

"We commonly refer to that as a 'temptation,' buddy." Bill accented the word 'temptation' as he said it.

I came back with a very quick, "It's *not* a 'temptation!' I'll accept the fact that it's an *opportunity* but not a temptation. I just wish the 'opportunity' didn't have such beautiful eyes."

"Man, you are really hooked," Kenny said as he shook his head. "You're hopeless."

"No, I'm *not* hopeless," I said with conviction. "You guys are giving up on me too quickly. Where's your trust and faith in me? Let me try this idea on you.

"How about if I just ignore Sister and avoid meetings with her? I can come up with an excuse for not being there. Then, I won't see as much of her and maybe my interest will wane and ultimately disappear. Good idea?"

Bill yawned. "Naïve, if you ask me. If you think that's going to quell your interest," he said, "you're blinded by the light.

That's just going to create a mystery, make you even more attractive to her, make her curious about what's going on, why you're avoiding her. It'll be too obvious. Man, you sure don't know much about women. How do you counsel a female in the confessional? You'd better go back to school. Or buy a book. Or do something that teaches you more about women."

"And that advice is supposed to help me?"

"I'm just being honest, Francis. You've got to come to grips with this thing rather than *hoping* it heals itself."

"I agree," said Kenny.

"Yeah, well, I agree, too. But neither of you has given me a single concrete idea on *how* to come to grips."

"Weren't you listening? I just told you. You've got to face her and explain this 'opportunity,' as you call it, and the fact that's it's dangerous because she's a woman and you're a man and you have tendencies to act on something that'll get you both into trouble."

"Don't you get it, Bill? If I explain that to her, she's sure to be frightened, probably run to her Mother Superior. Those religious women couldn't possibly comprehend what this is all about. They wouldn't be able to treat me fairly after hearing all that."

"Boy, they should hear you say that . . . 'those religious women.' What an insult. I never knew you were a sexist. You can do better than that, Francis."

"Okay, so if I talk to her and explain that I've got this 'thing' for her, this attraction to her . . . you don't think that'll stimulate her, force her to sort out her feelings and discover she's got the same 'thing' for me?"

"You have no choice."

"You *leave* me no choice, my two priestly friends. And I've got to be perfectly honest with you, there's a very strong incentive for me to do just that, to talk to her. Because it's appealing and intriguing to think about telling her how she affects me, about how I love all the little things she says and does. I don't know if you can understand that, but I'd very much like to do that. It's no hardship. I'd enjoy every minute of it. But in the end, I don't see how that'll benefit either of us."

"Like Kenny said, 'you're hopeless, man.'" Bill led our discussion into a pause and then added, "Okay, look at it this way. If you add a different color to your palette and skew your viewing angle, you could conclude that you're simply battling a scrupulous conscience, that there's nothing inherently wrong with your friendship with a member of the opposite sex. You think you're the only priest who's ever encountered that?"

Kenny took the floor. "That makes a lot of sense, Bill. But going back to what Francis said before, if talking to her about his true feelings is a 'turn-on' for him, then he should just let it ride and gradually start being less and less available, kind of like you proposed before.

He directed his last comment at *me*, "Just fake it. Make your unavailability seem accidental rather than deliberate. Then, slowly change your behavior. Don't insult her or hurt her feelings, but don't be so talkative, so animated when you're around her."

Bill added, "And don't be so melodramatic about your feelings. Convince yourself that it's natural and that you'll get over it. Look, pal, you're going to be thrown into other such exposures to women. This is the first but not the last . . . for you and for all of us."

"Okay, now you're making sense. I'd prefer to let it drift away rather than to try and explain it. In the meantime, it's going to be a struggle. Because she's wonderful and there's nobody like her in the world."

"Man, I've got to get out of here," Bill said in ultimate frustration, flailing his arms and grabbing his jacket. "I've been here way too long. I've got a huge stack of paperwork on my desk and it's close to ten o'clock. My pastor's probably watching for me. And now I'm supposed to focus on my papers? Boy, did you ruin the rest of my night. But that's what friends are for, right?"

All I could say was, "Sorry about that."

"Uh, one more thing," Kenny interrupted. "You mentioned a movie before. I've got a suggestion to help you get through this thing with humor. If you haven't seen the new Jerry Lewis film yet, go see it. It's called, 'Ladies Man.' It's hilarious and just what you need."

"What's it about," I asked, wanting to be forewarned.

"Well, this guy played by Jerry, he's just been ditched by his girlfriend and he wants no part of the opposite sex. He unknowingly takes a job in this huge house inhabited by a bunch of attractive, young ladies. What he endures from them will crack you up. It's just the kind of crazy stuff that'll straighten you out. Go see it!" Kenny was laughing so hard, he was barely intelligible.

I said I'd take his advice and see the film. Maybe it would help to laugh at myself.

I got up from the table and the others followed. I thanked them and said I'd repay the favor any time they needed me. (As it turned out, I did see Kenny's movie and enjoyed it as much as he did, superimposing my situation on that of Jerry Lewis as he dodged women and tried to avoid their smothering attention.)

I had built a ton of resolve after listening to the wisdom of my two friends. But the very next day, that resolve turned to mush. My intentions for a slow disappearing act dissolved quickly. This time, it was on the playground of St. William's school.

Sister Mary Rose was monitoring a softball game between two all-girl teams from her fourth grade and I was on an adjoining field umpiring a game between some eighth grade boys. Sister and I were ostensibly minding our own business, though I did sneak a glance and a wave toward her. As luck would have it, I was watching her game as one of the girls hit a 16" softball out of the yard and onto the flat roof of a garage that connected to a residence across the street.

The girls, led by Sister Rose, stood frozen on the field, not having any idea how to retrieve the ball. I couldn't let them lose the ball so I offered my help. My first idea was to simply walk up to the house, knock on the door, and get permission to climb the small building via a tree that leaned against the rain gutter. However, there was no response to my knocking. So I figured I might as well climb the tree without permission since it would take only a few minutes. Wrong on all counts!

My attempt to climb the tree was a gallant attempt to be a hero, to the kids as well as to Sister. Sister, not missing a beat when it came to my need to be noticed, called out in a loud voice.

"Do I detect a note of chivalry?"

"Not at all," I hollered back. "It's a chorus of the Notre Dame Victory March!"

The first limb I touched broke and fell about five feet to the grass below, with me still hanging onto it. An attempt to scale the rain gutter also failed as the gutter collapsed and broke into two pieces. Once again, I was left on the ground, with minor physical injuries but with enormous pain to my pride and to my *image*.

Of course, Sister and her girls enjoyed the scene, laughing and carrying on at my expense. It was great fun to witness the Parish Priest making a fool of himself with a sizeable crowd of spectators. I was wearing my black pants and Roman collar which magnified my failures and simply made me a more dignified fool.

Immediately following the recess, when the kids returned to their classes, Sister and I were left alone to relive "The Folly of Father Francis." She led me to the school *infirmary* and bandaged a couple of scrapes on my elbows. She worked at close quarters as she also cleansed a slight cut above my right eye. I controlled myself commendably but she showed no restraint in snickering at my humiliation. The entire mishap and its resulting personal medical repair by Sister were not consistent with my new plan to curtail our relationship.

All that notwithstanding, I had benefited greatly from the evening with Kenny and Bill. Talking openly about Sister Rose did me a lot of good. I actually slept better knowing that the reaction from the guys was civil. And though I was inspired to dissolve my relationship with Sister, I still had the desire to see her, like right now . . . to watch her talk, to stare at how she moved her lips and blinked her eyes, to smell the scent of soap . . . and to reprise my recent roll as the school clown.

I harbored those thoughts as I placed my head on my pillow for a night of unrest. Kenny was right when he said I was "really hooked!" I had to now disconnect myself from having personal encounters with a very lovely and holy woman. I had already committed several terrible errors in judgment and must rely on the strength of God to help me. I would surrender myself to Him.

Opportunity

It was a cold winter's night and the Chicago streets were covered with light snow and a layer of ice beneath it, dangerous conditions for any driver. But for a new driver only seventeen years old, the roads were even more treacherous and less forgiving.

On a remote highway in a western suburb, the new driver was Alice Sherman. She had celebrated her 17th birthday just five days earlier. Her only passenger was Becky, a younger sibling who attended the fourth grade at St. William School. Becky was a student of Sister Mary Rose and Alice attended a nearby high school.

The crash was horrendous! Alice was traveling slowly but she underestimated the sharp curve and the slick surface. The car began a skid that took it across the road and into a 20-foot ditch. Both girls were killed instantly. Alice could do nothing to avoid the accident.

The news reached the rectory about 1:30 am. I was on-call for emergencies so I answered the phone, wondering who would possibly be calling at such a strange hour. It was the father of the two girls. He was grief-stricken as was his wife. He was calling the rectory to ask for prayers for the souls of the girls and strength for his family to endure the tragedy.

I woke Monsignor Devereaux and told him about the deaths of the two students. Monsignor was deeply saddened and asked if I would contact the convent next door to explain the story to Mother Superior. She could then use her own judgment in passing it on to the other Sisters. I did as I was asked, telling Mother that I had something very serious to talk to her about and would prefer doing it personally rather than by telephone. She said I should allow her five minutes and she'd be waiting for me at the convent door, just across the street from our rectory.

I quickly slipped a sport-shirt over my T-shirt and a jacket over both of them. It wasn't my regular priestly garb but I didn't plan on staying long or removing the jacket. Mother greeted me at the convent entrance, invited me in, and guided me to a small room that she referred to as "the parlor." It was my first time in the convent and, honestly, I must say that it reminded me a bit of a Funeral Home . . . the smell of fresh flowers, complete silence, and no windows. It seemed appropriate for the sad news I was carrying to Mother.

The "parlor" was no more than ten feet square, contained three walls of bookshelves, a desk, two chairs, and a picture of the reigning Pope, John XXIII. Mother sat on one of the chairs and asked me to sit beside her. She wondered what brought me there at such a late hour. I gave her the devastating news and expressed my sorrow for being the bearer.

Mother had a reputation for being an excellent educator and a strict disciplinarian, of her Sisters as well as of her students. She was also reputed to be a tough administrator and restrained in expressing her feelings. Knowing that, I didn't expect her to become hysterical at the loss of the young girls but was still surprised by her unemotional response. She was sorrowful but changed the subject of the girls to focus on announcing the news to the other nuns in the convent. Mother explained that it was her wish to tell Sister Rose first since she was the younger girl's teacher. Later, she would tell the other Sisters.

Then came an unexpected request that I dared not refuse. Mother Superior politely asked me to spend a short time with Sister Rose, now and alone. She knew the Sister and I had been good friends for nearly two years and she reasoned that I was in a position to comfort her and help her face this deep and personal loss. I agreed but was uncertain of how to soften what I knew would be a crushing blow to the fragile nun. I had no previous experience in the area of bereavement counseling but would do my best to ease the pain. I waited for Mother to return with Sister Rose. I was very nervous, for a multitude of reasons.

Ten minutes passed slowly as I paced the small room. The door opened and Sister Rose entered. I was standing in the center of the room as she closed the door behind her and we were left to ourselves. Sister walked toward me slowly, then, spontaneously burst open, placing her arms around my waist and pressing her face into my chest. The movements of her head caused her habit to loosen around her face, thus exposing her hair. Her actions made it clear that Mother Superior had already told her the grim news.

Her erratic physical movements caused her habit to drop further and I could see very short dark brown curls encircling her face. Tears ran down her checks and moistened several loose strands of hair beneath them. I moved her head slightly and helped her remove the garment from around her head so she could be more comfortable. I looked into her face and wiped her eyes with my fingers. She was so vulnerable, so helpless, so pitiful (and beautiful) in my arms. I stroked her back firmly and withheld my own tears.

"I cannot believe what Mother just told me," she said. "I cannot believe my little Becky is gone. She was such a sweetheart."

"Whatever the reason, it's God's will," I said. It was a lame attempt to console her but it was the best that came to me.

"So young . . . she was only ten years old. So young."

"I'm really sorry, Rose. I'm very sorry for you. Is there anything I can do?"

"You can hand me that box of tissues on the desk." I did, without saying a word.

"Do you know that Becky was a special child?" she said. "She had a learning disability and I tutored her after school two days a week. And she was able to keep up with the class. So innocent . . . so fragile and lovely. And now she's gone."

Sister continued to cry and to keep one arm around my waist, clutching the back of my shirt with the fingers of her other hand. She looked so delicate, like the flower of her name. I held the back of her head in my left hand and pushed her hair from the front of her face with my right. I relished the opportunity to touch her short, soft curls. It was a rare moment I'll treasure for all my days, feeling no guilt and no regret for anything I was doing.

"Hold me," she said. "Don't let me go. I need you, Francis."

"I'm here for you, Sister. Here, sit down. I'll stay with you for as long as you like."

Sister didn't move, still gripping my shirt from behind and still pressing her head into my chest. I forced her to shift slightly while I removed my jacket. For whatever reason, the room had become uncomfortably warm. It was the first time Rose had seen me in any clothing other than my clerical suit and shirt. She looked up to me and stared, right into my face, inches from my mouth. I did want to place our lips together but prayed to God and to my patron saint, Francis of Assisi.

I wiped her eyes and her cheeks repeatedly until they were dry and she forced a smile. She was sniffling and her nose was running uncontrollably. I gave her a handkerchief from my pocket and she used it judiciously. She explained that she'd launder it before returning it to me. She thanked me but didn't release me, still staring into my eyes from very close range. I remained in disbelief at the transmogrification of this dear little Sister. I saw her now as *woman* more than *nun*.

"I love you, Father Francis Chase," she said in a whisper.

"I love you too, Sister, just as I love all God's people."

"Not like that," she said quietly but with assertion. "I love you *differently*. I know you love all women on earth. But you love your mother *differently*, don't you? I love you *differently*, too, like no other person on earth."

I was taken back, not expecting such a reaction. I knew it was rooted in sorrow and that she was not responsible for her actions at such a traumatic time. I tried to convince her that her feelings were prompted by sadness and grief and that she'd soon forget what she had just said. She refused to accept that as she slowly leaned back from my face. It was even more difficult looking at her from two feet away than it was talking to her with her face in my chest. At least from that previous angle, it was the top of her head that was more visible.

"Here, why don't you sit down?" I said, pushing her gently away from me and into a chair. I repositioned the other chair so that we faced each other. "You'll feel better soon." Her stare was discomforting. I was at a loss for words, though I didn't want to excoriate her.

"I love you, Francis," she whispered again. "You cannot change the way I feel. I love you more dearly than I could ever dream of loving any man."

"Even Jesus Christ?" I said through a sardonic smile. It was an attempt to shock her into reality.

"Even *more* than Jesus Christ!" she said instantly.

Sister was very sure of herself. My response was inane and meaningless compared to her certainty and conviction.

"You must remember your vows, Sister. You made those promises to Jesus who is your one true love. You must *conscientiously* remember the promises you made to Him."

"You can't be serious," Sister shot back. "When I made those vows, I was in a different life and time. I didn't know Francis Chase back then."

She sounded as though she was addressing a third party who wasn't present in the room. She had detached herself from everything in the world . . . except me. I tried again to disrupt her spell, to relieve her distress but still avoid being didactic.

"Sister, my dear Sister Rose," I said softly as I reached out and placed her hands into mine, pressing them together into one. We sat that way, still facing each other in the two chairs.

"You're grieving the loss of your lovely young student," I continued. "You're suffering a deeply painful experience. And it's hurting your heart more than anything you've ever felt. It's affecting your judgment and you're saying things you don't fully comprehend."

"I love you Francis. I've loved you for a long, long time. Don't you love *me?*" She withdrew her hands from mine and stared at me without blinking.

"Of course I do. I just told you that I love you like I love all women, all of God's children."

"And I told you that I love you *differently*. I love everything about you, my dearest Francis."

The traumatized Sister turned her head and looked away from me toward the bookshelves. I could see her tiny chest heaving from all the tears she had shed. Loose strands of hair fell over her forehead and covered her eyebrows. It was my unprofessional diagnosis that she was suffering from traumatic shock caused by an intimate loss of someone dear. But I was no doctor.

I watched and listened closely to a sound so soft and gentle that I couldn't determine its source. Sister was singing quietly. It was more like humming because I couldn't understand the words. The melody was familiar. It was the *Ave Maria*, the most common version by Bach/Gounod. As she sang, Sister rocked forward and backward in the chair, sitting on crossed legs in a *yoga* position.

The sound accompanying Sister's movements was, at the same time, beautiful and disconcerting. She had many of the symptoms of a nervous breakdown and an acute emotional collapse. She was out-of-touch with reality. And there was nothing I could do to help her. Since I wasn't qualified to offer effective psychological help, I tried a simple, direct approach that drew on our friendship. I wanted Sister to shed her hopelessness and wash it away with tears. I held her two hands tightly again as I spoke to her.

"Sister Rose," I said in a whisper. "You and I have been good friends for a long time, and I care for you very much. You are one of my best friends. But because we're both people whom God has selected to serve Him in special ways, we've got to obey the rules of our vows. Don't you agree with that?" Since there was no reply, I continued.

"We made promises to keep our vows. We've made commitments to Jesus to do special work for Him. And we can't do that, we can't answer His call if we . . ."

"If we what?" Sister interrupted. "Why can't we answer His call if we love one another, if we praise Him in our hearts by loving one another, you and me? I see God's goodness in you, Francis. I see His spirit shining forth from your heart and soul. There is nothing you can say or do to make me stop loving *that* and everything else about you." Now, Sister was displaying anger.

"But you don't really understand your feelings for me," I said. "It's a disorderly love you have for me, disorderly, untidy. Right now, I'm serving as a temporary stabilizer in your life and it's confusing you. Your love should be focused on something else."

"Like what?"

"Not *what*, but *whom*, Rose, *whom*! And I think you know the answer to that. Your love should be focused on Christ, on the One you married when you took your vows. He should be the primary focus of your love."

"I knew you'd say that," Sister retorted.

Even though she was contentious, I was most pleased to hear her speaking again. At the very least, our conversation had caused her to stop rocking and humming.

It felt emotionally healthy for both of us to resume our verbal dispute, to openly debate Sister's perspective. But it was difficult to accept this agitated and angry young woman who was once so bubbly and ebullient.

I assessed the strange, unorthodox scene that had unfolded. Here sat two dedicated people, a priest and a nun, arguing over personal issues of romantic love, raising their voices in anger and frustration. Strange, indeed.

"All right," I said, feigning surrender, "if you love me so much, then you must do as I ask. You must listen to me. You must take hold of yourself and understand that it was, it *is* God's will to take this little girl from your class, from her family, from *you*, into His merciful arms. You believe that. I know you do. Your friend, Becky, and her sister are in God's hands, happy forever. You can pray *to* her instead of *for* her. She is a saint in heaven."

I lowered my voice, paused, and whispered, "May I suggest that we quiet our voices, Sister. Mother Superior is sure to hear us shouting and she'll come in here to reprimand us."

As I spoke to this dear Sister whom I cared for so much, I tried my best to be unselfish. But I wondered with every word I said why God was punishing me at such an early time in my priesthood. My relationship with Sister Mary Rose had been so beautiful and uncommonly innocent. But now, with the death of this little girl, in a flash, everything became incredibly complicated. The story of our simple friendship had suddenly become a story of forbidden, romantic love.

"Why?" I asked of my God. "Why did this happen?"

I could not understand what purpose the heavy cross would serve. Was it punishment for my sins, things I did wrong? Was it a reward, a gift to reinforce my vocation? I was confused and, at the moment, did not hear an answer from my God.

I made still another attempt to help Sister. I moved my chair closer to her. We now sat with our knees touching lightly as I still held her two hands in mine. I looked into her eyes from only six inches away. And I spoke softly and deliberately.

"My dear Sister Rose," I said. "You've been so deeply hurt and it's left you angry and distraught. You've got to forget about me and focus on more important issues."

"Like what?" she again challenged, again in a tone of defiance.

"Like deciding how you're going to face your class, those wonderful little kids who'll look to you for help. They're going to need your love and compassion. They're going to be hurting even more than you. Are you prepared to face them?"

"No," Sister answered quickly. "No, I haven't given that a thought. What time is it?"

"It's 3:30 in the morning."

"Oh my. I've got to go." For a minute, it seemed that our conversation had been transformative, that Sister was regaining control and returning to reality. "We'll be meeting for vespers soon. I have to get back to my room, to meet the other Sisters."

I couldn't allow her to leave that quickly. "Look," I said, "give me another minute." I was insistent.

"Regarding your class . . . are you going to leave Becky's desk empty?"

"What? Why would you ask such a thing?"

"Because tomorrow that'll be a pressing issue. Think about it. What will you do about Becky's desk?"

"I don't know. Maybe I'll ask the children for their thoughts, like what would *they* like me to do. I guess we could leave it empty for awhile. Or we could have everybody move up so somebody else fills it. I have to think about the kids first."

"Yes, you do." I smiled at claiming a small victory. I was encouraged that Sister had left her self and was thinking more of her class of 10-year-olds. It was the first sign of relieving the trauma after hearing of Becky's death. All things considered, I thought she was doing quite well, except for her wanderings into the love story about Father Francis. But that story hadn't concluded.

"Francis," she said as she stared at me. Her eyes were blinking rapidly in a reprise of a performance I had admired early in our friendship.

"Please remember what I told you here tonight," she said. "I mean this *morning*. I love you and always will, Francis. It's a reality that's remained inside of me for so long and this was the catalyst that forced it into the open. These are not the thoughts of a crazy woman. These are the honest feelings of a woman in love."

"Do you hear yourself, Sister? Remind yourself that the woman you're talking about is a nun, consecrated to God, and the man is a priest, ordained by a minister of Jesus Christ."

I felt moisture gathering in the palms of her hands. She was nervous and uncomfortable with what we were both saying. I've got to confess, I was enjoying her in such a vulnerable position. I knew that was sinful of me. Perhaps I, too, was traumatized. I re-focused my dialogue, still desperately committed to help her.

"Don't you understand, my little Rose?" I asked. "Neither of us wants to give everything away, not now or ever. It's the life we've chosen. Think of all the years that we prayed for our vocation, that we nurtured and handled it so delicately. We can't abandon those years. Am I saying anything that makes sense to you? Will you answer me?"

"Of course," Sister said, bowing her head, breaking her hands away from mine and using them to wipe her eyes. "But no, none of this makes sense to me. I love my God so much and I want to be true to Him, but I also love *you* and I want to choose you, too. What am I to do? Help me."

Sister was pushing *me* to make the decision for her, to do something as difficult for me to suggest as it was for her to accept. We were both guilty of shifting our attention from Becky's death to a discussion of personal love. Neither was easily resolved. Sister was incapacitated and inconsolable. If I could get her to focus on her class, I knew she would put the pieces of her life back together and return to her role as an exemplary, holy nun and teacher. One more try.

I stood and began pacing. Sister watched every move I made. I walked back and forth in front of her. Her head and eyes followed me as if she were watching a tennis match.

"Sister, I want you to think about what you'd like your class to do for Becky, something special, some action they could take at the Funeral Home. Maybe you'd like to lead them in the rosary. Or maybe you'd like each of the children to read part of a prayer. Think about that."

Sister was quiet. She glanced at me from the corners of her eyes as I stopped pacing and returned to the chair in front of her. Then, she spoke. I was eager to hear if my attempts at redirecting her attention had worked.

"I think it would be good for each of the children to write a small 'goodbye' to their classmate," she said. "It would also be a beautiful experience for Becky's parents and family to listen to how the class appreciated her friendship."

"That's a great idea, Sister." I exhaled deeply but secretly. "You can also begin planning on what you'd like Becky's class to do at her Funeral Mass."

The situation had improved and I was breathing easier. Sister appeared to be regaining control of herself. She was better prepared to leave for vespers. She stood and reached out to touch my hand. Our four hands joined into one.

"My Lord in heaven," she gasped, realizing for the first time what she had been doing and saying. "Just look at me. My habit is a mess and my hair is hanging in my eyes. I've made a complete fool of myself. When Mother sees me . . . oh, my. I've never been so embarrassed in all my life."

I leaned toward my sad and pathetic friend. She was a sight that would have broken any heart. In a moment of pity, I bent down to minister a kiss of healing. Just as my lips arrived at her cheek, she spontaneously turned her head toward me. We kissed on the mouth. Its short length was disproportionate to its meaning. We both gave and received what we wanted, by accident.

The kiss was sincere and loving, without romantic overtones. If the move had been choreographed, it could not have pleased each of us more. It was, indeed, to our liking, a fitting end to a meaningful, albeit, seriously difficult chapter in our lives.

I watched silently as Sister left the room. She brushed against a vase of long-stem red roses on the desk causing one of the flowers to fall to the floor. I picked it up and studied it, smiling at the obvious connection of the gentle flower to Sister Mary Rose. The loose petals that had separated from the wounded flower symbolized Sister's separation from reality. But both the flower and the Sister had retained their inherent beauty.

On the next morning, I awoke early and exhausted, both conditions influenced by loss of a night's sleep and a stressful encounter with a distressed woman. But since my company and counsel did seem to help, it was worth the effort and deservedly rewarding. I enjoyed sharing that small piece of my life.

The good Sister wasn't seen much over the next few days. She was busy working with the family of Becky and Alice to assure a series of holy and memorable services following their deaths. The funeral home and the church were jammed with parishioners who paid their respects and offered prayers for the young girls.

Sister and I *did* make eye contact at the Mass. I was asked to assist Monsignor and our other associate and I saw Sister sitting with her class directly in front of me in the first pew. From time to time, when I glanced at her, I detected that her eyes were trained on me. Never had I participated in such a deft and wordy conversation with so much said through nods of the head and blinks of the eyes . . . without a single audible assist.

After seeing nothing of Sister over the next month, I inquired about her whereabouts. One of the nuns stationed with her at Saint William explained that she had been transferred to the Motherhouse for the BVM's in Dubuque, Iowa. The shockwave of that news led me to wonder if Sister had told Mother Superior details of our "friendly" relationship and if Mother wisely determined that the transfer was necessary.

It was difficult to forget Sister Rose. The good times we had spent together generated permanent memories that I had no reason to erase. I saw her face blooming in every rose over the next summer. I heard her laugh, breaking the silence of my quietest reflections. And I felt her breath on my shoulder as I prayed for her joy.

Eventually, I learned that Sister was working as a caregiver with older, retired nuns. Though it was not my business, I judged that her new position away from teaching was a waste of her gifts and her effectiveness with young children. But I quickly acknowledged that it was God's will and wisdom at work, knowing that He knew far better than me where Sister Rose was needed most. She would fare well without the distraction of a priest she loved. In the end, we both had passed serious tests of our vocational commitments. But it would not be the last of my challenges with women.

Wakeup Call

As quickly as Frank Chase fell into his coma, he emerged from it, fully regaining his consciousness and prepared to ask dozens of questions to satisfy his curiosity as well as to learn what he had missed while he was sleeping. His "Living Will" had been obeyed, following instructions to avoid the use of extraordinary measures to keep him alive; but in spite of no sustenance of any kind, he had lingered for over three days.

There was no witness to testify to just what caused Frank to awaken from his apparent deathbed in the ICU. Only he knew that when he opened his eyes, he saw a ceiling over his head. He studied that ceiling for a long time and slowly perused the area around the circumference of his bed. It was visual proof that he had endured a long, deep sleep and awoke without understanding how or why.

The very sick patient had, indeed, overcome incredible odds to still be alive while his physicians and family had feared the worst. After falling into the coma, it was most likely that he would never regain consciousness and/or never experience a meaningful recovery.

For the time being, however, the hospital room was just as Frank remembered it before his unexpected attack, with one exception. A single, long-stem, red rose lay on the pillow near his head. Seeing it out of the corner of his eye, he struggled to reach it and, eventually, hold it in his hand, deftly avoiding the thorns on its stem. He was unable to make sense of it but he examined its subtle elegance. There was a nagging recollection, from somewhere or sometime, that the flower had significance. Its fragrance did more than confirm that he was alive. It contributed to his discontinuity and disorientation.

The odor of medicine and the stale air of "hospital" still prevailed and overwhelmed the scent of the flower. The noises that ricocheted up and down the hallway were identical. All was the same as he remembered it before his coma. The only exception was the flower and an absence of the fluids dripping from tubes into that "port" in his right shoulder.

The annoying plastic tubing had been disconnected long before his awakening. He had been placed in Intensive Care just before becoming comatose. Frank Chase, the humble Dentist from the suburbs of Chicago was "born again" to continue his unique and exceptional experience of living.

After the encounter with the rose and the process of his passage into consciousness, Frank's next intentional maneuver was to search for his "call button" to summon a nurse. The device had been moved from under his pillow to his bedstand where visitors could call for assistance if needed. Now out of his reach, he needed to develop an optional means of notifying someone, *anyone*, of the dramatic change in his condition. So he gathered what little strength he had and cried out, "Help! Help me! Somebody . . ."

His cry was but a whisper; but since his room was electronically monitored, the urgent message was heard at a nearby nurse's station. There was a rush of personnel and frenetic activity around his bed as staff arrived. They immediately contacted the physician on duty who soon phoned Frank's oncologist and his primary care physician. The shock of the team led to a delayed phone call to Annie who wasn't at home to answer her telephone. But she did respond to a cell phone message. She was speechless and told the voice on the phone that she'd be there in 20 minutes.

Immediately afterwards, Frank's medical team continued to assist his breathing with oxygen. He was also ministered intravenous feeding and antibiotics. His condition was listed as "extreme exhaustion, weakness and malnourishment." One of the initial goals was to ensure that his swallowing mechanism was functioning well enough to allow the consumption of food and liquids.

Frank smiled throughout a tedious examination from his confounded medical team. His vital signs were excellent, though his blood pressure was higher than normal. Naturally, every member of the staff worked in disbelief as Frank slowly began to improve his intelligibility and to clarify his return to lucidity. From his perspective, he was as puzzled as everyone else but particularly joyful and grateful.

When Annie arrived at his bedside, she smothered her husband with kisses . . . on his forehead, cheeks and chin, wherever she could fit her lips between the tubes. She embraced Frank around his shoulders and pressed her mouth as near to his face as possible so she could hear his every word. Awkwardly, she mixed audible dialogue with emotional doubt. There were tears and a multitude of muddled questions. Nothing made sense to her.

She called each of the children and knew she could lean on them for balance and support. Two were on their way to the hospital and the other two would receive messages and arrive soon. Her recorded words and texts were simple, albeit dramatic: "Your father has returned from dying. He's awake and talking!" They all knew that he'd have a lot to say.

Frank held his hands in front of his eyes, flexing his fingers and watching their movement like an infant studying his fingers for the first time. He was fascinated by little things: the movement of the hands of a clock on the wall, the scene through a window as branches of a tree bent in the wind, and an orange sun about to set. It was, indeed, an *awakening*, to sensory stimuli that were each appreciated and treasured more than ever in all his life.

Of the elements he remembered from his past, The Prayer from the pen of Saint Francis dominated his recollections. As he assembled pieces of the puzzle that left him so confused, he recalled that his friend, Father Tony Tonelli, had personally presented him with The Prayer and he had faithfully repeated it many times before the coma. Now, as he tried to say it from memory, only the last several lines were recalled with ease.

He especially remembered the intention of The Prayer . . . his private desire and request to live another life as a priest. At that point, however, his reasoning was alarmingly troubled. He became additionally confused as he asked more and more questions about his three days in the coma.

Had he been asleep? Was he near death? Was he able to think and experience anything over those days? Or was he dreaming? Was every thought imaginary or a tangible part of serious mental (and even physical) activity? And were his comatose experiences rooted in real happenings or hazy recollections from another time? Was it a dream?

Frank struggled with each of the questions. He remembered some basic experiences, but didn't know how to describe them. Most of what he recalled was in the category of *feelings* rather than facts. He received only speculative interpretations but no concrete answers from his family and the hospital staff. The medical evaluation of his condition remained incomplete. At best, the team of doctors threw up its collective hands and pointed to the heavens exclaiming jointly, "We have no reasonable explanation for his emergence from the coma."

The reality of the situation indicated that Frank was still suffering from pancreatic cancer but that it had gone into a rare state of dormancy, remaining stable but no longer inexorably marching toward the destruction of his life in six months. That, indeed, rarified his case.

The medical team, in a lengthy discussion with Frank and Annie, determined that the most beneficial approach was to release Frank from the hospital and monitor his condition on a weekly basis. He would receive only *palliative care* at home, "applying any methods used to alleviate pain and anxiety without the goal of curing." In short, Frank would be made as comfortable as possible, continuing to avoid radiation and chemotherapy treatments indefinitely. Instead, he would enjoy as much of his life as possible with few restrictions. The prognosis for longevity was listed as "unknown." The odds of lapsing into yet *another* coma, high.

For Frank's future, there were no longer speculative projections of one year, six months, etc., but a *lifetime* length that was as indefinite as Frank's bucket list was long. The term "life expectancy" was deleted from his file. It was anyone's guess and God's exclusive privilege to know with certainty. And so, Frank returned home to ponder with his family the limited things he could accomplish.

The reluctant but grateful patient began the slow process of strength-building by obeying his doctor's order to walk each day. He generally made it around his block of one-quarter mile, but with great effort. With equal commitment, he ventured throughout the inside of his house by foot, as much as possible. No wheelchairs allowed. If he wanted something, he got it himself. If someone else wanted something, like from another room, he or she asked Frank to retrieve it for them. He lovingly became known as the family's "retriever dog." But the tiniest physical accomplishments were noted and his goals were being reached, literally, one step at a time.

One night, after completing his second month at home, Frank and Annie sat down for a serious conversation, one he had patiently awaited and rehearsed several times before uttering the words. The setting was anything but spontaneous: the room lights were off, a small candle burned brightly in the center of the kitchen table, and two mugs of decaffeinated hot tea were served by Frank. In situations like this, when Frank called for a meeting immediately prior to retiring for the night, Annie became suspicious. This time would prove consistent with the pattern. She was prepared for big things to come.

Over their fifty-seven years of marriage, Annie and Frank each enjoyed these sessions immensely. The creatively designed setting had been developed and nourished during their courtship: the candle was crucial and, even after so many years of changing other habits, the beverage of tea was preferred over all others. No distractions were allowed, especially not television or even quiet music. The air had to be completely clear and, since their hearing had depreciated over the past ten years, the rule of a silent background provided multiple benefits. On this special night, Frank began with *small-talk*.

"Well, darling," he said slowly, "are you proud of me? Bet you're surprised at how faithful I've been to my exercise regimen. C'mon, give me an attaboy or two. I deserve it."

Nervously, Frank began rotating his wedding ring with fingers from his right hand. As fast as it would spin, he twisted and turned it. Annie recognized the tell-tale action.

"You're doing that thing again," she said to him.

"What thing?"

"You're playing with your ring. It's obvious that you're about to say something that you're afraid to say."

Frank denied that but timidly continued the habit. Annie prepared herself for ominous news. She coyly went along with the deception but asked. "What is it you *really* want to talk about? Out with it, my dear!"

"Woman," he said, "how can you have so little trust in me? Here you are, suspicious, when I'm trying to be completely open and honest." He reached across to touch her hand lightly and stopped playing with the ring. He shook his head from side to side, ruffled his hair, and sipped from his mug. The tea was still very hot and he quickly jerked the mug from his lips. Annie smiled, pretending that he deserved the pain for his deception, then apologized for appearing so insensitive.

"I know you've got something up your sleeve," she said.

"Nothing bad, just a subject that I've been giving a lot of thought. I need your approval of an idea." Frank was preparing to move in for the kill but, nevertheless, he was worried and apprehensive about his wife's reaction. He didn't want her to veto his idea before he had time to explain it.

"So okay," she said, repeating the line, "Out with it!"

"All right," he said sheepishly. "I know you're going to think I'm crazy, but just hear me out." He clutched Annie's hand tightly and sipped from his cooler tea, procrastinating nervously. He was as stressed as he was on the night he asked Annie to marry him, over

57 years earlier. And yes, this was almost as important and crucial to his immediate future as his question was then.

"I want to go to Rome," he blurted out! "And I'd like you to come with me. There, now I've said it."

Annie recoiled and pulled her hand gently back from her husband's. She was shocked but not speechless.

"To tell you the truth, my dearest," she said, "that doesn't surprise me as much as you might think. After all we've been through together, I'm accustomed to getting ideas like this from you, especially at the eleventh hour, before getting into bed. But . . . *Rome?*

"My God, Frank," she continued, "you can barely get around this house. Do you know how much walking you'd have to do on a trip like that? Look at you. You're nothing but skin and bone after all the weight you've lost. You look like a skeleton. Your hair is nearly all gone. You just . . . I don't want to hurt you, my dear, but you look . . . *sick*. They might not even let you on the plane."

"I know all that. But I really don't care how I look. It's what's inside of me that counts." He pointed to his heart with a smug grin.

"I think you can do better than that," Annie said as she again pulled her hand back from his. She also smiled, but it was a facetious, exaggerated smile with the ends of her mouth drooping to her chin.

"Look, honey," Frank insisted, "You remember how over all these years I said that 'if I had but one city to visit before I died, it'd be Rome?' Remember that? Well . . . need I say more? I truly love that place. And on top of my deep sentiment for Rome, I now have this affinity for Assisi. I'd really like to visit there and meet the Brother who gave Father Tonelli that beautiful prayer from Saint Francis, the one I feel was, *is*, responsible for my still being here today. I'd like to thank Father's friend, Brother Pietro, personally . . . shake his hand, maybe even give him a big hug."

"Boy, you've done your homework on this one, haven't you, my dear? What can I say that you haven't already designed an argument and a rebuttal against?"

"Well, darlin'," he said quickly. "You know that over all these years, my sole purpose in life has been *you*. I always believed that my charge on this earth, the task given me by God, is to do all I can to assure your happiness and help you get to heaven. And let me say this right now, if you're seriously against this idea of mine, I'll forget about it this minute."

Annie shook her head, incredulously marveling at her husbands timing and his powers of persuasion, some subtle and some not so subtle. She had one last question, however, that could reverse the tide.

"Have you talked to Father Tonelli about this?" she asked. "If so, what does he have to say?"

"Uh, no, I haven't had a chance to visit with him long enough. He's been so busy with Lent and Holy Week. I thought maybe I could get him alone next week."

"Okay, then," she said, "I'll make you this deal. If you tell him what you want to do, and if he approves of it and doesn't think you're out of your mind, then, and only then, will I endorse your plan. If he's okay with it, we'll go to Rome."

"I can live with that, darlin' . . . and I'm glad you're keeping an open mind. You know I couldn't go to Rome alone. I need you with me, as always, for more reasons than helping me to physically get around. I need your moral support and your encouragement to do this thing. Plus, I've never done anything in my life like this without your stamp of approval. That's the only way I could go and feel that it's the right thing to do." Frank's heart was soaring, though he hesitated to show it for fear of implying a victory too soon.

"Why don't you ask Father to come along if he approves," Annie asked.

"You must be joking . . . come along with us?"

"Yes. Why don't you ask him to join us if he feels it's a good idea? Wouldn't it be nice to have him there to introduce you to this Brother Pietro, sort-of open the door for you?"

"Wonderful thought, honey. He just might be interested."

"So, okay, then. We've agreed. We'll wait to make the final decision until you've talked to Father Tonelli and gotten his approval, right?"

"Absolutely! We've got a deal . . . and I love you very much for at least going along that far. You'll see. It's going to be the best thing we've ever done. And it's going to make you much more accepting of this cross we're carrying.

"You know how much I've always loved the Eternal City. There's not a single place, no church nor palace nor cathedral anywhere in the world where I feel closer to God, or to my Church for that matter. It's an opportunity to thank God for the incredible blessings He's heaped on our family for so many years. And now this . . . my return after the coma. Maybe that's why He brought me out of it, to give me the chance to say 'thanks' one more time, to worship Him in His favorite places.

"I mean, Rome is where Jesus Christ lives. I can just feel Him there . . . in each of the Basilicas, for example. He's alive in the Pieta, on the ceiling of the Sistine Chapel, in the statues and murals of St. Peter's. It's always a great renewal of my faith in God and in our Church, *His* Church. So I'd like to consider this a pilgrimage, certainly my last opportunity to see with my own eyes, for just the second time, the gorgeous artwork of Michelangelo and DaVinci and all the great shrines of Rome."

"And what about the food and the other historical places in Rome that we love so much?" Annie said, smiling impishly.

"Of course, you know how I love every corner of that city. I'm going for that, too. But it's the spiritual pilgrimage that's most important right now."

Annie frowned and shook her head from side to side. Her only comment was, "I always said you missed your calling, my dear. You should've been a lawyer. The way you put convincing arguments together never ceases to amaze me."

"But do you know something," Frank added quickly. "I've always been the 'me, too' person in our marriage."

"What do you mean by that," Annie asked.

"You know, it's like you're always the one who initiates 'I'm sorry . . . 'I love you' . . . 'I'll try harder.' And I'm the one who replies with 'me, too.' It takes a lot more courage and love to initiate it like you do. It's a cop-out to get away with just a 'me, too' like I do."

Annie smiled lovingly and thanked Frank for his kind admission. It made little difference that he was right. But it made a huge difference that he admitted to his shortcoming. She loved him all the more for his demonstrable humility. He was ready to end the discussion with one final thought.

"Do you know something, darlin'? I had this idea the other night after we explained some dreams to each other. When I was falling back to sleep, I was loving you so much and thinking of how I miss you when you sleep. And I wished I could go along with you *into* your dreams. I'd enjoy it so much if I could walk beside you, drive with you, share in the places and thoughts of your every dream. It's the only thing we haven't done together, *dream*, and I wish we could do that."

Annie thought about that for awhile and said, "You mean you don't get enough of me while we're awake? Goodness, since your illness, we've spent almost 24/7 with each other. And you're saying you want more?"

"It hasn't been 24/7 because we're apart when we sleep."

"Speak for yourself, my dear. You *do* accompany me in my dreams. As a matter of fact, I sometimes laugh at how you stick so close to me, even while I'm dreaming. You watch and weigh every move I make, every word I say."

"Please take me with you," Frank implored with a smile. "That's the way we always wanted it, isn't it . . . together every possible moment of our lives."

Annie smiled, too. "Yes, it is, dear. But even in my *dreams?*"

"*Especially* in your dreams. Because that's the most private, most secret place of all. And I want to share that, too, just like we share everything else. Work on that for me, will you?"

"I'll see what I can do," Annie said as she again shook her head in amazement at her husband's persistence. She was moved by his devotion and desire and acknowledged to herself that his obsessive love for her was occasionally a burden, albeit a pleasant one that she accepted and appreciated.

But Frank wasn't ready to quit. He had one more thought, one he had recently heard at a parish "retreat."

"This visiting priest," he explained, "he told us about his belief that love is the greatest gift God has given us. Of all the wonderful things, love is the greatest of them all. It's great when we receive it, and then it's great when we give it away and share it with others. So it's a two-tiered, actually a *three-tiered* gift because we can also return it to God when we love Him back. Does that make sense, darlin'?"

"Of course," Annie replied as she leaned toward him and kissed his cheek. As usual, she wondered privately just when he'd run out of thoughts and words before the night came to a close. But she hesitated to stop him knowing it wouldn't be too long before she didn't have him beside her. She thought about that often but refused to allow it to become an obsession. They would enjoy every moment together until God called him to His side.

Selling the Dream

The discussion with Annie ended with Frank rising from his chair, moving around to slide her chair away from the table, helping her stand, and then giving her a substantial kiss on the lips. It was long and romantic. They were both ready to go to bed and to sleep as well as could be expected, Annie's only concern being the health and welfare of her husband if they went to Rome and working on his unique thought to take him along on her dreams. That idea was not conducive to sleep.

Actually, as far as his dream of visiting Rome, she was quite confident that Father Tonelli would and could talk Frank out of it. Frank would accept the priest's good reasoning as he had many other times when the ambitious dentist had come up with extraordinarily impractical ideas.

Conversely, Frank was equally confident that Father Tonelli, sharing a spirit of adventure, would take *his* side and approve of his visit to Rome and to meet Brother Pietro in Assisi. So, as it stood, Father controlled the outcome of this important step in Frank's life. The good friend thus retained the potential to emerge as hero, conspirator, or both.

Easter had come and gone and Frank invited Father over to the house to chat about his plans for international travel. In the meantime, he had enlisted the aid of one of his daughters-in-law, Maureen, who was vice-president of a travel agency in the Chicago area. She would begin studying itineraries for the trip to Italy even before Frank received confirmation from Father and Annie. (It was a sign of his confidence in his wife's unselfishness and in his own ability to sell her and Father Tonelli on just about anything he desired.)

On arrival at his house for an evening visit, Frank and his priest-friend sat on Frank's deck overlooking a stand of tall trees and a small lake. The weather was perfect for outdoor conversations with temperatures in the mid-seventies and the air heavy with the fragrance of spring flowers. It was a lot easier for Frank to sit rather than to walk while discussing heavy material, thus consuming a lot less energy and focusing more on his dialogue. Additionally, a Guinness and a Heineken were more conveniently handled, adding substantially to the genial ambience.

Frank had all he needed to "pitch" his idea. In fact, it was the first private opportunity the two friends were able to manage since Frank's wake-up call two months earlier.

The first item on the agenda was Frank's experience in the coma. Father had one question after another, most of them regarding Frank's feelings going into and coming out of unconsciousness.

"I'll tell you, Father," Frank began, "there's no way . . . there aren't any words to describe what went on, I mean, what it felt like inside my head."

"Was it like dreaming?"

"No. That's what was so strange about it. You know how sometimes when you dream, you don't recall the dream until the next time you lay your head on the pillow and fall asleep again?"

"Yeah. I've had that happen," Father answered.

"Well, it was like that . . . but then, it *wasn't* like that at all. The stuff that went on in my head while I was 'sleeping,' was *real*, like I was someplace else, in some other time . . . while at the same time, I was laying in the hospital bed. I'm telling you, it was surreal! I can't explain it in words."

"Do you think it was an 'out-of-body experience' like a lot of people describe if they've been in danger of dying or believe they have, indeed, *died?* Did you see a white light?"

"Nothing like that at all. This was totally different from anything I've ever heard."

"It sounds like you're describing something *paranormal.*"

"I'm not knowledgeable enough to answer that, Father."

"Okay, my friend," Father said, "let's come at this from another angle. Can you recall any single sight or sound, any *people* . . . any kind of conversation? Is there anything that stands out, clearly, as a part of that 'place' you were in?"

"Boy, I feel really stupid, Father. I just can't explain it. On the one hand, it was *me,* Frank Chase, but I was living another kind of life, somewhere else. On the other hand, it wasn't me at all, but somebody else inside of me acting like I would act and feeling like I would feel in all kinds of situations."

"Was it pleasant or frightening?" Father asked.

"It wasn't at all frightening. But yes, it was pleasant. I was confronted by all kinds of dilemmas, troubling and difficult decisions I was being forced to make. You know in a dream, sometimes you're caught in a situation when, well, you just can't seem to find an escape?"

"I read once, and I firmly believe," Father said, "that dreams are filled with puns, intense situations that suggest different meanings. A typical example that comes to mind is the classic case of being trapped in water that's over your head and you're hopelessly drowning. That can symbolize worries about getting out of debt or quitting your job because you're drowning in toxic relationships . . . or something similar that's characterized by that fear of drowning. Can you identify any such *puns* in your experience, any *plots* that give you some clue in discerning whether it was a dream or . . ."

"Or what, Father? I'm telling you that it wasn't anything conventional like the puns you're describing. I know all that about dreams. In the condition I was in, I felt like I was on a journey, going someplace I'd been before but in another context. I was, at the same time, the same man I am now but I was on a different road altogether."

Father made an educated guess. "Do you think there's any chance that your experience was related to The Prayer, to the intercession you're asking from Saint Francis . . . about wanting another life as a priest?"

"What a dummy I am. Yeah, sure . . . I think you've got something there, Father." Frank closed his eyes and tried to remember more details of his 'dream.'

"Maybe I'm getting closer to understanding you," Father said. "Man, oh man. You can think deeper than anyone I've ever met, Francis. You can . . ."

"What did you say?" Frank interrupted, reaching over and grasping Father's arm.

"I said you can think deeper."

"No . . . you called me 'Francis.' You've never called me that before. Where did that come from?"

"Well, it just so happens to be your name. Maybe that's where I got it, right from your actual name, *Francis*."

The two friends laughed. The conversation had been both tense and intense and the laughter broke the heavy thinking. It prompted Father to make a suggestion.

"Why don't we change the subject, Francis . . . uh, Frank. Let's talk about something else. You said you wanted to talk to me about something important. Was that it, your comatose experience?"

"No, not at all," Frank answered. "But you're right. I do want to talk to you about something else, something *urgent*, as a matter of fact. It involves traveling to Italy . . . Annie and me traveling to Italy."

"You and Annie? When?"

"Well . . . *now*, in a couple of weeks if we can put all the pieces together. I don't have any time to waste, do I?"

Father wasn't a bit surprised at Frank's determination in wanting to go on a trip to Rome, though Father was slightly reticent to encourage it without asking a ton of questions, all of them related to Frank's health and the risk of becoming ill in a foreign place. He was also considering Frank's age and the unknowns of distant travel.

"So you don't have any fears about making this trip at your age and in your condition? You're comfortable with traveling so far at . . . how old are you now, my friend. I lost count at 75."

Frank laughed and replied sharply, "I'm 77, a very *young* 77, if you exclude my cancer." He paused briefly and finished his thought. "I was watching one of my favorite reruns last night on *TCM*. It was an episode of *Gunsmoke* from back in the early 60's and Matt Dillon was listening to a couple of old guys yakking on about aging and ambition. And this one guy is being scolded for wanting to go prospecting for gold. And the other guy keeps telling him he's too old for something that physical. And this guy turns to him and says, 'Hey, there's plenty a good tune played on an old fiddle, ain't there.' Now that's exactly how I feel. I'm an old fiddle all right, but I've still got plenty a good tune to play. Which brings me to another point, Father." Frank said that with conviction. "Are you *ready* for more?"

Father nodded and responded, "You're on a roll, my friend. Just keep going. I wouldn't try to stop you for anything in the world."

"Okay, and oh, maybe I forgot to tell you. I also want to visit Assisi and meet your friend, Brother Pietro. I'd like to thank him personally for The Prayer. It's meant so much to me over these past months. That would be a very important part of the trip."

"I think I could set that up. It'd be no problem. I just hope Brother is still in good health. A lot would depend on that."

"I'd really appreciate your help. Okay, then, I just wanted to discuss one other thing that's on my mind. This is way off the subject, but since you're a captive audience, I'll bounce this off of you.

"The other night, we had a guest speaker at the Knights of Columbus meeting. He was a missionary with Maryknoll. Excellent speaker. But I didn't agree with everything he said. I'd like your 'read' on this."

"Are you asking me to take sides, Frank?"

"Well, sort of. See if you don't think I have a point here. The priest was trying to convince us that we'd all be better served if we'd focus on *today*, on the *present* rather than the past or the future. He said something like, 'The past is gone. It's over. There's nothing we can do to change it. The future is yet to come and there's nothing we can do about that, either. When the future gets here, it'll be *today*. And then, we can affect change and improve ourselves . . . on *this* day, *today!*'

"Do you buy that, Father?"

"Of course. It makes a lot of sense. I'm sure he was addressing the subject of making changes that can help us get to heaven. And *today* is the only time we can do that."

"Yeah, but . . . I want to argue the point that *yesterday* is as important as *today*. It was *yesterday*, figuratively speaking, all the past years of my life that made me what I am. It was the struggles, the accomplishments and the failures, all of it, that tested me and improved me. Plus, it was everything that Annie and I shared as we raised our kids. We had some great times and some bad ones, but we learned from each of them. We like to think we became stronger people as we advanced in age." Father listened, giving Frank's every word his careful attention as Frank continued.

"Now these days, at least for me, when every day is so precious, when it may be my last, I enjoy dwelling on the past, reminiscing about all the good times gone by. And while I consider both the good and the bad, it's a way of reliving my life, of savoring some wonderful times, especially those indelible times with Annie . . . the romantic times, the sickly times, the times we stuck together. No matter how the devil tried to break us up and come between us, we made it!"

Frank was using his hands to make his points, gesticulating freely and effectively. He went on. "So, in that light, I don't see anything wrong with living in the past. The past is a better friend that the present or the future. Because it's done, over, ended. All the problems have been solved or resolved. You can't say that about the present or future, now can you?"

Father shifted in his chair, having been glued to his friend's eyes as they became increasingly intense with each word.

"And I'll tell you another thing," Frank added. "Reliving the good times . . . well, there's nothing like it. Annie and I can talk about decades of traveling around the world, mentally revisiting dozens of foreign countries, all the capitals of Europe and the Far East, as well as the most beautiful places in our own country.

We can recall missed airline flights, terrible meals as well as sumptuous feasts, getting lost in foreign cities.

"When we sit together, we have great fun reconstructing our travels together. We can imagine, like it was yesterday, the smell of burning incense in the Casbah in Tangier; we can feel the bumpy movement of the ferry crossing Hong Kong harbor; we can hear the music of the Balinese people in the lobby of the Hyatt Hotel in Indonesia, all of that as we travel vicariously.

"Why, we can even taste the salty air as a beat-up old tug carries us across the straits of Gibraltar, passes slowly as we study the famous rock, then carries us from northern Africa back to the Costa del Sol in Spain. It takes some work to remember like that. So when somebody tells me I shouldn't live in the past, I don't buy it. I mean, the word 'memory' itself means to recall and keep things in the mind. And Annie and me, we're not going to give up that habit.

"Why, I even enjoy remembering some of the patients I served. I met and treated some of the finest people in this city. You know, the past is free, it don't cost a thing. So as long as my memory serves me as well as it has, I'm going to go right on using it as much as I can.

"I even enjoy reliving the very day before today, yesterday. Annie and I had a great lunch downtown, in *The Loop*. We drove down with two of our dearest friends that we've known for over 50 years. And we ate at "The Berghoff," one of our favorites, one of the oldest restaurants in all of Chicago. We had a most memorable time, one that all four of us will relive over and over again. Nobody can take that from us. That's the good that comes from *not* killing the past, from *not* being afraid to spend time *living* in the past.

"So now I'll shut up. It's your turn, Father," Frank said. "You can ask any questions, anything you'd like. You have my undivided attention."

"Yeah, right," Father quickly responded. "After you use up half the night narrating a 'Cook's Tour' of the entire world, you relinquish the floor." Father knew from the past, by Frank's own admission, that he liked to hear himself talk. This was no exception.

But at the same time that Frank felt totally *spent*, he slumped back in his chair and realized that he had expended more energy than he had to spare. He was pleased with himself, though, and everything he had said to Father. On the other hand, Father was exhausted from the tedious details of the lengthy monologue. Of course, he appreciated every word and wouldn't dispute anything his closest of all friends had just uttered about living in the past, not so much for the reason of *appeasement*, but rather, in *agreement* with everything he said. He acknowledged that fact and was grateful for Frank's candor regarding the trip to Rome. He would long remember the stories that were now a part of *his* past. He provided an addendum of his own.

"In justice to people who encourage others *not* to dwell on the past, don't you think they mean past *mistakes*, sadness or error that can't be altered? I'm not *disagreeing* with your point-of-view, Frank, but I think there are a lot of good people who don't relive their past because it's too painful.

"In cases like that," Father continued, "focusing on the past can prevent someone from seizing the opportunities of the here and now. A lot of people have experienced misadventures or have been guilty of hurting others, for example. I think those are what your missionary meant about forgetting the past and living for today, don't you?"

Frank gave that some heavy thought, albeit brief, and responded by agreeing with Father but still getting in the last word. "Yeah, I guess you're right. But I'm stubborn enough to maintain that my argument is stronger.

After almost two hours of such stimulating dissertation, divided *occasionally* with opposing as well as amicable thoughts from both parties, Father agreed that it was a good idea for Frank and Annie to make the trip to Rome. It would thus allow them to develop many more *new* memories. But he also knew how important it was for them to come to a quick settlement of the issue. What he *didn't* know was that their previous adventures would pale in comparison to the one ahead. Ultimately, Father deferred to Frank's medical team to make the "final call" on the trip.

Father was moved and touched by the request to have him join Annie and Frank, but he had major commitments over the next month and thought, too, that they should experience the trip together and alone. He knew them well enough to sense an air of anticipatory romance that just might permeate the trip.

But the evening's discussion was far from over. Frank had an additional subject he had not yet covered with Father. It concerned The Prayer. That subject was, after all, tantamount to his trip and the stimulus for his passage into another time and place. Or was it? For the first time since rising from his coma, Frank readied himself to broach the subject in detail with his friend/counselor/confessor.

"First of all, Father," he began, "you know that I was saying The Prayer two, sometimes three times a day before the coma. And you remember that I was praying that I'd someday get the chance to experience life as a priest."

"I don't mean to interrupt," Father asked, "but I'm curious. Did you actually want to *be* a priest? How did you position that in your prayer-conversation? What were you expecting, a 'flashback,' like going back in your life as a youngster and then . . . I don't know, *you* have to tell *me*. Were you expecting a second chance at choosing priesthood over marriage?"

"Yeah, I guess. That's the only way I could imagine it. Maybe a 'flashback' or something like that. Maybe even seeing it in the *future* somewhere, like after I died.

"And that remained the intention of your prayers?"

"Absolutely! I told you many times that I didn't want to erase any of the wonderful life I've had with Annie and the kids. My wish, my dream, my *prayer* was to be able to live a second life, if you will. I didn't know how in the world God would work that out. That part was up to Him. All I knew was that I wanted to have the privilege of making a second choice. I guess you could say that 'I wanted to have my cake and eat it too.' Not that I deserved that second blessing, mind you, but . . . you understand what I'm saying, don't you?"

"I'd be lying if I said 'yes' because I don't really understand it at all. But it was *your* personal prayer, *your* private request to God.

I assume that if He saw fit, if in His Divine wisdom, if He knew that the experience of living that *other* life wouldn't do any harm to you or anyone else, He has the power to do it, in whatever way He desires. He's the Master of Creativity, you might say. Nobody could second-guess His ways and means to answer your unusual request."

"Okay, I think you get the idea of what I'm talking about."

"And you think this is all connected . . . your request during The Prayer and that hazy *journey* you felt while you were in the coma. That stuff is all connected, right?"

"Yeah. But my problem now is . . . well, did God answer my prayer or didn't He? Is it over, complete? Did I have some kind of 'flashback' with details that I just can't remember? Or was I on some sort of trip into the future . . . or the past? What do you think, Father. You've had answers for me before, you've been able to solve complex problems for me, now I need you to solve this one."

"Good grief, man . . ." Father said in a halting delivery. "You sure can conjure up the challenges for me, can't you? I don't know how to explain your experience. I have to throw it back to you and ask . . . what do *you* think happened?"

"If I had but one answer to give, I'd say that . . ." Frank took several long, deep breaths before finishing. "I really don't have a clue! All I know is that I recall something about priesthood, really hard decisions . . . I can't tell you if those things occurred in the past or in the future."

"What about the present?"

"The present?" Frank asked while frowning and leaning far back in his chair.

"Yeah, the present. Maybe you were on some 'Magical Mystery Tour.' Maybe you were given a pass to travel *back* in time while you were still living in the *present time.*"

"You mean simultaneously? Like living parallel lives?"

"Exactly . . . *concurrently!*"

"Wow, I never looked at it that way. Maybe you're right."

"Look, Frank, anything's possible with God. He can answer any prayer in any way He sees fit. Beyond accepting that explanation, I can't give you any other help. Just be content to have had the experience. It doesn't really matter why or how it happened, but according to your feelings, you seem to believe it did happen. So then, just settle on the fact that God answered your prayer through the words of The Prayer of Saint Francis. End of discussion!"

"But it's *not* the end, Father. I only recall brief snippets from that experience and it *had* no ending, no resolution to the problems." Another long pause. "Actually . . . I just don't know. But if nothing else happens, I'll sure be disappointed. I guess I'll leave it alone and move on. For right now, it's 'To Rome and Beyond!' That's my battle cry."

The *Alitalia* flight was booked within the next week and scheduled to take Frank and Annie nonstop from Chicago to Rome in a little over nine hours. Two weeks before departure, their daughter, Margaret, who had just celebrated her 55th birthday, decided she'd like to accompany her parents on their journey. She made the decision based on two factors: first, her mom and dad could use a personal *travel director* to make certain that everything ran smoothly; and second, she'd never been to Rome or Assisi and would like to visit there with her parents while her dad was still capable of making the trip.

Margaret was never married, not because she didn't *want* to be, but because she hadn't met the right man. Now, after owning and managing her own brokerage firm for over 30 years, she could afford to take this vacation. She was a most trusted and loyal friend of her parents. She was also as straight as they come, in more ways than one, and got along well with all peers and most humans. Complementing her attractive appearance was her tall, thin frame, long dark hair and a mild Irish accent, acquired in Dublin where she earned her undergraduate and graduate degrees in Finance.

In Margaret's case, her relationship with her father justified the phrase, "The apple didn't fall far from the tree." She even resembled Frank physically and, more important, spiritually. She had her father's high ideals. She was a welcome partner and would prove extremely helpful on every step of the journey, more than she could imagine.

The anticipation of the journey had been significantly enhanced by Frank's invitation to speak at an important gathering of the Knights of Columbus in Rome. The irony was notable and appreciable.

Several years earlier, *The Knights*, the largest of all Catholic Fraternal organizations, led the opening of a special exhibit called, "The Knights of Columbus in Rome, Celebrating 90 Years of Friendship." The Knights were pleased that for so many years they had become an established fixture in the eternal city and continued to be at the service of the people and of the Holy See during the pontificate of Pope Benedict XVI.

The planners of a special event again honoring the ties between *The Knights* and Rome had been informed of Frank's recovery and knew that his story would be of interest and inspiration to those in attendance, especially since he was a Past Grand Knight and had gained recognition as an exemplary leader for over fifty years.

The proudest of all Knights, Frank was buoyed by the flattering invite and accepted it without hesitation. He would speak on the second day of the two-day affair and the second week of the family's visit to Rome. Though it did little to disturb him, he recognized that the speaking engagement added a small amount of stress to an already stressful journey.

Frank generally slept well on long, international flights and it was his plan to do the same on this pilgrimage to Italy. Just into the third hour of the transatlantic flight, 50,000 feet above the earth, he fell into one of his deepest sleeps ever, almost as fathomless as when he was in the coma. He stayed in that physical and mental state for over six hours and managed to recline comfortably in his *business class* seat. Annie expected that. He had taken his full complement of eight medications that day and the result was anticipated drowsiness.

Annie, determined to allow him his coveted peace and quiet, kept flight attendants away throughout the entire flight. Frank's extended sleep would minimize the effects of jetlag and provide the rest and energy he needed, not only to *survive* the rigors ahead, but to *enjoy* them. While he was sleeping, he again experienced a second life . . . concurrent with the first.

Another Rose

At the same time I celebrated my 36th birthday in 1971, I also celebrated my 10th year as a priest. I couldn't believe that ten years had flown by so quickly. For the most part, my life had remained consistent with the way it began . . . filled with a plethora of opportunities to write and to preach, my first loves of priesthood.

As a result, my resume of retreats, novenas and days of recollection continued to expand. It kept me very busy and there was not a single offer that I rejected. I say with utmost humility that preaching came easy to me. I enjoyed every minute of it. The ability to write and to develop creative thoughts and then deliver those thoughts to large congregations was truly a gift from God, one that I treasured as much as my vocation.

My mom and dad were very proud of all that and also proud and excited about my anniversary. They were so grateful for the joys that God, through my priesthood, had given them that they offered to send me anywhere in the world for a celebratory vacation. I chose "The Eternal City!"

To visit Rome had always been a dream of mine, far back into my childhood before I chose priesthood. My family loved the Italian people, even though there wasn't a single drop of Italian blood anywhere in the gene pool or the DNA of any of my ancestors. But I grew up sharing a family affinity for the wonderful people, music and heritage of *anything* Italian.

I had encouraged and invited my best friends, Fathers Bill and Kenny, to join me on the trip to Rome. They eagerly accepted and were honored that my parents would fund the airfare and lodging for all three of us over the ten-day venture. Neither of my buddies had ever been to Rome though Father Bill did have some "connections" in the great city. Through them, he arranged for our housing to be in a pension (pen-see-yown) run by the Sisters of Saint Dorothy. The group of religious nuns had maintained a presence on the tiny island of Malta and also in Rome for nearly all of their history which dates back over 100 years.

Before we left on the trip, I studied and learned a bit of worthwhile trivia about the congregation of Saint Dorothea. It was formally known as the *Sisters of Saint Dorothy of Saint Paula Frassinetti.* Saint Paula is the foundress of the order and revered as "the patron of sick people."

The nuns were obliging hostesses and the three of us became dedicated to their cause, especially after learning that Saint Paula had four brothers who all were priests. We were informed that Paula's incorrupt body is entombed at Saint Onofria, the Dorothean motherhouse where we stayed. She was canonized in 1984 by Pope John Paul II. To be sure, the good sisters would always be remembered in our prayers and us in theirs.

The location of this wonderful and holy place was just a half-mile from Saint Peter's Basilica and across the street from the North American College where American priests study in preparation for ordination. We were grateful to Bill for finding us such great lodgings when most of Rome was filled with thousands of visitors from around the world. Bill did his job well and reminded us often of the debt we owed him. I didn't let him get away with that, reminding him (jokingly, of course) that it was my parents who made our trip possible.

Of course, the first stop on our itinerary was a visit to St. Peter's Basilica, the largest Basilica of Christianity. I can't describe the exhilaration I felt when I entered the huge doors at the entrance and stared up at the magnificent dome. A large part of that was my pride in having stayed the course, completed my studies, and been ordained a Roman Catholic priest.

Everything inside this extraordinary place was more than I had expected . . . the paintings and stained glass, the altars and statues, the soft echoes of human voices, and the thrill of beholding the elegance of that spectacular dome by Michelangelo. This was somewhere that deserved better than to be called a *Church* or even a *Basilica*. For me, it introduced a spiritual realm that was more heavenly than anything I had ever experienced, indescribably uplifting and inspirational.

The *other* three magnificent Basilicas of Rome have their own distinctions. Though second on our list, we didn't consider them "secondary" by any measurement, save only in size. Their history and beauty is uniquely impressive.

That having been said for the *spiritual* side of Rome, my very favorite *secular* space was the *Piazza Navona*. Over the many times that Bill and Kenny and I separated to "do our own thing," it seemed that I always ended up in this diverse and colorful meeting place, one of the world's most famous squares. To me, it was everything that makes Rome such an incomparable city: throngs of friendly people, excellent food and drink, artists galore, gorgeous fountains, vocal merchants, even a beautiful church named Saint Agnes.

On days when the three of us separated, my colleagues and I shed our "blacks" and wore our "civvies" (civilian clothes). They were more comfortable and we felt less conspicuous. Throughout Rome, however, members of religious orders who are dressed in black dot the urban landscape, on the streets, in the plazas, and around the countless historic sites. The fact is that we felt more at ease in jeans or cotton trousers and light jackets. The only exceptions were our visits to the churches and our "general audience" with Pope Paul VI. Those were special times that required and deserved our best religious clothing.

In *Piazza Navona*, eating and drinking at an outdoor table in a highly-recommended cafe called Tre Scalini is relatively costly. But it offers a famed tartufo dessert that's one of the most delicious foods I've ever tasted. It's a rich, handsome, handmade chocolate ice cream roll topped with loads of whipped cream.

For me, the dessert was worth the splurge, as long as it didn't become a profligate experience. I would take my time eating it while absorbing the freedom of expression surrounding me. The price included the great outdoor entertainment of people-watching. There were also brief comments and conversations with passers-by. The international flavor was unlike anything in Chicago.

In spite of the cacophony of sounds and the busyness of the sights, *Piazza Navona* in general and Tre Scalini in particular were ideal places to enjoy the exceptional "people" scenery and also sort-out the more serious elements of my life. Noisy and exciting environments did that to me. They stimulated my imagination and increased my creativity.

Additionally, being separated from the rigors of daily living, I could meditate more profoundly and better develop fresh thoughts for my speaking assignments. I was also able to spend important time reflecting on my relationship with God and evaluating my performance as a priest.

So while I spent my time in that wonderful and happy place, Bill took in the antiquity of Rome: the Coliseum, Forum, etc. Kenny, on the other hand, enjoyed venturing into the art treasures, many of which were in the churches: the Pieta, Michelangelo's statue of Moses and his ceiling in the Sistine Chapel. While we three travelers were very much alike, we had slightly differing interests in the sites of Rome. Most of those were rooted in genetic influences and to our personalities.

I should have known that the heavenly peace I found in such abundance within the piazza was destined for an earthly disturbance, an inconspicuous, unwilling encounter with . . . a woman. It was on my second visit to Tre Scalini. I was sitting alone at the café directly in front of *The Four Rivers* fountain when I saw it coming, *her* coming in this case. I couldn't believe that another female was poised to present a monumental challenge to my priesthood.

At the very least, I was grateful that *this* female wasn't a nun. I had enjoyed a ten-year break from such dangers but the hiatus was over. This new woman suddenly climbed the first rung up the ladder to temptation and instantly rose to the level of *potential!*

It was late in the afternoon on a warm and sunny day. The shadows played nicely across the piazza and strategically placed the last empty table at Tre Scalini in enviable shade. A large, white umbrella over my head provided as much ambience as shelter from the sun. It was a great spot to enjoy my pastime of people-watching. The background musical score was the soft and pleasant sound of voices, all *kinds* of voices, from the lilting songs of children to the brash hawking of artists selling their works.

Just as I sat down, an ethereal image emerged from the moving crowd. An exceptionally beautiful woman glided across the piazza as if she were skating on ice. She was slender and tall and walked with the proud strut of a model on a runway. She wore just enough skirt to reveal ideally proportioned legs, a white blouse above her waist, and a dark blue blazer. Long, blond hair decorated her shoulders. No man, whether priest or pope, married or single, young or old, could have ignored the magnetism of this lovely feminine creation.

As she approached my private enclave, I turned my head away from her, fearing that she'd notice my stare. But then again, every male in the vicinity was beamed-in on her countenance. So rather than being as obvious as the rest, I focused on food. I had been patient and hadn't yet attracted a server. I was eager for the famous tartufo.

Just as a waiter headed toward me, the serene image of the woman did the same. She stopped, directly in front of me, standing like a leaning tower as she studied the vacant chair across from me. I was at a table for two and she chose the only empty chair in the outdoor seating area. I stood quickly to hold the chair for her as she placed several small packages beneath the table. The waiter arrived just as she became comfortable. She spoke to both of us.

"Do you mind if I sit here?" she said to *me*.

"Could you give me a minute?" she said to the *waiter*.

He and I answered simultaneously, "Yes!"

The waiter said he'd be right back and would allow the woman time to study the menu. She and I introduced ourselves, by first name only.

"Hi, my name's Rosa," she said, more softly than I anticipated after seeing the authority in her strut. I told her my name was Francis and I was from Chicago. She replied that she, too, was from the Windy City. At that particular juncture in the conversation, the irony of her name struck me like a bolt of lightning . . . *Rosa!*

Could it be that this was another occasion of destiny at my doorstep? Was it possible that out of the hundreds of thousands of people in Rome on that day, this particular woman stopped at *my* table? And she's from Chicago. And her name is *Rosa?* Sure, it wasn't exactly "Sister Rose" but it was close enough to launch me into a state of disbelief. Another "Rose" had dropped her precious petals in my path.

The woman noticed my blank expression. She knew something triggered that, left it alone, and simply replied that she was visiting Rome as part of a Convention. She explained that it was her first time in the city and then asked what I did.

Rather than making it more complicated than it had to be, I answered that I was in *counseling.* Naturally, she couldn't leave that alone.

"What kind of counseling do you do and for whom?" she asked, her bright blue eyes sparkling from underneath her abundant golden locks.

I squirmed a bit but continued to pull off my deception. "Well, I counsel . . . just about anyone who needs it . . . men, women, children, the elderly. You name the category and I counsel it, I mean 'them.'"

"And who do you work for?"

This woman was as inquisitive as she was beautiful. I don't really know why I concealed the truth other than not wanting to make a big deal out of being a priest, and perhaps, with grave guilt, to instinctively leave the door ajar for the future. I watched her perusing the menu and took the opportunity to change the subject.

"If you don't know what to order, I'll recommend the tartufo. It's to die for . . . chocolate ice cream with lots of whipped cream. It's made this place famous."

"Yeah, I see that. The menu says, 'Tre Scalini is known all over the world for our truffles and our kindness.' She smiled as I did. The only difference was that I sounded a discordant note by coming off like a know-it-all.

Craziest thing, even after my experience with Sister Rose, I continued to struggle with shyness when around women. I could work comfortably with moms of children in our school and with members of our choir or other women who had a functional place in my parish family. But when left alone with a female, I was intimidated. I really didn't know why, but it made me self-conscious.

If my inhibition was caused by anything, it was an onus of guilt at being alone with a woman when I was bound to my vow of celibacy. Kenny and Bill told me that some of my problem was rooted in a "scrupulous conscience." But that's the way I was created and I'll always be the same.

Here and now, at Tre Scalini, I swore to do better with a member of the opposite sex. With that thought, the waiter returned and Rosa and I both ordered the famous dessert with another popular item called *Caffe Noisette*. It was a non-alcoholic cold coffee that neither Rosa nor I had tried since arriving in Rome; but here, we heard everyone else requesting it and thought it a wise and safe selection.

We were both very quiet while we waited for our order. Our coffee was served first. Then, while sipping slowly, we passed the time of day with common niceties. I managed to avoid my occupation, but before regaining my confidence, I made a silly comment.

"*Caffe Noisette,*" I said, "what we're drinking here. It sounds like 'noisy coffee.' Do you think that's what it means? Does the coffee make noise?" As the words left me, I repeated to myself, 'Open mouth, insert foot.'"

Rosa was kind enough to laugh. She did try to conceal the rolling of her eyes but I knew she considered my comment clearly stupid. I decided not to speak again until spoken to. I was grateful to see the appearance of our desserts. Eating would be a distraction to help pass the time.

My companion then got more personal as she probed into my profile. She asked what my surname was, and in the rush of dialogue, I almost stumbled and began with "Father." I recovered in time to say only "Chase. I'm Francis Chase."

"Your first name is 'Francis?'" she said. "Isn't that a little strange for a guy to go by that name? How come you're not called 'Frank?' I've got a best friend whose name is the same as yours but *she* spells it with an 'e'."

In addition to being so blunt (maybe *honest* is a better word), Rosa demonstrated a vocal trait that was unnerving. She spoke extremely fast, punctuating words in sudden bursts, rolling one explosion into another. There were no periods in her sentences, no pauses to catch her breath. I could barely follow what she was saying. She was thus no help in bolstering my confidence. And trying to explain why I was called "Francis" offered me no solace. I took a minute to check in with myself and display control.

"Well, you see," I began, "when I was born, I was named after my father, and my family had to have a way to differentiate between the two of us. So they decided to call me, 'Francis,' and he remained 'Frank.' Then, later on, when I got older and needed a Social Security number, I used the same name and . . ."

At that point, Rosa giggled like a small girl who had just beaten a boy at his own game. She was *putting me on* all along. From that brief conversation regarding my first name, I learned that this quick-witted woman had a very subtle sense of humor. I would not take her so seriously again. I laughed and felt myself blushing.

How a grown man, 36-years-old, could behave like such a fool in front of a woman, was beyond my understanding. So far, though, I had skillfully managed to outwit her and conceal my identity as a priest. In an effort to turn things around, I asked for *her* surname.

"Marsinski," she said. There's an 's' in the middle that's pronounced like a 'z'. My full name is Rosa Marie Marsinski."

I didn't dare comment. But I was not expecting such a last name from someone with strongly cut Italian features. She knew that.

"In case you're wondering," she said, "my maiden name is 'Bellisario' and I changed it when I married a man named Laszlo *Marsinski*. I wasn't happy to surrender my obvious connection to Italy and such a musical last name for one that was so, well, guttural and Eastern European."

"I'm a little surprised to hear of your Italian heritage. You have the features of an Italian but the blond hair and blue eyes throw me, if I'm not getting too personal."

"A lot of people question the same thing. But you see, my mom and dad are both from the *northern* part of Italy where those qualities aren't unusual. Essentially, I can't help how I look and where my ancestors came from."

My response was a scratchy, "Hmmm." After a short pause, I decided to take a more gentle approach. "And so, Rosa Marsinski," I said, "tell me what *you* do."

"What do you *think* I do?"

"I have no idea."

"Just take a guess."

"I don't know. Maybe you're a teacher. You strike me as one who could lead a classroom full of kids. Maybe you're a model, judging by your stylish clothing. Maybe you're even an anchorperson on television. You seem to have the confidence for that."

"Do you always justify what you say, Francis?"

"What do you mean *justify?*"

"Never mind," she said with a smile as she rolled her fingers through her long strands of hair and placed the strands over her ears. That move left an accent on the perfect lines of her nose and chin. Rosa had made her mark. I still couldn't get over her first name.

An Innocent Time

Preposterous! Sacrilegious! Unconscious! I must have lost my mind to be behaving so disgracefully as a *man of God*. And flirting?

Rosa and I had just finished our dessert when I lost control again, this time of my curiosity. "Okay, I said, "so you're being kind of mysterious about your occupation and that makes me even *more* curious to know what you do. I apparently didn't guess it correctly but are you going to tell me . . . or not?"

"I knew that would intrigue you," she said. "I'm a Physician . . . Internal Medicine and Pediatrics. Now, are you satisfied?"

"You're kidding, of course."

"Nope. Do you want to see my credentials?"

"It's not necessary. But you can't blame me for being surprised. I mean . . ."

"Why are you surprised? Don't I *look* like a doctor?"

"Rosa, you're quite a woman. But I never figured your profession to be in medicine. It's so . . . *scientific*. And you look more like a, well, somebody who's creative, like an artist, or like all those guesses I made earlier.

I paused briefly, and then asked, "So do I call you 'doctor' now?" She slapped me on the hand.

"Not in the *Piazza Navona*," was her reply.

"What in the world attracted you to *medicine?*"

"Don't make it sound like I'm a freak, Francis."

"I'm sorry. I didn't mean it that way."

"I'm used to it. I got that same reaction throughout medical school. But to answer your question. When I was a small girl, I was already interested in medicine. I'd prefer to play with my brother's chemistry set than with dolls . . . hands down! And I'd be messing around with frogs and snakes, trying to keep them alive while my friends were trying to cut their heads off. Now I've got three kids of my own and they're the same way, protecting the entire animal kingdom." Rosa laughed as we shifted in our chairs and looked to the sky. It was turning grey and appearing to be in the mood for rain.

"And what exactly *motivated* you to study medicine?" I asked, undeterred by the threatening sky.

"It's too long a story to go into."

"Go into it. We've got time. If it rains, so be it. And besides, with your efficient delivery of words, it probably won't take much time at all." Rosa smiled and seemed flattered by my encouragement.

"Well, my dad stood on a high pedestal as my personal hero," she began. "He was always doing something to help other people, like at Church, neighbors of ours, people where he worked. He was peripatetic in raising money for *anybody and everybody*. And he could not tolerate indifference. Actually, he studied to be a priest for awhile and I think his generosity and love for his fellow man was nurtured in the seminary."

I didn't want to go *near* that one, so I switched gears. "And what about your mom?" I asked.

"She was the same as dad, a died-in-the-wool philanthropist. We learned at home, by example, that if you can't be doing something to make the earth a better place, then give up. So I had it in my genes, you might say, to want to do something worthwhile with my life. Both dad and mom felt that way, and I was cut from the same cloth. That was my motivation. Never consciously planned it that way. It all just fell into place.

"It was in my heart and I had a propensity for social activism, for making an effort to help people who needed it. Practicing medicine was the best way I knew to accomplish my goals. And I was pretty good at it right from the start. Does that sound phony to you, Francis, like I'm overly altruistic?"

"No, not phony at all . . . and yes, altruistic in a positive way. It's commendable. You deserve a lot of credit for sticking to your principles and working hard for what you believe in. Now, in my book, that's not phony. It's genuine. And I'm not saying that to inflate your ego." We both paused. Then I enthusiastically burst forth.

"Could I tell you something you might find amusing?" I asked. "Before I made the decision to get into *counseling*, I also had an interest in medicine. Not as deep as yours, of course, but I thought I'd like to study dentistry. It was attractive to me, as funny as that may sound. It was within the field of medicine, but it wasn't nearly as serious, didn't require as much study, and there was only a small chance of dealing with terminal illnesses and saving human lives."

"It's a bit of a stretch for me to picture you as a dentist, Francis."

"Why do say that? Don't I look smart enough?"

"It has nothing to do with intelligence. You just don't seem like the *technical* type. You know what I mean? You seem to be more on the creative bent, like you'd be good at generating emotion, doing imaginative things rather than evaluating X-rays and lab stuff. I cannot picture you cleaning somebody's teeth or filling a cavity. It just doesn't fit your personality . . . or your appearance."

I had a quick reply though it was a stretch to make it fit. "I'm reminded of a line by Henry David Thoreau, 'It's not what you look at that matters, it's what you see.'" I was proud of remembering that under such conditions.

"My, how erudite we are. I'm impressed," Rosa said with a puzzled grin.

I noted that her smile was extraordinarily beautiful, with the bright blue of her eyes sparkling like topaz. She had, indeed, been amused by my interest in dentistry. But it was time to change the subject.

"I want to return to something you said before, Rosa, if you don't mind my blabbering on here." I continued as she nodded positively. "You mentioned that your dad studied to be a priest? Was that a *Catholic* priest?"

"Of course. What other kind is there?"

"Now that's interesting. I've never known anyone whose father studied to be a priest. That's quite rare."

"He was the kind of man who didn't *have* to be a priest to be a good person and to honor his God. His faith was so strong and his trust in God so complete . . . it made him the best father and husband in the world. And it influenced my brother and me into being better human beings and better citizens."

"So you're Catholic, then."

"Yes, we sure are. Laszlo was also born a Catholic and he's stuck to his religion very faithfully, pun intended. I take it that you are, too, Catholic, that is?"

"How'd you deduce that?" I asked.

"Well, the city surrounding us *does* attract a lot of us Catholics, right? And your line of questioning was obviously structured by someone who appreciated Roman Catholicism. More important, you just *look* Catholic. Ever notice how a lot of people telegraph their religion through their physical characteristics?"

"You're kidding, right? Give me an example."

"Okay, I can spot a Lutheran from a mile away, a Methodist, too. Of course, Jewish people are a breeze."

"That doesn't answer my question."

I did frown noticeably at her remarks but decided not to question this forceful woman's veracity or her possession of special gifts of insight. Her presence alone was an ongoing learning experience. I welcomed new thoughts like hers because they represented fresh energy. And Rosa was endowed with an overabundance.

It was raining lightly now and I had to slide her chair in my direction to keep her shoulders from getting wet. We huddled together under the large Tre Scalini umbrella as if we'd both melt from the touch of water. It was great fun; but I was growing wary of this unusual woman who had entered my life with such strong self-assurance. She was quite remarkable and totally different from Sister Mary Rose. I had never met anyone like her, before or after ordination. Approaching with trepidation and caution, I still wanted to learn more; and this could be my last chance.

"So, I assume you have a very close family," I said. "But I imagine it's cumbersome handling so many responsibilities."

"It *is* difficult. But Laszlo, married to me for 18 years, well, he and I have such a great love for one another, such a perfect marriage . . . it makes it a lot easier. We share all the responsibilities. We each want to be with the kids every minute of the day. And with our faith as the primary linkage, we see eye-to-eye on the major issues that normally cause conflict in most marriages. It's trite to say it, but 'we're a team.' It's Laszlo and me and the three little ones."

I was delightfully surprised to hear that. I said to myself, 'This Rosa is at once impressive and authentic.' I said that repeatedly and privately. She asked if I was married and had any children.

I answered, "No, I'm single, a committed bachelor. I'm here with a couple of buddies of mine, just taking in the city for the first time."

She immediately, without pause, said, "Are you gay?"

That hurt my feelings and I let her know it. She recoiled, asked forgiveness, and offered a sincere apology, pressing her hand atop mine from across the table. As she asked again and again for me to forgive her error in judging, I settled back and forgot the incident. I did, however, squeeze in one last remark:

"Nothing subtle about *you*, Rosa, nothing at all."

"I don't like subtlety."

"It can be a virtue if it's handled properly. It's even been said that the sounds of subtlety are soothing. And your comment was anything but soothing."

This banter was getting more uncomfortable the longer I played the game of concealing my priesthood. Gay? I figured I had gone this far and had to continue the charade in spite of the price I was paying. Things were complicated enough and I dare not exacerbate the situation. So I simply sat quietly with Rosa, enjoying every sound and sight of *Piazza Navona*: the rain, the fountains, the merchants and visitors as they scurried to avoid the drizzle. It was quite incredible to be alone with my thoughts and, at the same time, to have Rosa beside me. The rare treat was as sumptuous as the tartufo.

Trying to explain the meaning of it all was difficult. At first, when I saw Rosa approaching my table, I thought she was an unmarried woman on a mission to find an eligible mate. That was before I saw her wedding ring. Then, I realized that my initial assumption demonstrated my naiveté when it came to women. Actually, when I reflected on that, Rosa's perceived flirtation was a convoluted product of an inexperienced virgin-priest.

But even though I had absolutely no intention of going anywhere with our limited friendship, I was flattered that Rosa was sitting beside me. It was an experience totally unfamiliar and completely unique to my life as a priest. Further, I noticed that every person who passed our table, every man and woman near us, made a studied glance at my striking friend. I liked that. I was proud to be associated with someone so attractive. *That* was a most unusual feeling, to be inwardly proud of the person sitting beside me.

But the flip side of that Roman coin was that I realized, though externalities beget initial conversational fodder and visual attention, it is the *internal* qualities of a person that are more profound and permanent. In this case, I was both a victim and a contributor to directional errors in perception.

Moreover, by being judgmental in any and either case, I had become an active participant in the ambiguous courts of human judgment, partaking in the practice of interpretation based on outward appearance. That was a suitable and apropos deduction. (Those thoughts and more would provide stimulating material for a forthcoming homily.)

The rain began to fall harder as we discovered that neither of us had an umbrella. I suggested we make a run for the nearest taxi stop at the outer edges of the piazza. Rosa preferred to stay where we were. She trusted that the rain would soon cease. So that meant *more* interesting conversation, albeit on the wet side. It was an unforgettable way to spend time in the frequent rains of Rome and it certainly wasn't unpleasant.

We continued talking. I asked how long she'd be in Rome and she said only two more days. She explained that tomorrow, she and a group from the Convention would be heading by bus to Assisi. They'd spend the day there and return the same evening. She was looking forward to the trip.

Once again, I was speechless. Because I was already scheduled on the same tour on the same day. Kenny and Bill had decided to revisit the four cathedrals of Rome because they had missed so much on the first go-around. For me, since I was named for Saint Francis, Assisi had been part of my life for as long as I could remember. When Rosa named her tour operator, it didn't surprise me that we were on the same tour, departing Rome at the same time and from the same place.

Coincidence? Serendipity? Destiny? Torture! At this point, I made no educated guess. All I knew was the fact that we would be picked up at our respective hostels around 7:00 am the next day and we were certain that we'd see each other again.

The night fell hard on Rome that early evening. With uncommon bravado, I placed my light jacket over Rosa's head and allowed her to remain relatively dry as we surrendered our chairs and ran for taxis. She thanked me and laughed as we ran together. I studied how attractive she was even with her hair blowing in all directions. I told her she looked nice like that and she thanked me more than once. I said above the noise of the rain, "I come not to be served, but to serve." That caused even more laughter and I hoped that the quote from Jesus wouldn't tip my hand.

We took different vehicles to our lodgings after a comfortable "goodnight." She gave me a short kiss on the right cheek, nothing more than a *friendship* kiss. It was appreciated, most especially by a man who was not accustomed to such favors. I didn't mention meeting Rosa to Bill and Kenny for fear I'd never live it down, plus . . . too much explaining to do. They'd never believe me or understand.

I slept well that night, thinking of and praying for Rosa. She had both hands full, caring for her patients, her three young children and her husband, with priorities assigned in the opposite order.

As I recalled the time we spent together at the *Piazza Navona* and Tre Scalini, I felt no guilt. In fact, I was convinced that God approved of my behavior. I didn't see anything wrong with my enjoying the attention and the company of a beautiful woman, the time being spent with no sinful thoughts, passions or ambitions.

I was reminded of Jesus spending enjoyable times with women who might have been equally as attractive and stimulating as Rosa, saints as well as sinners. Of course, He was God! That humbling admission, though it allowed for His distinct advantage, caused me to admire His control over human instincts even more. With such a consummate and exemplary leader as my paragon, how could I strive for any less?

I did admit that with Rosa, there was *potential*, the first rung on my ladder to temptation and sin. But I knew it would never reach the second, third or fourth rungs: *opportunity, temptation* and *the fall.* I also knew that with such conviction and certainty, I was making myself even more vulnerable to failure and/or futility. So I acknowledged that the situation could still develop into a serious problem. My conclusion? I'll worry about that when and if the time comes.

Plethora of Surprises

Rosa was already on the bus when it came to pick me up. Fortunately, the pick-up point was one block *away* from the Convent of the Sisters of St. Dorothy. The luck in my deception continued to favor me. Truly, this was the first time in my life that I deceived anyone for such a long time and so intentionally. It would be the last.

As I boarded the bus which sat about 50 passengers, Rosa jumped from her seat near the front, took my hand in hers, and loudly announced, "Here, Francis. I saved you a seat. Come sit with me!"

Predictably, my new-found friend was in control. She left me no options. I sat in the fourth row as I was ordered and she sat by the window beside me. It was a new experience to be forcibly led like that in public, by a woman, no less. But I figured it did me no harm and taking orders like that was good for my humility.

I expected a peaceful 2½ hour drive with the possibility of sneaking in a short nap. I should have known better. I was riding beside a very talkative and energetic person. A tour-guide spoke frequently about the history, geography, and demographics of the area but neither Rosa nor I paid much attention. Instead, we discussed everything from raising children to problems in our Church. I was reticent to be too knowledgeable in matters of religion.

I had no idea at the time, but this innocent spiritual journey into the heart of the Franciscan landscape was to reveal a lot more than my identity as a priest. There would be revelations beyond my wildest thoughts. They began with a series of events that were as exceptional as they were distressing.

We were only ten miles from the highway turn-off that led to Assisi when we heard a woman in the front row cry loudly for help. She appeared to be in her 50's and was traveling with an older lady that appeared to be in her 80's, at the very least. The older woman had slumped to the floor of the bus and lay motionless near the driver. Everyone gasped at once, half of the passengers jumping to their feet for better visibility of the unfolding scene.

The woman cried out again and again. "Someone help me, please. My mother's had a heart attack! Please . . . is there a doctor here? Would somebody please help my mother?"

Rosa reacted instantly, climbing over my legs to kneel beside the fallen woman. She placed her left ear to the lady's heart and held her wrist between her fingers to get a quick read of her pulse. Within sixty seconds, Rosa shook her head in negative fashion. She spoke to the daughter, quietly explaining that her mother had a weak pulse, difficulty breathing, and a very irregular heartbeat. She consoled her as the woman sobbed.

By this time, the driver had pulled onto the shoulder of the road, stopped the bus, and monitored the scene on the floor beside him. The woman said that her mother's event was not the first, that she had suffered three heart attacks before, and that it was one of her final wishes to visit Assisi before she died.

The driver advised that he could get to Assisi in fifteen minutes and take the fallen woman to the Emergency Room of a nearby hospital. He reasoned that there might still be a chance to save the afflicted woman. Rosa continued to shake her head negatively. She said, "I don't think it'll help."

Then, the daughter surprised everyone on board, especially *me*. She asked if there was a Catholic priest on board. She wanted her mother, a devout Catholic, to receive the last rites of her faith. Several heads on the bus turned and silently scanned the passengers. It was a moment of decision and I couldn't hesitate. I raised my hand and said, "I'm a priest."

There was immediate murmuring on board as the peering crowd opened a path for me. Rosa arose from the floor and turned to face me. She stared with her mouth open. Her eyes didn't blink once as she moved aside and dropped back into her seat.

I generally carry a small flask of holy oil in case of such emergencies and was prepared to minister the *Sacrament of the Sick*. As I knelt beside the woman, her daughter explained that her mother had already been anointed twice when physicians determined she was near death. I was now ready to perform the ritual again.

I asked those around me to pray the Our Father with me. I started the Prayer as others followed, "Our Father Who art in heaven, hallowed be Thy name. Thy kingdom come, Thy will be done on earth as it is in heaven." At that point, the afflicted woman's eyes opened and she joined us in prayer. "Give us this day, our daily bread and forgive us our trespasses as we forgive those who trespass against us." She completed the Lord's Prayer accompanied by a chorus of shocked passengers.

The busload of people almost stopped breathing. Each stunned person sat or stood motionless. Mouths opened, jaws dropped, eyes bugged out. Everyone, in a solemn whisper, completed the Prayer. Emotions ranged from skepticism to tears. The daughter embraced her mother on the floor, helping her slowly back to her seat. The driver again offered to drive to the hospital but the daughter refused, saying, "What more do we need? We've just witnessed a miracle on the doorstep of Saint Francis."

I heard unidentified voices saying, "Thank you, Father. Thank you." I said, "It wasn't *me*. There's Someone far greater at work here."

Everyone was amazed and the daughter was beside herself. It was a very special moment for me as a priest. It was special, too, for my traveling companion, Rosa Marie Marsinski. As I returned to my seat beside her, I reached over and touched her hand, saying not a word. She pulled her hand back until we reached the village of Assisi. She hadn't spoken in a long while.

"Why didn't you tell me?" she asked.

"The way our conversation went in the piazza, it seemed unimportant. I didn't want to trivialize our friendship by going through a wordy explanation. Everything else was so lyrical. This would have broken the mood. And, like I said, it was unimportant."

"But all that talk about being a *counselor?*"

"It was no lie, Rosa. That's basically what I am."

"I've lost all words. I don't know what to say. A large part of me is angry with you for leading me on like that. Another part is . . . I can't explain it . . . I've gained a different kind of respect for you . . . as a priest, but . . ."

"Why should it matter? You knew me as a man, as a person, as a human being. What difference does my profession make?"

"I have to let this digest for awhile before I can talk about it. Why don't you go your way through the tour and I'll go mine. We can catch up later on."

I couldn't blame such a sensitive woman for being angry and disillusioned. Her feelings toward me were my punishment for my sin. At least the deception was over and I could relax. I asked God for the same forgiveness I would ask of Rosa.

I toured Assisi with a small organized group and a guide who narrated interesting facts about Francis himself and about the various buildings we visited. My favorite place was the crypt in the area where the uncorrupted body of Francis was laid to rest. Throughout our walk, I developed a very special fondness for my namesake, especially his dedication to serving the poor. His humility was another virtue I admired and promised to emulate as I spread the value of his teachings to my congregation. I also purchased several small icons with the picture of the saint and a dozen prayer cards with his "Prayer to Saint Francis."

It was a memorable time spent in an unforgettable place. To say the visit was touched by the eventful bus ride would be an understatement. The woman who suffered the heart attack was helped through the tour in a wheelchair. She refused to stay behind. I remained near her and provided visible peace-of-mind. She and her daughter were deeply appreciative. Though I watched for Rosa, I didn't see her anywhere in the crypt, the Basilica, or on the outdoor grounds. Her absence worried me. It was unexplainable and unexpected.

After touring, our group from the bus was led to a nearby restaurant for an Italian luncheon replete with fresh bread and wine and a unique recipe of pasta with eggplant. Again, I searched for Rosa but could not find her with the group. That also worried me.

But I had "bigger fish to fry" as the saying goes. Rosa was a grown woman and could take care of herself. If she was so deeply offended by my subterfuge that she must avoid me, then so be it. I refused to allow her to ruin my extraordinary visit to Assisi, a trip that I had waited for all my life.

When we loaded back onto the bus for the return trip, I finally found the elusive and reclusive Rosa. She chose to sit beside me once again but said no more than, "Hi." I responded with the same word. It was a very quiet trip back to Rome.

I managed to fall asleep for over an hour, relieving the awkwardness of the situation. I awoke to find Rosa asleep. Beyond that, we endured only fifteen minutes of awareness together. Then, as we approached the Rome Cavalieri Hotel to deliver Rosa and her group who were staying there, the serenity came to a shocking halt.

We slowly drove up the driveway to the Hotel and I saw a commotion near the entrance. What followed was the most dramatic surprise of the day, far outdistancing all the others.

A group of six *carabinieri* (local police) stood outside of two vehicles marked "Polizio Municipale." Two of the uniformed men boarded our bus and approached three female passengers. One of them was Rosa Marie Marsinski. Handcuffs were placed around the women's wrists behind their back. I wasn't the only one who stared with mouth open wide, though Rosa herself smiled demurely and seemed unsurprised.

The three women were hurried into a waiting van that quickly drove them away. Rosa glanced over her shoulder, pursed her lips and threw me a kiss. It was an undignified gesture that I responded to, mostly out of astonishment, with a slight wave of my hand. I asked one of the *carabiniere* who had remained behind, what was going on. He motioned that he understood no English; but one of his colleagues shouted crudely, "Read about it in the papers."

I stood frozen in the Hotel driveway reflecting on what I had just seen. Rosa arrested? On what charges? Was she a criminal? What crime did she commit? Was it murder, theft, assault? Was this the same Rosa that I met in the *Piazza Navona?*

Rather than riding the bus back to my stop at the Convent, I opted to take a taxi from Rosa's Hotel. I needed time alone, time without conversation. But when I met my buddies at a preordained restaurant, I absolutely had to tell them about Rosa, yesterday afternoon at Tre Scalini and all the events crammed into this day at Assisi. The three of us downed a couple of *Peroni*'s throughout my telling of the lengthy tale. As the men ate and listened, I talked and watched. I couldn't eat so much as a bite of food. Of course, Kenny and Bill accused me of exercising my vivid imagination and concocting a very bizarre story which they found hard to believe. I acknowledged that I did, too.

I slept restlessly and awoke at 5:30, eager to get my hands on a local morning newspaper. At the Convent, there was only one paper delivered to the eating area each day . . . and it was published in Italian only.

After inquiring, I learned that there was a newsstand nearby that handled English-language newspapers. I walked nearly three blocks to find the place, hidden in a small alley behind shops and stores. After that extensive effort, I found readable news in only one paper, *The International Herald Tribune.* The only problem: it ran daily but was published in Paris and then distributed throughout Italy. So the only news I'd get out of that source would be *older* than yesterday's.

At that point, I was about to give up. But questioning why Rosa was arrested and what was to become of her, plus wondering if I could be of any help, was driving me nuts. In desperation, I asked the proprietor of the newsstand for the most up-to-date daily paper he had. He understood English quite well and handed me a copy of something called *Corriere della Sera* saying it was the oldest and most reliable paper in Rome and had been published since 1876 . . . in Italian only.

Since there were no other customers in sight at that early hour, I asked if he'd be kind enough to read me one news story. I had only to open the first page to see a spread of "mug shots" of six women, one of them being Rosa. It was not a very long story and the man said he'd oblige. I stood beside him, studying Rosa's likeness as he read out loud:

"Six American women were rounded up by police yesterday and held without bail for being members of a criminal group known as 'The Lifters.' They refused to speak to authorities until they had obtained legal counsel.

"The women were trained in special skills for stealing the valuables of tourists and businessmen. Essentially, they were professionally-trained pickpockets."

The proprietor paused to catch his breath and shift the paper in his hands. "These all look like beautiful women," he said in a thick Italian accent. "Very pretty girls. You know someone here?" I simply replied that I had an interest in the story and asked that he please read on. He continued.

"The six women were suspected of being members of an international ring of thieves who submitted their stolen monies to an unknown leader with Mafia ties. Authorities were informed of the group's activities in the Rome shopping districts and, once identified, each was picked up for questioning. Police expected to make considerable progress in breaking the ring through information provided by the six."

Though I was happy to learn that Rosa wasn't involved in *major* crimes, I was shocked to hear her name associated with *any* crime at all, especially as it related to an "international ring of thieves." The proprietor read the last paragraph of the article:

"Initial reports from those questioning the six women claimed that they knew each other well and all had professional careers in the United States. They admitted that stealing was a lark that offered risk and fun!"

I found it difficult to believe *any* of that; but I thanked my personal translator and returned to the Convent for breakfast. It was 8:00 a.m.

I shared what I had learned about Rosa with Kenny and Bill, and though still skeptical about the veracity of my story, they sympathized with my plight and the destiny of the women. They worried because, in general, American women condemned by the Italian system of courts did not fare well, in most cases being jailed for lengthy periods of time.

I decided to remove myself from that kind of worry and spend my last three days in Rome taking in the major historical sights I had not yet visited. I did that, but I also succumbed to worrying about Rosa and wondering if I'd ever see her again. With minimal effort, she would remain in my prayers but it would be hard work to forget her.

Taking Action

Two days before we were scheduled to depart Rome, I surrendered my pride and made a difficult phone call, on the urging of my two buddies. They knew I was in a high state of anxiety since no new news had emerged about "The Lifters." I phoned the Cavalieri Hotel and asked for the room of Rosa Marsinski. To my surprise, Rosa answered on the second ring.

There were several moments in which there was not a word spoken. I was so surprised to hear her voice that I couldn't speak. That instantly turned to intimidation as I fumbled for words, *any* words, just to say *something.* I thought I sounded pretty ignorant as I kept repeating, "Rosa? Rosa? Is that you?"

I was happy to hear her voice but angered by her deception and dumbfounded by her arrest. I could only speculate on the circumstances that led to such movie-like drama. I had grossly underestimated the outrageous story behind it.

Rosa first asked when I was returning home. When I told her the day after tomorrow, she suggested that we meet at Tre Scalini the next day around 1:00 p.m. She wanted to explain and encouraged me to refrain from judging her. With hesitation and doubt, but with even more curiosity, I said I'd be there at that time and place. I said I'd be wearing my *blacks* because we had to meet several other priest-friends for dinner to prepare for our general audience with the Pope on the next morning.

I arrived early and was able to secure the same table at which we sat previously. Rosa also arrived early and I watched her walk toward me from across the piazza, just as she had done before. This stranger who had walked so quietly into my life appeared no less beautiful. I remained a male human being as I continued to appreciate her femininity. I would pray to St. Paul for purity of heart. Needless to say, this was to be one of the most intriguing, most fascinating "counseling" sessions of my life, as a priest or otherwise.

When she arrived, Rosa gave me a short hug and an equally short kiss. She commented that she liked me in my *blacks.* She said I looked "cute." I smiled boyishly and probably blushed like one. I was happy that she had forgotten *my* deception in hiding my priesthood.

With her approval, I ordered *Caffe Noisette* for the two of us and we sipped slowly. I listened intensely, first asking if this was to be a long story. When she replied "yes," I told her to shorten it since I was on limited time. I was happy to see her but rather than show it, I acted like I was a bit irritated.

The story she told was so preposterous that I believed every word of it. No one could have invented such a complex plot without the brain of Einstein and the talent of Shakespeare. It was stranger than fiction.

Rosa and her five friends met at Columbia University College of Physicians and Surgeons when they studied for their medical degrees. After graduation and separation, they remained in touch, having stayed close friends for many years. As part of a tradition, they gathered once a year on a rotating basis, at one of the women's home towns in the Midwest.

After five years, one of the women proposed an idea. It was so bizarre and exciting that it was instantly accepted by all six. As Rosa told the story, she explained that the women had grown bored with their lives as doctors, wives and mothers and were searching for something to revitalize their spirits. They were type-A personalities and had become sedentary. They wanted a *rush*, an emotional thrill, a risk-taking adventure.

The woman's proposal provided all that and more. It was fraught with risk and danger . . . to their lives, careers, and families. That was its attraction, risk and danger. It was "just what the doctor ordered," they said. And the *modus operandi* was incomprehensible.

Seems that the woman with the birth of the idea had an uncle with a reputed connection to the Mafia. He was Sicilian, maintained a residence in Palermo but ran a clandestine criminal operation from a home in New Jersey. *Uncle Vincenzo* had created an international consortium of thieves but, not uncommonly, remained faithful to his Catholic Church. The motivation for his daring shenanigans was a commitment to support a Sicilian orphanage in need of financial aid to sustain its ninety children. That justified, at least in *his* conscience, a quest for adventure and the resulting booty. But at the same time, it sounded like a huge lie, a contrived *shelter* to camouflage his crimes.

The principal takeaway? Cash. The method? Picking pockets. The model? Robin Hood—"*Take from the rich and give to the poor.*" The women had all the qualities that conformed to Vincenzo's recruiting profile. They were smart, attractive and in need of excitement.

At the beginning, no one questioned the "orphanage" part of the story, though they discussed the fact that it had a ring of altruism not generally associated with his particular ethnic connections. They did, nevertheless, accept the word of *Uncle Vincenzo* and were content to perform their acts of thievery for his cause, hoping he was being truthful.

The first move for the women was to be trained in the art of stealing from a mobile public, things like purses, wallets, watches, even parcels carried by unsuspecting tourists at different sites in Western Europe. The training was conducted at a farmhouse in a rural area outside of Morristown, New Jersey. The trainer was a handsome, young Italian whose name was never given. He was a master of his art and an excellent teacher.

The women learned quickly, enjoyed tons of laughs, and were sent on their initial assignment, to London.

They focused on the high-end shopping areas. Following a successful start there, they visited Paris the next year, then Madrid, Zurich, Amsterdam, and now, Rome. Their families accepted the once-a-year, ten-day disappearing act with no questions. Husbands and children assumed their wives and mothers went off to have an innocent good time together. That was okay with those who remained behind as long as the doctors were faithful to their families and their practices.

During her story of "The Lifters," Rosa reminded me more than once that I was getting the *abbreviated* version. But I was so fascinated by the details that I actually wished I had more time to hear the *long* version. I asked only one or two questions as she narrated.

At each foreign scene of their crimes, the women worked for a full week, then spent two days relaxing on their own. All of their travel expenses were reimbursed by Vincenzo. At the completion of their assignments, they submitted the results to an anonymous stranger at their hotel, generally, a different teenage boy at each location. They took nothing for themselves, per the agreement with the mysterious *Uncle Vincenzo*. They counted their money, combined it and delivered it. When assembled, it usually exceeded twenty- to thirty-thousand dollars per visit to each country, most of that converted to local currency.

Naturally, the women had no way of verifying that the money actually went to a Sicilian orphanage . . . and they really didn't care. They each got their *rush*, had a rollicking good time, and always took their tasks seriously. That's what saved them time and time again. They were as cautious as they were cunning, deftly staying one step ahead of local law enforcement.

When the Rome authorities arrested Rosa, she had already turned her stolen cash over to the designated partner who readied it for *the drop*. The carabinieri had a search warrant for the women's rooms but were too late to obtain any evidence that connected the doctors to the ring of thieves.

They had been instructed to deposit any "leftovers" in designated places where it was collected by a member of the ring. Everything . . . handbags, wallets, money carriers of all kinds, everything was completely destroyed. Stolen property vanished without a trace, thus making material evidence non-existent. Cash was the name of the game and the only item retained.

At the end of a brief police investigation into the recent arrests, each woman was released and allowed to leave the country. As individuals, they would, however, remain under suspicion. Taking that to heart, they never visited a country more than once. So far, the operation was foolproof.

Rosa said there were confidential parts of the story she was "not at liberty to discuss." I accepted that and absolved her from playing me for the fool during the times we spent together. I also accepted a justified scolding for concealing the fact that I was a priest. Our relationship ended in a dead heat regarding who committed the worst (or the best) act of deception.

At the conclusion of her story, I was compelled to ask Rosa a key question: "When you approached me at Tre Scalini, was I to be a victim of your ruse?" She paused and smiled before saying, "At the beginning, yes. But then I studied you more closely and decided you were just too nice . . . and too poor.

"When I saw you sitting alone, I read you as a good mark," she said. "But when you stood up, I saw your dirty tennis shoes, faded jeans, the absence of a Rolex and no "designer" clothes, I realized I had misjudged. But I enjoyed our conversations so thoroughly that I never felt it was a waste of my time. I learned a lot from you, Father."

"Like what?" I asked.

"Like how to enjoy tartufo. Like how refreshing it was to discover an innocent and simple man. Like how I enjoyed answering your questions about my family and my past. Like how I appreciated your unique personality. Is that enough?"

"You found me *simple?*"

"Not in the sense of simple-minded, no. But in your humility and your unadorned eloquence. That was refreshing. And your behavior on the bus? You were so, well, heroic and stable and in control. And when you administered the sacrament to the woman . . . you were totally comfortable in your own skin, as a priest. I'll never forget that. And I'll never forget *you*, Father.

"But there's one thing I have to say, because I care about you. It's just a personal observation."

"What in the world is it?" I asked. "Such a serious and oblique statement. What is it?" I waited, moved by equal parts of curiosity and anxiety.

"I want to tell you something about yourself that I'll bet you've never heard before, Father Francis. Don't try so hard to be liked. Sometimes, you try too hard and it's obvious. Be more honest. Say what you believe inside of you, not what you think you're *supposed* to say."

I told Rosa that I didn't completely understand and asked if she could be more specific. She didn't hesitate one second.

"It's like . . . about my arrest, about my wanting to steal from you. Here I am involved in criminal activities, with you as a mark, and all you do is ask questions about how it's all done. You should've nailed me, chastised me, chewed me out, up and down, and then spit me out as trash. That's what I deserved.

"Through all of our conversations, Father, all the topics we covered, you justified everything you said. I'm telling you as straight as I know how to say it . . . don't apologize for breathing! Don't make excuses for your naiveté. It's okay. It's *you!* Say what you mean and accept the consequences. If somebody doesn't like you, so be it. Let them go. Chances are that if they don't like you, then you don't like them either. It's about compatibility and honesty, Father."

"Wow! Speaking of a chewing out."

"Everything I've said is true. Do you agree with me?"

I gathered my thoughts and expressed them in words. "Don't you think that in *my* profession, it's *important* to be liked, that it's something I've got to be aware of?"

"Of course. It's the same as in *my* profession. If I wasn't liked, even *loved*, I'd lose my patients. My practice would go belly-up, evaporate."

"I understand that. And the same is true for me. As a priest, I'd be useless without being liked. I'd have no congregation."

"You know, we could go on like this all day. If you don't get it and don't agree with me, you're hopeless. I'm just telling you that you should dig deep and *be yourself*. Be less intimidated and more up-front. Don't be scared to death of people, especially *women*."

I knew there was truth in what Rosa said. Yet I had never before recognized my *multiple* weaknesses. I should've been less lenient and more firm about her arrest and her actions with "The Lifters." It was wrong. The end didn't justify the means. As a priest, I surely knew that and I should have reacted differently.

Clearly, it was humiliating to listen to such a personal critique, especially from a woman. I knew that was terribly chauvinistic, but it's the way I felt. The part that hit me the hardest was the line about "Don't apologize for breathing." I wondered why Kenny and Bill had never noticed that about me. I promised not to obsess about it but to address it. I decided that, following Rosa's directive, I'd be a *work in progress* as I groomed and honed the shortcomings within my personality. It was an extraordinary prescription received from a competent and friendly physician.

After a lengthy and silent pause, I said, "Rosa, I'm grateful for all this, for everything you've said. I'll think about it. But I've got to run now. I can't afford to be late."

I paused again and stared at her quiet eyes. Then I said, "Do you know, I'm curious about something. What have you been thinking while I've just silently sat here?"

Rosa laughed and wiped her lips with a napkin. She surprised me once again with a reply I never expected.

"Have you ever studied the clouds here in Italy?"

"No. I don't believe I have."

"Well, look up there, toward the west. Do you see that huge, vertical cloud, the one that's leaning to the right?"

I acknowledged that I recognized the cloud she had pointed to. "Yes," I said. "And what about it?"

"Well, I've seen clouds like that before, clouds that had a shape near the top that looked like the huge face of an older man. Do you see his beard there on the right, and his chin and forehead?"

"Yes . . . and . . . ?"

"And?" she replied facetiously. "Do you see the face of an old man?" I nodded "yes" and wondered where she was going with her questions.

"Well," she said, "to me, that looks like the face of God, like the face that classic artists rendered, like the faces of God the Father painted by Michelangelo."

All I could say, as I studied the cloud which was now rapidly dissipating, was . . . "Hmm. That's interesting, Rosa. So is there a point to this?"

"Of course, there is," she answered. "You being a priest and all, maybe you should think about this before you answer. If the Bible tells us that we're made in the 'image and likeness of God,' what if, just what if God looks like *that*? Wouldn't it be a shock . . . if and when we see Him face-to-face, that God has all the characteristics of a human being? We were taught to believe that, weren't we . . . 'made in the image and likeness of God?' When all is said and done, maybe He looks like *us*."

I answered simply. "My friend, you certainly have an active imagination. I never figured that God the Creator resembled a human being. He's always been far removed from anything I could, you know, no human has ever described 'God the Father' that they've actually *seen*. He's always been the product of imagination and we just figure that He's entitled to that secrecy about His appearance. I don't believe that Michelangelo claimed that he *saw* God the Father."

"Another thing," Rosa said. "Think about this, too. If God created us in his image and likeness and He's our *Father*, then we have the same DNA as Him. It was inherited from Him, right? That's a way we can always feel close to Him, by feeling a kinship to Him.

"Like I said, think about it. I do have a point, you've got to admit. Maybe we're all in for the surprise of our lives if we see God in a human body. Maybe clouds are a way He uses to reveal Himself to us."

I slumped back in my chair, studying an amazingly beautiful face that resembled no cloud in the sky, but instead, a lovely flower, as delicate as the name she carried. Her creative mind was always on overdrive, pondering heavy thoughts I had never considered. The one about DNA was a particularly intriguing *spin*. I'd use that in a homily some day.

"I really don't know how to end this, Rosa."

"Maybe you don't have to, Father," she said quietly.

"Well, I'll make a standing offer that if you ever need a friend, a priest, that is, I'll always be available. I'm at Saint William Parish in the city."

"Goodbye, Father Francis," she said. "Thanks for listening to my ramblings and for being exactly who you are. You've touched me deeply, in so many ways. You've changed *me* more than *I've* changed *you*, only you've done it by quiet example rather than by noisy words. I'll never forget our times together. I've enjoyed your company immensely. And I do hope I've not offended you by being so nit-picky about your personal shortcomings. I wish mine were as easy to correct."

Rosa stood, pushed her chair under the table and put both of her arms around my neck, kissing my cheek firmly. As she walked away, she generously threw me another kiss from over her shoulder. Her last words were, "Until we meet again, *Father Francis*." I felt an emptiness deep inside. I was emotionally raw.

Another beautiful Rose walked out of my life, this one disappearing across the *Piazza Navona* in Rome, Italy, in the rain. As I ran alone to the place for transportation, I was soaked by a sudden downpour. It made me cold and very wet. When I later climbed into a taxi, I noticed a long-stem red rose drop onto the pavement from my jacket pocket. Apparently, Rosa had taken it from its vase on the table and surreptitiously left it as a memory. The gesture tempted a tear to fall from my eye. It welled there until I wiped it away. That was the second time that a *Rose* added to the difficulties in my life.

Frank's Awakening

Annie woke Frank after deciding that he had rested long enough after six-plus hours of sound sleep. She feared that, since he had slept so long, his senses might be mushy and his extremities the same. There was reason to alert him. She repeated the crew's announcement that breakfast would be served and the plane was only one hour from landing in Rome.

Frank lay covered with blankets while he occupied two seats during his long sleep. Annie had to physically shake his shoulders to get a response and be assured that he had survived. She recoiled, however, when she removed the blankets and saw the condition of Frank's body.

"My God, Frank," she said, just below the level of a shout. "You're soaking wet. Look at your hair. It's pasted flat like you've been in a rainstorm. And your shoulders and shirt . . . they're all soaking wet."

In her surprise, she retained enough lucidity to start helping her husband remove his wet clothing, beginning with his shirt. She handed him a towel to dry his head and hair. Then, she wiped the wetness from his bare chest, removed his shirt, and asked Margaret to get a clean one from his carry-on bag.

As Margaret reached for the bag, she couldn't miss seeing a single, long-stem red rose leaning against it on the floor. She held the flower for a few seconds, figuring a flight attendant or passenger had dropped it, then gingerly pressed it dry and placed it inside a book she was carrying.

Frank was shaking from being wet and cold and could not explain why he was in such a condition. Annie figured that he became feverish from the length of his sleep. He had no other answer. But they were all puzzled by the absence of any odor of sweat. They discussed that without resolution during the taxi ride to the hotel shortly after landing. They also discussed the rose that Annie and Frank saw Margaret pick up from the floor and place in her book. It seemed inconsequential.

The first order of business after checking into the Rome Cavalieri Hotel was for the three visitors to take a quick tour of the public areas. Annie and Frank had stayed there 25 years earlier before it became a Waldorf Astoria Hotel and prior to a major renovation. They were now eager to see the changes.

A member of the concierge staff led the way with Margaret and her parents following. Margaret insisted that her father sit in a wheel chair for the tour and Frank didn't object. His legs had become weak and shaky from lack of exercise. The others walked slowly but closely behind him. The brief tour covered the grounds and interior of the Hotel with many pauses to admire dozens of priceless pieces of art and antique treasures.

"From high on a hill overlooking Rome, the panorama has inspired visitors for centuries. Though only minutes from the city's great monuments, the Rome Cavalieri has the tranquility of an oasis. The Hotel is recognized as an extravagant home where guests relax in comfort and luxury.

"The first hotel in Europe to be part of the exclusive Waldorf Astoria Hotels & Resorts, the Rome Cavalieri Hotel is more than just a 5-star property. It is the pre-eminent luxury hotel in Rome, with an art collection that outshines many museums, a Grand Spa that would be the envy of a prestige health resort, and standards of luxury that set it apart from other Rome hotels." (The Hotel brochure did not exaggerate.)

The family spent the first two days near the Hotel adjusting to the new time zone and exerting themselves minimally. Frank did well and was getting around nicely without the wheelchair. On the second evening, following a wonderful dinner at a nearby *Tratorria*, Frank asked Margaret if she'd join him at the hotel's main lobby bar, the *Tiepolo Lounge and Terrace*, for a nightcap. Margaret agreed and, knowing her father as she did, suspected he had something serious on his mind. So did Annie who left them alone. They were both correct.

The setting Frank had chosen to tell his daughter about Brother Pietro and the consequential new prayer of Saint Francis was an apropos environment to explain something so dramatic. *The Tiepolo Lounge* was the focal point of the Rome Cavalieri. With terraces extending outside, cushioned wicker chairs and sofas overlooking the pool and the gardens, it was *the* place where guests mingled, *the* place to see and be seen.

Located beneath the soaring lobby ceiling, the ambience was enhanced by the spectacular Tiepolo *triptych* on one side and exquisitely crafted antique tapestries on the other. It was also a quiet place where *Frangelico*, straight-up and served in a classic brandy snifter, suited the two conversationalists. They sipped slowly and, conjoined by meaningful chatter, savored both the drink and the setting.

Classic music from a live pianist featured the melodies of Verdi excerpted from his most familiar operas. The music was played softly but with fervor, at just the right level. And the scent of fresh flowers on each table added another dimension of taste to the smooth drinks. Margaret and her father enjoyed a maximum level of relaxation together, something they had both missed over the past several years.

Against the perfect background, Frank took his time relating the story of his special prayer, omitting no detail. He explained the role of Father Tonelli in delivering The Prayer to him in the hospital. Margaret had been a good friend of Father's for five decades so his revelations about The Prayer and its origin were totally credible. Margaret took great pleasure at times like this when she and her father were alone in the world. She knew that such times were limited and she thus appreciated them even more.

Throughout the telling of the lengthy story, Frank and Margaret shared the rotating emotions of gladness, joy and sorrow. Margaret's Roman Catholic faith had remained as strong as her father's and her special devotion to her father's namesake was rich with sentiment and loyalty. She, too, was a great fan of Saint Francis and looked forward to visiting his renowned Basilica in Assisi. The trip was scheduled for the next day, none too soon for the two impatient visitors and Annie. Margaret had arranged for a driver to take them to Assisi rather than traveling in a group by motorcoach.

But first things first. The night was young and there was much conversation to be had by the duo of father and daughter. After ordering a second *Frangelico*, Frank decided to tell Margaret the story of The Prayer, especially about his personal intention to God as part of its purpose.

"Now, I'm going to tell you something so deeply personal," he began, "that even your mother doesn't know about it yet. You'll understand in a minute why I've been reluctant to tell her. She's so vulnerable to heartache these days, what with my being sick and all . . . it's too big a risk to take."

Margaret sat back and focused on the words of her father. "I'm honored, pop. I won't miss a word," she promised.

"I'll try to make this as short as possible because I could go on until we both fall asleep. So here's a shortened version."

"No need to shorten it, pop. We've got all night."

"Okay . . . well, you remember that I studied to be a priest at the minor seminary when I was a young teenager. And I decided that priesthood wasn't for me. I just liked women too much to commit to celibacy. Oh, there were other factors, too, like my unworthiness to celebrate Mass and minister the sacraments, but liking women as much as I did was the tallest mountain to climb on the path to priesthood. Ironically, as much as I liked ladies, I was always scared to death around them. Figure that out. Anyway, I deleted priesthood from my list of ambitious undertakings.

"So I chose a conventional life, married your mom and, well, you were around for the rest of the story. But in-between all the happenings over these past 60-plus years, I've had this curiosity about what it would have been like to be a priest. I told Father Tonelli about all these thoughts and explained to him, as I'll tell you now, that I never, ever had any *regrets* about choosing your mom over priesthood. It's just been a curiosity of mine . . . how would I have been, what would it have been like to be a priest? You understand that?"

"Of course, I do. I wonder about the same things. You remember that I talked to you many times when I was just a kid about becoming a nun. And I chose the secular life like you did. But I, too, wonder if I made the right choice."

"See . . . you're looking at it the wrong way, my dear. It wasn't that I *questioned* my decision or *doubted* that I made the correct choice, it was that I'm probably too introspective, just too darn curious. I'm greedy, you could say. I want to experience both sides of life, priesthood *and* marriage. I couldn't do that. I couldn't have both."

"Yeah, I know what you're saying. But my thoughts are a little different, closer to *regrets* than curiosity," Margaret said. "Get back to your story, pop, because I'd like to know where you're going with this and I'm curious about the ending."

"I don't have one. At least, not yet."

The two continued to sip from their drinks, enjoying the game of rolling the *Frangelico* around the inside of the snifter before each taste. They also enjoyed an occasional glance at passers-by in the lobby, interesting-looking people who gazed at the ceiling art and the sculpted figures on pedestals. In no way, however, did those isolated incidents become *distractions*. Margaret was riveted to her father's story.

"So, you understand . . . The Prayer that dropped from the ceiling of the Basilica was believed to be written by Saint Francis himself. And it's said to have been dictated to two of his closest friends while he lay on his deathbed.

"What impressed me almost as much as the beauty of The Prayer was the tedious effort the friars made while translating the document. Apparently, it was originally written in the Umbrian dialect of Italian and that gave the translators fits. It was a very difficult language to deal with."

"So they were all pretty convinced that this prayer did come from Saint Francis?" Margaret asked.

"They had a lot of evidence to support that. But then they submitted that evidence to the Vatican in 2007 and it's allegedly now being reviewed by linguistic experts and Church authorities who want to verify its authenticity."

"Sounds complicated. Don't you think it's going to take eons before they arrive at a decision?"

"Probably. The Church does move slowly when it comes to miracles or attribution of a prayer's influence on God's will. But I'll tell you something, Margaret. I've been saying that prayer three times a day now for over six months and some very strange things have been happening, inexplicable things that'll knock your socks off like they have mine."

"I'm ready, pop, whenever you are. Can I stay seated while I hear this, or should I stand and walk around?" Frank grinned at his daughter's facetiousness, then went on.

"I tried to explain to Father Tonelli what's been going on lately but I didn't do such a great job. It's hard to describe some of my experiences, to put them into words. I guess it was probably *my* fault for being a bad story-teller."

"Why don't you try me, pop? You've got a captive audience here, right now. Hey, I'm your oldest child, so I should be able to understand you, perhaps even *better* than Father Tonelli."

"Perhaps. We'll give it a try and see. First of all, this is all related to the *intention* I submitted while saying The Prayer, the *favor* I asked of God. As the story goes, this composition by Saint Francis was called, *A Prayer for the Dying*. So at the time Father gave it to me, it was quite certain that I was, indeed, dying. And only a dozen or so privileged people have used it to have a request granted. There's one stipulation: you can't ask to have your life saved. It has to involve something else. I'll tell you about my intention in a minute.

"Now, when I was in the coma," he continued, intensely focused and carefully selecting each word, "at that time, I experienced a lot of unusual mental and emotional stresses. It was like I was living as Frank Chase, but then again, I *wasn't* that person. The scenario was different, different *places* that I don't recall ever visiting in this life, different *people* that I've never met. But at the end, I hadn't really been anywhere because I was laying in my hospital bed in a coma. Where did these strangers come from? And what was I doing in those extraordinary places? I've asked myself those questions dozens and dozens of times."

"Do you want me to try to answer them, pop?"

"Not unless you think you have a credible answer."

"Well, you said that Father couldn't explain . . . well, what did *he* think was happening?"

"He was mesmerized by my story but completely baffled in trying to offer a theory as to the origin of my new experiences. He thought maybe it was like visions people describe when they've been near death . . . the 'white light' and stuff like that. But I told him it wasn't like that. My thoughts were of current, living sensations that were real. Father's longshot guess was that it was a *preternatural occurrence* as he called it."

"So he didn't speculate beyond that? He didn't give you anything more specific?"

"Nothing even close to what I had undergone. He hadn't ever heard of anything like what I was describing. So, something even he doesn't know about yet . . . on the plane flying over here, you witnessed first-hand that I fell asleep. I mean, it was a really *deep* sleep. And I swear, I had the same kind of 'visit' experience like when I was in the coma: people I hadn't met, places I hadn't been, they were right there, in my face, in current times. And the people and places, even though they were new, were still familiar to me. Contradictions ran amok.

"It wasn't like dreaming because I was actually somewhere else at the same time I was flying on the plane, when I was sitting right beside you and sleeping. It was like living two lives at the same time, absolutely inexplicable."

"It sounds like an 'out-of-body' experience to me, pop, some strange, extrasensory, paranormal activity within your mind. Don't laugh at me when I say this, but there are people, really intelligent people of sound mind and body, who describe such experiences and attribute them to . . . alien captures! You don't think . . ."

"Margaret, my dear, no offense. But I can't really believe my dream-like adventures can be attributed to aliens. No, I won't laugh at you, but c'mon . . . this is *me* you're talking to. You know I don't buy into that stuff about aliens."

"Okay. I'm just thinking 'outside the nine dots,' trying to come up with some attribution you've overlooked before. I've got to sleep on this one, pop, to see if I can imagine a reasonable cause for your dreams, uh, I mean *experiences*."

"You've got to rid yourself of any explanation that points to dreams, conventional dreams," Frank said. "I know about dreams and this *wasn't* dreaming, nothing like it at all. It was something much more exceptional, more unconformable."

"Do you have any theory at all, pop? Is there any clue you can give me to get into it, to understand the experience more clearly. I'm having a little problem getting ahold of this."

"Let's just leave it at that. Because I've got to move on to tell you about my personal intention. I'm convinced that it's connected to my 'dream-like' experiences."

"What makes you say that?"

"Well, here's why and how I see a connection. When I came out of my coma, maybe you didn't even hear about this, but when I awoke in my hospital bed, I found a single, long-stem rose on the pillow near my head. I couldn't make any sense of it at first, but the more I concentrated, the more I remembered that the flower had some significance, some *connection* to what I did and where I was during the coma."

"That's pretty weird, pop. The rose was a reference to something that happened during your coma and you don't remember what it was?"

"Well, I have a strong feeling that it had to do with a woman, somebody named *Rose*. And, darndest thing is, you know how I've always appreciated being around women, well, it was exactly the opposite in my comatose experience. I was terribly nervous in the presence of a woman named 'Rose.'

"Pop, I hesitate to mention this . . . but did that flower on the floor of the plane mean anything to you?"

"I never thought about it . . . the rose?" Frank closed his eyes, then opened them again and stared at the ceiling.

"It seems kind of ironic that you're telling me about a woman named 'Rose,'" Margaret said, "right after I find a rose lying next to your bag, right after your long nap. Don't you think those elements are connected?"

"All I can say is that's the way it is. But the woman named Rose does baffle me. Actually, I think there was someone named Rose in *each* of my separate experiences. Now try to explain *that*."

"Why 'Rose', pop?"

"I don't have a clue."

"Was there somebody by that name before you met Mom?"

"Hmm . . . now that you mention it, I sometimes called your mother 'Rosie' to honor the name of her grandmother. And you know I always loved raising roses for the same reason. Do you think . . . ?"

"Pretty remote, pop. I don't think it's connected."

"Well, there was never anyone named Rose that meant anything to me personally. You know, I should tell you this. Ladies in general . . . I've found it easy to talk to them, always liked being around them. I've told you how women kept me from becoming a priest because I liked them too much.

"But in this other life, I was scared to death of women. I couldn't talk to them with confidence and I didn't feel at all comfortable around them. The whole thing threw me because it was so inconsistent with the real me. It was like I was somebody else . . . but then again, I *wasn't* somebody else. To say the least, it was extremely paradoxical.

"I also saw myself in much younger years, felt a lot of the same things I felt when I passed through pubescence into adulthood. And, most shockingly, get this . . . through most of the adult experiences in my *other state*, I was a priest, an ordained priest, a man of God. Can you believe that? I knew what it felt like to be a priest after all these years."

"Pretty incredible, pop. Unbelievable! So that's the connection then, the relationship to your intention for The Prayer and the *other state*, as you just called it."

"You've got it, honey. My intention was exactly that . . . that I experience life as a priest, first-hand and with no qualifiers. But I didn't want to wait until I was dead. I wanted it now. I figured it was an impossible request, but then again, my faith in God led me to believe it could happen. I was driven by the quote of Jesus: 'Nothing is impossible with God.' And I was motivated by my faith in *A Prayer for the Dying*.

"I think you could and should tell mom about this. She might be able to explain it better than me. Maybe she'll have an answer, especially for that *Rose* thing."

"Don't think so," Frank said. "But it *is* bothering me because we've never had any secrets between us.

"You know, Margaret . . . let me digress here for a minute. Allow me to branch off on a tangential exploration. It's about *secrets*. It's always amazed me that you never kept any secrets from us over all the years of your life."

"How do you know that, pop?" Margaret laughed as her father gently struck her on the hand.

"Well . . . what I should've said was that you're clever enough to have concealed your secrets, maybe *disguised* them is a better way of putting it. But my point is that you've always been completely upfront and honest with us, even about your failings. And none of your siblings has been that way. They've all got secrets from their past . . . adventures, mistakes, all sorts of things they've kept from us. Every once in awhile, a little something leaks out about when they went off to 'find themselves.' And now, they still feel they have to cover it up. Why do you think that is?"

"Not a clue, pop. We were all raised in the same house with the same parents and had the same influences on our lives. I think when people have secrets that they can't entrust to their parents, it's a sign of some kind of weakness, a character flaw."

"Do you really believe that, honey?"

"It's only a personal opinion, pop. On the other hand, maybe they've kept secrets from you because they're afraid the truth would hurt you too much. Maybe they're just protecting you from some things you wouldn't want to know anyway."

"Well, I don't know if I buy that. But it sure puts a new spin on *secrets*." Frank agreed to give the idea more thought.

"Something else I've wondered about," he said. "Since you're in a question-answering mood, what's your opinion on the age-old dilemma of environment versus genetics? Which do you think is the stronger factor in human development?"

"You mean the 'nature versus nurture debate?'"

"Yeah. Any feelings on that? I'm curious."

Margaret answered quickly, though she marveled at her father's inquisitive nature. She pretended that her answer took no thought at all. "Well, uh, I think they both have a role, that's for sure." She and her father laughed.

"I'm no expert," she continued, "but I know the answer involves one of the oldest disputes among sociologists all over the world. Some feel strongly that environment is a greater factor in shaping a person while others feel just as strongly that the heaviest influence is genetic. Tough to answer that one, pop. But if I'm pushed, I generally cop-out and say that I personally believe it's a 50/50 proposition.

"Case in point . . . when you think about it," she continued, "it's obvious that the loving environment you and mom built in our home was crucial to how we developed. You gave us our independence, the freedom to make our own choices. But then again, I think all of us kids felt, and still feel, that the genes we inherited from you and mom and your parents, those, too, shaped us and influenced our behavior and personalities and perspectives. All of those things contributed to our formation.

"You know, pop, there's evidence that genes *do* control speech and language development. But psychologists and sociologists have been studying the conflict for at least five decades and they've still failed to resolve anything. We could sit here and discuss this for days and not come up with a valid conclusion, much less one we agree on."

Margaret exhaled deeply, leaned back in her chair and smiled at her father. "I don't have to tell you," she said, "in spite of the great wisdom emanating from my lips, as we sit in this marvelous place in Rome, you know that the identical environment and the same genetics led us kids in very divergent directions. So, I guess my answer is really no answer at all." She paused before adding, "How did we ever get into this discussion, pop? Is it really important right now?"

"My gosh!" Frank said with a huge grin on his face. "I can't tell you how much I enjoy listening to you. Your thoughts and words bring tears to my eyes. Your knowledge and conviction are amazing. But I've got to add to what you so generously said about your mother and me. We were *not* perfect. You know that. We made our share of mistakes in raising all of you. Sure, we did our best, but there were times we both regretted things we did as well as didn't do."

"That goes without saying, pop. There are no parents who ever walked this planet who were perfect." Margaret thoughtfully paused and with her eyes focused more on the ceiling than on her father, added, ". . . except maybe Jesus' parents, Mary and Joseph."

"You're right about that," Frank said with a broad grin. "But you know, all of your wisdom still doesn't explain how I can accept the annoying, the very *private secrets* of some of your siblings. It's one of those little things that drive me nuts."

"Look, pop," Margaret said with intimacy diluted with a dash of impatience, "my soundest advice is . . . let it go. The kids are who they are."

"C'mon, Margaret. You can do better than that." It was Frank's turn to show impatience. "That phrase bugs me," he said. "It's trite and overused. Give me something original."

"Okay, then," Margaret said. "They are who they *want* to be. Is that fresher and more accurate? You know you can't change that, pop. No matter what you say or do . . . you can't change that." With her voice raised, she finished with, "Like I said, pop, let it go."

"Getting a little irascible, aren't we?" Frank said. "But you can be irascible and reasonable at the same time . . . incredible. Now that's being who you *want* to be, right?"

"Maybe that's why men don't like me, why I've never been married . . . 'always reasonable Margaret.' How dull is that?" Her comment *nearly* concluded the dialogue. Father and daughter smiled, with deep respect for one another. It was a quality that remained a bond until the end of their lifetimes. But Frank so enjoyed conversing with his only and "favorite" daughter, that he opened the door to still another area regarding siblings.

"I know you're getting antsy, my dear," he said, "but I'd really like one more opinion from you . . . and then we'll move on. Who do you think knows an individual more deeply and more accurately, siblings or parents? Think about it and give me a short answer."

Margaret *did* think about it. It was the first time she had ever considered the question *or* an answer. A sibling or a parent, she said to herself. Who knows an individual best? Then she spoke, with much less confidence than before.

"Gosh, pop, I'd selfishly believe that I know my brothers from a better perspective than you or mom do. But to call it more *accurate* to what that person is all about, I don't know. You and mom obviously, as adults, knew your children before any of us knew each other. So you have to win from that angle. But to know them more *deeply*, to get into their hearts and souls . . . maybe we kids have the edge, because we developed together, grew together, learned all the private innuendos and intentions of one another. And a whole lot of *secrets*, too."

"You're giving me something to go on," Frank said. "I've got a 'yeah-but' to add, however. Don't you think parents have the overall wisdom, a better understanding of their children than siblings do? Think about the fact that, number one, we changed your diapers; number two, we taught you to speak, to walk, talk, eat; and number three, we consoled you in our arms the first time you suffered both physical and emotional pain. Doesn't that give us an edge?

"Don't you think that led to a better understanding, to a more intuitive and judicious insight into each of you. Think about all the years we dealt with your personal learning, with the stumbles and falls each of you made along the way, all of that stuff we observed and shared while your brothers were watching from the sidelines."

"Got me there, pop," Margaret admitted. "I guess you and mom have talked about this before. You seem well-prepared to fence with me on the subject. You win. Next question?"

"Thanks for being so kind," Frank said quietly as he leaned over, gently held Margaret's face in his right hand and kissed her on the forehead. "I appreciate your patience. It helps me so much to talk like this. It helps me understand all of you kids better and actually helps me understand myself better."

"Okay, back to your story, pop, if I can remember where you were. You have such an uncanny gift for changing subjects mid-stream. Do you remember where you left off?"

"Of course. I was telling you about my prayer from Saint Francis." Margaret shook her head in disbelief at her father's short-term as well as long-term memory.

The caring and sensitive daughter repositioned herself in a chair that was slowly becoming uncomfortable. "I think you had just told me," she said, "that you asked God to allow you to experience priesthood and you're convinced that He's doing it today, in this day and time and place, right now."

"I'm beginning to feel more certain about that, yes. But it's so bizarre that I'm embarrassed to verbalize it because people would think I'm nuts. You know what I'm saying? It's so crazy. They'd attribute my thoughts to drugs I'm taking."

"Well, actually, there's no reason to tell *anyone* about your experiences, is there, pop?"

"Now that you mention it, I guess not. But I'd so like to tell, like my Knights of Columbus buddies, friends like that. I think they'd be blown away."

"Maybe that would take something away from it, water it down and risk having the effects of The Prayer disappear." Margaret thought carefully before she said that. She did not want to offend her father but she did want him to appreciate his special blessing and not jeopardize receiving it. She had further questions, however.

"Pop, I'm interested . . . is there some kind of timetable on these 'events,' some precursor, some way you can tell when something's going to happen?"

"No, not at all. I told you the first one occurred when I was in the coma and the next one on the plane coming over here. Those were over six months apart. So only God knows, literally, when the next one will happen, if it happens at all."

"So you're convinced it's *you* in the scenes that you see?"

"In the scenes that I *live*. Absolutely." Frank answered as quickly as he was asked. "Absolutely! And it's not like I'm *seeing* myself in the scenes, it's like I'm *living* the action. I *am* the scene. I smell the scents, feel the rain, get my tongue singed by hot coffee; I've even felt a kiss or two every once in awhile, and I don't even know who gave it to me. I'm moved to sadness and happiness. I'm embarrassed, proud, everything and anything that's happening is happening to *me*. And though the experiences have occurred only twice, the periods *inside* them have seemed very long."

With that information, Margaret better understood what her father was trying to explain. But that made it no less incomprehensible.

"So I think I've got a handle on this," she said, not really trusting her own words. "You're convinced that you're living two lives simultaneously, at the same time as here and now, but in different places."

". . . and at different times in my life."

"How old are you in those events, those journeys into the other place?"

"It's crazy," Frank replied. "After the coma, I went from my childhood up to, I guess, my mid-twenties. The other time, I jumped to my mid—or late thirties. So it seems like that *other* me who's an ordained priest, is catching up with *this* me, the one who's 77 years old. Does that make any sense?"

"A little bit, I guess. But none of the other stuff does. You just have to accept the fact that these short journeys into another life are blessings. It's what you asked for. And if you look at it in that light, you should be proud that Saint Francis was your emissary and that God heard your prayer through him and answered it. What more could you want?"

"Well, it makes me feel terribly selfish," Frank answered. "Do you think it's selfish of me? I mean, maybe I should be asking favors for mom, for God to bless all the family with good health, prosperity, happiness of all kinds. I could ask for you to meet the man of your dreams. Wouldn't that be less selfish?"

"Pop," Margaret said quietly through a long sigh, "I think all those wishes are in your prayers anyway. For heaven's sake, you don't have a selfish bone in your body. All your life, as long as I've been around, I've witnessed and felt your self-giving love. God probably heard your prayer for that reason. You're a good man. In fact, I've considered you a saint ever since I can recall thinking of things like that. A saint, pop, a *giant* of a Saint. That's what you've been in my eyes, and in the eyes of a lot of other people who know you well.

"I've overheard people at church talking about you," Margaret continued with her praise, "and I've heard all the clichés: 'He's the kind of guy who would walk around a roach rather than step on it; he'd give the shirt off his back if somebody needed it; he'd give his last dime to a panhandler.'"

"Yeah, right," Frank replied. "Those people don't know me like your mother does. Ask them to talk to *her*. She'll tell them about my flaws and failings. I've got plenty of chinks in this old armor, Margaret. You know that as well as I do."

"I've told you, pop, you're as good as they come. I'm just telling you what people think of you. I'm always proud that you're my father. I know that mom and the other kids feel the same way. So don't ever beat yourself up over the intention of your prayer. It's something very personal, between you and your God, and you don't have to justify it to anybody, especially not to me. This is *your* journey, or I should say, these are *your journeys*. I encourage you to enjoy every minute of every event in your varied states of awareness. Hey, go along for the ride. The fact that it's inexplicable makes it even more fascinating. And that's okay. Because it's God's will."

Frank returned to his dissection of selfishness. "I'll share an observation I've made since I became seriously ill," he said. "When a person gets sick, I mean really sick, his or her focus is on one thing and one thing only . . . self. You can't help it. Illness begets deeper and deeper thoughts of self. When it hurts, it hurts *me*, not my wife or neighbors or children . . . *me!* When I'm uncomfortable, it's *my* body that feels lousy.

"So when you're sick, you come at life from a different perspective. You develop this different approach and attitude that's inconsistent with the way you've acted all your life. You lose your focus on *others*. They become secondary. Your entire world centers on, revolves around *you*. And as much as I'm aware of that, I can't seem to defeat it. My bodily condition rules my virtue. In short, I've become selfish."

Margaret verified her understanding of all that and added.

"Pop, here's an angle you may not have considered. You know, it's also difficult for your caregivers to witness that change in you. Yeah, we've all noticed it. But we don't love you any less for it. We adjust, accept the new you but remember what you're all about inside. You're the same person we've loved dearly all our lives even though your behavior is a bit skewed toward self. But none of it means that you're selfish in the sense of deliberately engaging selfishness as a sin."

"Well, nevertheless, I apologize for all that. I'm very sorry."

"Let me tell you something about selfishness, pop," Margaret said. "There was a time in my life when I was completely controlled by selfishness. It wasn't long after getting my degree from grad school. You and mom were off somewhere exotic in the world, my brothers were all involved in their own families, and I felt like I didn't have a single friend in the whole world, especially the male kind.

"I can remember waking-up early one morning and lying in bed wallowing in self-pity. I felt like climbing the highest mountain, throwing my arms open wide and shouting to the world, 'Does anybody hear me? Is there anybody out there who cares?' If you can believe it, I did that from an open window at my apartment on the 22nd floor down on Rush Street. Thank God the noise of traffic drowned out my voice."

"You actually did that?" Frank asked as he listened to his daughter in wonder and disbelief.

"I absolutely did," she replied quickly. "And I rid myself of those selfish thoughts. I felt better for shouting, kind of like purging the loneliness from inside me. And it shocked me into the reality of what I was doing and how foolish I was acting. From that time on, I surrendered, surrendered completely and without reservations."

"To whom?" her father asked, puzzled and confused.

"I surrendered, first of all, to God, to try to understand His will and His plan for me. I figured if I could crawl out of my *self* and rely more on the will of a Supreme Being, it'd be a start. So I did that. I knew it was going to be long process, but I recalled an old bromide I learned back in grade school. 'Think of others first, myself last, and God always.' It became my mantra. And I was a lot happier for it."

Frank had been noticeably staring deeply into his daughter's eyes, without blinking. He dare not risk distracting her. Then, he leaned close and said, "My darlin', where and how did you become so profound, so in-control, so good?"

Margaret laughed quietly, patted her father on the hand, and said, "You taught me all I know, but . . . well, I guess maybe mom had a role in that, too."

Frank gently wiped a tear from Margaret's eye and also one or two from his own. He was, at the same time, proud of her conclusions about selfishness but he was also exhausted from their lengthy dialogue. Margaret felt the same.

"Pop," she said as she stretched her shoulders. "As much as I love to talk and listen to you, I think we should go up to the room. Mom's probably wondering where we've been for so long. And I'll bet she's got your meds lined up like soldiers, nice and orderly on the counter, just like she does at home."

"Are you kidding? She's known us both long enough to know we've been having a good time."

"You've got a point there, pop. But tomorrow's going to be a long day for all of us. You're feeling okay right now?"

"Never felt better. Would you help me get up to the room, my dear? I don't need a wheelchair but I could use your arm to hang onto. I feel a little weak. My meds do that to me. It's no wonder I walk around half loopy all the time."

Father joined daughter in stretching arms, neck and back as they stood simultaneously. There was a serious *goodnight* at the doors to their adjoining rooms, but not before their arms encircled one another in a firm embrace. It was an habitual conclusion to their lengthy discussions. This time, Margaret's tears soaked her father's shoulder. Sadly, that once sturdy shoulder had become thin and frail as she felt only bone between her fingers. The evening would linger in the core of Margaret's heart for the remainder of her life. She and her father rested well, soothed by the memory of a time spent well. Their farewell on this evening was a synchronous, "I love you." At the end of it all, Margaret felt weary and careworn.

The Assisi Experience

The next day was their first full day in the streets of Rome. It was a day of reminiscing, visiting some of the favorite places from Frank and Annie's memories 25 years earlier. In addition to the typical tourist stops, they escorted Margaret to Tre Scalini. They had previously spent many hours in that place on their first visit to Rome and explained their recollections to Margaret. She enjoyed the tartufo almost as much as the dialogue from her mother and father. It was an exceptional day that prompted Margaret to employ the cliché, "There's no place like Rome." Her parents agreed but groaned.

Visiting the home of Saint Francis in Assisi was more than Frank and his family had expected. The atmosphere was inspiring and serene. Polite worshippers roamed the grounds as if without purpose but focused reverently on the fascinating architecture of each building. Frank, Annie and Margaret shared the desire of Father Tonelli as they walked *alone* and meditated quietly rather than listening to narrated recordings. They absorbed the impressive artistic and spiritual history of the holiest place in the life of Saint Francis. It was an excellent overture to the meeting of Brother Pietro.

Frank was edgy about that and prayed that the saintly Brother was in good health and willing to meet with him and his family. He had not received a confirmation from Father Tonelli that the priest had connected with the Brother to set up such a meeting. There was, indeed, cause for concern.

After their brief overview of the Basilica, the three made their way down to the crypt, the place where the body of Saint Francis lay in repose. They would return and spend more time at each of the many locations after meeting with Pietro.

This was an emotional time for everyone, but a *monumental* time for Frank. He remembered learning as a young child how he was connected to the Saint by name. Since then, his dream was to visit Assisi. It had taken a long time to get there. Now, as he walked the grounds to the soft chanting of male voices in the background, he was deeply and emotionally moved. More than several tears fell from his eyes. Was it the most important moment in his life? No. Was it the most inspirational? Yes!

Meeting the man who generously handed *A Prayer for the Dying* to Father Tonelli was no less moving. Brother Pietro was even smaller in stature than the pictures portrayed. And as Father said, he looked much younger than his 92 years. He was, indeed, the stereotypical Brother leading his life in a Franciscan Friary: bearded, bald, and sporting a perpetual smile that transcended all the other facets of his appearance.

From the perspective of Brother Pietro, he was delighted to meet Frank Chase and his family. Father Tonelli had described them well and told of their long and close friendship. At that point, of course, Brother did not know the nature of Frank's intention. But his human curiosity influenced one of his early questions.

The kindly Brother escorted his visitors into the same courtyard in which he had first met with Father Tonelli. The weather was chilly but clear and comfortable with an infrequent white cloud jogging across the deep blue Italian sky. The visitors were impressed with the abundance of flowers and the delicate fragrance of the moist, hillside air. Frank commented about the flaming bush of red roses he recognized from the photo of Brother Pietro standing in front of it.

Once seated on chairs and benches and carrying small *cola's* in their hands, the group sat in a circle with Brother Pietro in the center. He directed his attention to Frank. "I understand that you have been saying The Prayer Father Tonelli gave to you. Do you understand its implications?"

Though Frank was caught off-guard, he had a spontaneous answer. "Of course, Brother," he said. "I've been saying it three times almost every day since I received it. I'm humbled to use the words of your Saint." He was cautious not to boast of his special privilege but, nevertheless, to express his gratitude.

"I am compelled to ask if you have seen any result," the Brother said. "I am only interested from the standpoint of logging evidence that relates to The Prayer. We are working to have it authenticated and all evidence helps our cause."

"Well, Brother," Frank said. "It's a long story."

"I have time," Brother replied. "Would you like to tell me? Or would you prefer seeing more of our home? You may make the choice. You may do *both* at your convenience."

"To tell you the truth, Brother," Frank said, "I'd first like to explain the details of my intention. Perhaps you can help me understand if my request is valid and if it is being answered. Naturally, that depends on whether you have the time right now. As you know, my time here on earth is limited and I don't want to get to my next life any sooner than I must."

Brother Pietro smiled and responded. "I'm sure you've heard the old English proverb, the one about heaven and death." Frank frowned indicating he had not. Brother concluded, "Well, it says that everyone wants to go to heaven but no one wants to die." The visitors laughed, surprised at Pietro's sense of humor. Frank simply said, "That accurately describes my frame-of-mind right now."

Frank looked over at Annie and winked at Margaret as he sent a short and subtle message. "Maybe my family would like to do some more touring while you and I talk here, Brother. Do you have someone who could take them around?"

That was an obvious hint and a well-disguised order to his family. Annie and Margaret accepted it gracefully and were soon introduced to Brother Gerard, a Friar whose duty was to escort visitors through the Basilica and adjoining buildings. They would return in one hour, the time when some of Frank's medications were due. Most important, Frank wanted to speak to Brother Pietro privately. Besides, Annie and Margaret had heard his story so many times that they could recite it as well as he could.

Brother Pietro had one directive for the two touring women. "Remember," he said modestly and respectfully, "as you walk the length and breadth of our cherished home, as you see glimpses of the sky through our beautiful stained windows, remember . . . this is not a museum for Saints; it is, rather, a hospital for sinners." The women smiled and bowed their heads in unison. They noted and appreciated the profundity of Brother's words. They would long remember them . . . "a hospital for sinners."

Alone together in the inspiring surroundings, Brother Pietro and Frank exchanged compliments, confirming their admiration for one another based on the stories of Father Tonelli. Frank especially enjoyed sitting with the good Brother and listening to him speak in his thick Italian accent. He felt very much at home in this place and was grateful that God had answered his prayer to visit Assisi and that Annie had agreed on the sensibility of the trip.

Frank gave Brother an "abbreviated version," as he liked to call it. He explained his exceptional intention and the unusual experiences that he believed were an answer to his recitation of *A Prayer for the Dying*. Following his narrative, Frank had something *additional* to add.

"I want to tell you something," he said. "I've thought a lot about this over the past months. It goes back to some friends I had when we lived in the state of Florida in the United States. That was before I became ill." Frank gave a background of his friends who met for morning coffee after daily Mass.

"One of the men in our group," he said, "was a really solid Irishman with a great sense of humor. His name was Tom McArdle and he was an excellent Catholic with a strong faith.

"So this one day while we're all talking, Tom comes up with this 'observation,' as he calls it. 'Do you know,' he says, 'if you think about it, the Lord is really a 'show-off.'"

"Well, we all laughed and stared at Tom waiting to hear what he meant by that uncommon observation. So he explained."

"'If you study all the great things the Lord does around this world,' he said, 'all the miracles he works . . . like the babies He creates, like every sunrise and sunset . . . and the crops and seasons all over the world . . . and the . . .' And he goes on and on to list dozens of things we take for granted that we should consider *miracles*. And the Lord performs them every single day. Tom sees them as ways God uses to 'show off,' to demonstrate His power and His love for us. What do you think of that, Brother?"

Brother nodded favorably. "Amusing," he said softly, "perhaps theologically-flawed, but amusing, nevertheless. Its flaw lies in the fact that it presumes a God with *human* frailties like pride and conceit, doesn't it, Francis?" (Frank appreciated being called "Francis." He always loved the formal name but it was an uncommon experience.)

Continuing his story, Frank instantly defended his friend Tom's observation. "Tom was speaking figuratively," he explained to Brother. "He was personifying God, giving Him human characteristics. He opted to use a figure-of-speech." Brother smiled and continued to wonder what Tom's commentary had to do with him or anything relevant in the conversation. Frank sensed that and concluded his dialogue.

"So you know," he said, "this whole thing with me and my exceptional intention. It's clearly a miracle if God takes me into another life, if He is answering my prayer to live as a priest. Don't you think that's an act of God that demonstrates His interest in one undeserving human being? Can you imagine that, Brother? Maybe God Himself is enjoying every minute of my adventures. And if He wants to 'show-off' like that, far be it from me to question Him or scold Him. As a matter of fact, that perspective makes me appreciate what He's doing for me even more. It amazes me. Do you think it's crazy to believe that the Lord likes to 'show-off?'"

Brother Pietro laughed. He had found Frank's story entertaining and was laughing *with* him, not *at* him. He found the idea of God "showing-off" to be merely an interesting perspective on the mercy and goodness of the Almighty.

"No," Brother said, "I don't think it is a crazy thought at all. Your friend has a vivid imagination and must have a great love for his Maker. I must say, however, that I find it hard to imagine Almighty God as one Who needs to display His powers to the helpless creatures to whom He has given life." Brother labored to accept the unusual twist that Frank's friend, Tom, had given to miracles as being God's way of "showing-off."

"But what if His mother," Frank argued further, "the mother of Jesus, encourages her Son to show humans His love by working miracles like mine? What if she coerces Him to do it like she did at the marriage feast of Cana? What if *she* wants him to show-off just because she's so proud of Him?"

They had been talking for over an hour when Brother arose and asked Frank to follow him into the Friary. His patience, though sizeable, had been tested. He wanted to not only change the subject but at the same time demonstrate cordiality. He offered Frank fresh lemonade with slices of newly-baked bread. He was unaware that his simple invitation was a preamble to disaster.

When Frank got to his feet, he walked behind Brother who led the way. Brother did not see Frank stumble on the stone walkway and fall hard to the ground. He landed on his left hip and struck his head on the edge of a concrete bench. Brother heard the frightening sound, turned abruptly, and rushed to Frank's side. Frank lay motionless and bleeding from a large wound on his left temple. Brother shouted for help as loudly as he could. He struggled to raise Frank, but could not arouse him or lift him. The Brother was terrified!

Within minutes, two other Brothers responded, leading a tourist who was visiting with them. They all agreed that moving Frank even slightly could cause irreparable damage. All they could do to help him was to press towels on his open wound and try to stop the bleeding. At the same time, the tourist called an emergency number on his cell phone. Help was needed immediately!

As an ambulance rushed to the scene from the town of Assisi, the visitor ran to tell Frank's wife and daughter of the accident. Brother Pietro had given a description of the two and the man took it upon himself to stand at the pulpit near the front of the Basilica and use the microphone to call for the family of *Frank Chase*.

Naturally, when Annie and Margaret heard the name over the speaker, they hurried to the area where they had left Frank. They were stunned to find him lying on the ground in a pool of blood.

Annie cried out and knelt at her husband's side in shock, hyperventilating and unable to speak. She believed that Frank was dead . . . until she saw his chest move slightly. At the very least, he was alive.

Brother Pietro explained how the accident happened. He was extremely apologetic, blaming himself. Annie and Margaret quickly excused him and told him they knew he was not negligent or careless. Annie explained that Frank had been fighting dizziness on the ride to Assisi but it seemed to correct itself and he felt he was okay to be without them. They figured it was the common effect of his medicine.

When the ambulance arrived from *Assisi Hospital*, several attendants knelt beside Frank and recorded his vital signs. They acted quickly and professionally, stopping the bleeding and assuring Frank's family that his signs were strong.

It was obviously not a heart attack that felled him, the team offered, but they explained in a broken English dialect that Frank should be taken to the Hospital quickly. It would be a short ride of only 15 minutes. The driver who had driven the family to Assisi was summoned, instructed, and drove Annie and Margaret as he followed the ambulance.

Frank was hurried into an emergency room where several local physicians and ER personnel examined him. They verified that his heart was functioning well and pulse was good. They quickly closed the gash on the side of his head with 17 stitches and determined that the blow had most probably caused a concussion. The fall was an accidental stumble.

Time would tell the extent of Frank's injuries, whether lasting or temporary. His family could expect him to experience ringing in his ears, nausea and slurred speech as well as extreme fatigue. His condition of unconsciousness might last for several hours or several days. "And when he awakens," one of the doctors said, "you can expect him to be very confused, maybe even to display amnesia. Hopefully, those conditions will disappear once his traumatic injury is healed."

Margaret and Annie breathed easier after accepting the concussion as something that wasn't, at least for the present, life-threatening. Annie was reminded of a rather primitive healing suggestion that one of Frank's buddies used: "If you've got a really bad headache," he'd say, "drop a brick on your foot and watch how fast the headache disappears." She hoped that the recent physical injury might deflect Frank's attention from his cancer to a less formidable foe.

In the meantime, Frank Chase seized the opportunity of being unconscious to calmly but without intent, again transition into his tandem life as Father Francis Chase.

Second-hand Rose

The two decades following my trip to Rome passed even more quickly than the first. Before I knew it, I was celebrating my 30th anniversary as a priest. There were many significant events that had occupied my life; but in spite of them, or perhaps *because* of them, I continued to appreciate being a man of God. I recognized my calling and was grateful that I heard God's voice and followed its directives. Along the way, however, the Lord continued to place obstacles in my path, many that were increasingly difficult to hurdle.

It was 1991 when I began relishing studious reviews of "the good old days." I was only 56 but I enjoyed reflecting on both the good times and the bad that had shaped and affected my growth. Reminiscing had thus become a part of me, a mental pleasure, if you will, that kept me properly aligned and prepared for where I was going. Such private reflection also prevented a dangerous recurrence of missteps.

I had recently given a homily in which I opined on the subject of *missteps.* My recurring thought was, "The true sign of maturation is not only being aware of one's *mortality* but also understanding one's own *fallibility.* That personal observation was tantamount to my spiritual growth.

The three years of change prompted by Vatican II occupied a large part of my life until it concluded in 1965. The many alterations to the rituals of Roman Catholicism were welcome, especially the formal encouragement of greater lay participation in the Mass. Some of the changes were difficult to enact, but most of us within the clergy implemented them with enthusiasm. Importantly, the majority of our parishioners reacted with support and acceptance.

The worst event in the three decades since my ordination was the death of my parents. They passed away just six months apart when they were both in their early 70's. Mom couldn't live without dad so she followed him quickly. She simply lost her will to live, not uncommon for couples who believed that marriage was to last *until death do us part*, and then some.

The second cataclysmic event in my personal life involved one of my closest friends, Father Bill. You'll recall from my many stories that Fathers Bill and Kenny were classmates of mine from as far back as my earliest days in the minor seminary. I always admired Bill and thought of him as an iconic Catholic priest, totally dedicated to the causes of his parish and its people. To my shock and to the shock of his friends, Bill was accused of sexual misbehavior with six young people in his parish. The news shook the Archdiocese, the entire city of Chicago, and me. It was devastating!

Bill's fall from grace was clearly the single most disturbing event of my life. The allegations were substantiated when he was in his mid-fifties, the same age as I was. From the time of the accusations, he was removed from his parish and could never again return to public ministry. He received four years of therapy, including personal psychological help that concluded he was not a pedophile; but, according to canonical law, he was banned from ever working in a parish again.

The initial details of the story were extremely difficult for me to hear. They were, of course, even more difficult for Bill to endure. There was public disgrace and humiliation, the sadness from the loss of his priestly duties and most significant, of course, the trauma of facing and asking forgiveness of those people he was guilty of abusing.

I spoke to Bill shortly after the news broke. Since we had been such close friends, I was not afraid to confront him. I scolded him crudely rather than gently and told him it was the end of our friendship. He accepted all of that and made an attempt to explain himself, making no excuses for his sins. I had a hard time comprehending the nature of what he told me.

Further, it became a terribly hard time for our entire class from the seminary. We had become a close-knit family for over twelve years that carried us through to ordination. It was also the "canary in the coal mine" that introduced an incredibly strenuous time for the Roman Catholic Church throughout the world.

I leaned heavily on my other best friend, Father Kenny Zalinsky. We managed to help each other cope with the loss of a man we considered an exemplary Catholic priest. He was gone, out of our lives, out of the priesthood . . . dead! It wasn't for us to judge Bill. We realized that. But we did find it very, very hard to forgive him. Unearthing that forgiveness took a lot out of us. Miraculously, in the end, rather than destroying our spirits, we were strengthened.

When forgiveness *did* appear, it had evolved from a supreme test of our spirituality and our love of God and all human beings, especially those who struggle with the same personal demons as Bill's. In time, Kenny and I embraced the word of God which dictated, "Hate the sin but love the sinner." It became a motto that carried us through the remainder of our priesthood. The pain and the wound healed but the scar remained. In many ways, we felt betrayed, misled, deceived. Bill made fools of us.

In spite of those angry feelings, we felt unconditional love and sympathy. Bill did bad things, suffered greatly, and was paying a heavy price for his behavior. He would never be the same. His life had ended. For his recovery and his acceptance of a heavy cross he had fashioned for himself, we would remember him in our prayers. I made it clear to him that I would always be available to talk or to listen. I didn't hear from him until after our retirement at the age of seventy.

Going back to some of the *better* times: I remained at St. William for 12 years, spent another 10 at a smaller parish, and after 18 years as a priest, I was named pastor of my own parish, Ascension Catholic Church in Oak Park, Illinois, a suburb of Chicago. I was proud to reach that milestone.

At the time I joined the parish, *Ascension* was already known for the strength of its music ministry, for its outstanding school and Religious Education programs, and for its deeply rooted community. I was happy to be there. However, if I had known what serious challenges awaited me, I might have turned around and headed south, to some far-away island in the Caribbean.

This was the first time I had cause to doubt my confessor in the seminary, the one who told me that *priesthood* was the easy life and *marriage* the more difficult. Of course, I'll never be able to make an accurate appraisal of that, but at this point, he was off by 180 degrees.

I'll explain how things began at Ascension. Before I arrived, the parish had already set in motion a "Welcome Reception" where parishioners could meet and greet me. It was a gesture that meant a lot to any priest beginning his stay at a new parish. For me, it would help ease my passage into a new pastoral role and be an event at which I could personally meet many of the people I'd be serving.

The activity took place immediately after my first Sunday Mass at Ascension, about noon. It was set up in the parish hall for about 200-300 people who formed two "receiving lines." I stood at the front center of the room and remained in the vestments I wore to celebrate the Mass.

The two lines extended from the back to the front of the Parish Hall. However, I could see clearly only the faces of those who stood directly in front of me. Since I believed strongly in direct eye-contact, there was little else in my focus but the person I was speaking with.

The event was nearing its close with only five or six people remaining in each line. A woman stood directly in front of me and offered her hand to clasp mine. She looked familiar but

I couldn't place her, until she spoke and our eyes locked. The woman reminded me a lot of Meg Ryan whom I recently saw in the film, "When Harry Met Sally." But this *wasn't* Meg Ryan. This woman was taller and more classically beautiful. She talked *fast*, in the same pattern as the last time I saw her, in the *Piazza Navona*, at Tre Scalini. Rosa Marie Marsinski held my hand, for a long time, then spoke.

"Well, hello, *Father* Francis," she said softly, being certain to accent the *Father* part.

"Wow . . . Rosa!" I caught myself in a display of unbridled enthusiasm and returned her greeting. "I mean *Doctor* Rosa. I'm sorry. I forgot the last name."

It had been almost twenty years since our encounter in Rome. And so much had changed. First of all, I was no longer intimidated by her presence or her beauty. And she, too, seemed quite at ease. You wouldn't have known it, however, by our shared discomfort. After a moment of dead silence, with only smiles and shakes of the hand, she spoke again.

"Welcome to Ascension. It's great to see you. I heard you were coming to be our pastor. You look terrific. Staying out of trouble?" I was intimidated all over again.

Rosa's hair was cut very short but still blond with several tufts of silver. Her eyes appeared an even deeper blue than I remembered. And she hadn't gained a pound. She did appear a bit older but I would've expected that after the passage of twenty years. Later, I would reflect on the fact that, within milliseconds, I observed and evaluated so much.

Obviously, my antennae were up. The cause and effect of that instant response worried me, as did the fact that the two of us stood staring at each other and locked by the fingers of our hands for several minutes. I finally pulled back as I noted perspiration on the palm of the hand I used for greeting.

"I'd sure like to talk to you some time," she said, "just to hear about your adventures over these many years."

"It would be nice," I said. "But this sure isn't the time or place." People behind Rosa were glaring at us like we were involved in a terrible public sin.

"I'll wait until you have time," she responded discreetly. "But there *is* something that needs attention, like right now."

"Call the office tomorrow and set something up," I replied. "The secretary knows my schedule."

Rosa turned and walked away, smiling broadly and waving over her shoulder. Her departure was almost identical to the one in the rain at *Piazza Navona*. The only difference now was the absence of a thrown kiss.

She scheduled an appointment and arrived promptly at four o'clock two days later. She was escorted into my office by the secretary as I moved from my chair behind the desk and sat beside her on one of two upholstered chairs. We were both comfortable, at least physically.

"So tell me," I asked, "how are you and your husband and kids. If I remember, you had three little ones."

"Well, they're not so little any more. Josh, the oldest, is 25; Linda is 23; and Michaela, the youngest, is 21."

"And your hobby? Do you still travel abroad and . . . ?"

"No, I stopped that a long time ago." We both laughed and she cleared her throat loudly. "That was just a whim," she said, "a *dare* that I had to accept. No, I don't do pick-pocketing any more." We smiled and I rubbed my chin as if I was still angry over her deception. She seemed cool but unusually quiet. I asked why.

"Well," she began, "it's a long story that I won't bore you with right now. It happened exactly ten years ago this month. Laszlo, my husband, contracted a deadly, unstoppable form of leukemia. He lasted six months."

Naturally, I was saddened to hear that news.

"I'm really sorry, Rosa," I said. "That's terrible. How did you handle it? I mean, it doesn't get any worse than a mother being left with three young children."

"I told you it was a long story. Maybe some other time. What I'm here to talk about is my daughter, Michaela. She told me a couple of days ago that she's pregnant. And she's not married." I tried not to show disdain or surprise.

"She was going to a Community College, got in with the wrong crowd, met some scumbag of a guy . . . and now she's in her third month and the guy is long gone. I'm sure you're familiar with that one-act play."

"It's not uncommon," I said. "We'll get back to that. But there's something you haven't mentioned, your medical practice. Are you still in medicine?"

"Absolutely . . . but it's been difficult. After Laszlo passed away . . ." She paused to collect her thoughts, then continued. "Like I said, I'll explain the nitty-gritty's some other time. But yes, I still have my practice."

I was surprised to see her in jeans. A bright red sweater and white tennis shoes made for an attractive combination. The contrast of the sweater with her hair was striking. I didn't want to ask her age but I figured she was now in her mid-fifties, about my age. "Okay, so tell me more about Michaela. What has she decided to do about the baby?"

"That's why I'm here. She and I don't agree about that. She wants to keep the baby and I think she should put it up for adoption, at somewhere like Catholic Charities. I'd like to know what you think, Francis. Oops! Is it okay to call you *Francis* and eliminate the *Father* part? It feels more comfortable."

I was so involved in studying Rosa's features and the attractive elements of her persona that I didn't focus on her words. I tried to conceal that lack of attention but didn't do a very good job.

"So . . . what do you think, Francis?" she asked. "Francis? Did you hear what I said? Are you paying attention?"

"That's the problem, Rosa. Sitting here with you again, after such a long time, is kind of unnerving. It's a distraction. I thought about you a lot after we said goodbye in Rome. Then, after working hard at it, I managed to store you somewhere in the distance of my memory bank."

"Thank you. I'm impressed."

"Now, after all that time, you're *here*, like in my face, right in front of me, twenty years later. It's a lot to absorb. So give me a chance to adjust, at least a few minutes to get my bearings. Don't you find it a little strange to sit here with me, like we never met before? And you expect me to listen and hear what you're saying, to concentrate on *Michaela?*"

"Why are you uncomfortable with me, Francis? You're a priest."

"Yeah, I'm a priest all right. But I'm also human. And I'm a man, in case you hadn't noticed."

"Well, it *is* a little weird, I must admit," she said. "But you're more mature now. You've sat with a lot of other women since *Piazza Navona*, haven't you?"

"It's been different."

"I don't understand. Why?"

"Because I usually don't have a *past* with them. I mean, a shared experience . . . in Rome . . . and Assisi. That's a bit unusual, wouldn't you say? Those were deeply moving times for me."

"But it was innocent, just an innocent friendship . . . a couple of visits together. Didn't you get over that? It was just two innocent visits. No harm done. And by the way, I seem to recall scolding you for being so shy, for worrying about every single word you said, for apologizing for being alive."

"I can't make you understand. The fact is that I was attracted to you back then. And that was exceptional for me, as a priest or as a layman. Very exceptional."

"Get over it, Francis. We're just two adults re-examining each other. I have no evil intentions."

That disturbed me more than slightly. It sounded like I was having problems with this encounter because I had some sort of "thing" for Rosa. And that's not the way it was. At least I didn't think so.

My response was simple, "Okay, then. Let's move on and discuss Michaela. Forget everything I just said."

I gathered my thoughts and suppressed any personal interest in the woman who sat beside me. She was right. I was, I *am* a priest. And it's certainly not priestly of me to create tribulations over being alone with a woman.

This is something all priests face, I told myself, whether they want to or not. And I *had* learned to handle it over the past 30 years as a virgin/bachelor/priest. The discipline was well worth the effort to remain faithful to my God. It was a promise I meant to keep forever, with the help of the same God.

Rosa and I talked for over an hour, running right up to five o'clock when we close the office. I thought we had thoroughly covered the problem of Michaela and resolved the major issues. But when I explained that it was time to call an end to our meeting, Rosa objected.

"Couldn't you slip out for a little while, Francis? I'll buy you supper if you join me. We san stay in the neighborhood and I won't keep you very long."

It was a kind offer. I reached for my appointment book and perused my evening schedule. Since I was new at the parish, I didn't yet have any pressing assignments. My evening was clear and I hesitated to turn down the invitation. It appeared as though Rosa had additional items to cover. I saw nothing imprudent in accepting her offer though I recognized the dangers.

She told me that the restaurant was only two blocks away and that we could walk. Since it was new territory for me, I took her word for it. It was an Italian place that seemed appropriate after our initial meeting in Rome.

I wore my black, short-sleeve shirt with Roman collar and had no shame in being seen with a woman. Down deep, however, I hoped we wouldn't bump into anyone from the Parish who might think our being together was inappropriate. Of course, my hopes were dashed as we stepped from the office. I counted nine people who passed us on the street and said, "Hello, Father." Most likely, their first impressions were wrong. Or were they?

During a wonderful meal, the subjects of conversation varied, from more talk about Michaela to the death of Laszlo, and from my transfer to Ascension Parish to Rosa's escapades as a member of "The Lifters." They all kept my attention and made two hours pass quickly. We shared a small carafe of wine.

The server had already cleared our table of the food dishes and we found other things to talk about. I offered a subject she found particular interesting.

"During your life as a mother and Physician," I asked, "did you ever question your decision on your career choice? I mean, not that you regretted your choice, but did you ever wonder what another life would have been like?"

"Of course," she said. "Many times. I think most people reflect on that."

"What other choice did you ever consider?" I asked.

"Well, for one, when I was younger, even before College, I dreamed of being a travel agent. I loved traveling the world and really wasn't attracted to the life of a mom and wife. Then I became friends with a couple of girls in my senior year of high school. One was heading off to nursing school and the other was going to study medicine. They both had a great influence on me, so I was smitten by a career in medicine. Plus, I had that natural interest in science from childhood on."

"I remember you saying that."

"Now, I can't say I was crazy about that first choice . . . but then, after getting my degrees, I met Laszlo, we fell in love, and that was it. There went my life as a single woman who was free to travel the world."

"Did you ever wonder if you would've enjoyed that other kind of life more than the one you chose? I'm not suggesting grades of happiness . . . but do you wonder how you would have fared? Would you have enjoyed a life that was free of all the entanglements of marriage and children?"

"Sometimes, I think," Rosa said without hesitation. "I know I could've been happy like that, too. Why do you ask such a question? Aren't you happy as a priest?"

"I love being a priest. No question about it. It's just that, well, it's hard to explain. I told you before, in Rome, how I wanted to be a dentist. I remember how you laughed at that. But every now and then, I do look back at my decision to enter the seminary and I wonder if I should've waited a little longer to make a commitment. Like maybe I should've entered the seminary *after* I had spent some time in the business or scientific community."

"Actually," I continued, "the thing I wonder about most is would I have made a good father and husband? I love kids and I do find women a wonderfully attractive part of God's creative exercise. So that's the part I really would've liked to explore. In short, I wish I could have sampled *both* ways of life . . . priesthood and the life of a dentist, dad and husband. Do you understand that?"

"Sure. It's easy to follow," Rosa said. "But we all learn that we can't have it both ways. You make a choice and you have to live with it, figuratively and literally. In most cases, there's no turning back."

"There is a 'yeah-but' however," I said with a grin and my finger pointed upward. "Just what if a person could sample *both* choices when they considered a life-path. What if God allowed us to try more than one career . . . at the same time?"

Rosa pulled her head back, sipped from her wine, and stared at me like I was crazy. Then, she laughed, not in the manner that made a fool of me, but more like she found my idea unanswerable.

"You've always been a thinker, haven't you, Francis, a thinker with imagination. Not a myopic bone in your body. I remember some of our conversations at Tre Scalini. In the brief time we were together, even on the bus to Assisi, you were questioning, wondering, even *worrying* about things that could never be. I think you're the exact opposite of a skeptic. You believe that *anything* can be accomplished. If it were my call, I'd say you're a *dreamer.* Anyone ever call you that before?"

"Guilty!" I said quickly as I leaned my elbow on the table and raised my right hand. "But there's nothing wrong with that, is there? At the seminary, I was often chastised for being a dreamer. 'Priests shouldn't be dreamers,' I was told. 'You've got to be pragmatic.' 'Anything wrong with being a dreamer,' I'd ask?"

"Not at all," Rosa answered. "As long as you're a realist at the same time, and you don't ask for the impossible. You have to accept the fact that dreams seldom come true. Like this one about having two life choices and living both of them. It's just not rational or reasonable to dream such absurdities and expect them to come true."

"You have to have faith," I said. "Remember the phrase of Jesus. It's one of my favorites, "Anything is possible with God."

Rosa had a quick reply. "I thought it was, 'Nothing is impossible with God.' Isn't that the way it goes?"

"Now you've got me confused," I said, very quietly. I did a quick scan of the restaurant to make sure no one heard me. I was clearly embarrassed to be uncertain about such a familiar and famous quote by the Savior Himself. Looking it up later would do nothing to re-establish my credibility. Rosa got me so flustered that I couldn't even recall the words of Jesus Christ. We both paused for a break as Rosa excused herself to visit the *Ladies Room*.

Of all the fine points of this extraordinary woman, perhaps the most impressive was her ability to listen and to hear exactly what was being said. No one in my life, save only my mother and father, had ever listened to me so closely, so intently. And that isn't an admission of doubt or a lack of confidence. It's the absolute truth. That attention she gave my every word was more than flattering. It was *pleasurable*. It was a personal and pleasurable experience.

When she returned, Rosa had a pertinent question for me, pertinent but sardonic, I thought. She asked, "Are you a follower of Shirley MacLaine?"

"What does Shirley MacLaine have to do with anything we've talked about?" I asked bluntly.

"Well, you do know about her metaphysical beliefs, like in reincarnation, channeling, UFO's, stuff like that. It sounds like your thoughts about living two lives at the same time are right out of one of her books."

"You know, Rosa," I said with a smile. "I think I resent that. You're playing me for the fool again, just like you did at Tre Scalini. And I don't know if I like that."

"Can't you take a joke, Francis? I'm only kidding."

"Well, maybe I'm a little sensitive about the Shirley MacLaine question. My thoughts about choices in life are completely serious, not metaphysical. But I have to tell you something strange. When you said 'Shirley MacLaine,' it struck a chord with me. I've heard her name somewhere recently. But I can't for the life of me remember who said it. That's downright puzzling."

"Do you remember where you were when you heard it? Was it in church . . . or on TV, or somewhere in a public place?" I couldn't give an intelligent answer.

"It's useless right now," I said. "I just can't remember. But I know I heard it recently. It's not a name you hear a lot of, so it's odd that I recall . . . heck, I surrender. I'll try some other time. But a little thing like that drives me crazy until I solve it. Well," I said, still shaking my head, "we'd better get going."

Rosa and I decided to split the bill for our dinner. It seemed appropriate because that way, no one could ever accuse either one of us of being indebted to the other. We got a laugh out of our common sensibilities and our clandestine tendencies.

As we prepared to leave the restaurant, I did a quick flashback and recalled several people staring at us during our meal, perhaps because of my Roman collar and the company I was keeping. I decided to dismiss those and not to worry about any fallout from gossip. It was interesting to note that our companionship had, indeed, created many eye rolls.

In such cases, an occasional result is a handful of letters written and sent to the Cardinal Archbishop of Chicago complaining about "the scandalous example set by a man of the cloth who was seen in public with a beautiful woman." I didn't really care if that happened because I enjoyed myself so thoroughly and knew there was nothing wrong with my behavior. I felt like the little boy who sneaks an ice cream bar from the fridge when he knows he's not supposed to have it. He knows he'll be scolded for his thievery but he so enjoys every lick of the stick that fear doesn't deter him. I was that kid.

At the same time, however, I did harbor conscientious misgivings. I was uncertain about having this dinner and wondered if I was exposing myself to temptation. Again.

Then, something traumatic happened as we began our walk back to the rectory where Rosa had left her car. The restaurant was in a local strip-mall and we used a sidewalk that passed by several small businesses. Most were closed since it was after 10:00 p.m., but a small bar remained open.

As we walked past the door, a large man, no more than thirty years old, exited suddenly and struck my left shoulder. I fought to keep my balance as Rosa supported me. The man was angry. It was clear that his temper was related to excessive amounts of alcohol.

"Watch where you're going, pal," he growled.

I apologized but it didn't extinguish the fires burning inside him. "Take that bitch and get out of my way," he screamed, even louder than his first remark. I wore a light jacket over my Roman collar and he couldn't see that I was a priest. (I doubt it would've mattered).

Rosa held onto my arm and said, "Let's get out of here, Francis." Before we could do that, the man grabbed my right arm, the one Rosa was holding, knocking her away from me. I didn't like that and told him so. He became more incensed and pushed me against the window of a barber shop. Mercifully, the glass didn't break. But as I bounced back, my elbow accidentally struck him in the face.

At that point, I could see that the stranger towered over me. If I was 6' 2" and 170 pounds, he was easily 6' 5" and 250. I usually backed away from physical encounters, but in this case, I had reasons to stand my ground, other than to display my Christian ideals. I had to defend myself and move fast enough to stop his closed fist from striking my face.

Instinctively, I grabbed his arm in the middle of his swing and held it tightly. From a close distance, I stared into his bloodshot eyes and spoke softly. It seemed to unnerve him, especially when I asked why he was so angry. As I slowly released his arm, he took another swing but missed again.

"Look," I said. "Calm down. What's the problem? Is this about a woman?" His arm was free and he took a step away from me. Rosa held her purse tightly as she nervously watched from several feet away.

The man snarled as he stumbled to one side. "What makes you think it's about a woman?" he asked, in one barely intelligible question.

"Have you been arguing with your wife or girlfriend?"

"You got a problem with that, buddy?"

"I sense you're angry over something very personal," I said. "Why don't you just calm down and head on home. Make peace with whoever you're fighting with."

"You think she's going to make peace with me? She's in the bar there. She's raving mad. Insane. Crazy."

"Why?" I asked, figuring if I could keep his mind occupied, maybe Rosa and me had a chance of getting away unscathed and also helping a very disturbed man. So far, I was on the right track. I asked again why his woman was so angry.

"None of your business," he shouted as he pushed me away. So much for my perceived progress.

"Look," I said as I stared into his face. "If your girlfriend is . . . is she your *girlfriend?*"

"No, she's my wife. And she's spittin' mad at me."

"Something you've done to make her that way?"

"She says I flirt with every babe I meet. On top of that, she says I'm always angry. In fact, the guys at the bar here, they call me 'Angry.' It's a nickname."

"Do you and are you?"

"What does that mean?"

"Do you flirt excessively and are you angry?"

By answering "yes" to both questions, the man forgot about *me* and re-focused on the true source of his anger, himself. I could tell he was beginning to mellow.

"How about trying this," I said, digging deep for any solution I could suggest. "How about you go back in there and give your wife a big hug. Tell her you'll do your best to stop flirting and you'll try to stop being angry so often. She'll be so surprised and you'll be a lot happier. I'll bet she gives you a big hug right back. C'mon, you feel better already, don't you? You *can* do this. Just go in there and say, 'I'm sorry!'"

"You gotta be nuts, man," he said.

"Why don't you just try it." I spoke very quietly.

He thought for a few seconds, turned towards me, extended his hand and shook mine, suggesting that he'd try but didn't think my idea would work. He said his real name was Jake. He mumbled something as he pulled a handkerchief from his pocket and blew his nose loudly. Much to my surprise, he was reconcilable.

Rosa and I watched him closely as he straightened up and walked into the bar, throwing dirty glances at nearly everyone. We waited until we could see if his apology worked. From the window, we saw him and a woman at the bar hugging and kissing. We knew they were okay. Saint Francis had heard my short prayer for assistance.

Afterwards, Rosa told me several times how proud she was of my handling of "Angry" and a festering situation that was headed for violence. I explained that throughout my life, I had avoided physical contact with anyone, drunk or sober. It was pointless and any kind of attack or even self-defense could end in a fatality.

Unfortunately for me, in Rosa's eyes, I grew a foot taller, instantly taking on the aura of an untarnished hero. My wisdom in helping Jake? Speak calmly and rationally, placing the solution entirely in his hands.

Had things turned out differently, I envisioned front-page headlines on every newspaper in the nation, something like:

"PRIEST ATTACKED BY DRUNK AS HE
DEFENDS FEMALE PARTNER."

What was I thinking in having this private dinner with Rosa? Things were getting too close for comfort and I'd better mend my ways and act more responsibly. My dear mother would have been disappointed and merciless in scolding me for my capricious behavior.

"This is a wake-up call, Francis," she'd say. "Heed the warning or pay the consequences."

She'd also have recognized the potential fallout from this evening. The mere thought of my blessed mom witnessing the childish behavior of her priestly son increased my stress but awakened my senses. I realized again that in the context of interpersonal encounters, none was more important than mine with Jesus Christ.

Friendship

Over the next few months, Rosa and I remained innocent friends, though I was a lot more cautious. But I was new to the parish and she was a logical choice to introduce me to a host of parishioners. She had been a leader in tons of activities since joining Ascension twenty-five years earlier.

Eventually, Rosa brought her daughter, Michaela, to the office for consultations regarding her imminent pregnancy. Her mother and I managed to convince the girl that adoption was the best choice for the baby's future. I promised to remain in touch with her and to help make arrangements with Catholic Charities for the adoption process. Rosa and Michaela were equally grateful.

Just when I thought I had everything under control regarding my friendship with "The Woman from Tre Scalini," I realized that I had underestimated her zeal. She was someone who operated on her own terms and didn't pander to the whims of others, unless her action was "the Christian thing to do."

Though we limited meeting in public places for lunches and dinners, there were many other visits where we ended up in one-on-one situations. I knew those had the potential to become dangerous liaisons but I thought I was strong enough to withstand their forces. My mistake was placing too much trust in Rosa and not enough in the gut feelings with which I was born.

After one of our sessions with Michaela, Rosa invited me to her home for dinner on the next evening. She explained that Josh and Linda, the two children I hadn't met, would be visiting her on the same night. She said she'd appreciate my talking to them about the untimely death of their father. Since Laszlo passed away, neither of them had been to church. They were bitter and angry with God for taking their dad prematurely.

Feeling it was my duty, I said I'd be happy to talk to them but I didn't think it would do much good since the post-college-age children were so set in their ways. I insisted on her keeping the dinner "simple."

I arrived at Rosa's house at the designated time, 5:00 p.m. She had a very nice house, a two-story that she and Laszlo had built to their own specs years earlier. The only surprise as I entered through the front foyer was not seeing Josh and Linda. Beyond Rosa, there was no other human to be seen or heard.

The charming hostess welcomed me into the family room. Adjacent to it, I could see a dining room table set for two with candlelight flickering over the dimly-lit area. A subtle enhancement was the soft sound of Italian-flavored music, vocal arias by Verdi. The candles set off flares in my self-conscious, a message to be on-guard for additional romantic nuances. (Then again, maybe my suspicions were a misjudgment on my part.)

Rosa was dressed tastefully in a flowered dress that was tight enough to display the perfectly feminine shape of her body. She invited me to take a seat on the sofa in the family room and to make myself comfortable while she finished preparing the meal. She offered beer or wine, whatever my preference. Since she held a half-filled glass of wine in her hand, I opted for that beverage. She explained that she was cooking a *simple* dinner of pasta and Italian sausage.

As I accepted the glass of wine, she placed a filled carafe on the coffee table in front of me. I asked about the two children that I was, ostensibly, to speak with. She dismissed the question quickly and said only that "Things came up and they were unable to make it." Once again, my antennae rose and scanned the overtly romantic setting. This wasn't the way it was supposed to be. I may have been naïve in detecting subtle seduction, but this was a flagrant foul.

The inclusions of candlelight, wine, pasta, soft music, complete privacy . . . it was the stereotypical setup for an amorous liaison. Though I had never been there before, I had observed the scenario in dozens of films (my ongoing source of education). I had also counseled people of both sexes to recognize such signs of danger.

The dinner served in the next room was delicious. The cook and I chatted comfortably throughout the meal. We discussed general topics like politics, the weather, her medical practice, and just a bit about her marriage to Laszlo. She explained that their relationship started "going south" before he was diagnosed with leukemia.

She accepted part of the blame for the demise of the marriage but placed most of it on Laszlo's fascination with a divorced female neighbor. She had twice seen them kissing across the backyard fence (literally) and Laszlo was unwilling to break the *neighborly* friendship. That bothered Rosa immensely. However, the "number" she was now doing on me made me suspect of *her* bad habits rooted in the same weakness.

After dinner, to exacerbate the romantic ambience, Rosa suggested we move to the sofa in the other room. She carried two long candles and placed them in front of us on the coffee table. She sat closely on the left of me as my apprehensions began to expand. She then surprised me with an abrupt shift from the physical to the esoteric. She headed directly to a most unlikely discussion, on the subject of *heaven*. It was the most remote topic I could have imagined, given the circumstances. Once again, I marveled at the unpredictability of this complex woman who feared nothing or no one.

I received another full glass of wine as it was poured from the decanter without my consent. Rosa settled back and delicately moved closer, her right knee and thigh touching my left. I had worn a casual layman's shirt instead of my blacks and

Roman collar, thinking that Josh and Linda would find it less intimidating. Now, alone here with Rosa, the shirt made me feel un-priestly. That was not my intention.

The environment unfolding before me, inch-by-inch and sip-by-sip, rapidly became a place where I questioned my choice of celibacy. I was rudely awakened by an instant infusion of virtue. I rested my head backwards onto a pillow behind it and silently recited the familiar Prayer of Saint Francis. I had memorized the words early in my life but never needed the intervention of the Saint more than at this moment. The words flowed quickly through my mind.

> Lord, make me an instrument of thy peace.
> Where there is hatred, let me sow love;
> Where there is injury, pardon;
> Where there is doubt, faith;
> Where there is despair, hope;
> Where there is darkness, light;
> Where there is sadness, joy.
>
> O divine Master, grant that I may not so much seek
> To be consoled as to console,
> To be understood as to understand,
> To be loved as to love;
> For it is in giving that we receive;
> It is in pardoning that we are pardoned;
> It is in dying to self that we are born to eternal life.

Though I remained in control and was aware of all I said and did, I didn't like it that Rosa continued to slide even closer, in spite of my appeal to higher powers. She had removed her shoes and curled up like a feline with her right thigh still pressing firmly against my left. The only awareness of my priesthood was a sudden jolt of conscience and a few drops of perspiration. I realized that this was no laughing matter as I repeated the prayer a second time, this time faster. Even as I mentally raced through the words, Rosa moved her hand and began caressing the hairs on my arm, ever so gently.

I loudly cleared my throat and moved away from my heated hostess by several inches. Just as quickly, she shortened the distance and moved back to the leg against leg conformation. On the one hand, I knew I should not be enjoying that because I was a priest. But on the other hand, I *did* enjoy it, because I was a man. A nagging question: why was God allowing this? Was it a plot to test my resolve? Or was it entirely Rosa's doing without God's intervention? Either way, I tried to defuse the event through the conversation related to *heaven*.

"So what in the world," I asked, "what interests you so much about heaven . . . *right now?*"

She thought for a minute, sipped slowly from her glass of wine and said, "I read an article about a nomadic people in a place called Tirkanaland. It's at the northwestern tip of Kenya. The Christian people who live there believe that God, heaven and the sky were originally very close to the earth. But then, people got too loud and so God, heaven and the sky withdrew. The people now see Christianity as bringing God closer to them again. Isn't that fascinating, Francis?"

I was so taken back by that tidbit of irrelevant information that I had absolutely nothing to say. I just gaped at Rosa and closed my mouth quickly when I realized it was open. But that wasn't the end of our foray into a discussion of the "pearly gates."

"I'd like to hear your thoughts on the hereafter," she said, "your ideas about the next life. When Laszlo died, I faced a lot of confusion about heaven. It became an obstacle to my faith and to my peace-of-mind."

"What bothers you?" I asked. "I mean, Jesus spelled things out pretty clearly. St. Paul was the only human to ever get a glimpse of the place, if it is, indeed, a *place*. You'll recall Paul's description, "Eye has not seen . . .""

"I know the quote," she interrupted flippantly. I pulled my head back and looked her straight in the eye. It was an excuse to slide away from her, just slightly.

"I thought you wanted to discuss this," I said. "*You* picked the subject, my dear," I said with hostility. (Why did I say, *my dear*? I privately questioned that.)

"Sorry," she said as she stubbornly moved back to the position of pressing her leg against mine. "I just wanted you to know that I'm searching for some new material on the place we're all trying to reach. I mean, heaven's our goal, isn't it? It's the purpose of our existence. Then why don't we talk about it more? Why doesn't the Church bring it up more often? If it's our ultimate destination, then why doesn't the Church have more discussion about it? Are they hiding something?"

Over the twenty years that I hadn't seen her, Rosa had retained her ability to speak rapidly. I continued to find that fascinating, albeit challenging.

"Rosa, are you sure you want to talk about *heaven* right now? For some reason, I find the subject too serious, awkward, out-of-place. Besides, it's getting late and we're both tired from a long day. Maybe this isn't the right time." I allowed my head to drop back again onto the pillow behind it. I feigned boredom and yawned.

"I have to tell you," I said. "The wine's made my head cloudy for any discussion deeper than the news, weather and sports. Can't we just talk about something simple, like what you've been doing the past twenty years? That'd be a lot more interesting than the heavy subject of *heaven*. It's too much like work."

I paused to let her digest my rationale. She did. But I learned the hard way that I would've been better off to accept her initial subject of heaven.

"Okay," she said without wasting a breath. "I'll *show* you what I've been doing. Buckle up, my priest-friend."

Rosa reached across the table, using my knee as a brace for her right hand and took a large binder from a stack of magazines. Regaining her position beside me, she placed the book on her lap and pointed out the words, "Rosa Marie's Portfolio."

I didn't know what that meant until she opened it and used our four knees as a makeshift easel. She explained that the photos inside illustrated her adventure into the world of . . . *modeling*. My comment was ignorant and inane, "Isn't that a bit narcissistic?" I said. "Why would you be *modeling* at this time of your life?"

She was offended by the questions but admitted that the venture *was* quite unconventional for a female physician her age. She explained that she was forced into "moonlighting" after Laszlo died, needing the extra income to help the kid's with their college tuition.

For marketability, she used only her first and middle name. She said that she did it for fun, in the same spirit as her membership in "The Lifters" many years earlier. She also said that modeling was an important diversion from the trauma of her husband's death. I said to myself, "Open mouth, insert foot!" My unfitting inquisition was common to my awkward behavior with Rosa. I secretly shook my head in disbelief at how poorly I was coping with the scenario in which I was a primary player.

The first page in her portfolio was a minimization of Rosa's photogenic qualities. There was a close-up of her face as she sported a smile and looked directly at the camera. She appeared sexy but innocent. Beneath the photo was a paragraph explaining the model's physical measurements. It was done tastefully as an introduction to the woman on the following pages.

Rosa turned to the second page and said, "I hope you're up to this. Just remember, I'm doing this for money, nothing else. So don't start *moralizing* on me."

The photographs would have singed the eyes of any man. The first "spread" showed Rosa wearing casual clothing like jeans and sweaters. All I could discern is that the clothing was to be worn on the golf course, at informal dining or shopping excursions, and so on. Though they were very modest, the clothes adequately displayed Rosa's attractive physical endowments.

The next several spreads were photos in more formal clothing. Her appearance was head-turning in both long and short dresses. She explained that the shots were taken at a variety of locations around the *Chicagoland* area, everywhere from "The Loop" to Navy Pier to Michigan Avenue.

She said she enjoyed going on-location and was flattered that her agent was able to get her such quality bookings so soon in her career. She was, after all, in her early fifties, an age when most models are lucky to receive *any* work. She pointed out, however, that the primary use of her pictures was in local newspaper ads. She said she accepted whatever was given to her and was happy with the diversity. Throughout the page-turning tour, I nervously anticipated an inevitable spread on swimsuits or, even worse, women's lingerie. How would I handle that?

Though I was still enjoying all of this, I remained cautious but comfortable with her leg still pressing mine. Since she removed her shoes, she had placed her bare feet on the coffee table in front of me. It was a provocative sight for a guy my age who was still a priestly virgin. I had never before seen the color red painted on toe nails. Using the proverbial analogy, I felt like I was "rearranging the chairs on the deck of the Titanic." I subconsciously moved in her direction.

The next few pages *were* on swimsuits. Not that I didn't enjoy perusing them, but what in the world could I say, "Gee, that's great stuff, Rosa." Or, "Your legs are sure pretty." Or maybe, "You're so well-proportioned for a tall woman." None of those expressions made their way to my lips. Instead, I had to recalibrate my reaction.

I remarked about the surroundings. "I always did enjoy walking down Michigan Avenue. Nice bedroom!" Those comments were even dumber than the ones I *didn't* say. Inside, I was a roaring inferno, experiencing every sensation known to the male human, some I was discovering for the first time.

I silently repeated the Prayer of Saint Francis, so intensely pleading for help that tears fell from my eyes. At that moment, I felt self-pity. It was inexplicable. I guess I was embarrassed by my emotions, by my lack of experience in such matters of the mind, body and heart. I was happy that Rosa didn't notice.

My forced smile grew weaker from overuse as we turned the last page and reached the back cover of Rosa's book. It was a full-page shot of her on horseback wearing very tight riding togs. She looked equally as beautiful in such *manly* clothes. She lacked nothing that was effeminate and everything that was masculine.

The candles had exhausted all their wax and the wine decanter was empty, both spent from doing their duty as a backdrop to subtle conversation. Just as I was about to rise, the *model* hostess reached across my lap to place the portfolio back on the table. As she did, she placed her hand on my knee for leverage and left it there. It then took a lesser prayer and all of my strength, spiritually and emotionally, to lightly push her back and prevent her from kissing me.

She leaned forward and took my face into her hands. Though my resistance was weak and her lips inches from mine, I created enough disinclination to send a clear message: I wanted no part of this. It was time to stop. And Rosa knew why!

In an instant, she pulled back, stood-up, and broke the spell she had cast. "Would you like some coffee?" she asked. "Come on, Francis, follow me. I've got something to tell you." With that, she took my hand and walking fast and barefoot, led me into the kitchen. En route, she navigated a myriad of corners and turns like a sea captain who knew all the currents, with me in tow. As usual, she was in complete control as she sat me down on one of two chairs at a small kitchen table.

At that point, hot, black coffee sounded like the perfect antidote to cerebral confusion and a safe drive back to the rectory. I offered no resistance and sat down where I was told as Rosa brewed the beverage. I was curious to hear what she had to tell me, presumably something inspired by her usual flare for the dramatic and unexpected. I was upset and she knew it.

I watched her move about the kitchen in front of me. She danced beautifully in her bare feet with the short skirt of her dress flaring as she spun from cabinet to cabinet and counter to counter. During the performance, she recited a discomforting confession.

"This all started about a month ago," she said. "You know I'm a member of the 'Women's Guild' at church. It's mostly the older women of the parish, but there's a younger contingent that hangs out together, five of us, to be exact. Well, the girls all love you very much. They truly believe you're a saint. Plus, they think you're about the cutest thing that's ever hit Ascension Church.

"So the other day, one of the girls says you remind her of the actor, Greg Kinnear, but with grey hair. Even more important, they admire your gift of delivering great homilies and they know that every word is sincere and born from a perfect heart. Any questions so far?"

"One big one. Where in the world do they get the idea that I'm a *saint?* They obviously don't know me very well, not like God does. I'm so full of faults that I can't keep count. So tell the 'girls' that they're wrong in that assessment. And that's not false humility."

After my self-defense, I wondered exactly where on earth Rosa's monologue was going. She poured the coffee and sat down in front of me, illuminating her blue eyes and pointing them directly and deeply into mine. She appeared honest. And I suddenly trusted her.

She continued. "Well, the five of us girls were out one night after a 'Women's Guild' meeting. We went to a nearby pub, told a few stories, and got around to a lengthy discussion about . . . *you.* It was all positive stuff; but we got kind of silly and one of the girls, who shall forever remain anonymous, suggested a bizarre plot to confirm the fact that you *are* as good as you appear.

So this one girl gets the idea that we should test you, harmlessly but convincingly test your moral fiber. It was for the common good, mind you. We just couldn't accept the fact that anybody could possibly be as perfect as you. Not incidentally, we did feel a high level of confidence that you'd pass our test with flying colors.

"So . . . I was against this, by the way, but they elected *me* to be the one to administer the test since they knew that you and I had met in Rome in a previous life. It was a simple assignment: seduce the priest! It could only be valid if the test was legitimate and if you had no clue that I'd stop if and when things got out-of-hand."

I was stupefied, in a state of disbelief, that someone I trusted would instigate such a devious plot to tempt me. It hurt, angered, and flattered me at the same time. But I listened. My only question was, "So this entire evening was a . . . a test?"

"Yes, my dear Francis."

"You expect me to believe that?" I said. "Really."

I stood up and paced the floor. Rosa's eyes followed me as though she were watching a tennis match.

"I must say," I continued, "I'm suspicious of your 'test.' This story of yours sounds like a spontaneous concoction, a knee-jerk reaction to my rejection of your advances. It hurts your pride that I said 'no' and now you're trying to save face and retaliate."

"I don't know what to say, Francis. I'm telling you the truth. I was tempting you. I would not have gone any farther. I consider you to be a dear and close friend, and I love you in many ways. I respect you as a priest and a leader of my faith. I wouldn't dare be a part of some cheap romantic tryst.

"Believe me, Francis. I'm sorry. That's the bad news. But the good news is that you *are* what we believed you to be, a good and faithful man who loves his God more than he loves himself, more than he loves the power of his own flesh."

I continued to pace, murmuring to myself that it was my fault. I should have known from the start that Rosa's impish instincts were a part of her marrow. She had remained the same person who enjoyed deceiving me two decades ago. No doubt, that's the reason I found her so fascinating.

Silently, she stood-up in front of me, physically blocking my pacing. She took both of my hands in hers and stared at me as she had throughout her entire story. I turned my face toward the floor. Once again, I was humbled. I felt like the greatest fool who ever lived, but then remembered that Jesus, too, was ridiculed as the ultimate fool. I was in good company.

"I hope you understand and will forgive us," Rosa said. "You should be so proud. My four friends and me, well, we're committed to secrecy about this whole thing. And I speak for all of us . . . no one will ever hear, *nobody* will ever know how really strong you are. You're a gem, my friend. I never met anyone like you. I do love you and admire you in that way, but more like a sister than a lover. I wish I could someday find a man just like you, one who hadn't yet committed himself to someone as important as his God."

"I'm speechless, Rosa. You can imagine what's all passed through my head on this night: visions, words, thoughts that I've never had in my 56 years on earth or in my 30 years as a priest. I'll never be able to forget even a minute of this evening, though I'll struggle to forget . . . well, never mind. The toughest challenge you've given me is that I have to forget that this was all a ploy, a 'test' as you've aptly called it. The perk in all this is that I've learned a great deal about myself. I'm humbled but at the same time, I'm proud of the way I handled it. But only through the grace of God."

"Now you know, first-hand, the temptations that confront men," Rosa said, "whether they're married or single or priests, regardless of the role they've assumed. Their purity is tested throughout their lives. And what about *women?* We're not excused from living up to the same standards. And it's no easier for us."

"You're right," I said. "It's an excellent reminder of the temptations that exist in the 'real world.' I'll have a greater respect for those guys with families that I see in church, that I preach to, that I hear in the confessional. I'll be more compassionate and understanding. For the first time, I can truly *empathize.* Does that sound simplistic, corny?" I paused to wait for Rosa's reaction, but seeing none, I closed with, "For some reason, the difficulties that married people face, well, the awareness of all that has escaped me in the past."

"Nothing wrong with that, Francis."

I had turned my head to look into Rosa's eyes again. There were several tears trickling copiously down each cheek. I felt sorry for her but was grateful for her candor.

"Please don't do that, Rosa," I asked quietly. "Please. I don't like to see you sad. You know I have strong feelings for you, good, strong, *healthy* feelings. I hope we're friends for all the time we have left."

We had still been holding hands, but she withdrew one of hers to wipe away the tears. When it returned to hold mine, I felt the moisture. It was comforting, bonding, like sweethearts from some medieval story when the two lovers draw their own blood and mingle it as a sign of betrothal.

We said goodnight in the foyer by her front door. Rosa apologized again, briefly, without embellishment. An apology didn't come easy for *me* because I really didn't know what I was sorry for, other than for refusing her advances. And she wouldn't have wanted to reverse that. At least that's what she led me to believe. The evening would end that way: words only, with a light touch of her hand on my arm.

When I arrived home, I parked my car in the garage of the rectory and closed the metal door behind me. I stood inside for a full minute, pushing my weight against the door with my back and spreading my hands to each side as if insisting the door stay closed. And then I wept like a child, sobbing so hard that my body shook the door and caused it to rattle. I was frightened, just as I was before in temptations with Sister Rose and Rosa.

Genuine fear was the only emotion I hadn't exposed during the evening, the only one that gushed and rushed out of me now through my mind, soul, heart and body. I was truly frightened by the proximity of disaster and the noisy resonance of temptation. I must never go to that place again. I knew that this was not the first time I had made that pledge. But this time I realized that unless I was serious about it, it was just another meaningless semantic exercise.

The *positive* parts of the evening lingered. And I savored the opportunity to relive them. I so enjoyed the company of women, especially those who were charming and gracious. I seriously questioned my decision to become a priest. As hard as I tried, that recurrent thought was something I couldn't deny nor conceal. It was inherent to my spirit.

As I entered my room and prepared for sleep, for the first time since ordination, I seriously wondered if I had made the right choice, or if, perhaps, I would have been more effective doing God's work as a husband and father. Maybe I could have served His people through *that* vocation even better than priesthood.

I remembered at the start of my long journey to the altar of God, how I prayed over the options of either becoming a priest or a dentist. As silly as it sounds, dentistry made a lot of sense back then. I was exceedingly impressionable and my love for science and girls ran a close second to my love for priesthood. Behind it all, of course, was my love for Almighty God.

I began to view priesthood and marriage as equal habitats, recognizing that exactly *what* I was doing wasn't nearly as important as why and how I was doing it. I realized that I carry my habitat with me. I *am* the habitat. Whether a priest or a dentist, it is *me* who brings my self, my soul, to the table. In other words, married to either my God or to a wife, it is *me*, the person, who will answer for myself, whether my habitat is a rectory or a family home or the heart of a loving spouse.

Now, after 30 years in pursuing *one* of those habitats, I was intrusively reflective. It wasn't that I was unhappy in my work or disenchanted with serving my God and my parishioners, it was, well . . . it was that I wanted to do both at the same time. That wasn't asking too much of God, was it? "Hey," I said to myself, "anything is possible with God." Or was it, "Nothing is impossible with God?"

The questions now were: Did I love women too much to be a perfect priest? Was the distraction of women a negative influence on my priesthood? Could I handle my future as well as I handled my past, with the courage and determination received only from God? Though I would put it aside for the time being and focus on priesthood, the dilemma was one I would battle into my years of retirement. Through it all, however, there was nothing or no one I loved more than my priesthood and my God. That was a fact that would never change.

I once heard, from a source I don't recall, "The measure of love is what one is willing to give up for it." I willed to give up my life for the love of God. Period! I would pray more strongly for His assistance, and for His mercy in sheltering me from temptations with women. That's something I would sleep on . . . for many nights.

The Infirmary

The hospital environment was not new to Margaret and her mother. They were both familiar with the smell, the sounds and the noises. The only difference in Assisi was the punctuated cadence of the Italian language and the smaller size and scope of the facility. The rest was the same as St. John's in Chicago: sickly people suffering through varying degrees of pain and misery, many of them waiting to die.

Three days after his fall, almost to the hour, Frank showed signs of emerging from his unconscious state. As the doctors predicted, he was confused but his speech was not nearly as slurred as they had expected. Annie leaned close to hear his first words.

"How did I get here?" he asked in a whisper. "Where in the hell is this? Where's Rosa? Where'd she go?"

His wife answered softly, "I'm here, darling. I'm your wife and my name is *Annie*. You don't remember. You're in a hospital." She smiled while saying that, and then continued to answer his question. "Do you remember that you're in Assisi, in Italy?"

"Where's Rosa? Where am I?"

"You're in Assisi, the birthplace of Saint Francis. You took a nasty fall when you were with Brother Pietro at the Basilica."

"With who? Where's Rosa?"

Annie showed great patience with her amnesiac husband, continuing to remind him that her name was *Annie*, not Rosa. She again addressed his questions. "You were with Brother Pietro, the friend of Father Tonelli," she said, sensing the name might mean something to her husband. "We brought you here to this hospital in Assisi after you fell down. They're taking very good care of you. So just relax and be comfortable."

"What did they do to me? God, I've got a headache, worst I've ever had."

"You're on an *IV* right now, dear. You haven't been eating and they had to give you nourishment. They also want to guard against dehydration. They want you to rest. You've had a concussion from your fall and laying here is the best medicine they can prescribe. You've got a sizeable bump on your head that took a lot of stitches to close. So you're going to have those headaches for quite awhile."

"And how about you? You all right?"

"Do you remember who I am?"

"Of course, Rosa. My God, we've been married forever, haven't we?" Regardless of what Annie said, Frank intermittently referred to his wife as *Rosa*. She had no idea where the misnomer was coming from unless it was an adaptation of her grandmother's name. Or perhaps it was a subliminal reference, a dream—or drug-induced version of her name. She patiently overlooked the incorrect reference.

"I'm all right, my dear," she said. "Margaret is here with me and we've taken a hotel just around the corner. We've been spending most of our time with you but we've managed to see a little bit of this beautiful town. We've also eaten some wonderful Italian foods. As soon as you're better, we'll take you around to all the places we've discovered. In just three days, we've visited some wonderful galleries, restaurants, antique stores . . ."

"Damn!" Frank interrupted loudly. "How could I have been so stupid? I feel as dumb as a bag of rocks. How could I have let myself fall like that? Now I've gone and ruined all your fun. Margaret . . . where are you, dearest? Come over here and let me see you." Margaret walked to her father's bedside and clutched his hand. "I'm right here, pop," she said. "I won't be going anywhere till you're all healed." The grip of his hand was stronger than she would have guessed.

"Did I miss the Convention? What about my speaking engagement?"

"We took care of it, pop. It was supposed to happen yesterday. Your friends from the Knights of Columbus left a message at the Hotel in Rome. They wanted to confirm your appearance. So Mom called them back and explained that you wouldn't be able to make it. Naturally, they were disappointed but they wished you the best and said they'd be praying for you. Now, that's something you needn't worry about."

"What about your work?" Frank asked Margaret. "What about your business? You've got to get back there."

"It can wait. There's nothing urgent going on right now," Margaret said. "So I might as well be enjoying Italy with you and mom. Besides, I'd much rather be walking around the streets of Assisi than the streets of Chicago. We've got to get you back on your feet. 'We've got bigger fish to fry,' as they say. And the biggest is getting you well."

Frank dropped his head back with a lengthy sigh. He was breathing heavily and showing signs of exhaustion from the rapid conversation. Affected by a clumpy pillow, his sparse strands of white hairs were misarranged around his head, some stretching from right to left, others traveling in random directions. The thin, uneven pieces of growth had been limited by his chemo treatments and roamed his head like wispy patches of thin silk. Margaret lovingly rearranged the errant threads and softly stroked her father's head. She and Annie waited until he fell back to sleep before they left for dinner.

Though Frank's prognosis for a full recovery from his concussion was good, they knew that his cancer was advancing and that the number of his days was restricted. They had been preparing for that eventuality over the past year.

When they returned the following morning, two doctors were waiting to give them an update on Frank's condition. Both wife and daughter were eager to hear.

"It's our opinion right now," the physician said, "that your husband should remain in Assisi long enough for his head injury to heal, at least until he shows no signs of confusion or disorientation. Flying in an airplane would be dangerous at this time."

The neurologist had a similar directive. "It would be a terrible risk to increase the stress he's already experienced. It's possible that he might not survive an international flight with all its physical and emotional demands. Needless to say, the frequent changes in altitude would be difficult for him to endure. His headaches related to the concussion would only worsen. You must remember that he's suffering from a concussive, traumatic brain injury. And it takes more than a few days for that to heal.

"Your best choice right now is to settle down in Assisi for as long as it takes. We have a beautiful village here and I'm sure you'll enjoy some quiet time with some genial people who'll become your friends. My advice is to break this news to Frank in a day or two, after he's able to comprehend."

That afternoon, Margaret and her mother took the doctor's advice. They settled back at a restaurant they had already made their favorite, knowing several people by their first names, especially an attractive young server named Giovanni who showed Margaret an extraordinary amount of attention.

The two guests, led by Giovanni, sat outside on a lovely day, sipped slowly from glasses of local wine, and enjoyed each other's company. It had been a long time since the mother and daughter had such an opportunity to relax together. They discussed the options to help Frank through his muddled state-of-mind and to help make the rest of his life meaningful as well as comfortable.

"I can predict what's coming, mom," Margaret said.

"And what's that?"

"If pop comes out of this in any reasonably mindful state, and knowing pop, he will . . . he's going to want to get back to the Basilica and visit longer with Brother Pietro."

"You're probably right, honey," Annie said. "And I agree with you that he'll come out of this, if for no other reason than to get back to the home of his dear saint, or I should say, 'saints' if I include Pietro. So we've got to be prepared to address that, before it becomes a debatable issue."

"All we can do is give pop whatever he wants," Margaret said. "We've both got to face this thing, mom. He just doesn't have many more days left. The doctors didn't even bother talking about his cancer once we gave them his prognosis. Here they are, all concerned about his *concussion* and he may not even live long enough to have it heal. Right now, I can't tell if it's the cancer or the concussion that's making him so disoriented and out-of-touch. And what's this thing about calling you Rosa?"

"I've tried, but I just can't figure it," Annie answered.

"Do you think he'll recover from his fall?"

"Does it matter?" Just remember, you *are* talking about your father, here. You know how determined he is once he sets his mind to something. If he decides that he wants to spend more time in the home of his namesake, by God, he'll work it out. You know that as well as I do."

"What do you think about phoning his oncologist back home," Margaret asked, "telling him about what's going on here. We could ask his opinion about the cancer and ask about pop's chances of surviving these critical times in what's left of his life, right here in a country he loves so much, in Italy."

"Actually," Annie replied, "That's an excellent idea. I'm surprised the doctors here didn't think of that. Let's arrange a conference-call to his oncologist and physician for tomorrow morning if it can be done. We can both be on the line."

The two smiled and enjoyed their pasta with zucchini and fresh Italian bread dipped in garlic and oil. They were making the most of their time together, in spite of the desperate condition of the man they loved so dearly. Additionally, Frank would have been overjoyed at the blossoming friendship between Giovanni Marona, the server, and Margaret. The man was slightly younger, rather dashing according to Margaret's assessment, never married, and eager to meet with her later in the evening. In spite of the dire circumstances, Margaret did accept his invitation to rendezvous privately.

Giovanni and Margaret enjoyed each other's company immensely and agreed to make such private engagements habitual.

Their friendship would prove mutually beneficial. In fact, the relationship had already become familiar enough for him to suggest she call him *John*, the English name for Giovanni. "It will make things easier," he said.

During another luncheon conversation with her mother, Margaret took it upon herself to explain the entire story of her father's gift from Brother Pietro via Father Tonelli, the story of Saint Francis' *Prayer for the Dying*. Margaret thrashed through every corner of her conscience and decided that sharing the story with her mother was not a betrayal of her father's confidence. Annie listened to every word and was amazed at the details of how The Prayer was found and how it was passed through so many channels into Frank's hands.

With great sensitivity, Margaret also explained her father's private intention offered through The Prayer: the ability to live two lifetimes, one of them being the life he had initially rejected . . . priesthood. Nothing surprised Annie. Margaret was not surprised either at her mother's response to having an alternate career that *she* might have pursued.

"I wanted to play in The Chicago Symphony Orchestra," she said. "You never heard me play the piano when I was in my prime, because obviously, you weren't born. But I had many recitals, all by myself. I was a decent pianist and could have studied longer and made music my career. But I couldn't have marriage and that career at the same time. So, your father won-out over The Chicago Symphony. And here you are, with three others who followed."

"I know this is pretty personal, mom," Margaret said, "but I'm curious. Did you ever have any regrets, any second thoughts, any doubts that you made the right choice?"

"Not a single one," Annie answered. "Never once. Sure, it would have been nice to do both but it just wasn't possible. As a matter of fact, I really can't say that I was talented enough to join the Symphony. But I did wonder. With a lot more training, I wondered just how good I could've been."

"But if you could implement *pop*'s wish, his intention through The Prayer, would you want to sample both lives?"

"I guess, if it was possible, sure. It would be an incredible experience. But I don't understand. How is your father doing all this, this living the life of a priest? Is it . . ."

Margaret interrupted. "Mom, I'd really rather not go there. That's for pop to explain. I couldn't do it even if I tried. It's something going on in his head right now, and I can't possibly explain it. Even *he* can't. You know, you probably *should* get into it with him when his mind improves. I think it's something you should hear from him. You'd be amazed at some of his stories." Annie accepted that and the subject was dropped.

Since the day Frank fell and struck his head at the Friary, Annie and Margaret had stayed in touch with the other three children back in Chicago, notifying them of their father's fall and giving them periodic reports on changes in his condition. None of the three could get away at the time and Annie encouraged them to handle their own responsibilities first, caring for their children and careers. They were unhappy about that but respected their mother's wish. They all agreed to pray for their dad and stay closely in touch.

Also on the list of contacts back in Chicago was Father Tonelli. In his role as one of Frank's closest friends, Father was shocked at the news of the concussion and had expected, if anything, that his *cancer* would have felled him. The priest's immediate reaction was to come to Frank's side and visit with him in Assisi. It was a tall order for the pastor of a large parish but Father Tonelli would "give it his best shot," in his words. Of course, Annie told him it wasn't necessary but she was sure Frank would appreciate seeing him.

As it turned out, after appealing to the compassion of the Archbishop of Chicago, Father Tonelli was able to arrange for a priest-friend to come to his church and serve as a stand-in until he returned. He didn't expect to be gone for more than a week.

For Father Tonelli, then, his trip to Rome was much more than a vacation. It was a pilgrimage, an urgent trip to visit with his dying friend and give him his blessing, especially in the location where *A Prayer for the Dying* originated. Also, though it was but a dream, he would seize the opportunity to arrange a common visit with himself, Brother Pietro and Frank.

The conference-call with Frank's two doctors in Chicago came off perfectly. Margaret and Annie were both able to speak with the doctors, solicit their personal counsel and then attempt to implement their advice. But the latter would not be easy. They agreed that, if it was important enough to Frank, even critical to his healing, he could be moved to the *Sacro Convento*, the Franciscan Friary which stands beside the great Upper and Lower Basilicas. That would place him under the care of *The Friars of the Third Order Regular,* the formal name given to the Order of Brothers created by Saint Francis.

The influence and friendship of Brother Pietro was tantamount in getting Frank accepted as a patient in the "infirmary," a place of physical healing set aside for Priests and Brothers. Originally, in the 15th century, during the reign of Pope Sixtus IV, the *Sacro Convento* was extensively enlarged and used as a summer residence of the popes. But in the 17th century, the kings of Spain endowed the same area with a hospice so that the Friars could provide for infirmed pilgrims. Here and now, Frank was in the right place at the right time. He attributed that to his strong belief in *Divine Intervention*.

In his new home of rich and historic tradition, Frank was, indeed, in good company, in an excellent environment in which to connect with the spirit of Saint Francis. It was, after all, the earthly habitat, the *home* of the great Saint. When Frank first heard the news of his transfer, he thanked God for the blessing, knowing he was likely to breathe his last breath within the blessed walls of *Sacro Convento*.

The room assigned to Frank was Spartan but comfortable, designed in the style of a Friar's quarters. The bed was a twin bed in size, the frame hand-hewn from Assisi wood, and the old-style straw mattress replaced by a conventional mattress. The walls were bare save only for a crucifix hanging over a small wooden dresser. A single lamp and window allowed enough light for reading.

Since Frank would spend most of his time in bed, the only other place to sit was on a rather uncomfortable wooden chair. Frank would be taken to meals and to Mass in a similarly uncomfortable wooden wheelchair. Its construction and primitive design dated back to the days of Francis himself. For an unknown reason, its annoying creak pleased Frank and caused him to smile each time it was activated.

In that environment, the recovering patient improved slowly and slightly from his concussion. His speech was better and his confusion minimal. He even stopped calling Annie, *Rosa*. Though he was as sharp as could be expected and ecstatic at being moved to the grounds of his namesake, he was also aware of the progression of his cancer. He recognized, too, that he was rapidly losing weight and growing weaker each day. He had no appetite. Even the sight and odor of food made him ill and caused vomiting. He did, however, continue to drink juices for hydration. Though his mind understood all of that, his body was retreating. He understood that, too.

Seven days passed quietly after Frank entered the infirmary. The time was spent with Annie and Margaret and in frequent visits with his faithful friend, Brother Pietro. It would be a pleasant surprise to see Father Tonelli in just two more days. Family and friends hoped the shock of seeing his friend in Assisi was something he could handle emotionally.

One peaceful afternoon, while Margaret and Annie were visiting, the patient began discussing an article he had just read in an American periodical they had brought him. The discussion offered a unique topic, one that did not focus on death, prayer, or the next life. They had searched for anything to distract the patient from such subjects that were fast becoming obsessions for all three of them. This fresh and stimulating dialogue served the purpose well.

But before Frank began his lecture, he warned his audience of his current mental shortcomings. "You're going to have to be patient with me," he said, "because the last couple of days, I've felt like my brain is as frayed as an old rope. My thoughts just aren't clear. The mind's not clicking like it used to . . . so just bear with me."

In spite of that warning, Frank caught everyone off guard with his subject-matter. "Have you ever heard of a concept attributed to William of Ockham?" he asked. "Ockham proposed his original idea back in the 14th century." Both women were perplexed, figuring Frank had regressed to his amnesiac state. Margaret managed a sensible reply.

"Yes, I've heard of it, pop. I've always appreciated the theory. But does this have something, *anything* to do with, with what's going on here, I mean with your condition and Assisi?"

"Of course, my dear. Let me explain how I've made a connection between Ockham and our sad state of affairs here."

"Go right ahead, pop. Mom and I are eager to hear your thoughts." Annie settled back in the rock-hard wooden chair, wondering how long the discussion would take. Margaret leaned against the dresser and made herself as comfortable as possible. The subject was, indeed, a diversion, albeit an awkward one.

"Well," Frank began, "it's the idea that, in trying to understand something, getting *unnecessary information* out of the way is the fastest way to the truth or to the most accurate explanation."

Margaret and her mother coyly glanced a wink at each other as Frank continued with the unwieldy details of his complex topic.

"Here, let me read exactly what it says here," Frank went on. "'It's a philosophy that reconciles religious belief with demonstrable, generally experienced truth, mainly by separating the two. Where earlier philosophers attempted to justify God's existence with rational proof, Ockham declared religious belief to be incapable of such proof and a matter of faith. He rejected the notions preserved from Classical times of the independent existence of qualities such as truth, hardness and durability and said these ideas had value only as descriptions of particular objects and were really characteristics of human cognition.'" Margaret and Annie frowned at one another as their mouths opened wide at the depth of Frank's readings from the magazine.

"It also says, 'Ockham was noted for his insistence on paying close attention to *language* as a tool for thinking and on *observation* as a tool for testing reality. His thinking and writing is considered to have laid the groundwork for modern scientific inquiry.'" Again,

Annie and her mother were shocked at Frank's grasp of such complicated thoughts.

"Okay, pop," Margaret said. "Now where does that get us? Mom and I are ready for you to connect the dots."

"Don't you see, my dear? *Annie*, you get it, don't you?"

His wife rolled her eyes just enough to imply a negative answer but not enough to offend him. He then went on.

"Okay, the two of you listen closely. The *'unnecessary information* that I'm getting out of the way to get to the truth,' is this: the reason all this is happening to me here in Assisi, is that my passing will be easier on the two of you and the rest of the family if I die here."

Margaret replied quickly, "Doesn't seem to make sense, pop. That ignores the involvement of God. That's giving rational proof to your death in Assisi and that justifies God's existence. That's closer to the thinking of the early philosophers rather than Ockham."

"You're wrong, my dear daughter. It merely provides an explanation for this complex scenario. Don't you see that my death here will make everything easier on the family back in Chicago? It's always been God's plan. I feel that in my bones."

Margaret and Annie were not only confused by Frank's disjointed reasoning, but they were continually perplexed by his references to Ockham's razor. It didn't seem like the time or the place for such tedious verbal adventures. But loving him as deeply as they did, they excused him and attributed his ramblings to the proximity of death, the lingering discontinuity caused by his concussion, and his twelve daily medications.

At any rate, the diversion didn't cause any harm. It actually brought relief to the two listeners who thoughtfully journeyed through the labyrinthine discourse. But they never resolved the issue; moreover, they continued to wrestle with the premise that Frank's death in Assisi would make things easier on his family in Chicago. And that reasoning was attributed to Ockham's razor? The dissertation reminded Margaret of a similar chat she and her father recently enjoyed on "nature versus nurture." Perhaps both of the subjects were irrelevant but they were clearly active in the mind of Frank Chase.

All that notwithstanding, Frank's family was not privy to the power and the beauty of *A Prayer for the Dying*. Consistent with his habit, Frank had been reciting The Prayer three times daily since his consciousness, most of the recitations from memory rather than from reading. And "it was not an easy prayer to memorize," he once boasted.

Margaret and Annie acknowledged that there was a broad chasm between Ockham's razor and the special new prayer, the latter having considerably more impact on Frank's life. The family members were in agreement on that observation.

As the time grew nearer for Father Tonelli to make his surprise appearance, Annie and Margaret visited Frank twice daily. They continued their stay at the Hotel San Francesco, a most beautiful hostel near the historical center of Assisi and within view of the great Basilica. They had arranged for Father Tonelli to stay at the same location.

The San Francesco was a comfortable and practical choice. It provided all the amenities of European hospitality plus the most important benefit of all, location. It was an easy walk directly to the Basilica compound. They opted to handle it that way rather than maintaining a 24/7 vigil at Frank's bedside when his current condition was increasingly bleak. The Hotel also provided a place of preparation, a peaceful harbor of privacy for tearful outbreaks and unlimited embraces.

In spite of the impending tragedy, both Annie and Margaret accepted the reality of Frank's death and were not at all surprised by his heroic acceptance. Beneath it all, they feared not so much the known but the *un*known. In addition to Frank's dying, they struggled with a different dimension of disturbing feelings, of uncertainty, of another climactic event looming just over the horizon, one as dramatic as death itself. They couldn't explain their anxiety but waited impatiently for the "event" to occur. It was a nonplusing experience.

In the meantime, because Frank was no longer eating or drinking and death was so near, Brother Pietro had arranged to have one of his Brothers stay with Frank in his room, even during his sleep. Brother *Daniel* slept on a cot beside Frank.

On one occasion, the attentive Brother was convinced that Frank had passed away. He could find no visible signs of life for ten minutes, no sound from his lips, no twitch or shudder of any kind. Even when he gently placed his hand on Frank's chest, there was little movement. On the day before, Frank had experienced congested, heavy, and noisy breathing. He had actually stopped breathing for several seconds but still showed a pulse when Brother held his fingers to his wrist.

Brother Pietro appeared at 3:00 a.m. to visit his friend and to verify that he was still alive. Frank remained in an unusually deep sleep but continued breathing. Annie and Margaret were notified of his rapidly deteriorating condition and arrived at his bedside in early morning. They assessed his noisy breathing and determined that it was, sadly but mercifully, the predictable "death rattle."

In spite of that condition, his wife and daughter continued to repeat the phrase, "I love you." Each time, Frank responded ever-so-quietly with a gentle smile and the words, "Me, too."

Priestly Retirement

I retired as pastor of Ascension Parish when I celebrated my 70th birthday. It was the mandatory retirement age for priests in the Archdiocese of Chicago. Five years earlier, however, I received a wonderful honor from my Bishop. I was named a *Monsignor,* an honorary title which recognized my long-standing loyalty to the Archdiocese and my dedication to years of directing retreats and other engagements that involved public speaking. I was extremely proud of the honor but reminded myself that I was "merely dust and into dust I shall return." That reflection kept my ego in check. My *Reverend Monsignor* designation seemed to please my friends and associates even more than it pleased me.

At the retirement age, I was given several options. One was to purchase private property and live in my own residence. That was impractical and unaffordable since my mom and dad's small inheritance had evaporated a long time before. A second option was to move to Bishop Lyne Residence, a housing and care center for retired priests. I didn't feel quite old enough to live there though I had maintained a deep respect for those retired men who chose it for their retirement.

The third offering was, indeed, my preference. It allowed me to remain active as a priest by accepting an invitation for residence at Holy Name Cathedral and concurrently taking assignments as a temporary substitute at a diversity of parishes throughout the Diocese. It was a dream-come-true: while I had none of the pressing duties of a younger priest, I was able to celebrate daily Mass and administer the sacraments while working out of the Cathedral.

Importantly, too, I could continue my favorite priestly duty of delivering homilies and retreats at the various venues around the area. It was an exceptional situation that was supported by my perfect health. I took no medication, remained physically fit, and had controlled my weight. The Archbishop was pleased to have me in a flexible program through which he could send me where the need was greatest. Most of my assignments lasted anywhere from two to three weeks. If there was room at the visiting rectory, I temporarily shifted my residence to that location. I continued in that capacity until I reached my current age of 77.

The priest who replaced me at Saint Francis became a good friend. Father Jamie Quinn did his job well and we had many lengthy chats about the operation of the parish. We enjoyed each other's company and shared meals together at least once every month.

Father Jim was in his late 50's when he approached me with an offer to travel abroad with him, to two of my favorite cities in the world, Rome and Assisi. An excellent artist in residence at Saint Francis Parish had painted an extraordinary likeness of Saint Francis of Assisi and gifted it to the pastor with the request that it be donated to the priests and brothers at the Basilica. The parish governing body then raised money to send Father Quinn and a traveling companion to Assisi to deliver the painting in person. When Father Jim invited me to accompany him, I could not refuse. He made all the travel arrangements and we were soon on our way.

Since Jim and I had become such close friends, I shared most of the stories of my priestly life. I told him everything about my friendship with Sister Mary Rose and my encounter with Rosa of his parish. He made little of the intrusive *opportunities* to my priestly commitment and, instead, found the stories amusing rather than threatening. I explained about the incident on the bus ride to Assisi and the distraction of Rosa in Rome. I told him, "I was short-changed on my first visit to Assisi and this is an opportunity to make things right." He understood and agreed.

Father Jim had the 24" x 36" painting shipped before us and we picked it up at a *Fedex* drop in Rome. Once in our hotel, Jim opened it for me and I was overwhelmed by the unique treatment and the heavy and masterful brushstrokes of the artist. It portrayed the great Saint in complex, brilliant colors, contrasting to previously monochromatic depictions. It thus more accurately captured the essence of a man with extraordinary human dynamism rather than one who spent his life in pious and private meditation.

I was proud to accompany Jim on his delivery mission to Assisi, but only *after* we visited Rome for two days. Jim had been to Rome twice before but we still felt obligated to see our favorite spots. In just two days, we visited the four Cathedrals, the Sistine Chapel, the Fountain of Trevi and the Coliseum. I was compelled to introduce Jim to the *Piazza Navona* and Tre Scalini since those favorite places were still loaded with extraordinary memories.

I knew that Jim would appreciate the excellent ambience and the fine desserts and drinks. If I said I didn't think about my meetings in that same place with Rosa, I'd be lying. There were youthful thoughts that bore little resemblance to the mind and body of a 77-year-old priest. It was in 1971 when we first met there, when I was just 36 years old.

I recalled exactly how she looked as she confidently strutted across that piazza like a model on a runway, then turned toward my table and into my life. Though at the time, she was deceiving me and I her, our games hurt neither of us and my recollections were pure, colorful visions with fond thoughts of an extraordinary woman. Over the years, as we developed greater wisdom and judgment, we emerged into a deep but innocent friendship that continues to this day.

While Jim and I were passing time at Tre Scalini, eating our tartufo and chatting about each and every passerby, we also digressed and discussed personal topics. Case in point: I was interested in his "take" on a corner of my conscience that had been bothering me in my older age. Jim was most eager and willing to exchange such fathomless ideas, "meaningless hang-ups," he'd respectfully call them. I explained my views on what I considered the inherent selfishness of all human beings. I began with a question.

"Did you ever perceive human life to be one single act of self-indulgent pleasure-seeking?" Jim waited briefly to digest the relevance and the weight of the question.

"Are you referring to yourself?" he asked.

"Yes!" I replied. "I've been analyzing my own self and realizing that most of what I've done as a priest and most of what I'm all about is terribly selfish. Have you ever viewed your own life like that?" His answer was as I'd expected.

"Never really dwelled on that, Francis. But I don't see how you arrived at such a conclusion. What's your reasoning?"

"Well, most of what I've done, even the charitable works with the poor, the time I've given to the Unwed Mothers Program, working with the retarded, everything in that genre of my life . . . all of it can fall into the category of selfishness."

"How can you possibly conclude that?" Jim asked.

"It's as clear as can be. I enjoyed it so much and was feeling so good inside after each of those actions that I figure I primarily did them for myself. Doesn't that make it selfish?" Jim shook his head and smiled, indicating exasperation.

"You actually beat yourself up over such foolish little things?" he asked. "Don't you have more important things to reflect on? How about the fact that you began each of those acts to help someone else. You were doing it to make somebody *else* happy, weren't you?" The tone of his dialogue was more of a compliment than a chastisement. I argued that in my reply.

"That's not the way it turned out, Jim. In a lot of cases, the other person wasn't made happy at all. But *I was*. I always seemed to get more out of it than the recipient did."

"So how can you call that selfish if you didn't *intend* it to be that way? I assume that your intention was to give of yourself rather than to get something back, right?"

"Of course," I said. "But I think you're getting my point. Think about the charitable stuff *you've* done and tell me you didn't feel good about it afterwards."

"Yes, I did," Jim shot back. "But that wasn't my intention. My intention and your intention when doing something for another person, was and is to give of yourself. And that's not selfishness."

"So you say it's all in the *intention* of the giver, right? And I say that most of our actions in life are done for ourselves. How about eating, going to a movie, sitting here like we are now . . . even *sleeping* is done for our own pleasure, isn't it?

"Almost every single act you can think of is done for self," I continued. "How many of the people passing us in this beautiful Piazza, how many of them are *not* doing it for themselves? We're a hedonistic lot, we humans. We're inherently narcissistic. Ironically, some of those pleasures come back to haunt us, like the self-inflicted suffering of so many Americans these days through over-eating, a classic example of what I'm talking about. Living for self. Just study all the overweight people walking past us right now."

"For one thing, Francis, *you* don't overeat. I'll bet you're as thin as you were when you were ordained. In fact, you're so thin and healthy . . . why, you're a poster-boy for 'senior citizens in good health.'"

"See . . . everything you just mentioned is done for myself. Even the healthy things I do are done for *me*."

"Okay," Jim said, "answer this, my Monsignoral friend. Would you call Jesus selfish when He fed the multitudes with loaves and fish? I'm sure He felt good about relieving their hunger but He didn't perform that act for Himself. His satisfaction was the *result* of His good act.

"Here's another one for you," Jim said. "How about heaven?"

"What do you mean, 'how about heaven?'" I asked.

"Well, the whole *concept* of heaven . . . it's something God used to motivate us to obey His commandments. And getting there will certainly make us happy. Do you think it's *selfish* to want to get to heaven, even though it benefits us?"

I laughed out loud and acknowledged that Father Jim had me on that point. But I had a rebuttal, skimpy as it was. I cleared my throat and grunted once or twice before I said, "It could be that Him being God, He knew of our inherent selfishness and counted on it to help us save our souls and to reach our heavenly reward."

"So is there anything wrong with that?" he asked.

"Not exactly. But does the end justify the means?"

Throughout our discussion, Jim played with his spoon, twirling it with his fingers in anxious, perpetual motion. When I noticed that movement, I sensed that I was guilty of overkill in defending my point-of-view. The debate had unnerved my kind friend. And I was sorry for that. It was time to stop. I apologized.

In such discussions, it was not uncommon for me to push the envelope a bit too far. Jim quickly accepted my apology with a smile and remarked, "Now that you've finished, let's go eat," he said with facetious intent. "Let's get some *real* food. I've had enough of this delicate, little tartufo stuff. Let's go for some pasta, homemade bread and some Italian beer or wine, as long as it's all *loaded* with calories."

"Sounds like a great idea," I said. "I know just the place." We walked out of the Piazza and around the corner to diligently and pleasurably stuff ourselves.

Following two days of such good times in Rome, Father Jim and I headed to Assisi to deliver the Saint Francis painting. We had been invited far in advance to concelebrate Mass at the Basilica. An English Mass was scheduled every Sunday at 8:30 a.m. and for this one, we were joined by another priest from Chicago. It was a pleasure to meet Father Tony Tonelli from Saint Francis of Assisi Parish in Oak Park, Illinois, and to share God's altar with him. I was introduced only as *Monsignor Francis* from Chicago.

With Father Jim off to one side, Father Tonelli and I exchanged neighborly greetings and smiled at our chance meeting so far from home. Each of us deftly concealed several double-takes as we struggled to recall a previous meeting. In no more than a minute, I remembered the time and the place. It was during my early years as a priest at St. William on the South Side.

On a Fall afternoon, when the parish was celebrating its annual "Oktoberfest" on the church grounds, I was introduced to Father Tonelli by another priest who knew him well. He explained that Father Tonelli had a close friend who had the same name as mine but was a layman; hence, his name was simply Frank Chase. Initially, that meant nothing to me because I knew there were at least nine different people in the Chicago phone book who shared our same names. That was the first and last time I heard of Father Tonelli and Frank Chase. Until now!

I stared at my fellow priest as he verbally noted that my facial expressions and the movement of my lips did remind him very much of his friend, Dr. Chase. He explained that the man was in Assisi and near death in the infirmary as we spoke. I paused and pondered that extraordinary coincidence and remarked, "I'd like very much to meet your friend right after we finish-up here." Father Tonelli said that he hoped Frank Chase would still be alive by that time because he was in grave condition. We did agree, however, to give it a try.

That momentary distraction put aside, I reflected on the privilege to concelebrate Mass within the walls of the burial place of Saint Francis. It was a treasured opportunity. I was humbled by the once-in-a-lifetime experience, the fulfillment of one of the most ambitious dreams of my 56 years as a priest. We would celebrate at the main altar in the Upper Basilica, a glorious setting enriched by ceiling and walls of magnificent stained glass, mosaics and frescoes from the 13th century.

Adding to the visual beauty surrounding the altar was the vocal embellishment of Gregorian Chant provided by a small choir of Friars. The added ambience of the chanting deeply affected my sensitivities as I tried to concentrate on the words of the Mass and comfortably mix them with overwhelming shudders of personal joy. I was most grateful for such a blessing and let the Lord know it throughout the Mass.

Expected/Unexpected

Because of their resignation to God's will and the fact that they were taught to recognize the final signs, Frank's family and their friend, Father Tony Tonelli, stood at Frank's bedside. Frank awoke lightly to look into the sober faces of his wife, daughter, Brother Pietro, and Father Tonelli. They had all arrived just as the early light of day entered the window of his room. It was that light that awakened him, though his vision was blurred by clouded eyes.

Frank didn't recognize Father Tonelli who could visit for only a few minutes because of his commitment to celebrate the 8:30 mass in the Basilica. Father prayed he would return before anything dramatic occurred in Frank's room. Though he was uncomfortable leaving his close friend at such a critical time, he must honor his commitment to the Mass.

Moments after he left, Annie held her husband's hands and found them unusually cool to her touch. His fingers and lips were slowly turning blue. In one last enormous effort, while clutching his wife's hands, Frank slowly and softly whispered into her ear:

"I'll always love you. Very soon, I'll know if I lived twice."

At 9:10 a.m. on that 24th day of June, 2012, Frank Chase, the dentist from Chicago, Illinois, inhaled and exhaled his last breath. As he transitioned from human life at the age of 77, Margaret drew close to touch him one last time. He moved his lips and whispered the word, "Wow!"

For Annie and Margaret, there was solace in three elements of Frank's death; first, the place: Frank passed to his new life within the sacred edifice of his beloved Saint of Assisi, his namesake, the man called, *Francis*; second, the terrible struggle with his deadly disease had ended; and third, he would discover the absolute truth behind the mystery of living two lives. Those elements of his passage would forever remain sources of consolation to his family and friends.

Between the location of that final breath and the altar in the Basilica where Monsignor Francis and Father's Tonelli and Quinn were celebrating Mass lay a sprawling system of hallways, naves, walkways, corridors, and dozens of rooms of varying size and shape, all connecting the buildings of the *Sacro Convento* to the main Basilica. It took a considerable amount of time to follow the winding maze that challenged walkers with circuitous stairways and halls of deviating courses that appeared to end nowhere but in darkness.

Multiple levels added further confusion for those who would travel from one area to the other. Within the *Convento* itself was a complex of rooms that included a refectory, dormitory, Chapter hall, Papal hall and the huge scriptorium-library. So it was no surprise that Frank's family heard nothing of the frenzied activity at the end of the Mass in the Basilica.

Following the distribution of the Eucharist and after the last blessing, with only minutes of the Mass remaining, Monsignor Francis, standing on the highest level of the sanctuary in the center of the altar and facing the congregation, leaned forward onto the altar . . . and suddenly dropped backwards, collapsing to the floor. At exactly 9:10 a.m. on the 24th day of June in the year 2012, Monsignor Francis Chase, retired pastor of Ascension Parish in Oak Park, Illinois, died and passed to a new life . . . at the age of 77.

There were futile attempts to revive the elderly priest, first, from his concelebrants Fathers Tonelli and Quinn on the steps of the altar; then from a Physician who was a member of the congregation; and finally, from paramedics who arrived within minutes. The diagnosis was "death from massive cardiac arrest." The attack came without warning and without notable symptoms. It was instant and fatal, casting a dark pall over the Basilica and the congregation. The Chicago priest, Monsignor Francis Chase would never meet Dr. Frank Chase, the dentist.

The blinking lights of emergency vehicles painted the outer walls of the holy Basilica with rotating shades of blue and white. The vocal noise inside the building segued to voices that were silenced. It appeared for a moment that time did not pass.

Not surprisingly, the shock and sadness at the sudden death of Monsignor Francis was initially confined to the area of the Basilica. Even Brother Pietro at the *Sacro Convento* heard nothing of the tragedy until Father Tonelli returned to visit Frank, some 40 minutes later. With a more effective communication system, Brother Pietro could have arrived at the priest's side more quickly because he knew his way around the Basilica compound as well as a blind man knows his way around his room. Perhaps after this experience, Brother could more readily suggest cell phones for use by the Friary staff.

As it was, after learning of Frank's unsurprising death, Father Tonelli regretted that he could not have brought Father Francis to meet his friend of the same name. Both men had thus died simultaneously in the home of Saint Francis, together yet apart. In essence, the events comprised the traumatic endings to two concurrent lifetimes compacted into one person.

Though each had lived separately, they existed within the same spirit and soul of one human person. Unarguably, that fact was a mystery, a matter of faith, a Godly answer to a private prayer allegedly written by Saint Francis and discovered in the ceiling of his Church.

The effectiveness of The Prayer was arguable, but only a handful of people within the Basilica and the *Sacro Convento* knew of the metaphysical act of Divine Providence through which two lives were conjoined in a single soul, then reconfigured from two human deaths into one *life-after-death*.

If each *Frank* was privileged to witness the simultaneous death of the other, he would not have accepted attribution to serendipity or coincidence because both believed that an act of such timing and precision was most certainly an act of God's will. "Every good action on earth," they had stated separately, "has a purpose, a raison d'etre, a destination for which it is intended."

All of that notwithstanding, the beginning of the distinct journeys occurred many months earlier when Brother Pietro first explained the story of the manuscript containing *A Prayer for the Dying* and subsequently handed a copy to Father Tonelli for use by Frank. Father now recalled that series of events and the disjointed stories Frank shared about living another life as a priest. As it was, Frank's rambling, incoherent tales of entrance into a new and coexisting lifetime made little sense to the priest. Nor did he dare to superimpose the life and death of Father Francis over the scenario. It was too preposterous to entertain, even slightly.

Remarkably, it was only Father Tonelli among all the primary figures in their life and times who actually met both Frank's. Only an hour ago at the Basilica, he had encountered *Father* Francis when they each recalled meeting decades earlier. Since that time, he never connected the priest with his friend, Frank Chase. But then again, Father Tonelli was no youngster himself and many such pressing items challenged his mentality. Having missed the opportunity, he would never appreciate his unique gift to know both Doctor Frank Chase and Monsignor Francis Chase during their simultaneous lives on earth. That thought defied comprehension.

For Annie and Margaret, their dauntless love and their fondest thoughts of Frank's story-telling were intensified by memories of his originality and imagination. He would not have taken kindly to the use of such words, however, because he intensely believed his experiences were *not* products of his "originality or imagination," but rather, were actual segments of two adjoining lives.

Just when it seemed that the mysterious adventure of Frank Chase was about to end without resolution, with no witness to "connect the dots," his daughter Margaret came to the fore. At the time, there was no one else with enough accumulated knowledge about the incidents in Frank's life to arrange the puzzling pieces into a discernible picture.

So at the apparent conclusion of Frank's story, enter again, daughter Margaret, the single offspring who escorted her mother and father to the birthplace of Saint Francis. It is that *Margaret* who was driven to assemble critical information to satisfy her intense curiosity, fueled by a passion to seek answers for the unanswerable. Most certainly, that ardor was a trait inherited from her father.

Margaret was surely as qualified as anyone to act in behalf of her deceased father, even more so than Father Tonelli, Annie, or anyone else for that matter. Given Margaret's conscientious approach to most any act of value, her assumed responsibility was later to surface as a sizeable asset. She accepted the role as the most logical person to unearth evidence to support her father's claims of setting foot into a second lifetime while both feet were still planted in a first. If there were holes in his story, so be it. When Margaret completed her study based on the facts, any such existing holes would remain unquestionable mysteries for all time.

The immediate business at hand was for Margaret and her mother to arrange for the celebration of a Requiem Mass for Frank at the Basilica. Brother Pietro handled the details and Father Tonelli remained long enough to celebrate the Mass.

Largely because of his relationship with Father Tonelli and his acquired friendship with Frank and his family, Brother Pietro secured permission for the Mass to be celebrated at the *Papal High Altar* in the lower church, just above the crypt where Saint Francis lay in repose. This was a great privilege that would have made Frank proud as it honored his humility as a faithful servant of God in the Roman Catholic Church. Father Tonelli was assisted by Brothers who functioned as servers and doubled as the voices of a choir. Frank had always revered Gregorian Chant.

The setting of the Mass was most remarkable. The *Papal High Altar* is surrounded by dominant works of art, some that depict St. Francis' life in parallel with the life of Christ. The Altar itself features colorful mosaic designs and delicate columns topped by a marble stone placed there in the year 1230. The slab is believed to be from Constantinople. The 50 Gothic walnut choir-stalls are arranged in two tiers, carved and completed in 1471 and featuring sculptures of leaves, animals and humans on the armrests.

This same altar in the apse is sustained by a series of ornamented Gothic arches, supported by columns in different styles. The stained glass windows were also finished around 1471, each one unique in its intricacies and original designs.

The actual sacrifice of the Mass, the centerpiece for all the artistic accoutrements, was both spiritually reverent and emotionally touching. Annie and Margaret were enormously pleased as were the 20-plus visitors whom Brother Pietro invited to attend.

Father Tonelli was definitely in his element, enjoying every single prayer of the Mass, especially his personalization of the Requiem inclusions for his long-time friend and confidant. It was no less touching for him than for anyone else participating in the ceremony.

Father Tonelli was obviously in a state of rapture as he shared in the quietist Mass he had ever celebrated. The responses of the faithful were barely intelligible. The choir of five male voices chanted in Latin, in deep and serene voices that faintly supplemented the hush. The environment was so intimate that the slightest echo was notable. Even the soft breath of incense seemed to emit a thin whisper.

In-between the chanting, the absence of voices was so pronounced that if a person listened closely, he could hear the sound of melting wax dripping from the dozens of candles. No one in the inspiring setting would ever forget the holy and symbiotic relationship between all the elements. It would be impossible to reconstruct or to surpass.

Though Annie and Margaret wished that the rest of their family—children, grandchildren, siblings, aunts, uncles—could be there, it was willed that they be the only family members to be sitting, standing and kneeling at Frank's side during this special "celebration of life."

Following that Mass in Assisi, Frank's body was cremated and the cremains carried back to Chicago by Annie and Margaret. There, in his parish church of Saint Francis, a simple service was a prayerful memorial to Frank, thus allowing his friends and all members of his family to pay their respects in his parish home.

The ceremony was executed to the thoughtful plans of mother and daughter as they both grieved deeply for the best man they ever knew. They demonstrated their gratitude by making his final bow memorable. They were honored by the large showing of his friends from the American Dental Association and his "Brother Knights" from the Knights of Columbus. Frank would have been most proud at the tribute by his loyal companions who accompanied him on his journey. But his story was far from complete after his burial.

Margaret had placed her father's obituary in the Chicago Tribune to appear for three days. After the last day, the body of Father Francis Chase was scheduled to arrive at *Dunahue*'s, the designated Funeral Home in Chicago, having been shipped by Father Jamie Quinn as a service to the Archdiocese of Chicago. Father Francis was scheduled to be buried at St. Joseph's Cemetery alongside his parents and grandparents.

The obituary for Father Francis Chase ran in the Tribune for three days, starting on the day that Frank's obit stopped. So the announcements for Frank and Father Francis never ran on any of the same days. The Requiem Funeral Mass for Father Francis was scheduled to be held at Holy Name Cathedral. His Mass would be attended by as many of the priests of the Archdiocese as could be accommodated, easily over 300 members of the local clergy.

On the very morning of that funeral, Margaret was enjoying a quiet breakfast in her parent's home, sitting beside her mother as they shared the reading of the morning *Trib*. Since it was the first day of her father's obit *not* to appear, out of habit, she perused the columns of those who had recently passed.

In an instant, the startled Margaret stopped and stared at the name, "The Reverend Monsignor Francis Chase." It was followed by copy that traced the priest's local history from his birthplace in Chicago to his education for the priesthood, on to his first assignment at Saint William Parish and his subsequent work as the pastor of Ascension Parish in Oak Park, Illinois.

To Margaret, the nearly identical name seemed more than a coincidence. She was even more startled at the date and place of the priest's death: June 24, 2012, in Assisi, Italy! As she turned to reveal the column to her mother, Margaret became speechless, silently pointing to the words and dates following the name of the deceased. She unintentionally and momentarily ceased to breath. From that minute on, she and her mother had a front row seat to chaos.

Annie was astounded at the print before her. She recoiled and said to Margaret, "What do you make of this? My God, it's the same date and place that your father died just ten days ago. And the similarity of names. Is this all a coincidence, serendipity . . . some kind of sick joke? How in the world . . ."

Margaret reclaimed the newspaper and studied it further. The type didn't alter or disappear. The facts remained as cold and clear as they were before. And that struck a nerve! The inquisitive Margaret absolutely *had* to investigate for herself. Her curiosity would be a catalyst to either a confirmation or dissipation of the facts. She would begin with the people at the Tribune. She firmly believed that the obituary was either a misprint, a malformation of facts, or a superimposition of details that overlapped the information she had provided in her father's obituary.

Margaret spoke by telephone to the head of the department responsible for logging obituaries at the Tribune. The woman confirmed that all of the information about Father Francis Chase was correct. She verified that it was provided by two reliable sources: a friend of Father Francis named Father Jamie Quinn and the secretary to the Archbishop at Holy Name Cathedral.

Margaret had hoped for a quick and easy solution to the puzzle but it was not about to happen. Her mother commended her for having accomplished so much in just one morning, the actual day of the funeral for Father Francis. It was only noon and the Mass was scheduled for 1:00 p.m. Margaret could and would make it to that Mass.

The ambitious, dauntless woman hoped to meet with any blood relatives of the deceased priest and/or close friends who could verify and clarify some of the personal information. She refused to believe that the identical facts about both men in question were mere coincidence. Her motivation was to confirm a connection between Frank's tales of living two lives and the simultaneous deaths of him and a priest, both of the same names, at the same location in Assisi.

Margaret was running on adrenaline as she ignored speed limits en route to the Cathedral. She parked hurriedly in an illegal spot when she arrived, only minutes before the processional that preceded the Mass. She found an empty seat at the rear of the Church and worshipped in honor of *Father* Francis Chase. For her, it was a bizarre experience.

After Mass, Father Francis would be taken from the Cathedral to the cemetery. "Visitation" was held two days earlier at *Dunahue's Funeral Home* but the casket was closed to all who paid their respects. It was a wise choice that was advised by the hospital in Assisi and facilitated by the administrators of the Cathedral. The decision was dictated by the fact that Father's face was badly disfigured from the fall onto the concrete floor as he collapsed from the heart attack in the Basilica.

Margaret learned all of that from one of the usher's in church as she followed the casket and the congregation out the large doors following the completion of the Mass. Her goal was to view the body, at least once, to establish any or no physical resemblance between Father Francis and her father. Though it might be personally difficult under the circumstances of disfigurement, it remained a "must" on her list.

So, as the crowd passed out of the church doors, Margaret moved quickly to the front of the line to speak to the Funeral Director, an unattractive man who was morbidly obese and made it obvious that he was in charge. He was, of course, extremely occupied as he and his associates moved the casket from the dolly into the rear of the hearse. At that moment, Margaret broke loose from the crowd and pushed her way to face the Director.

"Excuse me," she said politely but with authority. She got his attention but elicited a quick rebuff. "Can't you see I'm busy here, lady. What do you need?"

"I need to ask you a favor," she said, pushing closer to the man who stood at the open rear door of the hearse. Just as he was about to close the door, Margaret stepped in and blocked it with her shoulder, a daring move considering the size of the person she was confronting. He was adamant as he took her by the arm and prepared to push her aside.

"I wouldn't do that!" she said bravely as she stared into his eyes. "Take your hand off my arm, sir," she insisted. He did so but was angry and belligerent. "So what's your damn favor?" he asked.

"I'll be heading to the cemetery with the rest of these people," Margaret said. "And I'll stay around after the graveside service. If you've got a minute, I'd like to ask you a couple of questions. Could you be available for me?"

The angry man glanced aside as if he didn't hear Margaret, slammed the rear door and quickly jumped into the driver's seat. He was already moving away as she leaned into his face from outside the window and mouthed, "I'll see you there."

A procession of over 40 cars flowed from the Cathedral to St. Joseph's Cemetery. The closest relatives of Father Francis who attended the Mass were cousins who were with their families. The others were friends who knew the priest from his assignment at Ascension Parish before his retirement to the Cathedral.

An unusually attractive woman who appeared to be in her 80's stood beside the few relatives at the gravesite. She received a lot of attention and had obviously been a very close friend. All that Margaret could learn was that her name was Rosa and she had known Father Francis for almost 50 years.

One other noticeable guest at the gravesite caught Margaret's eye. She was a nun wearing a short, white habit that covered her head and a normal-length skirt. Her clothing resembled the attire of many current nuns. She was addressed simply as Sister Mary Rose, another friend of the deceased. It appeared as a beautiful gesture that each of the two women named "Rose" placed a single red rose on the casket. No one needed to explain and no one gave it much attention.

When the service ended, with the casket still raised above the empty grave, the crowd dispersed slowly and Margaret made her move toward the Funeral Director. He saw her coming and walked quickly toward his car. She shouted, "Uh, sir, could you wait just a minute?"

He ignored her. She shouted louder, "Sir, do you hear me? Could you stop and talk to me for a minute? I don't appreciate being ignored like this. Would you please stop?"

The man turned to her and, from ten yards away, shouted obscenities. That got the attention of one of the motorcycle police officers who had accompanied the procession to the cemetery and still remained onsite. Seeing and hearing what was happening, he approached Margaret and asked if she needed help. She explained that the man refused to speak and had become rude and abusive.

The officer watched as Margaret took advantage of his presence and spoke to the man again. "I absolutely must," she said, "I *must* ask you a few questions about this man. It's extremely important. Will you please give me just a minute of your time? I'm a member of his family."

The officer faced the man up close and pointed into his face. "Did you hear what the lady asked you?" he said. "Would you answer her? She wants to ask you a few questions. Can you afford a minute or two to help her out? It seems like a reasonable request from a member of the family."

The man loudly directed his answer to Margaret. "You can throw any kind of fit you want, lady. But even if you show me a signed decree from the pope and another one from the President, not even *then* can I answer your questions." His extreme reluctance confused the police officer and seriously disturbed Margaret, making her even *more* curious.

"I want to see this body one final time. Why won't you do that?" she said loudly. "It's completely reasonable and it'll take only a minute." The man had grossly underestimated the fervor of a very determined and assertive woman who would not take "no" for an answer.

At this point in the conflict, a younger man wearing a name badge with the *Dunahue's* logo walked across the lawn and stopped to face Margaret. "Is there something wrong here?" he asked politely. "My name is Robert Dunahue and I'm the owner of this company. What can I do for you?"

The angry man immediately left the scene and the officer remained to hear if Margaret's request would be granted and to make certain she was not being verbally abused. Margaret repeated her request to see the deceased one last time. Robert Dunahue's answer was more than shocking. Since his words were whispered, the officer figured it was private conversation and moved back to his motorcycle. Margaret was not prepared for what she was about to hear.

"You have to give me your word that what I'm about to tell you will be kept completely confidential," he said. He asked Margaret to step to one side as the Cemetery staff was preparing to lower the casket and close the grave. She responded and gave Robert her complete attention, wondering what could possibly be justifying such clandestine behavior.

"You see, he said, "something happened here that has never happened to me in 42 years of business in the Chicagoland area. And I believe what I'm about to tell you will answer all of your questions."

"And what is that?" Margaret asked.

"Well, there are only four people within our organization who know this. And I'm telling you only because I believe I can trust you. You seem like an honest sort and seem to have a legitimate desire to get some questions answered."

"Please, I'd greatly appreciate it."

Robert Dunahue hesitated and spoke slowly and quietly. "I have to tell you this in private," he said. "There *is* no body in this casket!" He repeated the phrase two more times.

Margaret's mouth dropped open as she shifted to lean against an adjacent gravestone marker. "I'm sorry?" she said. "I don't think I heard you correctly."

"You did. I said . . . there *is* no body. It was and is the greatest single mystery I've ever encountered. The body was shipped to us via an international carrier, from Assisi, Italy, via Rome and New York before it arrived in Chicago. We assume the casket was not opened anywhere along the 7-day journey since there was no reason to do so. When it arrived at my establishment, we had to view it to ascertain that the embalming process, initiated in Assisi, had been properly executed. We also had to examine the corpse regarding its condition after traveling such a great distance.

"There were three of us standing near the casket when the shipping seals were broken by our staff. We were all in utter dismay to watch the lid lifted and to reveal only emptiness. There simply was no body, absolutely nothing inside at all."

"But what did you do? What did you think had happened?" Margaret asked her question with typical speed and candor.

"We had no idea how to handle the situation. We could only speculate that the body either had never been placed into the casket at its point of origin in Assisi, or, if it had, it had been lost or stolen somewhere along the way. But we investigated thoroughly and found not a single person who could provide an answer. Everyone was dumbfounded, especially those at the location where witnesses swore they saw the body enter the container. An added mystery was, well, the shipment was sealed with multiple international logos that verified that it was never opened on its transit to America. We broke those seals in our facility before we opened the shipment."

Margaret was shocked to hear such details and had no reason to disbelieve Dunahue's story. "But then," she said, "everything at the Cathedral, the Mass and the service, they were all part of a charade, a service performed before an *empty coffin*, a container without the body of the man whose life was being celebrated?"

"Yes. It was the only method we could devise. No one along the line of shipment or communication was daring enough to take the responsibility for 'losing' the body of a very distinguished priest, one who was loved and revered by so many hundreds of people."

"Then, the bottom line in all this?" Margaret paused.

"The bottom line is clear. The service was performed with honesty and integrity, to honor a fallen hero, if you will, a wonderful and loyal priest with many years of service to the Archdiocese of Chicago. We honored his spirit and soul, not his body.

"My dear," Dunahue quipped, "if we were to attempt an explanation for this entire, absurd story to the Archdiocese, it would cause immeasurable damage. It would be scandalous. There are people in this town who would wallow in glee for 'taking down' the Archdiocese and all it stands for, people like families of abused children, militant groups who despise priests, and others who would cause such terrible grief to so many good people . . . it just isn't worth the risk.

"At this point," Dunahue continued, "and after great soul-searching, my partners and I would rather be part of a cover-up than to answer to God for being part of a horrendous scandal producing nothing but bad press. Do you understand that? Can you agree with me? Can you support this reasoning? Will you swear to keep our secret?"

Margaret slowly walked away from Dunahue to clear her head and absorb the staggering news. "The body was . . . lost?" She kept repeating the phrase to herself. It was a most bizarre situation but it appeared to be true.

Then, she answered. "Since you trusted me with your story, the only choice I have is to live up to that trust and commit to keeping it to myself. Although you're asking a lot, I'll honor your request. I may tell only my mother who's deeply involved in all this, but the story won't go beyond us. I promise. And thanks for the courtesy of explaining it all. I appreciate it more than I can say. I see where you had to keep it quiet, to protect *everyone*, especially the Church itself and Father Francis."

As Margaret left the cemetery, she planned to stop by her mother's house to tell her what she had just heard. The worst news she had personally received was the fact that her investigation into the life and death of Father Francis had ended abruptly, hitting the proverbial brick wall. She still strongly suspected that there was a connection between the priest and her father.

Just when she thought she was getting closer to solving the mystery, this terrible news crushed her efforts. It was an incredible tale Dunahue told, and it could have been a lie in order to protect himself from any fall-out from the story of a "lost" body. On the other hand, if he was telling the truth, he had good reason to shelter himself and keep the story quiet.

As she "rewound" some of her father's observations, one of Margaret's recollections was his whimsical speculation that God was performing the entire exercise of two simultaneous lives to "show-off" his miraculous powers. If she was to believe that, then why did such a "show-off" dictate that one of the two bodies disappear when both would be greater evidence to support His capabilities? That mystery alone, though difficult for Margaret to accept, left her increasingly stupefied.

Elusive Answer

After emerging from a mountain of frustrations and entertaining wildly imaginative thoughts, Margaret was convinced that the disappearing body was related in part to the miracle Frank claimed he had experienced, with attribution given to *A Prayer for the Dying*. If her father had, indeed, lived a secondary and simultaneous life as Father Francis Chase, then the designer of such a miracle could have been responsible for the vanishing body. Unfortunately, that body was the only piece of material evidence that Margaret could use to prove that a profound miracle had occurred. Or was it? Margaret's insight and intuition, fueled by her inexhaustible persistence, recognized one other element of evidence that could conclusively erase the obscurity . . . DNA!

If the ambitious sleuth could obtain a sample of the DNA of Father Francis, that sample could be compared to the DNA of her father. If the results were a match, it would be proof that both men were one and the same. She could easily obtain DNA samples of her father. But obtaining them from a person whose body no longer existed would be a bit more difficult. She had one chance. It centered on her server/friend from the restaurant in Assisi. She would call on John Marona for help.

It had been several weeks since Margaret and John were together in Assisi. Her phone call came as no surprise to him because the two had committed to staying in touch. This was much sooner than John had expected but he welcomed the opportunity to speak to the beautiful American woman who's company he so enjoyed. For now, a long-distance telephone call was an unearned pleasure. But he was clearly unprepared for Margaret's challenging request.

She knew little about the on-site death of Father Francis, only that it occurred at the main altar in the Basilica. To her credit, she quickly learned through the local Assisi hospital, when, where and how it occurred, but little else. Her request to her friend John was for him to arrange to meet with Brother Pietro and then secure detailed information from him about the priest's collapse and death. She was certain that the good Brother would cooperate. She phoned him first to explain exactly what she needed.

It was, after all, that same brother who introduced *A Prayer for the Dying* to Frank through Father Tonelli. She knew that her father had explained to Brother Pietro the details of his intention to live the life of a priest. All of her efforts were to support the manifestation of that intention through her father's belief that The Prayer had been answered and that Frank had led two lives at the same time.

In speaking to John by telephone, Margaret tirelessly explained every detail of the situation, asking him if he personally believed that her father could have lived two simultaneous lives. After a lengthy silence, John provided an honest opinion.

"While many physical things are impossible," he said, "I believe that nothing is impossible in the human mind. I would not be surprised if you found his story to be true, but perhaps not in the *physical* sense." Margaret would remember that explanation though she accepted it in a *visceral* sense, as a result of *reasoning* rather than as a God-induced miracle.

During their telephone conversation, John explained to Margaret that since he "grew up in the shadow of Saint Francis' home," he had nurtured a special dedication to the great Saint. To Margaret's surprise and delight, John recited a short poem to her, John's favorite of all those authored by the Saint of Assisi:

> "I hope that I so blessed will be
> That every suffering pleases me."

Margaret quickly wrote that down and soon had it memorized. She interpreted the poem as consistent with the focus of Francis on suffering and dying.

After briefly reflecting on Margaret's need of help, John agreed to accept her request, primarily because he knew it was extremely important to her. The goal of his inquiry was to personally and physically examine the main altar to see if any traces of the priest's blood remained on the altar's steps or on the floor where he fell. It was not an easy assignment but anything John did would be as detailed and well-executed as anything Margaret did if she were in Assisi. Most important, she had complete trust in her friend. She would wait patiently, or perhaps *not* so patiently, for word on the success or failure of his actions. She was reminded of her father's favorite prayer for patience: "O, Lord, teach me to be patient, but hurry!"

After seven days of no contact, Margaret could no longer control her patience, or lack of same. She telephoned John. He explained that Brother Pietro was in a *closed retreat* and he hadn't been able to take any messages. He would return in two more days. Margaret and John, nevertheless, took the telephone opportunity to speak to each other for nearly an hour. The conversation was enjoyable for both of them with brief sprinkles of laughter alternating with sobriety. Margaret ruminated over the fact that so much geography separated them from becoming closer friends. John felt the same.

Margaret had great faith that John could accomplish his goal and that she could get 100% accurate test results from even the smallest sample. She expected that any blood stains around the altar would be dry by this time but that John could scrape enough fragments to make collection of a sample likely.

Having done her homework, Margaret knew that obtaining DNA evidence through local testing labs had been eased in recent years and that court-admissible evidence and test results were even available through on-line inquiries. All she needed was a tiny sample to secure a forensic DNA analysis. She knew also that such a test wasn't important to anyone but she and her mother but that it would clarify a deeply inspirational experience by her father. Brother Pietro and Father Tonelli would find it no less interesting.

John met with Brother Pietro and then examined the site of Father Francis' collapse and death. He was assisted by several Brothers who helped him comb the area on their knees for any stains of blood. For two days, they diligently searched every inch of the floor near the altar but found nothing resembling blood. John was hesitant to phone Margaret with such negative results. But just as he was about to leave the grounds of the Basilica, Brother Pietro called him back and with great exuberance explained that he had an alternate idea, one that might provide the DNA sample they needed.

The humble Brother passed his suggestion on to John: the answer to the mystery might lie in the *chalice* that Father Francis used to concelebrate Mass on the day he died. It was a very notable ciborium set aside for special occasions and used only by visiting priests. Brother was certain that it had not been used at any time following Father's death. Since it had not been cleansed or rinsed other than with the cloth called the *Purifier* during Mass, it might still contain enough residue of saliva to produce DNA evidence.

After phoning Margaret with the bad news/good news, John enthusiastically went to work. He had a friend in Assisi who had a graduate degree in forensics. He contacted the man and secured his help in collecting a sample from the ciborium.

The drinking utensil itself was a beautiful work of art with inlaid rubies and gold trim that made it as unique as it was valuable. It was a collector's item, to be sure. While Brother Pietro held the goblet in his hands, John's friend, Salvatore, wiped all around the inner lip with small swabs. He repeated the procedure several times before feeling certain that he had enough to provide an accurate sample.

The three men performing the examination knew that the accuracy of the test was contingent on the fact that the chalice had not been used between the Mass by Father Francis and the test they had just executed. To assure the purity and safety of the swabs, Salvatore would hand-carry them in sealed plastic bags to a laboratory that worked in conjunction with the hospital in Assisi. It would take two days to obtain the results.

Not surprisingly, Margaret and Annie were extremely nervous as they waited at their home in Oak Park to hear the outcome of the tests from Assisi. Margaret felt comfortable in having the tests done there rather than in Chicago. John and Brother Pietro were responsible friends who would take all precautions to assure the validity of the samples. Everyone involved trusted the integrity of the Assisi laboratory.

Naturally, to support a legitimate comparison of DNA samples from each person, Frank and Father Francis, Margaret and Annie would be required to provide a DNA sample from Frank. While awaiting the news from Assisi, they went about that task. Under advisement, they were told to submit used toothbrushes that Frank carried on the trip to Italy, any that had not yet been rinsed. They found several that provided the needed evidence.

On the long journey to Italy, Frank and Annie carried enough toothbrushes to brush with a *new* one each day. They had fears of contracting an illness from local water through a hotel faucet so they discarded each toothbrush after a use rather than rinsing it.

There were two or three toothbrushes, however, that Frank used before his death that had not yet been rinsed or discarded. Most certainly, being a dentist, the man was scrupulous, even *paranoid*, about caring for his teeth. Being near death was no exception. His habit of brushing and discarding the brushes would prove crucial in supporting his story of living twice.

Truly, the entire investigative process was one of the most enthralling actions Margaret had ever initiated on behalf of her father. She felt she owed him her effort, to prove that he was richly rewarded for his faith in the special prayer by Saint Francis and that he had been gifted a second, simultaneous life.

As Margaret and her mother saw it, living two lives was a miracle. It was an extraordinary event, a meaningful blessing, a lesson in faith, hope and love the likes of which not many *believers* had encountered before.

Margaret constantly replayed the joy of her father whenever he spoke of his other life. That joy permeated his existence throughout his final months. He insisted that his happiness and sense of well-being were a result of his daily recitations of *A Prayer for the Dying*. Margaret knew that he was captivated by the intrigue that characterized her investigation. In her words, "I'm sure that pop is enjoying himself as much as I am, simply having a jolly-good time watching me stumble through a lot of worldly obstacles."

John phoned Margaret around noon, Chicago time, as she and her mother waited for his news. It was near five o'clock in the afternoon at the laboratory in Assisi when the test results were made available. John held in his hands a report that the DNA samples were pure, providing 100% accurate test results as verified by the laboratory. A notarized hard copy would be sent directly to Annie's home. It would be hand-carried by Margaret to a highly-trusted laboratory in Chicago.

Both mother and daughter were elated, most eager to provide the samples from Frank and those from Father Francis for a final analysis. Results from that comparison would confirm or deny Frank's claim to have lived two lives within one person.

Another week passed slowly. It was time for more waiting. Annie and Margaret were unwillingly developing a great deal of patience. The two women closest to Frank, however, admitted doubts as to his credibility over the last six months of his life. He was, of course, susceptible to the side-effects of his plethora of medications and he also believed what he *wanted* to believe about the effectiveness of The Prayer. To be sure, those influences were strong enough to affect his judgment, though neither of his favorite women would allow him to know their doubts while he still lived.

Margaret and her mother were spending a lot of time together during the days and weeks since Frank's death. Margaret hadn't appeared at the office of her brokerage firm in weeks but she did check-in periodically via an assortment of social media, telephone and email. She had convinced Annie that the firm "Is actually doing better without me than when I recently hung around watching every move people made."

During one of their most personal moments, while discussing the subject of life and death in general and Frank's life in particular, Margaret asked for her mother's insight in dealing with Frank's death. Annie was eager to share her most intimate feelings.

"I'll long remember a most important lesson your father taught me by example during his final months," Annie said. "He always told friends, everybody he knew for that matter, that he didn't want any books or lectures on 'death and dying' but rather wanted to learn more about 'life and living.' It was a powerful lesson, indeed, and it made his leaving so much easier for me. As he neared the end, his 'life force' sustained him and absolutely refused to surrender.

"Another of the deep principles he believed in," Annie said, "and another that I've had reinforced by his example, is the reality that the human heart is an amazingly resilient place. If you open it and surrender it fully to God, the heart can endure pain with such courage and bravado, that it defies explanation. Oh, it may heal less quickly than other organs in the body, but once it does, it bounces back with such strength . . . and it surprisingly leaves no scars or after-effects from its psychic exposure to suffering.

"And forgiveness . . . my, oh my . . . how the heart battles over that one. The Lord knows what tough adversaries we face in hatred and anger; but He also knows how fully the heart recovers from those nasty devices that can cause such great harm. Forgiving those who've hurt us terribly, that's certainly an area of the heart that also has the capacity to bounce back, to demonstrate its elasticity, if you will, and to return stronger and with a greater capacity for endurance than even before the infliction of sorrow and suffering. And, take it from me," Annie concluded, "there is nothing as wonderful as the feeling of healing . . . nothing in this world." Annie paused and stared at her daughter.

"You've been so quiet, my dear," she said. "Are you okay?"

"Of course, mother," Margaret said. "I'm overwhelmed by your sensitivities, by your absolutely delightful outlook on the heaviest of subjects. You diminish the complexities that get people so wrapped up in themselves, the harbors of suffering that attract all boats, the reefs of fear and self-pity that tend to destroy rather than to rescue."

"My goodness," Annie responded. "You speak of the ugliest of subjects in such lovely and prosaic discourse. I always said that you received your gifts of writing and expression from your father. No doubt about it." Both of the poised conversationalists smiled, bathing in a greater understanding and admiration for one another.

In that instant, Margaret's cell phone rang, only once. She picked it up quickly and listened to the voice of a lab technician. She looked at her mother. Tears formed in her eyes. She spoke quietly and with great difficulty, but her exuberance shone brightly.

"Mother," she said, "They've found that the two samples are a near-perfect match, just as if they were from one human being. The technician was so amazed that he asked if there was a mistake, if they were, perhaps, taken from the same source."

Margaret closed the phone and walked to Annie's chair. She and her mother had traveled a long road together to face this truth. They embraced, clinging forcibly to each other's arms and shoulders. They sobbed uncontrollably, joyfully, for a very long time.

As they separated, Annie said to Margaret, "I don't know if the impact of what we just learned has really sunk in. It's going to take awhile."

"Yes, it is, mother. Do you realize that this verifies pop's story. It validates what he said all along about *A Prayer for the Dying*? How about we give the Saint his due. How about we salute him with an attaboy or two." The two women leaned toward one another and slapped their hands together in the customary 'high-five' gesture, concluding with the words, "Attaboy, Francis!"

"Do you know what this could mean for Brother Pietro?" Annie said. "We know that Saint Francis has had his miracles for many centuries, but this new attribution, this could mean so much for the Church, for the millions of people who could use a boost right now when the Catholic Church is facing so many problems. And probably most important of all, can you imagine how much comfort and courage The Prayer could provide to dying people all over the world?"

"Let's not get carried away, mom. You know how long it takes the Church of Rome to authenticate these things. Let's just get the news to Brother Pietro as quickly as possible and leave the rest up to him. But before any of that, I've got to call my friend, John, and tell him the incredible news. He was so good, so important in helping us resolve the common identities of pop and Father Francis.

"I can't believe I said that, can you? 'Common identities!'"

Creating a Title

In the weeks following the dramatic discovery of indisputable proof of a biological kinship between Frank Chase and Father Francis Chase, a serious reaction took place in Assisi. After receiving the call from Margaret announcing the news, Brother Pietro traveled to the Vatican to meet with the team evaluating *A Prayer for the Dying*. He added the information from Margaret to help affirm The Prayer's effectiveness and, therefore, to strengthen the case declaring authorship by Saint Francis.

It had been almost six years since the initial documents were submitted to Rome. That was still considered a short time for such matters to pass through the Vatican. In fact, Saint Francis himself had run into the notorious red tape and beaurocratic delays of the Vatican on several occasions.

In this case, however, Brother wanted to waste no time in making the investigative team aware of the recent results attributed to use of The Prayer. Frank's case did not suit the criteria for a text-book "miracle," but it was, nonetheless, an extraordinary event, "inexplicable through natural reasoning and attributed to a supernatural agency."

The Brother believed deeply that The Prayer was responsible for Frank's unusual experiences. Unfortunately, after Frank's death and the simultaneous death of Father Francis, there was no one to support Frank's affirmations that he lived twice. The clearest evidence was from the DNA samples retrieved from both men. But that was only *part* of the story. There was a lot more needed to prove that two men actually walked the face of the earth as one person.

At the outset, it was clear that there would be no help from the Vatican in proving that story. Previously, the Vatican team was assigned *only* the task of showing that The Prayer was written by Saint Francis. That in itself involved a tedious investigation that occupied several scholars and theologians over a five-year period. If and when they announced certainty of authorship, it was still unlikely that they would refocus their energies on proving Frank's story, a tale which relied heavily on hearsay from those who were nearest to him, especially on testimonials from members of his own family.

Despite those negative issues, the DNA news had an instant and positive impact on the life of Margaret. She became rededicated and re-energized as the strongest proponent of her father's story. But she admitted that her work was incomplete until she secured more evidence. The result of that acknowledgment was a research effort to compile her findings and to copiously arrange them in an organized format. Since quitting wasn't an option, she would . . . write a book!

Because her brokerage business was, for the most part, running itself, Margaret had plenty of spare time. Her renewed motivation was to gather as much information as possible, and then, to present her findings to the Vatican in hopes of prompting an expanded investigation. Providing details of her father's story in the form of a book and relating them to *A Prayer for the Dying* might attract interest in the *story* as well as in the *document*.

Moreover, the self-proclaimed journalist was determined to publish The Prayer as a part of her book and, thereby, to help others in the same way it had helped her father. Since she was a realist, she new *that* undertaking would be arduous. But buoyed by the inspiration of her father, she remained positive.

Margaret also realized that she needed more than inspiration and faith to substantiate a story that was, at the very least, incredulous. Further, it was improbable and unfathomable. In street-talk, it was far-fetched. If Margaret could overcome those staggering obstacles with facts, she might have a chance. But those facts became less and less attainable as the key witnesses who were touched by Frank's and Father Francis' life passed away. Only Father Tonelli survived. And his memory had slipped so significantly that he was unable to recall much of Frank's life and/ or details of his last days.

So in the year 2013, both Margaret's father and Father Francis died; Annie followed by two months; Brother Pietro also passed away; and shortly after Margaret interviewed Sister Mary Rose and Rosa Marie Marsinski, they also succumbed to illness. It was as though the two women waited to tell their loving stories about Father Francis, fulfilled that wish and then passed away.

The entire deathly domino-effect of the principals in her story got Margaret's attention, resulting in more than a furrowed brow and chewed fingernails. It again raised the question, "serendipity or Divine Providence?" Her distress at losing the significant people in Frank's life and in the life of Father Francis transcended her investigation into the story.

Undaunted, Margaret pursued her efforts to seek relevant facts. She shifted her focus from the characters and turned her attention to the simultaneous deaths of her father and Father Francis in the Basilica. That was, after all, the most mind-boggling element of all . . . and it deserved further scrutiny.

She first examined the death certificates and verified accounts of the date, time and place of the deaths. More objective investigators recognized the extraordinary concurrence as "coincidence." Her *Divine Providence* theory remained unimpressive to Vatican examiners who quickly dispatched God's involvement as, "whimsical synchronism."

In a bold and life-altering move, Margaret sold her business and, with the encouragement of her friend, John, moved to Assisi. Three months passed quickly and the two recognized that they had fallen in love. Not long afterward, she and John were married and John became a devoted collaborator in his wife's endeavors. In spite of their joint efforts, however, after nearly two years, there was not enough hard evidence to prove Frank's claim that he had, indeed, lived two lives.

During that period of struggle and frustration, the newlyweds relocated to the tiny village of Aulino, just to the south of Assisi but in the same Province of Perugia. Margaret had made a substantial adjustment in moving from Chicago with a population of nearly 10 million to Assisi with around 25,000. Even that eventually proved "too crowded and busy" for she and John so they moved to the quieter climes of Aulino with a population of only 750 permanent residents.

Aulino thus became home. It was a place of immeasurable peace among friendly villagers, the kind of place her father and mother would have appreciated and the kind that Margaret and John treasured. Its serenity was an excellent backdrop in which to concentrate on writing.

Margaret's friends and family, including her husband and her three siblings, argued that she should settle for less than her original goal in writing her story. It should be shorter and contain fewer details. She should surrender her idea of proving the existence of two lives in one. The settlement worked best for those who were predisposed to the holiness in the lives of Frank Chase and in the life of Father Francis.

If their most ardent followers believed the story that *A Prayer for the Dying* had been secretly stored in the ceiling of the Basilica for hundreds of years, if they trusted the gifts of those who translated The Prayer and attributed it to the great Saint, then those people would also believe in Frank's claim. That group included every faithful member of his family down to grandchildren and great-grandchildren.

For those who did not accept the predispositions, Frank would remain a highly respected, greatly admired leader of his Church and community. He was known to say, "If people remember me only for being a good man and a nice guy, I'll be pleased." He achieved that and more.

The same statement was legitimately applied to Father Francis. His goodness was unquestionable and he also qualified as

". . . a good man and a nice guy." His reputation and legacy were untarnished. Though he was subjected to multiple temptations against his priestly commitments, in the end, "He was a priest forever, according to the Order of Melchizedek."

There remained one part of the mystery that baffled Margaret more than other elements. The newly-discovered prayer the Saint himself called *A Prayer for the Dying* was never allowed to be published. With heavy hearts, the members of *The Friars of the Third Order Regular* who lived in the *Sacro Convento* never felt in conscience that they should release it. They continued to believe it was the intention of their great Saint to distribute The Prayer only to those who were close friends and also facing death.

That rationale seriously disturbed Margaret. She viewed it as selfish and egotistical. It was unfair of the Brothers to deem themselves exclusive judges of specifically who deserved The Prayer. Distraught and frustrated, she said, "They're *playing favorites* if they select only friends and followers as suitable recipients." She recanted those words, however, when John convinced her that the Brothers were the living caretakers of Saint Francis' home as well as his legacy. He also pointed out that if she felt that strongly about it, then *she* was the one who was being judgmental. She reluctantly accepted that.

After poring over the document for over 15 years, the Vatican still hadn't resolved the issue of the writing that claimed it was Francis' intention to distribute The Prayer sparingly. That was a great disappointment to Margaret who had hoped to proliferate the powerful effects of The Prayer. The exact reason for that request by Francis was never fully understood, by Margaret or anyone else.

Even without The Prayer at her disposal, Margaret persevered in the completion of her book about her father's life as it conjoined with the life of Father Francis Chase. The title became a joint effort of her and her husband as they struggled to make it both memorable and appropriate. It emerged brightly one crisp night as they sat in the *Piazza Navona* in Rome after a day of satisfying one of Margaret's greatest addictions . . . shopping.

The only element of her life in Aulino that she found difficult to accept was living *without* shopping as she knew it, in the streets of her beloved Chicago. There was no *State Street,* no *Michigan Avenue* and no multiplicity of suburban malls. She did, however, manage to feed her appetite by frequent trips to Rome with areas no less chic than the best of Chicago.

There were dozens of places that pleased her. Among her favorites: the Via Condotti, Via Veneto, and the historic center with the Parthenon and *Piazza Navona,* surrounded by a network of small roads and other piazza's that glorified the high styles of Europe's best fashions. John was the designated driver on such jaunts, generally concluding at Tre Scalini.

In Margaret's lengthy and detailed interview with Rosa, Margaret was first exposed to the loveliness of the place at which Rosa first encountered Father Francis. For Margaret and her husband, this was now a perfect fall evening to do some recollecting, a private time when she and John could relax over a *Tartufo* and enjoy discussing the life of Father Francis and her father.

Margaret delighted in what she had learned from Rosa and from the nun, Sister Mary Rose. Of special note was the eerie and frequent appearance of the name, *Rose,* in the story of both men. Margaret explained it to John who was not aware of the intimate connections.

"First, you know that my mother's name was *Annie,*" she said, "but she had a nickname inherited from her grandmother on her mother's side. *Her* name was Rosita. Many times, pop was known to call my mom, *Rosie,* to honor the memory of her grandma. Because of that, pop placed great importance on the rose and always had a seasonal garden of red roses as a tribute to his wife's family." John agreed that the family occurrence of the name, Rose, was, indeed, something unusual and notable, but hardly relevant to Margaret's case. He was to learn more.

"Then there was the name of *Sister Mary Rose* in the life of Father Francis," Margaret continued. "She represented the first serious temptation in the priestly life of Father Francis. The Sister told me that. And then, the name of the woman Father Francis met at the *Piazza Navona* when he was a young priest, *Rosa* Marie Marsinski. How about that?" Margaret rhetorically asked the question as she thumped her hand on the table and continued her thought.

"So the name of the beautiful and delicate flower strangely and ironically touched *both* men, beginning with Frank and permeating the life of Father Francis. Or maybe it was the other way around," she said thoughtfully. Her husband listened closely but continued to show skepticism about the significance of the "rose connection."

Margaret struggled to maintain her point. "But don't you see, John," she said. "Do you think that all those inclusions of roses and flowers are serendipitous? Or are they providential and meaningful?" Margaret expressed the opinion that she personally believed the latter. "There was something far greater at work than simple irony," she said.

She completed her defense with a final argument. "Would you believe there are even *more* flowers involved, John? Wait 'til you hear this. In my research, I learned that there is a written work called, 'The Little Flowers of Saint Francis of Assisi.' It's a delightful collection, actually a rather *extensive* collection, of noteworthy events in the lives of Saint Francis and his followers. It was compiled by one of those followers whose name was Brother Ugolino. In it, the Brother points out similarities between Jesus and Francis. But more important for us as we argue a connection between Saint Francis, Father Francis and Frank Chase, there is yet another angle that suggests a relationship between all three men.

"You recall, John, that *A Prayer for the Dying* has always been shrouded in the mystery of its translation from the Umbrian dialect to Classical Latin and then to English. Well, it's a *fact* that the original Latin text of 'The Little Flowers of Saint Francis of Assisi' was lost. Just imagine, it was *lost*, just like The Prayer was lost after it was hidden in the ceiling of the Basilica for hundreds of years, and just like the body of Father Francis was lost en route to Chicago.

"But in the case of the 'Flowers' work, a team of very patient and persistent scholars was able to reconstruct it. Now don't ask me any more details about the flowers because my research stopped there. At that point, I had absorbed enough and I was convinced that the connection between all of the flowers, especially the *rose*, was a significant point of light that was more than fascinating. It was evidence that connected the principals to one another and became as inexplicable as pop's compelling story of living two lives."

At the end of their stimulating, candlelight conversation, just before exiting Tre Scalini, Margaret and John flippantly threw some ideas around for the title of her book. Margaret first suggested, *Francis and the Roses*. That didn't go anywhere because John still wasn't convinced of the *rose* significance.

John came up with, *Attaboy, Francis!* That bloomed even less than the rose idea. Another try, *Discovering Francis*, was scarcely less a bomb than the others.

Then, Margaret mentioned an idea she had considered over the past several days. Her focus was on the unusual *intention* of her father's prayer. That *intention* during the recitation of his prayer was arguably the central theme of the story. Also, it was a most extraordinary request. It was . . . *exceptional!*

Softly and humbly, Margaret dared to verbalize her idea to John. "It seems most logical," she explained, "that the book be called, *Exceptional Intention*. What do you think?"

John pondered that for slightly longer than a minute, then concluded it was too cumbersome a phrase. "You know," he said, "if you really think about it, your book isn't as much about Frank's 'exceptional intention' as it is about *A Prayer for the Dying*. I mean, isn't *that* what it's all about, the newly-discovered Prayer written by Saint Francis?"

"I'm confused," Margaret said. "No, it's not all about The Prayer." It was Margaret's turn to do some introspecting. And it took her no longer than it took John to reveal still another product of brainstorming. "Here's a new idea that just came to me," she said. "The Prayer was a miraculous gift, right? And my father's second lifetime was another gift. And everyone who's been touched by this story has been given a gift. How about *"Gift of a Lifetime?"*

"Too common," John said instantly. "I'll bet there are a hundred books published with that name. And it still focuses too much on your father's request."

"Okay," Margaret said. Now this is it. This fits perfectly because . . ." John interrupted and said, "This had better be good, my dear." He gratuitously cupped his hand over his right ear and leaned toward her as he awaited the announcement.

Then, so quietly that John could barely hear her, Margaret whispered, "How about *The Francis Connection?* All of the principal characters in the story did make a connection with the Saint. And that connection tied them all together into a spiritual family. What do you think, John? You like it?"

After thinking for only a moment, John signaled with a high-five against his wife's hand. He smiled at the working title of her book, *The Francis Connection*. It fit perfectly.

Ending the lengthy conversation, John added, "Did I ever tell you how much I love to watch the movement of your mouth when you're speaking so intensely? It dances like a butterfly, up and down and around . . . a butterfly dancing a classic waltz. So beautiful."

"Thank you, my dear," Margaret said as she rewarded him for the loving compliment, kissing him fully on the lips and *waltzing* her fingers through his hair.

Publishing

Margaret and John lived a happy life in Aulino, traveling throughout Italy accordingly by auto, train and bus with each mile programmed to the voice of John's Italian dialect as he narrated stories of his homeland. From Venice in the north to Naples in the south, with dozens of charming villages and cities in-between, Margaret was comfortable in her adopted country.

She remained close to her two sisters and brother who ventured *across the pond* for a visit when their schedules and budgets allowed. Margaret and John returned the favor by visiting Chicago as frequently as possible. On such trips, Margaret managed to schedule important shopping excursions to *The Loop* with one stop in particular at *Watertower Place*, an absolute necessity.

It took only six months after her father's death for the wannabe author to complete her manuscript. John was her harshest critic and strongest advocate. He believed in her passion for writing and her commitment to an original style reinforced by hard work. He also believed that she would one day be a published author.

When she owned and managed her brokerage firm in Chicago, one of Margaret's closest friends was Ellie Magnussen, a talented woman with many gifts beyond those in her field of money management. She was as successful in business as she was in raising two young children and sustaining a happy marriage.

Margaret recalled that Ellie's father was a Literary Agent who maintained offices in New York, Los Angeles and Chicago. On

274

a trip to the Windy City, Margaret emailed Ellie beforehand and arranged to meet her for a downtown lunch. Both of the women missed their business and recreational times together. On this visit, however, Margaret came bearing an unannounced favor of Ellie. Admittedly, she was taking advantage of their friendship.

During an enjoyably informal meal at *The Cheesecake Factory* on North Michigan Avenue, Margaret told her friend about the book she had written. Ellie was deeply interested. She had met Frank Chase on several occasions and was amazed by the tale Margaret told of his adventure in claiming to have lived multiple lives. She suggested that Margaret give her a copy of the manuscript. She would read it first and if she felt it was consistent with the fiction her father represented, she would pass it on to him. It took only three days for that to happen. Ellie liked the book very much.

Margaret prepared to personally meet at the office of the Stan Miller Literary Agency in the John Hancock Building on North Michigan Avenue, at a meeting set-up by Ellie. The location was inside the same building where she and Ellie had their lunchtime discussion.

From what Margaret knew, Stan was a kind and compassionate man but the nature of his business dictated honesty and explicit opinions of works submitted, even though some of the commentary might seem cruel and harsh. He was highly discriminating in the authors he represented and extremely cautious in appraising their work. His success and reputation for candor preceded him. Having been briefed on all that by Ellie, Margaret was as nervous as she was intimidated before her meeting with Stan.

She arrived at the street-level entrance to the Hancock Building carrying two copies of the manuscript in her briefcase and a sizeable amount of stress in her head. She walked slowly enough to allow the revolving door to carry her in circles several times before electing to be launched onto the other side. Her normal courage and feistiness were absent because of her discomfort in representing *herself* in an awkward new business arena.

Eventually, the well-dressed, attractive woman overcame the obstacle, gathered her strength and made it through the entrance, up the elevator and to the reception desk of Stan Miller. She was on time for her appointment but she had never been this uptight in all her life. She felt gathering beads of perspiration under each arm and hoped they weren't visible.

The receptionist escorted her into Stan's office, introduced the two and offered Margaret a chair directly in front of him. He spoke first.

"I've read your manuscript, Margaret," he said, "and I think it has potential. A couple of things I'd like to talk to you about."

Margaret was awestruck. She had no idea that Ellie had passed the manuscript on to Stan so quickly and that he had already read it. It was a pleasant surprise. But she was skeptical about the "couple of things" he wanted to talk about. She thanked him for the kind remarks and waited for him to speak again.

"Let me ask you something, Margaret," he said. "If you had read a story about a war between two world powers but you never learned which of them won the war, wouldn't you find that a major omission? Wouldn't you feel cheated?"

Margaret thought carefully before she spoke, trying to sense what Stan wanted to hear. "I'm not sure," she said. "But I'd like to know who the victor was before commenting on the war itself, yes."

"Wouldn't on obvious omission like that affect the credibility of the entire story . . . *and* its marketability?"

"Of course. But I don't understand. Just what are you saying about *my* story? Did I omit something that critical?"

"You sure did, Margaret. And I think it's the first question any publisher will ask."

"I thought I was very thorough in my research and plot."

"You were. But no publisher in his right mind would accept your story without reading *A Prayer for the Dying*. People would have a right to challenge you on that. Why would the author *not* reveal The Prayer, an instrument that was so *crucial* to the outcome of the story? And who would buy it *without* The Prayer?"

"If that's what you need to get it published, I'll go to work on it right away and . . ."

Stan Miller interrupted. "Hold on," he said as he rose from his chair behind the desk and stood directly in front of Margaret. He was a large man who knew how to deliver an intimidating stare through riveting dark eyes.

"A few comments," he said brashly, "before you run off to Italy and 'go to work on it.' "I'm compelled to ask . . . why in the world didn't you include The Prayer as part of your original manuscript?"

"Because the Brothers at the *Sacro Convento* still believe that Saint Francis wanted it made public with restrictions. They believe, from their hearts, that their translation of the documents indicated that Francis wanted it reserved for the dying and confined to personal friends of their family of Franciscans." Under her breath, Margaret quietly said, "Didn't you read that in my story?"

"Excuse me?" Stan said. He hadn't heard Margaret's last remark and was angered by her effort to purposely make it unintelligible.

"Look," he went on, "you don't have a saleable product here without *A Prayer for the Dying*. And if you go elsewhere to find an agent, you're going to hear the same thing. 'No sale without The Prayer.' Accept that, Margaret. Stan paused, then continued.

"Do you understand what I'm saying?" he asked. "Any reader would feel cheated without reading The Prayer. My God, it's the central point of the story. It's the determinative factor. It cries out for clarification, explanation. I must say . . . it sounds like quite an exceptional prayer. Do you have it? Have you personally read it? It belongs in the book. It's the only way I can represent your story with any hope of getting it published."

Margaret humbly bowed her head at Stan's brief but powerful diatribe. She was embarrassed at appearing so foolish. The agent had another biting comment: "Hell, write the damn prayer yourself. Don't be such a purist. I need that Prayer to get your book published. But if you *do* write it, don't ever tell me and I can always claim ignorance."

Margaret sat speechless as Stan returned to his chair and slouched down behind his desk. She knew it was a tall order for her to obtain The Prayer from the Brothers at the *Sacro Convento*, especially since her only contact was with Brother Pietro and he had passed away almost two years ago. She began gathering her things and was about to leave when Stan made a bold suggestion.

"For God's sake, have you ever thought about *channeling* your beloved Saint Francis yourself?"

"You don't think I already have?" Margaret asked.

"Well, do it differently," he snapped back. "For God's sake, go out and get yourself some gypsy, some medium who specializes in that sort of thing. Try to channel your Francis in the traditional sense. Talk to him, ask him where you can find a copy of that prayer of his. Ever thought about that?"

Margaret shook her head from side to side and frowned at Stan's irreverence. For personal reasons, she had dismissed his approach to "channeling" because it reminded her of Shirley MacLaine and her book, *Dancing in the Light*. While she smiled and didn't take Stan's suggestion seriously, he turned his back to her and began typing on his computer. Then, he paraphrased what appeared on his screen.

"Here," he said. "Here's some stuff about channeling. It says ' . . . seeking spiritual advice or healing.'" Under his breath, he muttered "blah, blah, blah" and continued. ' . . . to bring philosophical and theological teaching from a disembodied entity.'" There were more "blah, blah, blahs," then, 'It's a contemporary term for the earlier Spiritual idea of mediumship.' So there, now you know everything I know about 'channeling.' Like I said, get yourself a medium."

"How could you so insult me?" Margaret said. "You don't have to read me the dictionary meaning of "channeling." Don't you think I know what channeling means?" Things were getting personal and out-of-control. Once again, this man whom she had just met made Margaret feel ignorant and foolish. "Mediumship?" "Disembodied entity?" She could not let that go without a comment or two . . . or three.

"For your information, Mr. Miller," she said, "I do *not* need a medium to converse with Saint Francis. My father didn't need one either. This book is all about his *friendship* with Saint Francis. And friends converse. They talk a lot. In fact, I speak to Saint Francis frequently. I've *already* asked him for help in finding a copy of his special prayer."

Stan made a frowning face and said wryly, "What did he tell you? Did he answer?" Stan retained his smirk with his hand resting under his chin. It was an unflattering pose that irked Margaret. She judged it as *nasty.*

"Yes," she said quickly as she rose from her chair. "He did answer me. He simply told me, 'Not yet!' So I'm willing to wait until he and God are ready. Does that answer your question?" She turned her back to Stan and headed for the door.

"Sorry if I offended you," he said. "Sit back down here a minute." He gently took her by the hand. "I *do* like your story," he said, "and I think it has potential. Just get me The Prayer and I'll go to work on selling it."

Since Margaret badly needed Stan's influence to get her book into print, she swallowed her pride, glanced over her shoulder as she walked toward the door, and said, "Thank you. I'll be back."

At that point in her plunge into the Publishing Industry, Margaret felt like a jilted lover. She had a right to feel rejection because that's exactly what it was. Her story had been "rejected." And that was hard to swallow. Stan was okay, she opined, but if his attitude reflected his industry, she was in for a rough ride. She licked her wounds and decided to make a pilgrimage to obtain a copy of the elusive *Prayer for the Dying.* She hoped that it had, perhaps, been already approved for public release. Her father would have expected no less an effort as she tried to get her book into print for unselfish reasons.

After returning to Aulino from her trip to Chicago, Margaret began her newest investigative journey at the birthplace of The Prayer, the *Sacro Convento*, part of the 3-building complex attached to the Basilica of Saint Francis. It was the logical place from which to investigate the origin and existence of *A Prayer for the Dying.*

Her first step was a simple *internet* search from her home. From that source, she learned the name of the current Custodian of the *Sacro Convento*, Father Paulo Delisi. It would be the start of a lengthy adventure into the uncharted waters of 20th century Franciscan history. Her resourcefulness provided an excellent beginning. It was the first time she recognized the importance of securing a copy of The Prayer for her story.

Planning her strategy well, Margaret wrote a "summation" that she sent to Father Delisi prior to phoning to arrange a visit. The document explained her father's story regarding A *Prayer for the Dying* including the information about the existence of Father Francis Chase, the simultaneous deaths of he and Frank at the Basilica, and the mysterious absence of the body of Father Francis as it was en route from Assisi to Chicago. (She thus broke her promise of secrecy to the Funeral Home. But her rude treatment at their hands deserved no further loyalty, she reasoned.)

The Custodian had already studied several of those key facts but the disappearance of the body was a new revelation. Margaret waited one week after she mailed the papers to the priest, then phoned him and spoke to him personally. He had read her papers and was kind and gracious, agreeing to consider her request for a meeting.

Serving as an initial step, the priest referred Margaret to Brother Angelo Colardi, his personal assistant whom he delegated to be her contact as she explored details of the unpublished prayer. Little was said in the phone conversation. She detected hesitation from the Brother but he did agree to meet with her, responding to the revered name of Brother Pietro. Her previous friendship with him was the only reason she was allowed to venture into private Franciscan territory.

Margaret drove alone for the short ride to Assisi for her meeting. She was met in the front narthex and escorted by Brother Colardi into the *refectory* to join with other visitors for *prauzo*, the main meal of the day. She would also have a private conversation with the Brother following the meal.

The word "refectory" doesn't do the dining room justice. It is structured along the lines of a traditional Franciscan or monastic dining area with the tables and benches lined up along the wall. Moreover, it is the size of a large hotel ballroom and artistically dominated by a huge painting of the Last Supper. Over it is the word *Silencium* featured on a scroll, a relic from the days when meals in the Friary were taken in silence except for table-reading and prayers.

To the left of the painting is a large plaque with the following: "Lord, what do You want me to do?" Francis spoke those words to the Lord while traveling to the Holy Land, believing himself called to the Crusade. The Lord spoke to Francis, telling him to return home. 'Return home. You have misunderstood the former vision. Through Me it will have a different fulfillment.'"

As Margaret read the historical plaque several times during her meal, she wondered if *she* was receiving the same message from the Lord. "Return home. You have misunderstood the former vision. Through Me it will have a different fulfillment." The irony of that message as it applied to Margaret's personal mission demanded serious attention . . . but it didn't stop her from proceeding.

After dining and then visiting privately with Brother Colardi for over one hour and having explained her need for The Prayer, the Brother agreed to communicate the details to the Custodian and, if needed, to other authorities higher on the ladder within the Order. He would do his best to secure permission for the use of The Prayer in her book and to provide an approved copy to Margaret. He explained that, "In most cases such as this, it takes much time for the Franciscan hierarchy to grant approvals. So please be patient."

Margaret wasn't sure how long "patient" meant. Was it weeks, months or years? It was the most serious and the greatest test of her willpower thus far. But she had been well-prepared through the previous rigors of the journey thus far.

A Day of Reckoning

At just about the time she had given up on the Franciscans after nearly two months of waiting, Margaret received a letter from Father Delisi. He said he was prepared to speak with her. He suggested a meeting in his office exactly two weeks from that day, a Thursday. The "patient" author monitored the slow passage of the next fourteen days.

When the time arrived, Margaret again made the trip to Assisi alone. Once there, she was escorted into a precipitous assemblage of clergy in a Conference Room near the priest's office. She struggled to distinguish between priests and brothers but guessed that the gathering was divided about equally between the two groups of religious. There was not one who appeared to be less than 70 years old and Margaret, rightfully or wrongfully, equated their age with wisdom.

Feeling threatened by the eight men seated around the large, circular table, Margaret remained confident that she would face them as an equal, even without John at her side. What followed, however, was nearly two hours of the most painful dialogue she had yet endured in the fact-finding missions for her book. She equated her situation to encountering quicksand: the more she struggled, the greater became her chance of drowning.

Father Delisi began by introducing each of the men. Margaret made no attempt to remember names or titles but was impressed by how many were preceded by "Father." The titles included "a professor of," "a scholar of," "a director of," "an expert in," "a linguist in," and other such delineations far too complex for Margaret to recall much less comprehend.

The impressive gathering included highly-respected Franciscans from other parts of Italy as well as from The University of Muenster and the University of Hamburg in Germany. Some were already visiting Assisi for other reasons but all had, indeed, spent time working on the project of ascertaining authorship of Francis' newly-discovered prayer. Margaret was awed by the importance placed on her request for its humble use in her book.

Then came a lengthy and tedious disclosure, one she was unprepared to accept, especially in such a sensitive and spiritual setting. Father Delisi first handed Margaret a printed piece of paper. He told her it was an item posted on the free online encyclopedia, *Wikipedia*. Before he gave it to her, he asked if she had ever researched the internationally popular *Prayer of Saint Francis*. She responded "no" and began to read from the paper:

"The Prayer of Saint Francis," it noted, "is a Catholic Christian prayer. It is attributed to the 13th-century saint, Francis of Assisi, although the Prayer in its present form cannot be traced back further than 1912 when it was printed in France in French, in a magazine called La Clochette (The Little Bell) as an anonymous prayer, as demonstrated by Dr. Christian Renoux in 2001. The Prayer has been known in the United States since 1941 when Cardinal Francis Spellman and Senator Albert W. Hawkes distributed millions of copies of the Prayer during and just after World War II."

"Wow!" Margaret said out loud. "Do you mean to tell me that the famous, 'Lord, make me an instrument of thy peace' cannot be attributed to Saint Francis?"

"The fact doesn't receive much publicity," Father said, "but from time-to-time, we're forced to disclose it to people who are interested in its publication. It is no secret. Though it appears to be inspired by some of Francis' themes, the syntax of the prayer is not consistent with his favored Umbrian dialect."

"So, okay," Margaret said, wondering how that disclosure was related to *A Prayer for the Dying*. "That has nothing to do with . . ."

She stopped in mid-sentence, speculating on what the connection might be. Then, her eyes and mouth opened widely as she expressed a conclusion. "Are you telling me that The Prayer I'm so interested in publishing is similar to the famous prayer in that it was *not* written by Saint Francis?"

The priest responded: "In all the research these reputable men and others have done over the past years, there has not been one single piece of convincing evidence that the writing is genuine, that it can be undisputedly attributed it to our founder. As a matter of fact, there is evidence that points *away* from our Saint just as it did in the familiar Prayer of Saint Francis."

"But what about the signature on the new prayer?" Margaret asked quickly. "Wasn't it thought to be his? Isn't it authentic?"

"His signature, perhaps. But the rest of The Prayer, no."

"Then you must have some idea who did write it, who had it placed in the ceiling of the Basilica. Do you know who authored The Prayer? If you do, I'd greatly appreciate knowing at least that much."

As Margaret's voice trembled, Father Delisi answered. "Within the many discussions we've shared together and in our private investigations, these men and I surmise that one of the closest companions of Francis is likely responsible. That would have been either Brother Angelo or Brother Leo, in 1226, when they cared for Francis as he lay dying. They were familiar with his writing and speaking style. They knew him more personally than anyone else and they frequently quoted his words from other writings."

Margaret was devastated. She became noticeably agitated and restless. She excused herself and asked if her hosts would allow her to stand and stretch . . . actually, more like *pace*. They smiled and approved of her American habit of *pacing* while absorbed in serious conversation. It was an obvious attempt at multi-tasking.

She walked back and forth slowly behind her chair. That way, she was certain every man could see her face and she could also see theirs. The room was silent until Margaret broke it noisily. It was akin to shattering a piece of glass in the silent surroundings. In the vernacular, she was "becoming unglued!" Disappointment was not an emotion she was prepared for at this critical meeting.

"I'm very confused," she said. "If I understand you correctly, Father, what you're saying is that your conclusion is really . . . a *guess?*"

"An *educated* guess," the priest responded. "But it is rooted in logic and reason, in many hours of dialogue and deliberation. Our intent is to ascertain the author of The Prayer. Thus far, that cannot be determined from the evidence now in our hands."

Margaret continued to pace, chewing on her plastic pen as she walked and shaking her head in dismay. She also laughed softly and facetiously under her breath, just enough for the men to detect.

"Brother Pietro felt certain," Father said, visibly irritated by Margaret's attitude, "that the work was penned and signed, with notations concerning its use, by Francis himself. But since Brother's death and our examination of the document, we do not agree with his opinion. While we admit that it is influenced by some of the themes of Francis, as I said earlier about the famous *Prayer of Saint Francis,* this Prayer's syntax does not match the Umbrian dialect that he used so freely. That is a very strong point *against* its attribution to Francis.

"Further, every one of us at this table loved Brother Pietro with our hearts and souls. But we also knew his human shortcomings as he aged. We feel that his failing memory and his personal opinions were guided by his abiding faith in God and in the Saint he followed. There is nothing wrong with that, of course, but he followed Francis with subjective loyalty rather than with objectivity and rationality."

Margaret sat down again. Her futility was manifesting itself in anger. "Do you have any idea how important this document is to me, to my father's legacy?" she asked rhetorically. Her voice quivered and rose loudly, disturbingly.

"That man lived the last year of his life believing that *A Prayer for the Dying* was allowing him to live a second life, as a *priest*, no less, as a man of God. That was clearly a miracle he believed was due in large part to his namesake, Francis of Assisi. And you 'experts' sit there and calmly tell me that my father was crazy, that his stories were no more than an old man living in ignorance. What harm could possibly come from allowing me to use that prayer?"

Father Delisi rose to his feet and faced Margaret as the other scholars shifted uncomfortably in their chairs. But Margaret had not finished being unreasonable. She was clearly not the same woman who entered the august chambers of the *Sacro Convento*. Moreover, she was a *woman*, speaking loudly in the presence of acknowledged *male* leaders of their Order, scholars in the history of language, handwriting and evidential interpretation. Chauvinism was not dead in this place.

"My father's faith dictated," Margaret said, "that he trust in the power of God so thoroughly that his faith justified an exceptional wish. I don't understand how you can tell me in such cavalier fashion that Saint Francis did not write that Prayer. It *had* to be him. Who else would have had such a connection, such a *friendship* with God to intercede and receive a positive answer to such a monumental request? Who else?"

Silence enveloped the men at the table. The uneasiness increased. The religious men were at a loss for words, with the exception of Father Delisi. Margaret underestimated the Priest's verbal and intellectual prowess. He was transmogrified into a formidable foe.

"Ms. Margaret," he said, emphasizing the *Z*.

She stopped to correct him. "I am not a *Ms.*," she said as she *also* emphasized the *Z*.

"My name is *Mrs.* John Marona."

"It is unimportant," Father snapped back, adding, "And now, it is *my* turn to speak. Listen to me very carefully. And please sit down." Up until now, Margaret had been fearless. Right now, the feeling instantly evaporated.

"First," Father said. "Do you believe that we have discriminately rejected the notion that Saint Francis wrote The Prayer? We are equally as disappointed as you that we cannot ascertain its origin and thus attribute it to our great Saint.

"Monsignor Richard Legerman, here on my right, is an orthographical scholar. He has examined the document over many months and is adamant in his stance that the very material The Prayer is written on may not be accurately dated to the 13th century.

"On my other side is Monsignor Rufus Hoffman, a noted papyrologist. He concurs with Reverend Legerman and, too, has questions regarding the age of the manuscript.

"Understand, every person seated at this table has critical items on his desk right now. Since we are all aged men, our time is very important. Why would we meet here today if we did not care for you and your father's legacy? We are all bound by a sense of loyalty to your family because of your kindness to Brother Pietro. He spoke often of your friend, Father Tony Tonelli, and of your father.

"Understand that Pietro's friends are our friends. So there is no reason that we could, in Christian conscience, purposely impede your progress in getting your story published. We do not have time for that sort of tomfoolery. Besides, we would be honored if the world read about the miracle of your father's simultaneous lives."

The more that Father talked, the more embarrassed Margaret became. Suddenly, she viewed her performance as if she was watching it from the ceiling, looking down on the austere setting. She saw the table of eight, quiet, humble men recoiling at the loud and boorish behavior of an angry woman. She admonished herself for "behaving like a spoiled brat."

Margaret knew that she deserved the pain of being publicly eviscerated, although coming from a holy and wise man like Father Delisi reduced the agony. As she listened to the thoughts and words expressed by the dedicated priest, Margaret reflected on just why she had placed herself in such a vulnerable position. She wasn't, after all, *ordered* to write the book. She had a wonderful life with John in the romantic little village of Aulino, didn't crave any special attention, and this assignment certainly wasn't an ego trip. She had been content to live quietly with a man she loved dearly.

But as she continued to absorb the punishing words of Father Delisi, she recalled a favorite expression of her father's. It was a quote from author John A. Shedd: "A ship in harbor is safe, but that is not what ships are built for." Shedd must have had Margaret in mind when he wrote the phrases because *she* was not meant to be in harbor. It was during her hardest times that she was the most energized and the most satisfied.

Her father inspired her, as he did each of her siblings, to take risks. He advised them to challenge themselves: "What's the worst that can come of this?" he would say. "If someone says 'no' to your request, then you're rejected? If there's no risk of *dying,* then take a stand. It's okay to push your limits. At the very least, you'll discover what you're all about."

She altered her mind-set and returned to the issue at hand, the explanation being given by Father Delisi. The priest summarized the stance of the Order of Franciscans: "It is our conclusion," he said, "that The Prayer in question was *not* written by our great Saint. We cannot, therefore, authorize its use in your book, even if you only *imply* that it is the work of Francis. Further, it has far less significance if it cannot be attributed to our Saint.

"Also," he continued, "if your father's repeated recitation of The Prayer was in some way instrumental in God's granting his request, then so be it. It is a mystery each of us will resolve only when and if we address our God face-to-face."

Margaret was willing to accept the final word of the good priest and a collective response from an elite committee that nodded their heads in his support. She said in her personal conclusion, "So you would admit that this extraordinary Prayer did, indeed, please our Lord. It did appear to have a special attraction to Almighty God or its intention would not have been granted."

"Any good prayer from God's faithful people pleases the Lord," Father said. "There are no heretical statements in The Prayer and it is, therefore, approved . . . but only through the limited use that we've discussed." Margaret surrendered, acquiescing to Father's dictate. Arguing was senseless.

"I must explain that I do not have a copy of The Prayer," she admitted, "nor have I ever seen it. My father memorized it and told his family he would never expose it. He considered it far too precious to make public without permission of the Franciscans. And since the Order followed the rule that it not be made public, he honored that request, presuming it was made by Saint Francis."

"You and your father have made wise choices," the priest said.

"But if I might ask," Margaret continued, "why can't I use The Prayer, especially since you don't attribute it to Francis?"

"Because, my dear woman, there still remains a small chance that someday it may be proved that Saint Francis *did* create The Prayer you seek to place into your story. If we obtain that proof, you will hear from us. But for now, we cannot authorize its use. It is a matter of integrity associated with Francis himself. In other words, if Francis wrote it and demanded how it should be used, we must honor his order.

"We thank you for coming to see us. We appreciate your candor and we forgive the minor indiscretions within your thoughts and words. We know where to reach you if our decision is reversed by any new facts discovered by the people in this room or by the Vatican staff who continues to examine the original document. There is always . . . hope."

After that final commentary, Margaret thanked the group of eight, apologized again for her impudence and imprudence and asked for Father's blessing on her family and on her work. In departing the grounds and walking to her parked car, she could not control the tear in her eye or the tear in her heart.

The personal disappointment would remain, moderately diluted by the fact that the scholars did not *completely* close the door on giving her The Prayer or attributing it to Saint Francis. The acceptance of that emotional deflation was manifest in a silent sigh of introspection. "I guess this is what pursuing sainthood is all about," she said to herself, repeating the phrase with a smile, several times.

Alone with her thoughts, it was Margaret's first admission that she aspired to sainthood, a humble but noble pursuit that mirrored the goal of her father. With his living spirit as motivation, she slowly and carefully drove toward the mountains and toward her home in Aulino. Quite by accident, the CD player in her car was cued to a rendition of the "Hallelujah Chorus" from Handel's Messiah. She said out loud, "A bit heavy, but I'll take what I can get."

To that triumphant musical score, Margaret observed vivid clouds that slowly rolled into the shape of tall mountains. They reached high into the sky, from the road in front of her to beyond the edge of the earth. She studied one cloud in particular that resembled the face of God as rendered by Michelangelo on the ceiling of the Sistine Chapel.

Clearly under a spell, Margaret interpreted that as a sign, a foretelling of imminent success. In that moment, she faithfully submitted her project to the will of God, impacted by the crescendo of music and inspired by the majesty of the sky.

Margaret wept openly. It was a cleansing, a relief from the stress of a long day. And it felt good. For the first time, the would-be author felt confident that *The Francis Connection* would become a printed novel and that it would include The Prayer. She was buoyed by her father's positive nature as she heard his voice quoting the old bromide, "No one can ruin your day without your permission."

Finality

During yet *another* waiting period, John distracted his wife as best he could. "Do you know," he said out of the blue one day, "last year, before we met, I traveled to Paris for my first visit to the place called 'Disneyland.' It was celebrating its twentieth anniversary in Europe and in Paris.

"I went with some friends from Aulino and it was the first time I ever saw what you call, a *rollercoaster*. I went for a ride on it. It was a delight. I never laughed so hard in my life but at the same time, I was also frightened.

"The reason I tell you this, my dear, is because it reminds me of what you are experiencing in your life right now." Margaret listened closely to learn the connection between John's experience and her recent disappointment.

"What one enjoys on the rollercoaster," he explained, "is the ups and downs, the unexpected twists and turns. And I am sitting here looking into your beautiful, sad, brown eyes and thinking that what you are experiencing at this time is like the rollercoaster . . . ups and downs, twists and turns, all of them unexpected. But that is what makes the ride so marvelous, its unpredictability, the fear and anxiety that it generates. And that is also what makes *life* exciting . . . unpredictability and fear. Isn't that correct?" Margaret appraised John's words.

"So," he went on, "you should not be so unhappy. This is simply one of those times when the rollercoaster is down. But it will soon come up, carry you over the top, and fill your lungs with air and your heart with energy and excitement. You will see. The rollercoaster will rise to the top again. In the meantime, allow me to help you. Continue to brighten my life with your laughter and your love.

"Something else, my dear," John whispered. "Nothing pleasures me more than to see you happy."

There had never been a time when Margaret loved her husband more. He had demonstrated his compassion and his empathy. And to honor that, she must break from her somber mood and shift her emotional gears. She must get back to a quick tempo and the positive stride of her "triple-A" personality. In short, she must redevelop her eternal optimism and not submit to "ruining her own day." But before accepting what John had suggested, she had to slightly edit his discourse.

"Darling," she began, "I accept your analogy of the rollercoaster. But I'm compelled to 'add another color to your palate.' I perceive my current struggles more like *waves*, ocean waves. My challenges have always come in *waves* rather than like a rollercoaster. Hear me out. If you picture waves, they can be enormous at times but dissolve gradually, deceivingly, to become small swells on the surface of the water.

"My struggles and surprises aren't greater than I can handle because I see them approaching slowly. And I prepare for them and protect myself with a shift in my response to the upcoming wave. Do you understand what I'm saying? Or is this a bunch of mishmash? Am I merely 'singing to the choir' here? Do you agree or disagree with my picturesque analogy?"

Margaret laughed out loud at herself. John did, too, though he appreciated his wife's dissertation on handling *unexpected change*. Such displays of imagination and energy attracted him even more to Margaret's unusual spin on life.

Consistent with John's appraisal, Margaret spontaneously proposed an idea. "Let's go to Chicago!" she said in a shout. "And let's do it quickly. I need the energy of that place and I have an ulterior motive. I want to try another approach in retrieving a copy of The Prayer. Would you go with me, like as soon as I can get tickets? It'll serve as a good distraction for both of us and I just might be able to resolve the issue of The Prayer. That hangs over my head like the sword of Damocles. It's an obstacle to my life as well as to my book." John made an enthusiastic reply with a boisterous "Yes!"

Empowered and motivated again, Margaret and John departed for Chicago ten days later. They would be staying at her mother and father's house rather than at a customary downtown hotel.

After Annie passed away, the *Chase Estate* as the children called it was divided into equal portions to the four children. Brian, the oldest sibling and the only male, soon bought-out his three sisters and retained the house for himself, his wife and three children. But an offer stood for all of his siblings: "It's still your house and you're always welcome to stay as long as you'd like," Brian said. "The five bedrooms are furnished and it'll always be *our* family home."

As it turned out, Margaret and John had the large house all to themselves, not by accident, but rather, because Brian felt they'd like some *alone-time*. He and his family left town for a short vacation and would return the day before Margaret and John left. The plan conformed perfectly to Margaret's new idea to search privately for a copy of The Prayer . . . within the walls of her parent's house.

The determined daughter had to see for herself, dig into the nooks and crannies of hidden places where her father might have placed the document. He absolutely *must* have retained a copy before his death, she reasoned. She was convinced that somewhere in that house was a private place where Frank concealed The Prayer. Her search began with faith and gusto.

At the same time, the sleuthing wannabe author knew nothing of an extensive investigation that was occurring with a simultaneous passion in Assisi.

At the Basilica of Saint Francis, two years earlier, the area of the crypt which held the incorruptible body of Saint Francis had been closed to visitors for a major restoration. When it was reopened, it was accompanied by a formal celebration. Franciscan priests and Italian culture ministry officials were proud to show-off the results of the tedious and difficult work.

The task had been to clean away decades of candle smoke and ash and to allow the original pink stone of the walls to shine through. Originally, the crypt was designed in precious marble in a neo-classical style. Then, between 1925 and 1932, the area was re-designed in bare stone in a neo-Romanesque style. The cleaning project removed the caked-on soot that had badly darkened the luster of the pink stone.

The actual tomb of Saint Francis was found in 1818, but it dated back to 1230, four years after the Saint died. There were many revelations and discoveries throughout the current restoration, some nearly as startling as the one that revealed The Prayer. It seemed a good time for great surprises. Margaret would learn more later.

At Frank's home in Chicago, the search began with the uncovering of dozens of cardboard boxes from the basement, all labeled "Frank" or "Dad." They were mostly items from his collection of sports memorabilia: trophies, news clippings, pennants of his favorite teams and other trinkets that everyone wanted to keep. But there was nothing of personal value like The Prayer. The investigators gave up on the basement and moved to the attic. That also proved to be an area void of anything meaningful to Frank, at least superficially void.

But then, while examining the deepest corner of Frank's closet in the master bedroom, Margaret found an old and weathered wooden cigar box. She remembered that it was a gift to Frank from his father before the elder passed away. The paper glued over the surface was worn, discolored and pealing and the top was held shut by a tiny but adequate nail.

Margaret and John paused to consider exactly what they were doing. They silently glanced back and forth at each other. Margaret held the box and pressed it to her chest. Her heart beat like a drum against the thin wood. There was hesitation, a question of disturbing her father's most private possessions, a move that could reveal something meant to be kept very secret. The box was obviously overlooked until now.

As Margaret shook it gently, she and John listened to shifting papers inside. The contents were lightweight, perhaps letters of love from Annie during courtship. It was a cliché but a logical guess. She asked John to remove the nail and open the box. He did so with great care as well as trepidation.

Inside, Margaret took several small envelopes into her hands. As suspected, they did contain letters with the return address of Annie's home before she married Frank. They were obviously "love letters." But just below them lay a wallet, a billfold that Margaret had bought for her father some years earlier when he and Annie lived in Florida. It appeared to be unused. Margaret recognized it instantly. It was made of American alligator, a favorite material of Frank's despite the increased sensitivity of owning the hide.

Margaret purchased the billfold from an online wholesaler for $350.00 knowing how much it meant to Frank. He treasured it just slightly less than his wedding ring, using it only on special occasions. It even remained safely at home when he and Annie made their final trip to Rome. He was afraid of losing or misplacing it on such a rigorous journey.

John encouraged Margaret to open the wallet. Again, she hesitated for fear of violating Frank's privacy and crossing the line to a place never touched by anyone but her father.

At that very time in Assisi, a similar exploratory event was marking a most unusual but relevant discovery. It was the divination of a very private possession belonging to Saint Francis, one that *also* had been secretly secured. Now, it was being unearthed by accident, similar to the manner in which The Prayer had "fallen from the ceiling."

In this current case, renovation workers were cleaning the pink stone behind the crypt on the wall adjacent to where the body of Francis rests in the Lower Basilica. As one of the men gently and meticulously cleaned the stone, one of the stones moved, slipping no more than an inch horizontally.

The worker investigated more closely and called on a fellow worker to witness the occurrence. The mortar between the stones was crumbling from age. As it did, it exposed a small empty space behind it. In the space was an aged wooden drawer no more than six inches wide. When the worker carefully pulled on the drawer, he was surprised to see that it went back into the wall a distance of nearly twenty inches. A small handle made it possible for him to pull it toward himself and to delicately remove it before the wood disintegrated.

At that point, all work in the area ceased while Father Delisi was called to remove the contents . . . one small piece of parchment. Over the next two days, a team of Brothers carefully scrutinized the document, eventually determining beyond any doubt that it contained the words of Saint Francis. The document was titled, *A Prayer for the Dying!*

Since the evidence was unarguably clear, the deduction was that Francis personally wrote The Prayer while he was dying and gave it to someone he trusted for safe-keeping. That individual must have arranged to place it in the drawer behind the crypt. And there it lay, overlooked for centuries.

The copy from the ceiling of the Basilica was just that, a *copy*, most probably dictated by Francis to Brothers Angelo and Leo. As a pragmatist and realist, Francis had thus provided his friends with a *backup* of his original writing. If the original was lost or destroyed, the other would suffice. The Saint had thus treated The Prayer preferentially, subtly revealing that it was in great favor as a personal treasure.

Because Francis was known through other writings to be intensely interested in death, it was also a notable fact that his last words, from the 142nd Psalm, were *"Bring me out of prison!"* His followers believe that it is good for all to remember that Saint Francis taught, "Even death is a part of perfect joy when it opens the gates of paradise."

What was of special interest in the newly discovered document was the omission of the *Introduction*, the several sentences preceding The Prayer that appeared in the Basilica copy. It was there that it was suggested to limit the release of The Prayer and to reserve it for friends and families of the Franciscans.

The solution to that part of the puzzle emerged quickly: it was likely that Brothers Angelo and Leo didn't want the responsibility for releasing the document. Instead, they created the small segment of writing as a conservative *directive* to its use, assuring that they would not dishonor or disgrace their founder by releasing the holy document against his wishes.

The latest discovery was met with elation throughout the *Sacro Convento,* the Basilica, and all corners of the town of Assisi. Father Delisi tried repeatedly to notify Margaret but the best he could do was to leave voice messages on her answering device in Aulino. "Call as soon as possible," he said. "I have news that will bring you great joy!"

Margaret was about to experience her own "great joy" many miles from Assisi. Inside the cigar box with the alligator wallet, buried by letters of love, were two *Corona* cigars with the cellophane wrappings still intact. Frank had apparently snuck a smoke or two after he had promised Annie he quit. It was an innocent secret that caused no loss of luster to her father's image and a minor digression from the wallet.

His nervous daughter then ventured further and opened the wallet. Unceremoniously, considering the importance of the activity, she removed a small piece of folded paper. Judging from the condition of the creases, the paper had likely remained that way since it was placed there. Margaret unfolded it slowly, until the top of the paper was visible. It read, *A Prayer for the Dying.* Judging from its location in the wallet, it was the last item placed there.

Margaret leaned towards John and showed it to him. Together, they shook their heads in amazement. Margaret shed quiet tears of joy as John gently wiped them from her cheeks. Her dream, her prayer had been answered. Frank's legacy was complete. She would include The Prayer in a new draft of the book, ship it immediately to the Stan Miller Literary Agency and hope that he would now consider her effort complete. The beat of her heart was thunderous, though she knew, of course, that she must still obtain the permission of Father Delisi before including it in her manuscript. And that task still worried her.

At the moment, Margaret's attention was on the words of the Prayer itself. As she and John read it, they realized that it was more beautiful than they had imagined and equally as touching as any of the other works of the great Saint. They humbly appreciated that they were two out of only a handful of people in different parts of the world who had been touched by the inspiring thoughts and words. It was, indeed, a privileged and exclusive group.

It had been two days since Margaret picked up messages from her land-line telephone in Aulino. As John continued to peruse The Prayer, she sat beside him and returned the call to Father Delisi. She was confused but eager to know the meaning of his messages. The tone and inflection of his voice was urgent so she wasted no time in phoning him. John remained at her side as she dialed directly to the priest's private office at the *Sacro Convento*.

It was seven hours later in that part of Italy, around four o'clock in the afternoon when she made the call. She guessed that Father would be available at that hour. Margaret placed the call on the speaker-phone in her parent's bedroom so that she and John could listen to the conversation together. That proved to be an excellent idea. Because neither one of them could have handled the wonderfully shocking news alone.

Father was happy to hear from Margaret so soon after he left his message. Not only was he extremely intent on telling her of the news but he was, as a friend, eager to make her and her husband extremely happy. Slowly and deliberately, he chose his words based on their content and efficiency. There was no need for hesitation, no attempt to make the issue more dramatic than it was by its nature.

It didn't take more than an instant for the news to travel many thousands of miles with every important detail included. Father's unmistakable "certainty" was his most important word. He was not surprised to have his message greeted with absolute silence. It didn't happen often in Margaret's life, but now it had occurred twice in one hour: she was thrust into total verbal silence. Not a single word could make its way from her mind to her lips. She was joyfully stunned and helplessly without speech. It was confirmed that The Prayer was written by Saint Francis of Assisi!

Father heard her shriek, crying out her husband's name repeatedly. "Giovanni . . . John! Did you hear what Father said? They've found another copy, uh, the *original* of *A Prayer for the Dying*. They've found the original and the one that came from the ceiling was just a copy. It's been authenticated. The writing is in the hand of Saint Francis. And it is *his* signature. It is absolutely, most certainly the work of *his* mind and heart. *A Prayer for the Dying* is *his*, confirmed . . . the Spirit-inspired creative effort of Saint Francis. Did you hear me? John continued to remain silent but smiling, overjoyed for his wife.

Father, too, was rendered speechless with tears in his voice. But because he had expected such a sizably emotional reaction, he made his conversation short. He suggested that Margaret and her husband allow the news to *sink in*, to permeate their senses together as a family. He asked her to phone him on her return to Rome and Aulino. She was pleased to have special time alone even *before* she called her siblings with her grand tidings. They would also be proud to share in the joy of re-establishing their father's credibility.

To say that Margaret was experiencing an adrenaline-rush would not have done justice to the level of her exhilaration. It exceeded any other ecstatic emotional event in her life. She would explain later that her efforts to bring this all about were not an obsession in winning but an adventure in love, an expression of her deep feelings for her father and mother with emotions that exceeded measurement.

Within an hour, she had talked to every one of her siblings, informed Stan Miller of the news, and typed and emailed The Prayer to his office. He said he would go to work immediately at trying to market her manuscript. He already had two publishers in mind the instant she told him that she had The Prayer and that it was confirmed as the work of Saint Francis of Assisi. It may take him a few weeks, he said, to have a publisher read the material and then get a contract. But her wait this time would be easy. Her prayer had been answered.

She and John planned to leave for Italy in two days. The Prayer was folded as it had been for almost two years and tucked carefully back into its nesting place in Frank's alligator wallet. The precious cargo would be hand-carried back to Aulino and never leave Margaret until she was home.

That night before retiring, Margaret and John sat by the fireplace and stared at bright orange embers popping in a slow rhythm to quiet music in her parent's den. A glass of wine for each of them warmed the room even more. The gentle stimulation reminded Margaret of an unbelievable story she had kept to herself until then.

On the recent flight from Rome to Chicago, she explained, when she slept for three continuous hours, she had a dream. The dream involved *alligators!* She couldn't recall the exact details but she saw herself on an alligator hunt in the Florida everglades with her father. (He had done that more than once when he and Annie lived in the State. The wild game was open for hunting once each year.)

At the time, Frank loved every minute of the unique adventure, not the *killing* part, but the fun of tracking alligators with a guide. He bagged only one gator and wanted to do something special with the hide. Instead, Margaret came up with the more practical idea of buying the wallet. Frank appreciated her thoughtfulness. It proved sufficient to satisfy his need. In his words, "What goes around comes around," he had said. Strangely, the phrase also fit the sequencing of the dream, the wallet, its contents and its discovery.

At the time of her dream, Margaret made nothing of it, even forgetting to tell John. But now, in this solitary time beside the fireplace, the thought of the dream recurred.

John was as surprised as his wife when she made the connection between the dream and the alligator wallet. It was an extraordinary coincidence. Or was it? Had the dream been a premonition? Was it a message from Frank? Was it directing her to the cigar box and the wallet? Neither Margaret nor her husband made any attempt to answer those questions that simply became conversational fodder for another chapter in the amazing story of *A*

Prayer for the Dying, a tale rife with undecipherable, unexplainable mysteries and miracles.

On the eve before leaving for Italy, Margaret phoned her brother and two sisters with a farewell message. She was happy to speak "live" to each one of them, expressed her love and thanked them for their prayers in helping her find The Prayer. Each of them offered to drive her and John to O'Hare International Airport the next morning, but Margaret opted for a taxi instead. Because of the time of day, "It would be easier on everyone," she insisted. Her decision would prove questionable later on.

When the two awoke to an alarm at 3:30 a.m., John rolled over and kissed his wife gently on the forehead and mouth, in that order. She smiled and turned her head toward him. "Umm," he said quietly, "You taste so good."

"John, my dear," she said through a large and noisy yawn. "How can you be so romantic . . . at this hour of the morning?

"It's not just *romantic*," he said. "It's that sometimes I don't appreciate you enough. I love you so very much. You know, the other day I heard a song . . . I didn't even get the name of the performer . . . but the refrain was 'I want to spend my lifetime loving you, if that is all in life I ever do.'"

"How can you remember such nice things when you just wake-up from sleep? That's beautiful, John. Thank you," Margaret whispered. "I feel the same. I should appreciate you more, too." Margaret paused and glanced at the clock on the bedstand. "Right now," she said, "we best be getting out of this bed and head east . . . toward Italy." The loving exchange had been an excellent preamble for a day of unforeseen events.

It was a cold November morning in the Chicagoland area. A light snow had fallen without an early sun to encourage it to melt. The taxi headed for O'Hare at 5:30 a.m. Less than two miles from the airport, a 16-wheeler with a full load of wooden pallets entered an intersection. It traveled straight through a STOP sign. Suddenly, while braking, it went into an uncontrollable skid and struck the taxi broadside. The weight of the cargo and its carrier sliced the taxi in half. Both drivers of the vehicles were killed instantly.

Margaret and John lay helpless on what little was left of the rear floor of the taxi. They were on the doorstep of death.

In their mind's eye, they saw nothing but a tapestry of dense, solid black, a complete sensory void in the absence of all imagery and sound. Within that emptiness, the vast and dark silence projected the sudden voyage beyond life.

In less than ten minutes, in that frightening, bloodied place, the seismic noise of metal cutting metal shattered the darkness and broke the silence. The "Jaws of Life" chewed through the roof of the taxi and exposed the two passengers inside. Carefully guided by "responders," the *Jaws* helped free Margaret's bloody leg and then John's arm, enabling the EMS crew to extricate them from the torn vehicle and manually stop their profuse bleeding. Each of the victims heard the harsh noise of the tool and welcomed it as a song of joy.

For several more minutes, the teeth of the saw continued to cut. But to Margaret and John, the sound was no longer *noise*. It was a triumphant symphony, a discordant series of notes that signaled *rescue*.

With the roof of the taxi peeled back, the two survivors were carefully lifted to freedom and rushed to nearby Resurrection Hospital by the EMS team. They were immediately admitted into the Intensive Care Unit. Their condition was listed as "critical" and they both were placed on life-support. They had fared better than the two drivers who lost their lives. The name of the hospital proved to be prophetic . . . they were, indeed, *resurrected*.

On the third day in the hospital, after major improvement but still reeling from physical and emotional trauma, John and Margaret were moved from the ICU and placed side by side in a conventional room. On the fourth day, just at sunrise, they awakened to a silent alarm. It was a human presence at the foot of their beds and it stubbornly denied the early sun from shining through their window. Since the figure was back-lit, it formed a shadowy, unnerving silhouette.

Even more eerie than the ill-defined image was the warmth filling the room. Both patients turned toward the door, expecting to see someone adjusting the wall thermostat. There remained only the dark figure standing in silence.

John and Margaret bravely lifted their heads. When the figure moved slightly to one side, they discerned that it was a uniformed Chicago Police Officer, a male in his mid-fifties.

The man formally removed his hat and placed it under his arm. He wore a beguiling smile that transferred friendship. Brown, quiet eyes glowed from beneath thick, grey brows.

"Good morning," the man said. "I hope I'm not disturbing you." He moved into the light where they could see him even better. He was actually older than they first thought. He spoke.

"I'd like to explain something about your rescue."

"Come in, Officer," John said. "Let's hear what you have to say. Pull up that chair." The Officer preferred to stand and John and Margaret honored his choice.

"I won't take a lot of your time," the man said. "I'm here to tell you a story that I think you'll find interesting."

Each of the patients raised the backs of their beds to place them in a more upright position. The stranger had gained their attention *and* curiosity.

"On that morning of your accident," he started, "I received a report of a serious collision in my area. I arrived just seconds before EMS. They started to work on the vehicle and I saw you on the rear floor. I didn't think you were alive. You were lying in pools of blood and your clothing was badly torn."

"I saw your purse, ma'am, on the floor beside you. An EMS female handed it to me. I opened it and started to retrieve your driver's license. I saw your leg and it was gushing blood. It was very bad. I'm sorry to be so graphic.

"The EMS people stopped the bleeding but it appeared that you had lost too much blood to survive. And you, sir. Your arm was badly crushed and you were unconscious. I didn't give you much of a chance either.

"When I lifted your purse, ma'am, a wallet fell out and hit the pavement by my foot. It was made of alligator. When it hit the ground, a piece of folded paper fell from inside. I opened it and saw the words at the top . . . *A Prayer for the Dying.*

"I didn't know if the two of you were alive or had already passed on so I said the prayer because it was for the dying. I read fast and finished it twice before you were put onto stretchers and taken away."

Margaret and John lay speechless, motionless, intrigued by the Officer's sensitivity and diligence. "I knew that only God could save you," he said. "It was the worst wreck I ever saw."

The man continued to stand at the foot of their beds as Margaret and John held back tears. The man spoke so quietly that they had to strain to hear his words.

Margaret told him that the author of the prayer was Saint Francis of Assisi and that the prayer had special meaning to them. They expressed their overwhelming gratitude for his personal, compassionate action.

"I knew you'd want to hear this," he said, "so I had to see you in person . . . because I've been witness to a miracle."

Margaret struggled to form words. "It sounds like you're *part* of that miracle. And we don't even know you."

"It doesn't really matter," the Officer said under his breath.

"For starters, what's your name?" Margaret asked.

"Francesco." There was a pause in the conversation as Margaret and John noted that his name was the Italian equivalent for Francis. They stared at each other and smiled.

"Okay," Margaret stammered, "it's clear that reciting that prayer had a great deal to do with saving us. If you knew its background, you'd understand why we're so sure of that."

"I have a question," the Officer said with a frown. "This Francis of Assisi is a friend of yours?"

"This is how it is with the reign of God," Margaret said. "In Francis, we've found one of God's dearest friends. In so doing, we've become closer friends with God *and* with Francis. So yes, we are all close friends, *family* friends."

"I'm happy to hear that."

"So how can we reach you when we're released from here?"

"Do not worry," the stranger said. "I will be in touch."

Margaret scrambled to detain the man, "But I . . . we . . ."

"I must go now, my friends," he said softly. "God be with you. Thank you for the light of your single candle."

"We love you, Francesco. Thank you. Thank you."

Margaret and John couldn't quite *place* the man's words about ". . . the light of a single candle." There was a memorable connection but no recollection of its source. They watched in wonder as his image disappeared slowly and faded again toward the light from which it came. The light pulsated several times; then, in an instant, it faded to darkness.

From her hospital bed, the day after the stranger's visit, Margaret began a search for the identity of Officer Francesco. She had little to go on and her attempt to obtain his address and phone number was time-consuming and fruitless.

She investigated the dataset of employee names at the online data portal of the City of Chicago. As deeply as she dug, as many questions as she asked, she could find no record of a Chicago Police Officer by the name of *Francesco*, either as a first name or surname. Nor did his name and description ring any bells with members of the Hospital staff. So for the time being, Margaret and John were content to know only that the stranger was a principal player in their miraculous recovery.

The story of the man's actions traveled fast in the "city of neighborhoods." Word-of-mouth was the first carrier. A feature article in the Tribune hastened the spread. It was a happy story that the public feasted on as they sought good news. From Chicago, it flashed through social media and, eventually, to the national and international news scene. The unidentified "miracle man" became a silent, unknown hero.

At the Basilica in Assisi, after speaking personally and at great length with Margaret, the miracle was recorded in the archives as the first case in which the recitation of *A Prayer for the Dying* was instrumental in saving lives. Whoever willed it at that time and in that place had fulfilled a mission. The story of *The Francis Connection* would thus have a happy ending.

Margaret and John wrestled with a resonant question: who was the unidentified visitor in the hospital? Was it, indeed, a Chicago police Officer? It didn't seem likely.

One lead was the name "Francesco." Perhaps it was not coincidental. Initially, Margaret believed the man was her re-embodied father, Frank Chase. After all, he was the one who believed that The Prayer had miraculous powers. And he was the one who facilitated those powers in living a second life. Surely, he might have intervened to help save his daughter and her husband.

John, on the other hand, speculated that the man may have been Jesus Christ. But he and Margaret quickly reasoned that if the man was Jesus and He recited The Prayer, He would actually be praying to Himself. That made no sense.

They also ruled out Father Francis because he had no knowledge of them or The Prayer. There was no motive for him to appear in that situation. Nor was there a personal reason for a visit from Brother Pietro.

After lengthy deliberation and examination of all the facts, the two survivors concluded that the visitor just might have been their friend, Francis of Assisi. Perhaps his visit was a tribute to their tireless efforts in confirming his authorship of The Prayer and in helping release it to the public. That rationale made sense. But a smidgen of doubt remained.

Finally, exasperation and frustration exploded in resolution. The visitor was convincingly identified. Margaret's memory served her well as she finally *placed* the man's parting words:

"All the darkness in the world
cannot extinguish . . . *the light of a single candle.*"

The words were paraphrased from the writings in "The Little Flowers of Saint Francis of Assisi." Margaret and John rested well with attribution confirmed, at least in the private places of their hearts.

It was in the next year, in 2013, that Margaret's book was released and distributed internationally. Uncannily, the date coincided with a major event taking place in Rome. Pope Benedict XVI retired from the papacy and Cardinal Jorge Bergoglio of Argentina was elected to replace him.

The 266th Pope chose the name *Francis* in honor of the humble Saint of Assisi. As part of the announcement, veteran deputy spokesman for the Vatican, Thomas Rosica, said that Cardinal Bergoglio had broken historic ground in his precedent-shattering choice. He said it was most appropriate since ". . . Saint Francis was known throughout the world for *connecting* with fellow Christians." The circle of friends thus grew to global proportions, united in faith, hope and love.

The Francis Connection was complete.
And all is as it should be.

A Prayer for the Dying

I beseech Thee, O Lord, that the fiery and sweet strength of Thy love may absorb my soul from all things under heaven, that I may die for Thy love as Thou didst deign to die for love of mine.

Father, keep the dying in Thy Name, all those for whom I pray. And I ask, Father, that they may see Thy glory in the kingdom of heaven. Honor those who die with Thy presence.

Thou art holy, Lord God. Thou art strong. Thou art great. Thou art most high. As I will to see You and to end my suffering, I beg the mercy of my omnipotent Saviour.

Praised be my Lord for my bodily death. Blessed those who shall find themselves in Thy holy will. They are peacemakers who amidst all they suffer maintain peace in soul and body for Thy love.

Most high, omnipotent Lord, Hail Thou Your palace. Praise, glory and honor and benediction are Thine. Praise be to Thee, my Lord, with all Thy creatures. Give grace and strength to me.

God, Living and True, with a pure heart and mind, admit me into Thy Kingdom. Show to me Your tabernacle. There the Lord guards the house and the enemy finds no way to enter.

O how glorious and great to have a Father in heaven! O how holy and lovable to have a spouse in heaven! O how joyous to have a Friend Who, in death, will clothe me in a new robe of life.

I pray for all who lie dying, Lord. Bless and sanctify them. And for them I sanctify myself that they may be sanctified in one. In no tribulation or anguish or pain may I turn away from you.

O great and admirable Lord God, Thou art my eternal life!

Author's Note

At the outset of this story, the writing was defined as a work of fiction. As such, *A Prayer for the Dying* on the previous page was composed by the author. However, it is excerpted and assembled from *The Writings of Saint Francis of Assisi.*

The paraphrased thoughts and words have their roots in *Praises of God*, *The Canticle of the Sun* and *The Praises of the Creatures*, all undisputed works of Saint Francis of Assisi.

Edwards Brothers Malloy
Thorofare, NJ USA
April 10, 2014